Tricks in Captivity ©

a novel by

Julie Locascio

Table of Contents

Preface

"...as there is no condition in
which man can be happy and
entirely free, so there is no
condition in which he need be
unhappy and lack freedom...
suffering and freedom have
their limits...very near together."

Leo Tolstoy, *War and Peace*

Part I

Tricks in Captivity

... Mexico, 1994 ...

Chapter 1

My senses abruptly snap to attention, overwhelmed with awe as the dolphins hurtle out of the depths of the water into the sunlight, each dolphin carrying one of the perfectly balanced legs upon which António stands as he too is launched upward through the spray into a surreal ski-lap around the shimmering, bright blue pool. My heart clenches as every instinct I possess propels me to jump into the pool and let the dolphins lift me up, too. I want it so immediately and so achingly and so primally that it takes a long time for me to realize it has riveted and wounded me so much because none of my own flying dreams have ever come true--or even seemed remotely possible until I saw António whisked effortlessly through the enchanted water and tossed into a dazzling trajectory through the air before landing again on solid ground.

Mesmerized, I cannot stop watching the show, and at the end I have to go buy another ticket to see it all again, desperately wondering how António had ended up swimming and soaring with dolphins while I had ended up so motionless. Why were my flying dreams something from which I always awoke, whereas here was an actual person who got to swim through water and soar through sky every day? It is unbearable, and I leave the park miserable, with tears suppressed, vowing to come back every Saturday to watch until I can figure out a way to get into that water myself.

My job is insufferable, like the ones that preceded it, but in Mexico it is a thousand times worse: fetching the Center's mail while untold myriads of families wait for money to be sent to them from their relatives in the States, making the Center's photocopies while generations upon generations are copying the poverty-soaked lives of their forefathers, shelving the Center's books and journals that speak so much about socioeconomic injustices in a library only perused by a handful of well-meaning souls without any power to do more than hand out fifty pesos to the next beggar at the door. I long to forget my impotence and drench myself in typhoid-free water, closing my eyes until every last bit of dusty grime has been washed away, opening my eyes in pleasure as Mother Nature lifts me through the spray into the brisk air and warm sunshine of the joyride I have dreamt of all my life.

Instead, I head back to Casa Dolores to eat something and drink half a gallon of water from our water filtration system. As I slowly absorb the water, I think back to the first month I was here, when the water filter had been set wrong and I had quickly come to know the cramps, nausea, diarrhea, and feverish migraines so common in the tropics. For weeks, I could scarcely lift my head at an angle sufficient to read a book, and I had pondered the reality of the afflicted peasant trying to muster the strength to till the soil, to till any sort of life here.

It was not just the filter set wrong, either--so many things set wrong, so many nauseas in this place. I had come here to help fight poverty, but instead I was chained in service to a madman whose lifeboat operation had so many holes that we could barely keep ourselves afloat--financially or psychologically--let alone save the desperate numbers of Mexicans in poverty. My hopes were dying with them.

Chapter 2

The desperate peasants in faraway Chiapas had suffered in a media-imposed silence for ages until the Zapatista revolutionaries stormed four towns on New Year's Day. Only a few weeks have passed since then, and I am already sick of hearing about it. My mind sneers at any attempt to analyze it, dissect it--for God's sake, it is El Salvador, it is Nicaragua, it is everywhere, over and over again! How many more governments will pretend not to understand, will pretend that nothing can be done? I am as tired of hearing about simple solutions as I am of hearing that there are no solutions.

The rest of the staff is electrified by the revolution, outraged at the government response, and ready to do whatever they can to help the oppressed of Chiapas, but not I. I am sickened by the violence--men with guns telling other men with guns it is time to redistribute the resources. It is the same conversation men in every region of the world have had every century for the entire history of human civilization. It is not the solution. No men every really surrender: they just bide their time until ready to wage war again.

***

For days on end my mind races forward and backward in time, forward and backward, desperately searching for clues to make my peace with the world before my youth runs out and I no longer have the energy to be doing what I really should be doing, whatever it is, wherever it is. Something...something to live for without cynicism, without despair, without boredom, without.... Then the phone call comes: would I like a job in Brazil? I accept it instantaneously, no thought at all--another job, another chance,

3

another place! When I hang up, I am not sure the phone conversation really took place. I will not really believe it until the day I get off the plane in Brazil and the shock of hearing all that Portuguese spoken confirms it.

Shit! Brazil! Brasília, Brasil! How am I going to tell Stephanie I am going to Brasília? When Fernando did not take her to Brazil, she fell apart. For the first and only time in our lives, my sister had fallen apart. I will be going there, where her dream did not come true. Every letter she gets postmarked "Brasil", every "Brasília listed on her phone bill, will remind her of Fernando and the two letters and five telephone calls they had exchanged before he had changed his mind and decided she should stay in Washington after all. I had almost believed in them myself--I could picture them dancing around in that Milton Nascimento/Duran Duran waterfall love fantasy video world. I still cannot picture her with the D.C. lawyer who is dating her now. Where's the waterfall?

Latin lovers--she should have learned from my mistakes. I had already transferred my romantic idealism from Latin American men to Latin American politics by the time Stephanie had met Fernando. By the time he split with her, I had split with the politics and was rushing headlong into an on-the-rebound love affair with Latin American flora and fauna--so beautiful, so lush, so vulnerable and sensitive.

Brazil is a wounded creature, worthy of my attention and efforts and love. Mexico has already betrayed me too many times, in too many ways. I watch the evening news on television--could Los Angeles really be burning again? The Big One? Maybe if I threaten to move to a major disaster area, my mother will be more relaxed about my merely moving to a military-coup vulnerable, quadruple-digit inflation country. She always worries about the wrong things in my life--if she only knew what she **really** should be praying to the saints about.

I shut off the TV and retreat to my room to listen to Stereo Nova's latest Yankee discovery--New Age. This music is way too serene and pleasant for Mexico, and it teleports me back to Chapel

4

Hill, where it was the only music I could study to–all those hours reading and writing, thinking and analyzing, preparing myself to save the Third World, and now I wonder why I did not just try to earn a million dollars, then give it to charity. Surely that would have been easier than this path! What do non-homicidal, non-suicidal people do with their frustrations? I never figured out how to get rid of mine--they always had to die a slow, natural death. How long in Brazil before the Mexican pain would be over? Would Brazil be enough to make up for all I left behind in North Carolina? Would it be enough to help me face Washington again?

Everybody is sure I will be back in Washington sooner or later. Stephanie has now lived there longer than I did, but she still acts as if I am the one who belongs there. How can I tell her that I have begun pondering Hawaii? It looks nice. Hawaii! Of course! That is where Hollywood can go after Los Angeles is burned to the ground, or after the Big One! I wonder if they have already thought of that? It is so logical. No, I guess I will not fit in there, not if it is going to be overrun with starlets after California crumbles into the sea.

Why is my mind always wandering so much? I used to be so focused. I had my college major picked out before I ever arrived on campus and never ever changed my mind: now I am seriously pondering whether cavorting with dolphins should be considered a viable alternative to returning to the paper-pushing nightmare of D.C. Brazil--this could really be an unknown commodity! I cannot picture a 10:15 a.m. or a 3:45 p.m. there at all.

Chapter 3

I wake up dreaming about blood transfusion thieves in the night, thinking, "Why would they want to steal **my** blood?" I do not even know what type it is, it might be borderline anemic on any given day, and possibly has remnants of dengue from the one black cloud of the blue sky that had been Costa Rica. God, I wish I could get a job in Costa Rica. Must not think about that now--that glorious month in paradise. That was then, this is now--or so I told Stephanie.

Our time together in Washington scarcely overlapped: I had already been accepted into graduate school by the time she graduated college and moved there. After hearing my admonitions about the traffic problems and high rate of mental illness in Northern Virginia, she bravely opted for the aesthetically pleasing--if somewhat dangerous--neighborhood of Adams Morgan. Every visit to her neighborhood was a sociological survey--how many new refugees had set up shops and restaurants, how many had moved on to the upscale melting pot of Georgetown? I steadfastly refused to dine at the Ethiopian restaurants, ostensibly in solidarity with the hordes of people starving in the Horn of Africa, but actually because it was embarrassing to admit that Ethiopian food was too spicy for me. Stephanie and I stuck mainly to the fare of the Cambodian and Lebanese refugees.

I hated the fact that Washington fit her like a glove. Not that it did not fit me like a glove, too--like a surgical glove that had to be tugged and pulled and stretched over my suffocating skin. My years of studying history, public policy, and international relations had gotten me nothing but lowly positions in non-profit organizations

6

there, whereas her generic computer programming degree had immediately landed her in the center of the statistical research division of the United Nations Development Program. She met Fernando there two weeks after she began the job. It was a great year for her--great from the start.

My thoughts return to Brazil. Still awaiting job confirmation, I am already ninety percent mentally removed from Mexico. How long it seems since I took the plunge into Cuahtemoc, Mexico! I had walked all over town, wanting so badly to immerse myself thoroughly in Cuahtemoc life, but ten-foot high walls barred me from seeing anything but street vendors and beggars, spastic cabbies and manic bus drivers. There was no bus schedule or route map to help me navigate the city--I had to rely on others who had already made the journeys to tell me where to go. Everything worth seeing in Cuahtemoc was hidden behind high walls--parks, schools, churches, houses. I had to pay money just to see a duck pond.

My heart cried out for the rolling lushness of Chapel Hill. I desperately missed the proud and lovely manses on East Franklin Street; the profusion of azaleas, dogwood trees, giant magnolias, pear trees, redbud, and crape myrtle; the softly wooded lawns all over campus; the sweet smell of honeysuckle walking home from class. More than anything else, I missed having them all right at my fingertips--not hidden behind a wall, or, worse, tauntingly placed on top, like the bougainvillea draped invitingly over the broken glass and spikes cemented into the wall tops to deter Cuahtemoc burglars.

Only the rich live well here, and my job--far from being a beacon of education and assistance--seems of little use to the poor (though of great benefit to my boss, the Prophet/Profit). I had turned from it dejectedly, seeking to immerse myself in something else here--a music scene, an art scene, a student scene, any scene-- but I could find no scenes, could not figure out behind which wall they were hidden. The only aspect of Mexico I would ever know like the back of my hand was Casa Dolores--and that because of all the hours spent mopping up dust, mud, cat hairs, ants, cockroaches. My Mexican cultural immersion is limited to the Center's delightful

Mexican cooks; my wildlife safaris are limited to hunting expeditions against rats and scorpions.

***

Still no confirmation of the new job in Brazil at the end of the next day. I sink into a warm bath, all the way down to my...tail bone, the maximum depth allowed by the quantity of hot water available in a given half-hour period. I wonder how much more quickly Sylvia Plath would have committed suicide in Mexico–didn't she say that a steaming hot bath up to her neck was required therapy at the end of a rough day? I alternate soaking one leg, then the other; I prop up my knees to soak my lower back; I slide all the way down with my legs in the air in order to soak my upper back and neck as best as possible. When the ants start falling in and the chilly breeze from the partially unshuttable window hits me, I have had enough.

The next day, the Center staff is abuzz over the nearby filming of a scene from the next Harrison Ford movie, wondering if they can get a good look at it. I think instead about how I wish I had been here when they had filmed "Romero", which was such a cathartic and inspirational movie to the cast and crew that they had done daily devotions together. All I can picture the Harrison Ford bunch doing after each day's shoot is knocking back margaritas at Larry's Bar and Grill--the "bright spot for shady characters". Would the crew see any more of Mexico than the Palace of Cortés, across the street from Larry's? Do they know that "margarita" means "daisy"? (Should they know that? Is that important?)

I reminisce about our last celebrity visitor, when a Nicaraguan band had spent a couple days in our guest rooms during their benefit concert tour to raise money for war orphans. Comandante Omar Cabezas was the one shepherding the group through their tour, and I was stunned that evening when I had walked in to see the author of *Fire From the Mountain* eating supper in our dining room. When introduced to me, he had asked if we had not already met. Some of my coworkers had assumed it to be a macho come-on line, but I suspected he had met too many sympathetic gringas to tell them apart.

The Nicaraguan benefit concert was as disastrous as the Nicaraguan war had been, with a huge storm blowing in to knock out the electricity before the end of the opening act. The group--unaccustomed to acoustic performances--hung back while members of the local warm-up band strummed guitars and told jokes by flashlight. The electricity finally returned hours later; the Nicaraguan band played a couple songs, then left. The speech by Cabezas had been a disappointing homage to Cuba--I would have preferred a brave affirmation of Nicaragua.

***

Three weeks have passed since I returned from my Christmas vacation in the U.S.–the best Christmas in years–yet it already seems half a year and half a world away. The three weeks I had been gone for Christmas had apparently been a feline eternity for Chillona, who was in shock when I returned to Casa Dolores--probably having already decided I was dead. Now, she is incessant in her demands for daily affection: if I do not let her spend an hour or so curled up in my lap every night, she meows pitifully until I give in. Every night, I spread the towel carefully--trying not to get her allergen-laden hairs all over me--and let her hop up. She only likes being petted around the head: fingers wandering down her legs get a sullen look, and fingers stroking her back and heading down towards her tail usually get a nip. She knows exactly what she wants: under the chin, behind the ears, nose-to-forehead. I know exactly what I want, too, but have never found the obliging lap.

Chapter 4

Michael had been the antithesis of my ambitions, the anachronism of my desires, and one more frustration of my hopes. I had met him shortly after starting graduate school at the University of North Carolina, scarcely four years ago, though it already seems an eternity. He was the featured speaker at our Amnesty International meeting in September; his topic, human rights abuses against the indigenous. Part Cherokee, Michael Proudpine discussed the current human rights issues affecting American Indians. The catalog was long and depressing, and he topped it off with a few acidic comments about human rights abuses against the indigenous of other countries.

Our Group president followed up with an outline of the new AI indigenous campaign we would be working on, and as he handed out briefing papers, I approached Michael to ask him to clarify some of the generalizations he had made. He had quickly been engaged in a heated debate with a UNC history professor about the American Indian Movement, and I had to wait until the debate and its audience finally waned. He eyed me warily at first, and showed marked relief when I posed a question on a completely different subject. He suggested we head over to the Columbia Street Bakery to talk about it.

It proved to be the first of many meetings there talking about religion, politics, music, and life–over shortbread, granola, and chocolate chip cookies, washed down by clear glass cups of the best hot chocolate in town. There was no place in Chapel Hill more politically correct than this vegetarian, intellectual, folksy coffeehouse for a date with a part Cherokee, part African, part

Scotch-Irish man. Drinking him up, drinking the cocoa up–nothing had ever been sweeter...until the moment I choked upon his telling me he was in the army. He had immediately seen my hostile reaction to that information, and had launched a preemptive strike to explain it before I could attack.

"Every firstborn son going back from my father, to his father, to my great-great grandfather, has been designated for the warrior role. It is a tradition that thanks and honors an army soldier who protected my great-great-great grandmother's family from being expelled to reservations in Oklahoma when Andrew Jackson ordered the deportation of the Cherokee Nation from the Atlantic states in 1838. This soldier, David Gallagher, hid my great-great-great grandmother's family, in return for my great-great-great grandmother. By the time the Trail of Tears was over, he had finished building a cabin up in the mountains for her family, and then he left. Maybe he didn't like having all those Cherokee fugitives as neighbors out there. Maybe he missed white people--I don't know. He never saw his son born, but he sent money for him every Christmas."

I could restrain myself no longer, even though I knew he was not finished. "What, are you kidding me? You think that guy was some sort of hero, just because he hid away a woman for himself? You think he spoke up about the injustice of it all, or about how the Supreme Court had ruled against the deportation, or about all the Cherokees dropping dead on the march, or ever did a thing about how shitty the Cherokees were treated after they had sacrificed their homes and marched all the way to Oklahoma, or--"

"No."

"No, what?"

"No, he was not a hero, but he did a good thing. He didn't have to save her whole family, you know--he could have just dragged her off. He hid her parents, her brothers, an old grandmother, cousins. And he sent them money every year--how many white guys do you think were doing that?"

11

"Not a lot, I guess-they didn't have DNA testing back then, you know!"

"What is your point?"

"I hardly think he's worth forcing generations of firstborn sons into the military for!"

"That's 'cause you don't get it. He showed bravery--"

"He showed--" I wanted to yell "horniness," but something in Michael's eyes stopped me.

"What?"

I suddenly wanted to believe that some Scotch-Irish soldier had really fallen in love with that Cherokee woman, had risked death to pull her away from the Trail of Tears, had risked death over and over again until everybody in her family was safe, too. No, it was just horniness...wasn't it? I stared into his eyes--did he love her?

"What?" he repeated.

I kept staring into his eyes. He would not be alive today if that soldier had not fallen for that Cherokee girl.

"Look," he had given up waiting for me to finish my sentence, "everything you said might be true, but he **had** done a brave thing. And my family had learned from him that there were a lot of soldiers who didn't like what was happening, but had to do it because the orders were handed down from Washington."

"And all the Nazis were just taking orders, too--"

"And he wasn't! That's the point! An institution can be bad, it can be evil, but that doesn't mean all its members have to be."

"Ok, ok, but why can't you just have an annual picnic--David Gallagher Day? Why do you have to make all these people join the army?"

He shook his head. "Nobody made anybody join the army. It just happened. And I wanted to, too." He sighed. "There's a lot of shit in the army, but there are good people in there, too. People who believe that some things are worth defending."

12

"Beautiful women or land? You know, most armies have actually opted for land."

He looked at me quietly, and I could not believe he still had not lost his temper with me. He sipped his hot chocolate and stared at the whipped cream for a moment, then looked up at me again. "I think a really good soldier is somebody who can decide anew every day what is worth defending and what is not." I stared blankly at him. "And how." He cracked his knuckles. "Sometimes it's not the battles you expect.... My dad said the hardest battle he fought in Vietnam was convincing his platoon not to burn a village of two-hundred people where some Vietcong weapons had been found." He looked down again at the dregs of his whipped cream, dissolving slowly in the steamy chocolate.

"Well...that's good but...he still must have killed a lot of Vietnamese...."

"I don't think he killed any, actually."

"What?!"

"Well, he was discharged pretty early on."

"For what?"

"I'm not sure. He never really explained it. He just always said, 'if I had **seen** the enemy, I **would** have fired my gun, but I never saw him.'"

"He never shot anybody in Vietnam?"

"I don't think so."

"Wasn't he court-martialed?"

"That was pretty early in the war--it wasn't even really a war yet. They discharged him quietly the day before Kennedy was shot. He was in the plane heading back, and I guess the pilot got it over the radio, and announced over the intercom that Kennedy was assassinated. He said he had been feeling sorry for himself until that; then he started crying. He said he saw burly Marines crying, three-star generals crying."

13

I stared at him, dumbfounded, lost. "Why are you in the army?" He did not reply, and we gazed at each other. "Do you think soldiers really get to decide for themselves what is worth defending? Do you think you can do this without killing anybody?"

"I hope so." He smiled at me, slowly: the lips started to move, the eyes started to soften, the dimples slowly opened up. "You're a pinko pacifist, aren't you?"

My head was spinning. In the back of my mind, I could not erase the image of a brave soldier risking his life to defend his lover. "I hope so," I replied, smiling uncertainly. My heart was thumping, and I got scared. I wanted him to defend me, somehow. Not with a gun, but bravely...no, I did not know what I wanted...I was confused. I just wanted him on my side, not to have to kill somebody but just to be with me, on my side, with me. I wanted him to fight for me, I did. Not with a gun, but somehow. Somehow so that I would know he really wanted me, really...loved me. I wanted him to love me.

14

Chapter 5

Michael had grown up all his life in North Carolina's Smoky Mountains. He was amazed that I had seen so many different places and thought North Carolina was the best; he had never been elsewhere, but was sure there must be something better out there. He had gone to college at UNC on ROTC money, and, much to his frustration, had ended up based at Ft. Bragg, in the heart of Carolina. He still had never been outside of North Carolina when I met him, except for short camping trips into Tennessee--which did not count, he said, because they were the same mountains.

Chapel Hill, at least, had been a new world to him, and now he found himself returning again and again to spend time with me. He never let me visit him in Fayetteville--if certain soldiers had seen him with a white girlfriend, it might not have been well received. Not that he would have been lynched--Carolina racism was much subtler than that. In a land where very few farmers had ever owned slaves, let alone owned enough land to be considered plantation owners, the poor white farmer of North Carolina had way too much in common with the freed slave to face up to it. Times had changed, of course, but Michael never let me forget that Chapel Hill was in another social dimension, and outside of the Research Triangle, I could not really take **us** for granted.

Racism, to be sure, was still emitting some dying gasps in Chapel Hill, too, and the counter-offensive was like a pack of wolves on the fallen-but-still-cussin' hunter. The showing of "Do the Right Thing" on campus was followed by a university-sponsored rap session on racism. The free-wheeling debate ranged from thoughtful comments to pure venom. "Why didn't any whites die in this movie?!" hollered one particularly light-skinned, European-featured, African-American student.

Wondering if mob violence was about to erupt, I was only a little consoled when Michael wrapped his arm tightly around me. He gave me a quick smile, then turned back to the source of the broadside, furrowing his brow and parting and reparting his lips in preparation for what he wanted to say. He did not have to say anything: an African-American student issued a stern rebuke, and the conversation got back to the realm of the rational and intellectual.

Later, over pecan pie and Beethoven music at the Carolina Coffee Shop, Michael asked me what the worse thing was that I had personally ever seen done by a white to a black. I could not think of anything beyond racial slurs--I had only seen racial violence in books and on film. He started telling me the story of his one African-American ancestor--why she had fled to the backwoods of Snowbird, NC, and pleaded for the Cherokee there to hide her. He started telling me about how his relatives had found her--in shredded, bloody clothes.... I put down my fork, and he abruptly stopped. "Are you going to vomit?"

"No."

He smiled in relief. "Well, I guess I'll stop anyway."

"Good." I turned my chair and put my head between my knees.

"Oh, my God! Are you gonna pass out?"

"I won't," I declared confidently, well practiced in the heart of nipping faints in the bud. I suddenly felt freezing water flooding the back of my head and jumped up, screaming.

"Are you OK?"

Everybody in the restaurant was staring at us as I wiped the napkin across the back of my neck. I just smiled at him, feeling very alive.

16

Most of that fall semester was very happy. Michael's jaded eyes saw Carolina in a rosier light when he was with me, the jolly refugee from the North. I raved about how much prettier the wooded hills and lush gardens were in Carolina than in the corn-covered flatlands of Illinois. I raved about how progressive and caring UNC was in comparison to my first alma mater, the traditional, pompous and pretentious University of Virginia--where pearl necklaces and polo shirts were the norm, not the friendship bracelets and Guatemalan pullovers of UNC. I raved about how cheap Chapel Hill was compared to Washington, in terms of cost-of-living, yet so much richer in quality of life. Having never been outside of North Carolina, he was sometimes surprised to hear how wonderful his home state really was.

He loved to point out my suburban inconsistencies, of course. I loved flowers, but loathed earthworms and spiders. I could write term papers on sustainable agriculture in South America, but could recognize no plant at the North Carolina Botanical Gardens. I shopped for organic foods, but pulled out the Raid whenever I saw a creepy invader in my home. He said the only time I ever seemed completely in harmony with nature was when I was near water. Paddling on University Lake, swimming in Jordan Lake, reveling in the Atlantic Ocean waves--these were the times he said I was most at peace.

He was a mountain man, himself. I agreed that mountains were beautiful to look at, but they could not envelop you the way water could. "They're sacred," he tried to explain. "They do envelop you, but only if you let them." Those words haunted me over and over again when he returned from the invasion of Panama. The warm, embracing, nurturing water I had found in him before was gone: he had become a hard and steep and rocky place where my feet faltered with every move I made to get close to him again.

***

17

When he had called to tell me about Panama that December, I was hunkered down in Illinois for my Christmas vacation with the folks. Relieved to be over my first semester of graduate school, I was relishing the vacation but missing him terribly. I had only had the distance of four days to step back and begin analyzing what I had or might have with Michael Proudpine. I wanted to hear him say, "I love you, I miss you."

What I got was, "We're shipping out tomorrow for Panama." His voice receded in my mind as my thoughts flailed away at the incomprehensible. I shakily leaned my forehead to the wall and had to muster every ounce of will I had to continue paying attention to what he was saying. "I guess Bush wants Noriega bad." I strained to hear fear or horror or disgust in his tone, but, as much as I tried to deny it, he only sounded excited. "I'll probably be back in Carolina before you are." He'd never even been on a plane before. "What do you want me to bring you from Panama?"

I kicked the wall and snapped. "How can you be so cavalier about invading another Third World country? We don't have the right to do it, and--"

"Look, I'm just going to nab a drug lord--I'm not gonna do anything else."

"You believe that shit?"

"No, but **I** am not going to do anything else!" He was angry-- really angry.

I spoke as quietly as I could. "Don't go." Dead silence. Was he considering that idea or debating how to tell me politely to shut up? My heart was pounding, and I leaned on the wall again.

"You know what the sad thing is? You sound more concerned about the Panamanians than about me."

"Michael! God, if you only knew how I felt, my heart's...." I choked, the hot geyser of tears overwhelming me.

"I'm sorry. I'm just not in the mood for a political debate today. I just...I just wanted to hear your voice before I left...and tell

18

you...I love you." I told him I loved him too, but I was not sure if he could hear what I was saying in between sobs. He had heard me cry plenty of times before--watching sad movies, reading sad news stories, sucked into sappy sentimental TV commercials--but he had never heard me cry over something real before. Maybe he did not know I was really crying. He said other guys were waiting to use the phone and hung up. I collapsed on the floor.

***

He did not die in Panama. Not really. But he did not really come back, either. The first few weeks, whenever he could, he would head up to Chapel Hill to see me. He never wanted to talk. We shot a lot of pool and caught a lot of bands at the Cat's Cradle. The winter was occasionally mild enough to permit strolling around the campus, holding hands. Whenever he temporarily lost my hand--in a crowd, a turnstile, a revolving door--he would quickly grab for it again. My face, he stayed away from. I think he would have kissed me more if he could have been assured that my eyes would be closed, but I could not help probing his eyes every time he turned his face toward me.

As the weeks went by, he slowly told me some of the details, but he always told them as if he had not been involved--he never said exactly what he had done. Whole neighborhoods had been burned to the ground, as U.S. troops searched for Noriega's cronies, and hospital records had been deliberately destroyed to hide the true extent of mortalities. Sometimes I would regard him watching a newscast or reading an article about it--how the CIA had been bankrolling Manuel Noriega for years in return for his connivance vis-á-vis Nicaragua and El Salvador, how George Bush was probably in it up to his eyeballs, how it had suddenly become important to get a different puppet installed in the canal-of-drugs zone--and he often nodded, but he did not want to talk about the politics, and he would not go to any more Amnesty International meetings. He did not want to go anywhere people might be discussing the invasion of Panama.

I dreaded the summer at the same time I welcomed it. I feared our separation might be the final nail in the coffin, but I could not help being excited about my research grant to study refugee

19

programs in Costa Rica. After a month there, I would spend two months in Washington interning in a refugee agency. I would be learning a lot, and I needed a break from his melancholy. No, that was not really true--I needed a break from mine.

Chapter 6

I cannot get from the Post Office back to Casa Dolores: the south end of the plaza has been roped off for more filming. I ask a guard about it, and he says they are shooting some close-ups for "A Clear and Present Danger". I ask if the movie shots will include the formidable Palace of Cortés: no, the movie is not even about Mexico, but actually set in Colombia. Ah, Tom Clancy must be forced to write about drug wars now that the Cold War is over. I make a mental note to tell my parents, the spy novel fans, about the shoot three blocks from where I live and work.

If it were actually about Mexico, "A Clear and Present Danger" would have to refer to the North American Free Trade Agreement--at least, that is what most of my histrionic colleagues here think. I think we need to stop pretending that propping up fallen industries can prop up fallen people.

I do not see it the way my boss sees it: the Prophet/Profit would rather encourage Pedro to keep his family in the Indian village high up in the mountains--making cheap baskets for our visitors and students--than help him come down from there and get the education he and his wife and children need to survive into the next century. We buy scads of his baskets months before we even need them in the inventory, just to keep food in his one-room mud-floored hut. My boss has known Pedro a decade. I want to work for someone who, after a decade, would be able to come up with some way to get his friends out of a hovel, out of a cholera-racked dying village.

21

My boss will not discuss this issue with me: he will listen to nobody and nothing except the little voice in his head which he has identified as God's. Anybody that disagrees with that little voice is disagreeing with God and can safely be ignored! Our boss is a prophet, after all! Social work he leaves to somebody else--not us, of course, since we are employed full time in keeping the spotlight aimed on the Prophet/Profit.

***

I take a long detour to get back to Casa Dolores, and my thoughts wander back to Michael again. When I returned to Chapel Hill that fall, Michael was happy to see me, but not happy. He still loved me, but he was not in love. I knew immediately that the most I could hope to salvage was a friendship. He was too scarred, and I could never be the balm he needed deep in his soul. He did not need to tell me that: he was the only man I had ever loved, and I knew I was not enough for him. He seemed relieved, actually, when we both admitted it, and we began to grow close again, in a different way.

We finally started really talking about Panama. I told him about the Panamanian atrocities I had learned about while in Costa Rica that summer, and he finally told me what he had done there. He had wanted to speak up--at first to point out the absurdities of what they were doing, and later to stop the horrific violence being waged in the invasion--but he could not do it. He was astonished at the bloodthirstiness all around him, how many men were eager to torch every last neighborhood in Panama City until Noriega was forced to surrender. Nobody was considered a civilian--everybody was assumed to be Noriega's accomplice and deserved to lose their homes and their lives. He wanted to speak up, but did not know how to speak to that kind of blind rage.

When it was his platoon's turn, he hung back as the flamethrowers went to work. He saw men, women, elderly and children running out of burning buildings as his fellow soldiers ruthlessly swept through their assigned neighborhood looking for hiding places. He saw a woman trip, and he ran forward to scoop up her baby girl before she got trampled by the others fleeing their

22

burning houses. She screamed, "NO! NO! POR FAVOR!!!" at him, and he burst into tears as he looked into her eyes and realized she actually believed he was going to kill her daughter. He shifted her baby to one arm and used his other arm to pull her up from the ground. He handed the baby to her, and she turned and fled.

He threw his gun down and used both hands to try to control the stampede. As the size of the crowd diminished, he noticed an old woman crawling on the ground and realized her leg had been broken. He picked her up despite her screams of protest and started trotting after the crowd. He had no idea where they were going. He could hear somebody calling his name but did not turn back.

When he caught up with the crowd, he realized they had run straight into a Marine platoon. The soldiers had raised their rifles and were ordering the refugees to drop to the ground. They looked over the prostate bodies, saw Michael standing there with the old woman in his arms, and the commander screamed, "What the hell do you think you're doing, boy!?" He put her on the ground, turned, and bolted. "Desertion is treason!" he heard being screamed at him as he ran back to his own platoon.

By the time he got back, they were already hosing down the neighborhood and searching the still smoldering houses. "Proudpine!" "My God!" "I can't believe you did that!" "The commander almost saw you!" A chorus of voices assailed him, and he did not know what to do. One of his buddies grabbed his arm and pulled him away: "Hold this hose, NOW!" He helped steady the stream of water, his arms shaking. "Where's your gun?" his buddy whispered. He said nothing. He did not say another word until the day they shipped out of Panama. As the commander was reviewing the platoon prior to departure, he stopped in front of Michael and stared at him quietly for a few moments.

"Where's your gun, soldier?"

"I lost it."

"Why didn't you request another one?" He did not answer. "I said, why didn't you request another one?"

"I was too busy."

"TOO BUSY TO GET A GUN!? This is a WAR, soldier!"

"Yes, sir." His commander spit on the ground and stomped off.

Michael told me he was racked with guilt but confused. When he got back to Ft. Bragg, he thought of a thousand things he should have said and done in Panama, and did not understand why he had not done them at the time. Now that I was finally understanding, I tried to tell him that he **had** done plenty--much more than he realized--and was lucky not to have gotten in trouble, and just to forget about it now.

He could not forget about it, and when he found out there was a Hollywood producer preparing a documentary on the invasion, he secretly started supplying her with information. By the time the documentary started winning national awards, Michael was in prison.

***

One year after President Bush had given Michael Proudpine his first trip outside of North Carolina, the President asked him to take his first trip outside the Western Hemisphere. Four-hundred and ninety-nine years after Christopher Columbus had bumped into the New World, Michael Proudpine declined an all-expenses-paid trip to the Old one. No, he would not pack his duffel bag to defend the oil wells of Kuwait.

My final semester of graduate school was a nightmarish merry-go-round of sleepless nights and stressful days. I was constantly riveted to the television set, trying to understand how the SCUDS and the Patriot Missiles could be flying in this pathetic war for oil decades after the blueprints had already been laid for solar cells, wind power, geothermal energy, and electric cars. How could people still think they needed to shed blood for oil?! I knew it spelled doom in more ways than I cared to count, but count them I did, every restless night, instead of counting sheep. Night after night, I counted the dollars that would now be unavailable for the refugees already languishing after other Third World wars, I counted the scientists working on "smart bombs" instead of sustainable development, I counted the hours I had spent preparing for a career whose funding and political hope were surely going up in smoke in the Persian Gulf, I counted the numbers of hard-working volunteer organizations in the U.S. who could kiss their long-awaited "Peace Dividend" goodbye, and I counted the hours Michael was spending locked up at Ft. Bragg.

I marched for peace, I attended lectures on the historical roots of the problems in the Persian Gulf, I wrote every elected and appointed official I could think of, and I still felt completely powerless. Several peace organizations were waging legal battles for the rights of the conscientious objectors at Ft. Bragg and elsewhere, but I held no hope for Michael. By the time graduation came, it was clear that the war and the recession had defeated any chance of my landing a job in the shell-shocked non-profit sector of Washington; it was also clear that Michael would not be free anytime soon.

I got a job at the University and stayed in Chapel Hill. It was a bittersweet time: I was not where I thought I should be, I was not doing what I wanted to do, but I was still near Michael and still in the sentimental womb that was Chapel Hill. I played volleyball in the parks, ate pizza and licked ice cream on Franklin St., swam every chance I got, watched the stars on parade at the Planetarium, and reveled in the blooming of the roses in January, and all the other flowers that followed in progression until the chrysanthemums and pansies of the fall. I prayed and prayed and prayed, I walked my new roommate's dog, I cried without knowing why every time I heard Nikki Meets the Hibachi sing "Bluest Sky", and I could not get Michael out of my mind for a minute.

Michael wanted me to fill him in on everything I was doing, but he was never jealous of my freedom--he was proud of the choice he had made. When his appeals were exhausted, he made his second trip outside of North Carolina--Zanesville Federal Prison in Ohio. Before he left, I gave him a copy of Leo Tolstoy's *War and Peace*. He took one look at the formidable bulk of the novel and burst out laughing. "The biggest book you could find, huh?! I won't be locked up forever!"

"No, it's the **best** book I could find." It said a lot of things I wanted to say; it held a lot of ideas I still wanted to believe. His subsequent letters from Zanesville were always sprinkled with quotes from Tolstoy about war. He never writes me about prison.

The next year, I finally landed a job in Latin America, and packed my bags for Mexico.

Chapter 7

Bored and frustrated, I head to the opulent Las Mañanitas for a drink with a co-worker. We are hoping that a glimpse of the movie stars staying here will jolt us out of our blue funk. The only jolt I get is from my right fallopian tube--that mistress of torturous ovulations. I flee to the ladies room and double over in pain, incredulous that my right ovary has again produced an egg the size and texture of a walnut. I feel it pushing and scraping its way down the fallopian tube and shudder to think what a right-ovary baby might come out as-- hunchbacked and nineteen pounds? A second thought crosses my mind: perhaps my right ovary produces in huge batches and I am actually passing potential quintuplets? I make a mental note: pregnancy only with left ovary!

I feel better the next day. The unorganized and unprofessional ecology committee--for which the Prophet has consented to diverting part of the Center's office space and subcontracting part of my own work time--has finally made arrangements to print the graphics I prepared three weeks ago. I copy the files to a diskette, and hand it over to the secretary. I wish I were already in Brazil. I wish I could have a real job with a normal organization. I wish they would telephone me again because I am starting to think I dreamt it all.

It is hard to believe that in the first month I was here I saw pyramids, cathedrals, murals, rural villages, rivers, lakes, mountains. Now so many people have quit that I work six or seven days a week, sometimes twelve hours a day. I never get to go anywhere, anymore, and my snatches of free time are barely enough to answer a letter, read a book, or watch a TV program. Mexico has nearly disappeared from my sight, except for the Post Office and the shops where I run errands for the Center. It makes me crazy to think I will never get out of this town again until I quit. If only I were suffering **for** something, someone--I can redeem nothing and nobody working in these bozo operations.

I sit at my desk, staring out the window, remembering my first trip to a Mexican slum. No amount of grisly television footage really prepares you for it--the overwhelming stench of excrement, the muddy paths whipped into a frenzy by the rainy season outburst, the immediacy of filth and vermin. The first home I saw was draped in spider webs and every other cliché, down to the naked toddler playing on the dirt floor. These are the children of God, the rejects of human society.

I think back to the visitor from St. Louis who asked me if I get angry. To whom could I direct such anger? The list of candidates is way too lengthy. The man who fathered the "second family" that lives in the cobwebs while he still lives with and spends most of his money on his "first family"? The unemployed, uneducated woman who has let this jackass get her pregnant five times? The society that taught men to be macho studs and women to treasure motherhood above all other things? The incredibly wealthy Mexicans who never give a peso to charity? The government that has always squandered its wealth in corruption and vanity? The foreign "investors" who have reaped the fruits of undervalued resources and paid slave wages to the landless laborers with no marketable urban skills? The conservative Christians who keep insisting that the cry of the poor is coming only from communist agitators?

Everyone under arrest: I cannot find many good guys in Mexico, let alone genuine heroes. There are certainly a lot of loud do-gooders, though. They spend a lot of time sitting around complaining and criticizing. They hatch grandiose schemes in their minds. They take justifiable outrage and turn it into impotent self-pity. They think it is an all-or-nothing struggle, but if they get it all, I know they will then be the oppressors. Compromise seems to be a

28

dirty word for Mexican activists: sometimes I think they would rather accomplish nothing than settle for the small gains possible in such a repressive society. All of history has been the struggle for resources, and in a country so torn by haves and have-nots, nobody seems to believe that a middle-class allocation of resources is possible. Maybe they are right: the U.S. has certainly not achieved it.

The director of the ecology committee enters my office and interrupts my thoughts: he wants to have a rap session with me. It will be the first time he has spoken to me in over three weeks. He is concerned because I am spending so much time aloof in my office. Am I uncomfortable working with Mexicans? I am stunned--what Mexicans!? The secretary and I are the only ones here most days! I remind him that he himself asked me to prepare this office for eight Mexican students with whom I would be working on a research project, and I have been patiently waiting for weeks for them to show up!

"Ah, yes...." He explains to me that they have been "out in the neighborhoods", and are working out of a different office. He adds that I should feel independent enough to "go do my own thing". I remind him that he had told me repeatedly in the fall that I would be working on a very specific project by now--what happened to it? "Well...", but there is no real explanation. "The financing has been delayed, blah, blah, blah."

He adds that I seem defensive. Apparently it has not occurred to him that I might be feeling quite annoyed since the first project he gave me blew up in my face through his own inaction. Apparently he has already forgotten the wrath of the architect left twisting in the wind after I had interviewed him about his ideas for low-income housing and extended to him an invitation from **this** ecology committee director to do a presentation for us. After the architect's presentation materials sat on display at our Center for weeks without the director's ever confirming an actual time for the presentation, the architect got furious, vented his anger on me, began believing that this director did not even exist, and began making threatening inquiries about my legal status to work in Mexico. The

29

architect only calmed down when a senior member of our organization finally telephoned him to explain the delays and eventual cancellation of his presentation. I, myself, have still never been told why they canceled the presentation I had been specifically instructed to arrange.

I say nothing about that now, trying to keep the conversation focused on the present. I have already accepted the fact that the Prophet will never give me anything worthwhile to do, and I am determined to make something of my hours lent out to the ecology committee. I point out to him that--financing or not, students or not--I could be spending my time doing something useful, perhaps research at the government's ecology agency or the university library?

He suggests instead that I go out in the neighborhoods and "talk to people". Inner groan: this is baloney! The do-gooders have already organized this town's neighborhoods to within an inch of their lives, and there is no point in having a non-Mexican who will only be here another six months doing additional community organizing. They need to figure out what actions to take to address the local environmental problems, but, instead, he just wants me to keep networking to see how many more people will join his do-nothing movement so that they can have even bigger and more grandiose meetings to discuss how bad the ecology situation has gotten, and apply for bigger and better grants to do even more networking.

If Mack had not shown me his plans to do an organic farming demonstration project, I would never have believed anybody on this committee had a concrete plan to do anything. Of course, the cynical rumor going around is that they had to let him do it because Mack had become so frustrated with the ecology committee's inactivity that he had threatened to return to California, and they desperately need his credentials on their grant applications. Every time I have broached the subject of potential projects, I have been airily dismissed: "We already have many people with ideas." Yes, indeed. You want money. Ideas can become superfluous, but you can never have too much money!

I frantically grope for a way to bring this absurd conversation to a close before I start screaming. "I quit," would be the most preferred option, but I am reluctant to do that until Brazil is solid as a rock. I tell him that I would like to meet with the students, and he agrees to that.

I cannot recover from this conversation. If he is right, I am culturally retarded, "just don't get it," and have no clue what is really happening on this ecology committee; if he is wrong, I am working with a bunch of morons. Either way, it is bad news. When I get back to Casa Dolores, I close my bedroom door, and put The Sundays on the cassette player.

*And I've been wonderin' lately just who's gonna save
me?....I could have been wrong, but I don't think I was .*

I lie on my bed, trying to use music to calm my nerves and avert the still-hovering anxiety attack.

I'd marry you, but I'm so unwell .

Who **are** these people? How is it that these faraway people can express exactly what I am feeling, while people right around me have no clue in the matter?

Well, that is not exactly true. Many of my coworkers here-- Mexican and American alike--have quit in disgust and gone on to other jobs in Mexico. They agree with me about the institutional sickness here, the hypocrisy, the repression of intellect and creativity, the prevalence of deceit and backstabbing, the madness of the Prophet. Yet, they got out of here sane--beaten up a bit, but sane. I truly "don't get it": I do not know how to hold onto my sanity and continue to work here.

*We are who we are, and what do the others
know?....But I keep hoping that you are the same as me .*

The hope that never dies: it seems we all wander around this world in a state of astonishment at the outrageous behavior of others. Princess Helena spent a decade trying to figure out if she was crazy or the in-laws were; I will not even make it ten months here.

I try to remember what it was like when I first got here--when everything was fresh and new. Was it ever fresh and new? I got two colds the first month here, amoebic dysentery after that--always tired, nauseous. I did get to see some great places, though, before I started to have to pull extra shifts. I did meet some fascinating people, before my tasks increased and I had less and less time to spend with visitors. It already seems so long ago--I can scarcely remember the joyous expectation and excitement I felt at the beginning. Dancing, swimming, sightseeing--yes, I used to do all those things. I struggled to convert my classical Spanish to Mexican colloquialisms. I tried to make friends, but my coworkers kept quitting, and our guests were never around long. He was right, in a sense: I **am** defensive now. With so many people who hurt me still here, and so many people who befriended me now gone, I prefer to be alone. I want to shut it all out.

I suddenly remember being told once that, if I were ever to do drugs, my drug of choice would be heroin. Too true. I get up and switch the tape to Pink Floyd.

When I was a child, I caught a fleeting glimpse...

out of the corner of my eye.

I turned to look, but it was gone.

I cannot put my finger on it now:

The child is grown, the dream is gone.

I...I have become comfortably numb.

I yearn wistfully for the days when I was too young to understand that song, but fight off the longing for blissful numbness one more time.

Tomorrow is my day off, and I vow to immerse myself again in the dolphin show. I can think of nothing else to do. I struggle to find the patience and wisdom I have never known. Many times before I have underestimated my own strength, and I hope this is such a time, too.

Chapter 8

The next week, I am astounded after lunch when Fr. Francis smilingly hands me a ten-page fax. His desk is closest to the fax machine, and he is one of the few people to whom I have confided about my job hunt. "Is this what you've been waiting for?" I glance at the cover page: Brazil is mine pending outcome of a telephone interview! I tell him it is, and he smiles again before heading back to his desk. I will miss him.

I set aside my translation work and spend a lengthy time perusing the details of the research institute and its job opening, my heart pounding. When the prophet's new Associate Director realizes I am reading a personal fax on work time, she goes ballistic. I try to point out that the fax has just arrived, and everybody here gets and reads their faxes at work--not to mention their mail, newspapers, personal phone calls, chatty conversations (of which she, herself, is the queen)--but she will have none of it.

"This place needs to be run more efficiently!" My blood starts boiling: she has been here two weeks and has done nothing but tell other people how to do their jobs, while actually doing nothing herself. A staff this small and over-worked does not need a full-time manager: it needs a full-time masseuse or hypnotist! Where was she when everybody else quit or went on vacation while I worked twelve-hour days, seven days a week, for five weeks straight !!??!! Where does she get off yelling at me for reading a personal fax?! If she wants efficiency, I will whip out the calculator to show her how much comp time they owe me...and start keeping track of how many hours of other people's time she wastes gabbing her

33

head off.

***

Saturday arrives at last--my blessed day off--and I return to my addiction: dolphin shows at 1, 3, and 5. In between shows, I contemplate the other animal attractions in the amusement park--the birds and the monkeys. I decide to rent a boat today but then find that the lagoon has been temporarily drained, so I sit down in the ancient Aztec amphitheater and bury myself in one of these currently popular attorney-authored thrillers. They are so dry, so jaded, so sick. No pretense of love in these sex scenes. The men are always decades older than the women--wow, what a turn-on.

I have already read every good and fair novel our library here has--another reason to quit! Things seemed so much more poignant when I was reading *Les Miserables* or *Death Comes to the Archbishop* in my spare time: my American-abroad, woman-on-her-own psyche wanted to develop, not escape. I read piles of nonfiction, too, reveling in the act of **learning**. Now I know that there is no outlet here for such knowledge, so I am constantly trying to empty my mind, reading as quickly as possible lest there be any chance for my brain to sneak in a stray thought.

The anxieties exiled from my mind take up belligerent residence in my bowels, no matter how hard I try to tell them this is my day off. It is of no use: by the end of the second show, I know I have to quit, as so many disillusioned coworkers have before me. I will try to stick it out one more week to see if I get a concrete offer from Brazil. If I do not, I will surely be too depressed to stay on, in any event. My intestines start settling down as I walk alongside the pool, and I feel I have made the right decision.

After the final show of the day, I hang around, hoping to see some of the post-performance practicing and horsing-around that I glimpsed last week. This time, I am in luck--no guards chase me out! The trainers are practicing the dolphin surfing technique with two new staff members. After awhile, one of the assistants comes over to where I am, and I smile sweetly at her, hoping she will not kick me out. She stuns me by inviting me over to the "stage" to see the

34

dolphins up close! As we walk around the pool, she tells me that everyone has noticed what a big fan I have become, and I realize it would have been hard for them **not** to notice that I have probably seen their show a dozen times now. I am a dolphin groupie!

The assistants chat with me a bit, and the trainers flash smiles at me in between antics. The trainers climb up to the high diving board, and Alejandro places António upside-down like a sack over his shoulders. António spits water through Alejandro's legs, and everybody laughs at the perfectly simulated urination. Then they topple towards the water, separating with a surprising smoothness in mid-air before they enter the water, one head-first and the other feet-first.

I long to jump in the pool, too--get one of these dolphins to flip me high into the air, as they are doing to the staff. I must settle for António's parting invitation to pet them. They are unique animals, and they awe me. After lots of strokes on my part and playful spits on their part, I sheepishly attempt my first "trick"--I imitate António's signal to get the dolphins to talk. It works! I **can** do this! They chatter happily at me.

Yet the supervisor tells me it is not as easy as it looks. Moreover, all the animal trainers that he prepares are young, the eldest being twenty-three. It is almost as if he has read my thoughts and is telling me it is too late for me to prepare for this career.

I ponder how much I love spending time with these people-- not because of or in spite of their being Mexican, but because they are open and honest and caring and joyous--all the qualities lacking in my workplace and staff house. Thinking about leaving them before having had a chance to explore their friendship saddens me. Many people I have liked in Cuahtemoc have said goodbye to this place; soon, I will be the one saying goodbye, and only then will I know how hard it is to bid farewell to the silver linings as well as the black clouds which have been my Mexico.

***

On Sunday I put in six hours of tedious translation work for the Associate Director. Even though several others supposedly have Sunday work shifts, I am the only one in the office. Whenever we have no visitors and things are slow, the unwritten rule is to relax, try to make up for the nightmarish weeks of twelve-hour days, but I will store this day of stupid, unimportant translation work as ammunition for the next time she attacks me. I knock off in time to see the second half of the Super Bowl, but it seems superbly irrelevant here.

On Monday, I wake up with a cold, terrified that I will be incoherent should the Brazilian institute telephone me for the interview. As the cold takes hold of my senses, I become drowsed enough to calm down. They do not call during my entire shift at the ecology committee office.

Before I return to the Center, I flip over my Greenpeace calendar page to February and am greeted by two dolphins! My first reaction is that it is an excellent omen. My second reaction comes after reading the captions about the continuing threats to dolphins: the oceans are becoming increasingly hazardous places for them. Are they better off in captivity?

Later, I lie down and try to finish my legal "thriller", but it is bogged down in what must be its fiftieth description of well-fitting jeans and a baggy sweater. Ohhhhhh, there is a twist this time! Her bra strap, for the first time, is peeking through! This story should have been finished two-hundred pages ago. The descriptions of the law student's hair alone surely account for one-hundred pages. At least this one is not as sadomasochistic as some of those other legal thrillers. I suspect the plot of this one was hatched in a beer stupor at a fraternity pig-pickin'.

Tuesday arrives--still no phone call. Panic is lurking in the back of my mind, held off somewhat by the constant distraction of sneezing. At least I have survived a couple more days without any incidents.

***

36

My cold gradually exits, and Friday arrives without a call from Brazil, but the ecology committee director surprises me with a visit by some of the long-missing students, a research assignment for the coming week, and an appointment with a government agency. At the end of the morning, he comments in a self-congratulatory manner, "I hope now that you feel incorporated into the movement." Well....

A week after my resolve to quit, I chicken out. The Brazilian institute has not given me a phone interview yet, but the American university trying to arrange this assures me they are still interested-- the Executive Director there just happens to be a very busy man. I will go see the dolphins tomorrow and try to endure my tortured thoughts. If Brazil falls through, I truly fear a nervous breakdown.

***

I fall asleep thinking about the trouncing of the Duke Blue Devils in the Southern Part of Heaven--Chapel Hill. Watching UNC basketball on cable TV here was beyond surreal, and bittersweet, as I searched the faces of the fans in the crowd, trying to find traces of the life I led that already seems light years in the past. I lie in bed thinking of the rose blossoms surely blooming around the sundial of the Morehead Planetarium, academic conversations, wacky new sounds at Schoolkids' Records, fried okra and butter beans at Time Out, squash casserole and yeast rolls at Mama Dip's Country Kitchen, eggs at Ye Olde Waffle Shop. Tomorrow, the basketball fans will stroll proudly through their campus, the home of the 1993 NCAA basketball champions and launchpad of Michael Jordan, the best basketball player that ever lived. They are proud of him, proud of it all, proud of UNC. They will walk and talk and kiss and cuddle and play dog frisbee next to the research offices and laboratories of the first public university established in the nation. Many of them will not leave during their summer vacations; many will not leave after their graduations. The reasons I had for leaving seem smaller and smaller in my mind every day.

***

37

I wake up from another nightmare about my job. Thank God it is my day off--the dolphins give me a reason to arise, and I am quickly off to the Magic Jungle. The dolphins as well as their kissing cousins, the sea lions, have learned several new tricks in the past week, and I am humbled by their constant upward spiral of excellence. After the final show, the guards harass me mercilessly, but I finally evade them and sneak down to the stage. They are only practicing a few dives and miscellaneous items from the act this evening, and several of the staff pause to chat with me.

I learn that António is from Costa Rica, and his father is the one who prepares the sea shows throughout Mexico. I am sadly unsurprised. I adore this park so much because it is like a little piece of Costa Rica in Mexico--a place where there is pride in trees and plants, birds and monkeys, dolphins and sea lions. This uncommon, hard-to-find park in my Mexico reminds me of the parks I saw in abundance in my Costa Rica, reminds me of how many Costa Ricans I had met striving to achieve harmony between man and environment. Costa Rica was more lush at the end of the dry season than Mexico seems even at the height of the rainy season. In Costa Rica, you could breathe the air. In Costa Rica, the people actually got the President for whom the majority voted. Costa Rica, like North Carolina, was never monopolized by fat cat plantation owners, and does not suffer from the class extremities of Mexico. It suffers from other things, to be sure, but it was not insufferable to me. If Brazil falls through, the gutsy thing would be to return to Costa Rica and look for a job there.

How few times have I done the gutsy thing! The gutsiest thing I could have done would have been to become an accountant, marry a normal guy, live in the suburbs, and learn to play bridge: I was so sure it all would have suffocated me. We flee the terrors we know, not foreseeing the unknown terrors lurking in our gilded daydreams.

Chapter 9

Sunday is another overlong and depressing workday, but on Monday I get a fax from Brazil asking me to send some academic papers. Joy and agony! Joy because they are definitely interested; agony because they are definitely not in a hurry. It takes me two days to find a decent photocopy place and an international package express company, and in the meantime I can scarcely sleep.

That night, I watch on TV for the fifth time Fanny Flagg's Southern masterpiece "Fried Green Tomatoes", and cry again for the fifth time when Ruth Jamison dies. I am briefly enveloped in Southern homesickness, but the bittersweet spell is quickly broken by the scorpion awaiting me in my bedroom. Tired and aggravated, I miss him nearly ten times before my hurled flip-flop finally dislodges him from the ceiling. I use the other flip-flop to beat him to a pulp.

On Tuesday, I call my sister. "Just be patient," she coos. "Make the best of what you're doing **right** now." **This** from the woman who holed up with her VCR for six straight weekends watching Kevin Costner lose the girl in "Fandango" over and over and over again after Fernando told her not to come to Brazil? "You know, there are two kinds of people in the world--"

"People who **think** there are two kinds of people in the world, and people who **don't**," I interject.

"Why did you call me if you won't listen to me?"

"I was hoping you'd come up with something revolutionary to say," I mutter.

"How about, 'stop feeling sorry for yourself'?"

39

"Don't you ever just get totally fed up with the pain? I mean, why does God get to be thanked for all blessings, but absolved of any responsibility in our suffering?"

"Well...."

"You know, the secretary at the ecology committee stopped being nice to me when I asked her to stop giving me Jehovah's Witnesses magazines? She probably thinks I'm going to Hell because I'm unconcerned that Christmas and Easter are celebrated on old pagan holidays! Who cares?! Why is that important? People can't even be nice to each other. I'm tired of forgiving jerks. I just want to be around **nice** people for a change."

I stop to catch my breath. Stephanie is slow to respond. "You can't be around nice people all the time: there's no challenge in that. Anyway, getting so angry only turns you into a jerk, too."

"Thanks."

"It was a warning--not a criticism! Look, I know you're in a crazy job and a lot of terrible things have happened, but what's important is what's happening **inside** you."

"Exactly," I reply. "I'm losing my mind."

"No, you're not. You're just under a lot of stress. You need to get out more."

"You know what my schedule's like."

"Try meditating."

"You know I can't do that."

"Then listen to your favorite tapes."

"I do." She is running out of gas, but I feel a little better. "Look, I just wanted to hear your voice--I'll be OK. How are things with Peter?"

"He's loosening up a bit. Last weekend I got him to go roller skating! Of course, we had to do it in Annapolis--he was so afraid he'd run into somebody he knew if we went to some roller rink around D.C. Personally, I think some of his bosses' snotty kids deserve to get run over by a novice skater, but he didn't want to be the one to do it. Did you ever find a place to go horseback riding?"

"Nope," I respond. I have not been on a horse or at a piano in way too long. She is stalling now, and I realize there is something else she wants to say.

"Umm, you haven't said anything about Michael," she finally says. "When you called, I figured that was what you wanted to talk about."

"What?"

"Didn't you get his letter?" No. "Oh.... Well, he called me last week. He wants to move to D.C. when he gets out of jail--he might get out sooner than expected. I told him he could crash with me until he finds a job. You don't mind, do you?"

"Mind?! God, that's great! Why didn't you tell me as soon as I called? I'm so happy for him!"

"You really don't mind?"

"Stephanie! I think you should be asking Pete that, not me!"

"Well, I haven't yet. I figured there was no point, if you didn't want me to."

"We're just friends now," I say.

"I know--it's just...kind of weird. Anyway, I don't think Pete could get jealous of somebody like Michael--no offense. I just mean--."

"I know what you mean!" Half-breed, ex-convict.... "If he doesn't mind, I don't mind--I think it's really nice of you to offer that! I'm just surprised he wants to go to D.C."

"Well, he's a surprising person, isn't he?" Yes, he is.

***

I leave work sick. I writhe in agony on my bed, trying to keep my headphones on to concentrate on the music. REM is singing about the horrible things they have seen, about how you must hold on when everything hurts, about how it feels when a loved one dies,

41

about black-eyed peas and candy bars and swimming on a warm Southern evening, about leaving because "...nothing is going my way." REM is Michael's favorite group. My body is punishing me for wasting another ovulation. Every muscle in my abdomen is squeezing the life out of me because I have, yet again, failed to give them a baby to which they can direct their pent-up energies.

I cannot get the heating pad to work; maybe I should go find Chillona to heat up my lower abdomen. I hate her dander, but I love her warmth. Last night she set a record--one consecutive hour of sitting on my lap without freaking out. She trusts me more and more. It has taken a very long time, but she now lets me caress her from head to tail without getting upset.

She will be a nervous wreck again soon: three new staff members are moving in this month. It took Chillona months and months to get used to me. I still have not recovered from the staff turnover myself. This Friday I have been invited to a party at which there will be seven former co-workers in attendance! It is absurd. I miss them. Perhaps I should bring my camera. I took rolls of film the first couple of months I was here. Lately, there has been nothing and nobody new to photograph, except the dolphins--happily framed on my desk in front of my radio.

I change the tape to Jon Secada and slowly fall asleep, listening to him sing to his child about how he shall be his best *amigo*. My heart breaks when he sings about the courage of his *angel*--a sick little boy, his son?--in facing the future that Secada is afraid to face.

***

The week continues, downhill. By Thursday night, I am dreaming of impending death. I race through the hospital corridors, desperately trying to find the emergency room before the miniature twin babies I am carrying in tiny Tupperware containers die. They do not seem to be breathing. When the alarm clock goes off, I am panting for air.

The ecology committee director, whom I have not seen all week, shows up Friday and decides to get chatty while I am printing letters off the computer. He asks me if I have just washed my hair. I give him a quizzical look. He adds, "You have trouble understanding me, don't you?" He is referring to his Spanish, but I have, unfortunately, "understood" every word he just said. I reply that I always wash my hair, wondering if I should feel insulted that he has perceived it as dirty on other days. "But, it looks as if you **just** washed it." There is nothing different about my hair, and I say nothing.

He then asks what color my eyes are, and now I am very concerned. I answer him in a matter-of-fact voice that they are green. He elaborates on how they look different in certain lighting conditions or with certain colors of clothing. Is he bored with the eye color of his wife? I say nothing.

He abruptly changes the subject and asks if I have seen "A Perfect World". (Yes, in the U.S., during my Christmas vacation.) What about "Like Water for Chocolate"? (Yes, in the U.S.) "Don't you go to movies here?" (Yes, but I saw those two in the U.S.) I have finally finished my letters and promptly turn the computer off to leave for lunch, even though I am not hungry, afraid he will start quizzing me on specific love scenes.

Chapter 10

I finally get the letter from Michael. He wants to get a public policy job when he gets out of jail. He is torn between working for other conscientious objectors or working for an American Indian group. He knows a lot of D.C. doors might be closed to an ex-con, but he wants to try. His folks want him to return to North Carolina, so he may go spend a month there before trying his luck in Washington.

I irrationally want to believe he is doing it for me, as much as for himself. I want him to slay that dragon for me--that nostril-flared, smoke-hurling, teeth-bared city of political viciousness that chews up optimistic public servants and spits them out as hardened cynics obsessed with covering their own asses and paying those ghastly suburban D.C. mortgages. The truth is, I fear for him--I cannot even imagine what D.C. will do to him. At least he will have Stephanie-- that is a lot more than I had when I arrived there.

***

I head to the bizarre party of past and present co-workers. I know all the enmities and all the alliances, and it unnerves me to watch the fake smiles exchanged by certain conversationalists forced to talk to people that drove them away from the Center, or vice versa. I have a reputation for honest and open behavior, so the backstabbers avoid me: they know I have had no difficulty figuring out whom to trust around here, and they know I will not fake pleasantries simply because we all work(ed) for a "Christian" organization. I have the clearest of friendships and clearest of enmities of anybody here. I avoided hurling daggers for as long as I could, but I too have begun to take sides, something of which I am not proud.

I talk to Rosa, who is starting a new job on Monday, and I am thrilled for her. She tells me she sees me going through the exact same struggle she did with the Center and the way the Prophet/Profit runs it, and I know there is nobody in Mexico who understands me better than she does. I am sad that her new home is far away from the staff house. I confide in her that I might get a job in Brazil, and she is happy for me. I know she will tell nobody.

***

On my day off, I again return to the sea show. It is two weeks since I resolved to quit. A couple of faxes have enabled me to procrastinate that decision, but I remain tormented by the thought that Brazil could still fall through.

The show is exceptionally funny today because the rebelliousness of the animals is making even the trainers laugh. I have never seen so much misbehaving in all the times I have been here, but the dolphins and sea lions come through with the big-ticket items.

At the end of the day, I go down to the stage and learn they have just gotten a new sea lion. Alejandro feeds the new fellow his supper while Blondie and Toto look on with agonized expressions of envy. I know the other sea lions have already eaten, but it seems torture for them to get nothing while the newcomer dines. I also start feeling pangs of guilt, knowing that these two had to perform a trick for every fish they ate today, but the newcomer does not...not yet, anyway. Maybe Blondie and Toto never enjoy it at all--maybe the fun is all just an illusion, maybe they will do anything out of desperation for food.

I go to the edge of the pool to play with the dolphins. We splash each other over and over again. The physiology of a dolphin's face, unlike that of the mournful looking sea lion, seems eternally locked in a grin, but I wonder how much of this is genuine play and how much of it is hope for fish. If they were suddenly given a choice between the magical pool and the open sea, would they stay here?

45

My mind wanders to the monkeys chained in the trees near the entrance. They have a decent range of motion available, but not enough to play with each other. They all have to sleep in private huts, and I ache thinking about that while I watch the dolphins chase each other and knock each other about in the pool. If life is all relative, then these dolphins actually have it pretty good, better than the monkeys...I think.

I am a monkey that knows how to cut my chain, but I am not sure which tree should be my next destination, so I hang on. I wish I were trapped in a dolphin pool, instead--sentenced to a life of jumps, somersaults, water polo, acrobatic stunts. Their room and board is earned far more cheaply than mine is...I think. I head back to Casa Dolores, soaked to the skin, wishing the sun had not already set.

***

Sunday is a brutally long day, culminating in a marathon solo session of cleaning up supper for thirty people while everyone else mixes with the guests. I am enraged. I am so exhausted I become feverish.

Valentine's Day arrives--it means nothing to me. Mardi Gras arrives--it means too much to me. I must start thinking about forty days in the desert, Lent. I do not want to suffer anymore.

I go with a coworker to a pancake supper hosted by the Anglican community. This is WASP Central. Everything is "lovely", "yummy", or "splendid". My ethnicity and Catholicism rise up in alternating bursts of amusement and disgust at these happy, bubbly people. What will they do for Lent? Give up chocolate? Give up one of their servants?

The mariachi band is the youngest I have ever seen; after inquiries, I learn that they are from a large orphanage I visited last summer. When they are finally given plates of food after everybody else, they wolf down the pancakes and sausages in a fervor familiar to orphans the world over. Do these Brits and Brit descendants ever think about Oliver Twist in this Dickensian Mexico?

I go home. I cannot help but wonder how differently I might have passed Mardi Gras in Brazil--Carnival! However, Mardi Gras is ending, and I must think about Lent. Logistics first: will I be able to squeeze mass in between my two jobs, or will I have to try to go in the evening? Sinfulness second: will I succeed in growing closer to God in the next forty days? I have my doubts on both counts.

I enter the guilt trip: I am a bad Christian, I do not forgive, I pity myself for my sufferings, I get angry about bearing my cross, I am fed up with trying to discern God's will in my life. I tell myself that I would endure any suffering at all if I could see the redemptive power of it, but I prefer trying to save the world to trying to face my own scary self. I am a hypocrite, and even more so because hypocrisy is the one trait I refuse to tolerate in anybody else.

Judgmentalism, selfishness, hard-heartedness--these are the flaws I must address over Lent. Yet, it is a fine balancing act, trying to flail out against my faults without toppling off the tightrope which is my self esteem. I must take positive actions, not negative ones: Bible readings, prayers, and good deeds–not sackcloth and ashes. It will be hard. I am angry at God because of all I had to give up to come to this place, a place which has not given me the opportunity to redeem the poor and suffering of Mexico, or redeem myself. A good Christian would trust that God had a reason for bringing me here, but the doubting Thomas in me fears I will break into little pieces before I see redemption here. I have no desire to enter Lent; I want out.

I go to bed thinking about today's phone call: the Executive Director of the Brazilian institute has taken steps indicating the likelihood of my hiring, but it is still not definite. How long must I live in this twilight zone? Some man I have never met, in a city I have never seen, in a country I have never known, will decide whether I belong in his world or not. The last man who made that decision–the Prophet/Profit–misled me about the reality of this world, this work. Still, I take refuge in the hope of the hopeless: it cannot get any worse, can it? Last night, I had to listen jealously to vacation tales about the Yucatán, Vera Cruz, Guatemala, flamingo sanctuaries, and archaeological sites that I have never had a chance to see. Would I end up chained to my job in Brazil, too? If I did, would I at least see some redemption for the suffering of hard work?

The next day, the Ash Wednesday church bells ring on and off all day long. I picture the throngs of Mexicans asking forgiveness of their sins and deliverance from hunger, thirst, illness, fear. I have many blessings, and I am ashamed at how often I ignore them. I am ashamed of how rarely I am a blessing to others. I am ashamed of my shame, at my difficulty believing in God's grace.

The office phone rings, and it is for me. The Brazilian institute **does** want me to come--the sooner, the better! They are now only awaiting the approval of a couple officials at the donor agency which will be funding my placement. I am delirious, near tears. Easter has arrived forty days early for me! Well, maybe not quite yet. Perhaps I have just seen the boulder removed from the cave: when the next fax or phone call comes, I will know for sure my resurrection is a reality.

I am giddy, but purposefully dampen my own spirits by remembering it **could** still fall through. These higher-ups **might** just see something in my application, something in my resumé, something in my papers too offensive to sign off on my hiring. I must remain cautious until I know for sure. All afternoon, I work like a mad dog, frequently fighting off the huge grins which keep threatening to erupt on my face. Every now and then my lungs seem to squeeze my heart--rejoice! No, not yet. My feet are killing me at the end of the day, and I change shoes to walk to the cathedral.

The Ash Wednesday service begins with the priest's asking us all to turn around; then he talks about how people often turn their backs on God. Next, we are asked to turn sideways, and he talks about how we turn our backs on one another. The service is excellent: my Spanish is not perfect, but I sense he has distilled the essence of Lent perfectly.

As I walk up to receive my ashes, an adorable little girl in her mother's arms keeps tugging on my shoulder strap. Every time I turn around, she is completely mystified as to why her action is causing me to look at her. I finally hang the purse on her shoulder,

48

but she is even more stumped. She regards my smiles and laughter with complete bemusement. I want a child. So many Lents I have gone through, but I still have so many desires, and most of them end so badly. I will not have a child until I know it will all turn out fine. If Brazil turns out badly, I may be afraid to pay heed to my dreams ever again.

Chapter 11

When will I leave Mexico? What will I take with me when I leave? I want to remember the good and forget the bad, but how? I ponder the good things: the sunshine, the palm trees, the guitar music, the churches, the pyramids, the lush swimming resorts I used to visit when I actually had weekends. I ponder the good people: departed and non-departed coworkers, professional acquaintances, the housekeeping and maintenance staff who have taught me so much Spanish and even more kindness, the desperate vendors of the zócalo that seemed to range in age from 3 to 93, the death-defying political protestors, the pious at the cathedral, the joyous in the parks, and the happily beloved children everywhere are the people I will never forget.

I have learned a lot and seen a lot, but *basta--no más*. The Executive Director of the Brazilian institute told me on the phone that I may lose my Spanish after switching to Portuguese. There is a hurting place inside me that would probably be happy never to hear Spanish again, but I know that will pass, eventually. One day it will make me happy to listen to the Mexican songs I have on tape, to watch a Mexican program on TV, to chat with a new Mexican acquaintance--but not now.

In the evening I head out to pick up a ton of bread for supper--53 people! I am accosted in the plaza by a student of English who would like to give me a survey as part of a homework assignment. Name, age, why am I in Mexico--then he goes right for the kill-- "What do you hate most about Mexico?" I am momentarily stunned--has he been reading my mind all day?--and he prompts me with, "some people say things like 'there are no garbage cans'"! **That** would not even make my Top Ten list!

"Sometimes people are very rude," I say. What do I like most? "People are very committed to their families." How do I greet people in the U.S.? "I say 'hey!'." What do I think of the way Mexicans greet each other with a kiss? "I like it."

In the evening, we all watch the faraway Winter Olympics on TV at the staff house. I do not like snow or winter sports, but it is a thrill to see these crazy people flying down the mountains at breakneck speeds, and these figure skaters occasionally breaking out of the mold to do something stunningly original or beautiful. Today is a day for many favorites to fall down, and many upstarts to triumph. The announcers are, as usual, unabashedly for the front-runners, and scarcely comment on the others unless their performances are too superb to be ignored.

The Winter Olympics always seem such a European affair: the imperialists brought many things to their Third World colonies, but they did not bring snow and ice. Aside from the famed Jamaican bobsled team, I have yet to see any competitors from Latin America or the Caribbean, and it seems odd to be watching the Winter Olympics in Mexico. It is only in the Summer Olympics that former colonies can embarrass their ex-masters by triumphing in track and field, soccer, baseball....

It is hard to go to bed, and I settle in for another nerve-wracking Thursday night: if the Institute does not call on Friday, I will have to suffer through yet another weekend without any confirmation. I awake on Friday with another huge stomach ache-- three trips to the bathroom before breakfast, two more after.

I try to go to work, but the ecology office is locked until someone I have never seen before finally shows up at 10:30. I, the only person who has actually come to the ecology office every week since 1994 began, have no keys! Who is this stranger with keys?! It is going to be a long day.

51

For some reason I start thinking about Michael's letter again. He always complains about the injustice of being in jail, but he never actually complains about the results of being in jail. He must be suffering so much. I could break my own chains if I were braver, stronger, but he has no choice--he **must** serve his time. He has made a handful of major life decisions, and lived with the consequences; I have acted and reacted a thousand times, and continue to complain about the consequences.

Friday drags on. I have already begun preparing letters and change-of-address cards to announce my exciting twist of fate, but I still do not have the green light to send them out. Am I living in a dream state? I try to wake up, I try to open my eyes, but I seem to be paralyzed. I cannot wake up. I need a trumpet blast or something to put me in motion. At times I feel the butterflies welling up from my inner depths–hope mixed with fear of the unknown. Delirium, elation, hysteria, panic--I am flooded by emotion. I can file books in the library, answer the door, and work on the computer, but I am not really here at all. I am in a daze. There is no reality left for me but that one, particular communication I await.

Father Francis delivers another fax to me after lunch: they are still awaiting the final approvals, which they anticipate will not be a problem, but they do not know how long it will take. Nonetheless, they want me available in three weeks! This must be a cruel practical joke: after I give notice and mail off all my changes of address, they will tell me that--surprise!--Mr. X and Ms. Y have vetoed me, after all.

I am a nervous wreck and have no idea what to do. Perhaps other people in my position would completely assume that everything would work out fine and proceed with that expectation, but I always expect calamity and proceed with a caution bordering on paranoia. This is ridiculous! I must force myself to draw a line here: I need to tell the Institute that I will not give notice or make travel arrangements until they say everything is completely confirmed. I will call on Monday. I cannot go on like this.

***

The dolphins and sea lions put on the worst performance I have ever seen. It is still good, but I am shocked at its variation from their usual excellence. The petite sea lion, Blondie, scarcely performs at all: she keeps diving back into the water for five-minute stretches at a time, leaving Alejandro alone with the veteran, Toto. Perhaps she is unnerved by the new sea lion in their living quarters, the one who does no tricks at all but gets to eat fish, anyway.

I have no clue about the dolphins; they are simply a mess. After the last show, I watch them being fed up close. I had no idea dead fish produced so much blood: the bucket is drenched in it, the open jaws of the dolphins are awash in it, and the pool water shows streaks of it. I look at these five bottlenoses chowing down, and it is now much easier to picture them ganging up on and devouring a shark. Yet, they never attack their fellow mammals--humans. Why? Horses, dogs, and cats have all been known to turn on their owners, attacking with teeth or claws, bites or kicks. There are no dolphin horror stories. Would there be atrocities if they understood what water pollution has done, how many brethren have been snared in tuna nets, how many sisters have been overexploited in sea shows?

Sunday's workload is surprisingly easy. I finish my tasks quickly and start making phone calls to friends in the U.S. I also write out a careful fax to send to my prospective employer in Brazil: I want a green light, not a flashing yellow or a merge sign!

The Center's office manager decides to take a mini vacation this week, and I will be swamped with work covering for her--what terrible timing. I can scarcely imagine how I will drag myself through the tedium of endless office chores this week. Everything will seem unbearable, and I fear it might not take much to make me blow a gasket and bite somebody's head off.

I sleep very badly, and Monday is an exhausting eleven hours of duty. I learn that somebody is heading back to the U.S. tomorrow and can take letters; I ponder it all day with my sleepy and barely functioning rational process, and I decide to go ahead and send my mail-forwarding notifications--they will go into effect one week from now! Two weeks from now, will I be getting forwarded, too?

Today is the first day of peace negotiations between the Zapatista revolutionaries and the Mexican government, fifty-one days after the rebellion in Chiapas began. In the U.S., they are celebrating President's Day--George Washington, the famed revolutionary, and Abraham Lincoln, the famed counterrevolutionary. Schoolchildren are always taught that there are good rebellions and bad rebellions. This rebel army has named itself after one of Mexico's most-revered revolutionaries and is, in fact, rebelling against a government run by the supposed inheritors of Zapata's revolution many decades ago. The Party of the Institutionalized Revolution will now negotiate with the Zapatista Army of National Liberation. In my heart, I want to believe it could be a win-win situation, but in my mind, I have my doubts.

Tuesday night arrives with no response to my fax, and I am near tears, terrified it will all fall through. I retreat to my room and listen to the Boomtown Rats sing on the radio about a woman who really did have a nervous breakdown one day and shot to death a bunch of children in a schoolyard.

> *School's out early, and soon they'll be learning, and the lesson today is HOW TO DIE...And you can see no reason, 'cause there are no reasons. What reason do you need to die? Tell me why! I don't like Mondays....I wanna shoot...the whole day down.*

There are millions of things I would love to shoot down--but schoolkids?! God, could I ever go that berserk?! Yet, I know how it feels to have rages and fears and anxieties growing to unmanageable sizes, to know an explosion is coming without knowing when or where it will happen. How many implosions can I take before I explode into a million pieces?

***

I get a phone call from the American university on Wednesday: the wheels are turning, but, for some reason, those higher-ups still have not signed off. They will push it all back a

54

couple weeks, but in the meantime, they are going ahead with the visa application, the computer importation process, and the other things they need to do to coordinate my placement at the Brazilian institute. I am stunned, and flee out of the office to get a grip on myself before the hysterical sobs erupt. Why, oh why, oh why?! Why so long?! Who are these people that are too busy to read a memo about my hiring and sign off on it?! Would it help if I called them up and cried hysterically on the phone, pleading with them to deliver me from this loony bin?!

The Center's office manager is late in returning from her vacation, but I insist that I have already spent too much time away from my other job, so I desert the Center office and go back to the ecology committee the next morning. I cannot remember the last time anybody had a discussion about ecology here--it is all meetings and computer reports, and meetings about reports, and reports about meetings. The last time my ecology supervisor spoke to me was to encourage me to get some sun on my white legs. Still, there is less stress here, and I do not have half a dozen people pulling me in a hundred different directions as I do at the educational center. If I were a violent person, at least three people over there would be sporting black eyes right now. I am a nonviolent person who still has no clue what to do with her anger.

I settle into my ecology office desk and think about Chillona's nervous breakdown last night. There has been too much change, and too rapid, at the staff house. With two new staff members arriving and the office manager being away on vacation, Chillona has suddenly taken to following me--the still familiar face--around Casa Dolores all the time. Last night, she spent over an hour darting around for no apparent reason, repeatedly diving for cover under furniture to escape invisible assailants. She finally relaxed enough to snooze a couple hours on my lap while I watched the Winter Olympics.

It was the ice skating match of the decade. The woman who was viciously attacked in January has made a complete recovery and managed to skate into first place; the woman linked to the attackers but swearing her own innocence will enter the finals from a tenth-place standing. Good has triumphed over evil; Cinderella, over the evil step-sister! Or so it would seem.

Yet, if we have to let go of the myth of Cinderella, we also have to let go of the myth of the "evil" step-sister. Maybe she is not so bad. Maybe she is innocent? Maybe her only crime was poor judgment in picking friends and lovers? It happens. She has tried to refocus on her skating, to talk with her feet, to prove she can do it with or without that rival. Her pride is in her blade skills, but nobody will judge her by what she wants to be judged. I know how that feels, too. Stephanie and Michael are the only two people who have ever judged me on what I wanted to be judged--and been proud of me.

***

On Friday, the office manager returns, and I am jubilant. Late in the afternoon, we have a chat about how things are going for me. She knows I am unhappy and has done everything she can to make it better for me, but she, too, is being pulled in too many directions. She, too, is looking forward to the day when she can move onto something else in her life. She is exhausted from her trip, but manages to stay awake for the finals in the ladies free skate.

It has become, improbably, even more melodramatic. The Ukrainian and German competitors had a terrible collision in practice and will be skating with injuries. The femme fatale in tenth place breaks her shoelace minutes before her performance and cannot get her act together; she pleads her case to the judges, in tears, and they grant her a respite. Even so, she ends up out of medal contention. The Ukrainian orphan, sixteen years old, is permitted a local anesthetic for her injuries, and skates magnificently to a gold medal. Cinderella also skates beautifully, but loses by a tenth of a point and takes the silver.

Poor femme fatale. My nightmares are always like that: it is not that I cannot perform, but that I am late for the test, or cannot move my legs fast enough to get there, or have a flat tire....There is always something holding me back, marring my abilities. Give me a chance! I can do this! So many excuses.

***

I awake on Saturday morning with knots in my stomach, thinking about all the angry things I want to say in the big meeting that the office manager has planned with the Prophet to discuss how I am being used and treated here. Over breakfast, I listen to one of the brand-new employees start voicing her miseries here: it is Rosa all over again, it is me all over again. I struggle with what to say to her, reluctant to encourage her down the road of acrimony I have trod. I tell her not to take it personally: everybody gets the same treatment here. My big meeting will probably not even take place.

I decide I should take a break from the Magic Jungle sea show and head out of town to a swimming resort where fields of sugar cane have been replaced by fifteen different types of swimming pools, and the colonial architecture built by Indians and owned by Spaniards now hosts hundreds of pleasure-seeking mestizos. It is a lovely place of bamboo and palm, flower bushes and blossoming vines, fountains and waterfalls. Happy people abound, and I, too, love it.

My ecological mind is embarrassed by the fact that I truly love the smell of chlorinated water, but I cannot help it--swimming has always made me happy. Of course, I cannot swim today because I am alone: my things could get stolen, or I could drown and nobody would notice. The last time I came, I was with a friend, and we tried out pool after pool--volleyball pool, lap pool, slide pool, waterfall pool, Roman bath pool, and, of course, the mighty toboggan pool. Today I will have to settle for vicarious pleasure and aesthetic sensibility.

By the end of the day, I realize I have made a terrible mistake: I had so much fun the last time I was here that every minute today has only served to remind me of that friend's absence, of how alone I am now that she has returned to the U.S. I resent the happy families and friends here, I begrudge them their joy mere miles from the ravine of precarious shacks and shanties that the bus passed on the way here, I am jealous of their volleyball games and laughter. What am I doing here? There is nothing for me here.

I need to move on, but already I am losing the ability to imagine myself living in Brazil. It is again becoming easier to picture myself ending up back in the horror of D.C., pounding the pavement. It has been another week in which I did not quit, in which I got a fax and a phone call implying I would be "wanted" very soon, but nothing real. I could have gotten married, pregnant, and divorced during the time I have been courted by Brazil. The thrill is gone.

I do not know the clinical definition of a nervous breakdown. I do know that, more and more frequently, I am seized by sudden urges to smile or sudden urges to cry. Both feelings begin in the exact same way--with a sudden arrest in respiration, followed by a constrictive feeling in my chest--and end with a sensation of some force being thrust up my esophagus into my throat. It all happens in about one second, and it is only when it reaches my throat that I know if it will dissipate into a loony smile or into a frowning swallowing-back of tears. Many times in my life I have beaten back my unhelpful emotions with every weapon of denial and detachment I could muster; never before have my emotions fought back with such guerrilla tactics. I am under siege from within.

Chapter 12

I will force myself to make some sort of decision, some kind of baby step towards confronting the absurdities of my present existence. Today is the last day of February, and the ecology group is already six weeks behind in paying my measly salary and expenses. I will not return until they pay up: these people and these activities are not worth voluntary labor. I could do more social good walking around the city, handing out coins to the beggars. I could do more personal good hiding out in my room, listening to the radio.

Now, what to do about the educational center? I hate working there, but they will be busy enough in March to consider bargaining for more hours from me. I decide to make them an offer: I will work more hours for them **if** they "loan" their sister organization--the ecology group--the money to pay what I am due, as well as assuming responsibility for my future salary. If they say no, I will not work one hour over my current agreement with them. I have done overtime for them every week I have worked for them-- *no más*.

Brazil, Brazil--I still do not know what to do about Brazil. I have puzzled it over in my mind again and again, but it seems there is nothing I can do but wait. I take down my Greenpeace calendar from the ecology office I am abandoning. March's photo will be a wise owl; I reluctantly bid farewell to February's dolphins, and struggle for life's wisdom.

***

The sneering reply to my previous leap of faith--the mail forwarding order I sent a week ago--arrives in the mail. It has been

59

mailed **to** me!! I check it over and over again for mistakes, but there are none. Some other stupid bureaucrat has hit the delay button on my life, refusing to activate my mail forwarding request. Who is playing this cruel joke on my life? Again, I am near tears, but fight them off.

I will make a phone call tomorrow to my suitor in Brazil--tell him that FATE has delayed my mail-forwarding order, but I would like to send it again, **if** he would be so kind as to give me another, more certain date. One of these days I will not be able to store one more tear, the dam will break, and I will cry a torrid river.

***

It is March 1st. I telephone my suitor in Brazil. I get the green light. I have awaited it so long–I can scarcely believe it is true.

I head to the educational center to tell the office manager. She is thrilled for me--happy, excited, jubilant. I am not feeling any of these things. It feels good to write my resignation letter, but the dam is still firmly in place. It is as if the wedding date has been set, but I half expect the groom to jilt me at the altar. When will I relax and be happy? I am detached from my own life: I will probably end up fractured into ten personalities, trying desperately not to deal with the realities of my life, my emotion.

I have a long list of things to do, but I get shanghaied into working seven hours instead of my "part-time" three. By the end of the day, I am exhausted from running around on so many errands, but I telephone a couple friends in the U.S. I tell them that before going to Brazil I will go to the U.S. for orientation with the American university coordinating this, and the sponsor agency funding it, and thus have time to see them before going on to the Institute in Brazil.

I call Stephanie, too. She is ecstatic for me, and it is touching to hear the most familiar voice in my life bursting with happy emotions on my behalf. I will see her in a couple weeks in Washington!

Chapter 13

The next day I set in motion all the things I have been waiting and waiting and waiting to do. I was thoroughly organized and prepared for this day, and I know exactly what to do. I just do not know what to feel, or rather, how to bring my feelings to the surface, and so I continue to wander around in a fog.

I run into the newest ecology committee employee--the one who showed up that day, out of the blue, with the office keys--and she asks where I have been, because they have something for me to do! Apparently my resignation letter has not made the rounds yet. I tell her I will no longer be working there, and point out that they have not paid me for six weeks' worth of salary and expenses. I do not have time to try to explain my other grievances to her.

She replies that the "communication problem" with the bank has been resolved, they have access to their money now, and, in fact, have already cut me a check! "Gracias," I reply, a little stunned. It is fortunate that I wrote the resignation letter before they paid me-- otherwise it might have been difficult to strike such an indignant tone. Still, they had never explained to me that they had been having "communication problems" with the bank--they had merely stated they had *no dinero*, which I took literally as "no money". They never explained anything to me.

When I stop by later to pick up the check, the ecology boss wants to talk to me. He is terribly sorry that nobody ever explained to me the banking delay--he thought I knew the situation. I want to scream, "you never explained anything to me!" I hold myself back and try to be gracious--my weak suit. Then he tries to talk me into doing a manuscript project before I go. Inside, I am groaning, but I tell him I will think about it, see how much time I have available--in a couple days I will know if I am on schedule or not for being ready to go in less than two weeks.

Then he adds that he would like to take me out to eat before I go. Now I am hedging desperately, and he asks me pointblank if I do not want to. I decide it is time to answer truthfully: I do not feel comfortable with him because he is a married man who has made many comments about my anatomy. He is incredulous--he never meant that! "It is just a cultural thing!" Yes, indeed, men the world over have clung to sexist behavior as their rightful cultural heritage. He is apologizing profusely, so I accept his apology as best I can. I tear myself away as soon as possible.

Surely there is a place in this world I will fit in, where everything and everybody will all seem natural and normal to me? This afternoon I heard the allegedly very religious Associate Director make prolific use of the F word; sometimes I feel I have spent my entire time in Mexico cringing at one inexplicable nastiness after another. *Basta*.

***

I have less than two weeks to go, and what am I panicking about? The dolphins! They only perform four days a week, mostly in conflict with my work schedule! I may only be able to see them a couple more times! I ask the Center if I can come on duty a wee bit late tonight, so that I can go this afternoon. I have never seen a Thursday performance! I have never seen anything other than Saturday shows. Missing it last Saturday has weighed heavily on my mind. It does not help that the novel I am currently reading has a special focus on dolphins, and a TV program on Sunday speculated about the ability of dolphins to communicate therapeutically with human beings: my obsession just keeps getting fed! I will have to quit cold turkey soon enough--this afternoon, I will indulge.

I furiously try to finish off my correspondence in the morning, then head out in the afternoon. I am still not sleeping well, I am nervous all the time, and I am constantly suffering from fierce stomach pains. I am close to tears over and over again, and it finally registers in my conscious brain that it is my loneliness which is driving me crazy. I have begun to anticipate being alone again in another strange city. I have tried to view it as glamorously and enthusiastically as I can, but I am picturing myself again working unbearably long hours with little time or energy or opportunity to get to know anybody but fellow slaves and slave-drivers.

The park is practically deserted: the Thursday crowd is a pale shadow of the Saturday throng. When I try to enter the dolphin show, one of the attendants starts commenting on how many times I have come and what they do when somebody comes so frequently.... They have made no move to open the chain for me to pass, and I wildly conclude that they have realized my insane obsession, labeled me a dolphin stalker, and are going to deny me my addiction! Instead, he concludes his chat by telling me that they do not charge people who come so often. I am stunned. I have come virtually every weekend for seven weeks, and now, finally, when I can probably only come a couple more times, they will let me in free?!

I thank him for being so kind and tell him I love the show, but actually I do not mind paying and I will be leaving Mexico shortly anyway. They open the chain but refuse to take my ticket, which I had already paid for and cannot use any other day since it is stamped with today's date. I suspect the trainers noticed my absence last Saturday and instructed the attendants to let me in free, in case I had run out of money or something.

The show is very weak. It may be in part because it is the first day of their performance "week", but it is probably because the staff really do not feel like pulling out all the stops for an audience of fewer than ten people. I feel sorry for the other audience members when I realize they have missed a few of the really nice tricks. It is far from the best show I have seen, but I am thrilled because it has been a whole twelve days since the last one.

In between shows, I read some more chapters in my fantasy novel. In a book full of mysteries, one of the key mysteries seems to be, why have all the dolphins disappeared from planet Earth? The scientist who knows more about them than anyone else realized far too late that his efforts to learn their language were irrelevant, since the dolphins actually **could** understand humans fine but just chose not to bother communicating with them–that is, did not bother until they left Earth with the parting message etched in glass, "so long, and thanks for all the fish." Well, I suppose a truly intelligent life form **would** probably avoid communicating with humans: we are strange and dangerous when unpredictable, boring and dangerous when predictable. We are rarely content, let alone truly happy.

The first time I saw this dolphin show, I **was** really and truly happy. I was thrilled to be alive, filled with the wonder and awe and instant love and adoration usually found only in children. I ache with the thought of never seeing these beautiful beings again.

I head to the second show. I have it committed to memory so well now that I will not forget it for a long time, maybe never. I hope this level of detail does not make the memory excruciatingly painful. There is one odd addition today: for some reason, during part of their chat with the audience, the trainers mention where the dolphins were captured. I cringe at the word *capturados*, picturing large men with nasty nets dragging these innocents away from their friends and family. They did not want to come--surely they did not. I hope fervently that they have ended up happy, anyway.

I rush off after the show to buy dinner rolls for the Center's guests. The dolphins and I both work for room and board, and though I have never been threatened with a cutoff of food or removal from my bed, I am acutely aware that I am a peon here, working long "part-time" hours for bare survival. When the workload turns out to be uncharacteristically light this evening, I half expect to be told "no supper tonight, young lady".

Later, I open my map of Mexico to see where my idols had been captured. Out of my map falls my hand-written note about all the places I wanted to see in Mexico when I had the chance. No chance. One of the places was, actually, a famed dolphin-inhabited bay on the Pacific side of Mexico. Soon, I will throw the note away.

Chapter 14

It is Friday night, and the newest, most recently miserable, employee wants to go out to a fancy place to pick up rich Mexicans. I am happy to suggest Casa de Campo, with its beautiful gardens and birds, and its lovely three-piece orchestra. On the way there, she bangs her too-tall *gringa* head viciously into a traffic light control box. While I am consoling her, some creep hikes up my dress and takes a deep grab at my butt. He runs off before I can kick him where it counts, so we resort to pathetic screams and curses in Spanish. As we arrive at Casa de Campo, we are laughing at our own ineptness.

The crowd is quite small, and the only available men seem to be the middle-aged musicians and teenaged waiters. I have made up my mind to get sloshed, even though I know the doctors were right to warn me against it. I have had more liquor in Mexico than I drank in my entire four years in North Carolina. We are having a good time, entertaining the band with our silly requests and staring down the flamingoes and swans in the garden. By the time we leave, my stomach is in agony, and my neck and shoulders are in knots from the anguish of trying to pump fresh blood up to my befuddled brain.

We wander home, and I make garlic bread for my head-injured companion. She starts pumping me for explanations about our workplace, and now I am sorry the alcohol is already wearing off. Still, I can tell she is one of those people that can find happiness, or at least a boyfriend, anywhere she goes. She will survive this place.

***

Saturday I do not see the dolphins because I have a lunch date with yet another friend who used to work here at the Center: she, too, is leaving Mexico, but after years of employment at a better workplace. After lunch, I spend a few hours downtown trying to find dress shoes and a blazer, to no avail. I will have to set aside precious free time this week to go to the mall. Sunday is yet another goodbye party for a couple North Americans in town who are leaving Mexico. So many goodbyes at this place.

The final new staff member of the spring hiring frenzy has arrived. I am shocked to learn he is a mere nineteen years old. His Spanish is excellent, and if he likes to drive vans and buses, the Prophet/Profit will be more than content. The Prophet/Profit does not care how many years of work experience and academic degrees have walked out since last year because he never really wanted them in the first place. The 1994 staff is collectively some three decades younger than the 1993 staff. Two of the newcomers have made commitments of six months or less--they have no illusions of grand career development here. The older and better-educated of us were the real naive idiots. The newest staff member's main work experience was in a grocery store, which would have prepared me for almost half of my workload here, I now realize.

***

Time is flying now. The washing machine breaks down on my dirty clothes. I sleep badly again, anxious nightmares haunting me. Again I awaken too early, stomach in knots, unable to stop thinking about all the things I need to do here and back in the U.S. in the next three weeks. People keep asking me if I am excited. The day something is handed to me on a silver platter, I will be excited. For now, I am too afraid of making a wrong step--not having the right clothes to make a good impression on my unseen employer, not having adequate books and notes and computer manuals to enable me to remember all the things I "learned" in graduate school, and a thousand other worries.

I spend Monday morning packing up a box to ship to Brazil. The shipping company seems quite decent, modern, and reliable, but they refuse to take my credit card. I am stunned, even though I should not be, after all this time in Mexico. I must cab it all the way home to pick up the cash, and cab it all the way back again. Everything in this country takes longer than I expect, and Murphy's Laws always accelerate when I am in the process of moving. I worry excessively about losing my precious possessions in transit, about not having enough suitcase room at the last minute and staying up half the night trying to get it to fit, then of being too tired to get out the door on time. I have shipped the "least" important components of my life, but I will still be devastated if they do not arrive, even as I am already eyeing what is left, trying to visualize it fitting into a small enough amount of luggage to leave me carrying capacity for the computer being prepped for me at the University.

At lunch I give away some clothes and miscellaneous things to the Mexican staff. Moving so many times has been like a sift through the contents of my life. In every new apartment, in every new town, I take on some better possessions, and shed some older and less gratifying ones. My papers have been reorganized so many times that I can find anything--allergy prescription, last checking account statement, housemate Chilli's poem, latest resumé, list of natural pesticides--in a matter of minutes. My belongings get better organized with each passing year, even as my psyche splinters with every move.

Finished distributing well-received hand-me-downs, I head off to the courier service office. It has been a week, and the manager still has not inquired to their U.S. branch about the gaffe in sending my forwarding order back to Mexico. I am furious, knowing I will miss a lot of letters. I hate missing my mail, my friends.

Tonight, I seem to be the only one at home, and Chillona cannot even sit patiently through my peanut butter and carrot sandwich and my cantaloupe without mewing pitifully for my lap. When she comes up at last, she is ecstatic to receive my caresses. She even strains up to face level to gaze fondly into my eyes. In one week she will lose me cold turkey, and it is killing me. Although I have always known my life was too nomadic to get a pet, I have fallen in love with a circumstantial pet once again.

I have never lived completely alone. There are many times when I **felt** alone--unaided by the schizophrenic housemate, the manic-depressive housemate, the other less-than-comforting housemates--but I have never come home to dead silence day in and day out. In Brazil, I will probably be living alone for the first time. Two years. Surely that is enough time to justify a couple of dogs? Surely, when my two years are up, I will finally have my act together enough to know that my dogs could go wherever I go?

Chapter 15

I have been asked to translate some articles about Subcomandante Marcos before I leave. I have been avoiding reading about him, knowing instinctively that the Zapatista rebel leader is no Robin Hood, and that he will disappoint me. He claims in an interview that he learned his English from reading *Playboy* and *Penthouse*. Enough vocabulary to launch a revolution, perhaps, but possibly not the one he claims to be launching. Sex and violence, hand in hand--exactly what every woman dreams of. The rest of what he says is just melodramatic poetry: he would rather die as a dignified human being than live worse than a dog. Which side of that equation holds the hours of pornography?

Is this guy really what the desperate peasants need? What would he do with power if he got it? He claims he does not want any power--he just wants to see justice done--but when in history did an army ever willingly give up its weaponry or power? I think what the peasants really need is a woman leader, somebody driven by more than testosterone, somebody who does not think killing is an ethical and efficient option to resolve grievances.

***

Another bad night's sleep. It is International Woman's Day, and I have to spend the morning tediously shopping at the mall. I get hopeful about half a dozen pairs of shoes, but none of them are available in my size. Nor are long-sleeved navy blue blazers in abundance in Mexico--or anything else I could respectfully wear in the thirty-degree weather to which I may be heading back, since winter is still in full force in the U.S. I helplessly think of all my nice

69

winter clothes stored with friends and family: it is too late, but I should have had them ship me a couple of those things. I will have to go to the University orientation wearing only my sunny Mexican wardrobe.

I am exhausted from the heat and exertion and lack of sleep, and can barely drag myself through some more translations and letters in the afternoon. The office manager wants to know what I want to do for my farewell party. I try to get out of it, but she will not allow that. I pick a "folk music" bar for Friday night. At night I dream I am in a ship on the ocean and someone is forcing me to dump oil in the water. I get a sick feeling watching the oil slowly diffuse through the clear blue water.

On Wednesday I work ten hours, repeatedly ready to flip out and run screaming from the endless aggravations--except for the consolation of knowing that tomorrow will be my last day. With less than twenty-four hours until quitting time, I have a glimmer of hope that my sanity has not been irrevocably damaged here, and will, in fact, survive until Thursday afternoon.

I return to the staff house at 9:00 p.m., one of the earlier ones to escape the harried workplace. Chillona is frantic for company and leaps to the doorway to greet me. I keep thinking that I should ignore her or be mean to her so she will not miss me so much, but I cannot bear to do that. She will just have to wonder at my abandonment, and try to love again.

Thursday arrives at last. It is, unequivocally, my last day of work. I do the Post Office run; I do not care at all if I ever see this Post Office again. I type on the computer; I definitely do not want to see this office ever again. When I finish, I help the office manager take the computer into the shop because the a:drive has ceased to function; I do not care a fig. We stop at the grocery store; I hope never again to have to lug fifteen pounds of bread back for supper. My only joy is the fax from my future employer giving me some happy logistical details. Is this new adventure really beginning?

I meet Rosa after work for our last farewell. By the end of the conversation and the bottom of my wine glass, I am choking back the

70

tears. I am mourning for her, still struggling to rebuild her personal and professional life after her disastrous time at the educational center, and I am mourning for our friendship, torn apart so prematurely. If things were different, we would still be working and living together. She is one of the friends I fear will slip through the cracks--letters unwritten for her lack of time or undelivered for lack of reliable postal systems. I will really miss her, and I really hope to see her again.

I intend to do some more shopping on the way back, but I cannot cope with the suppressed sobs heaving in my bosom, so I head home. I pick up my photo enlargement--three of the dolphins giving "handshakes" out of the water--and I almost burst into tears again. It is gorgeous, this photo. I should give it to the trainers as a farewell gift. I cannot stop thinking about that Gordon Lightfoot refrain, "there never seems to be enough time to do the things you wanna do once you find them." Maybe I can adopt a dolphin in Brazil--a dolphin, two dogs, a horse, and half a dozen street orphans. I am bursting with love to give. When I leave here on Monday, I will have been here nine months, and I wish to God I at least had a baby to show for it.

Friday: I awaken to near freedom. I also awaken to some intestinal bug wreaking havoc in my system--one last farewell from the Mexican critter community. Today I check things off my to-do list right and left: buy bus ticket to Mexico City airport, get photos taken for Brazilian visa application, get gifts for friends I will see while in U.S., fill out University employee forms and read orientation manual, share supper with some other former employees. With every item I cross off from my list, I feel ever so slight a relaxation of the vise that has had a chokehold on my heart for so long.

In the evening, we head to the folk music bar. The turnout is surprisingly good for my farewell party, considering how swamped everyone is at work. First we hear a talented Andean band, and then, like a good omen, a Brazilian guitarist takes the stage. His first song is in Spanish, but it is a Spanish far more delicate than the Mexican version. His next song is in Portuguese, and it is just enchanting. The words seem to hold some of the best qualities of both French and Spanish, and I feel a glimmer of excitement growing within me. I had forgotten how much I loved to learn new languages, and get acquainted with new cultures, and it is slowly dawning on me that maybe life does still hold some new surprises and inspirations for my weary soul.

It is Saturday, and I have done everything except one last load of laundry, so tomorrow I will actually be able to pack quite leisurely. I can take the time today to go to the Magic Jungle one last time. I want to remember every detail, so I force myself to look at every animal in every cage, in every chain, in every binding.

Environmentalists are sharply divided over the value of zoos: the animals do not belong here, they are not free to do what they want, they may even be mentally ill from the captivity, yet they delight and soothe the human spirit, they enable people to see and learn about exotic animals, and they may even survive in these sheltered environments better than they could out in the unsheltered world. Is it better to have an endangered species locked up for safekeeping, or let it die out in a polluted or encroached habitat? I still do not know, but I know I love this place. It may be a bittersweet affection, but it is stronger than any I have known in a long time. This is the only place in town where I can hear roaring water, smell floral breezes instead of car exhaust, find shaded resting places among hundreds of trees, and see animals that are not street dogs or beheaded market carcasses.

The first dolphin show has a severe handicap--no electricity. Berenice invites the audience to come very close to her so that she can emcee the show without a microphone. To make matters worse, Alejandro is not here today, so António must do the sea lions and the dolphins too. It is very odd to watch it all without the music system playing. I realize now that the music has nothing to do with the animal training: it is all whistles and hand signals. The staff carries on remarkably well, and the audience is perfectly pleased. In fact, the sea lions and dolphins perform better than I have seen them perform in a long time. Perhaps the music is a distraction to the animals? After the show, a dozen technicians swarm over the place, trying to fix the electrical system. I hope to see the show with music and with Alejandro one last time.... It is not to be, at least not for the second show: Alejandro must be sick or on vacation, and there is still no electricity. Berenice has a megaphone this time, so it is a little easier to hear her. It is a good performance, again.

I go buy a sandwich and walk down to the lagoon to watch the ducks until the last show. I stumble upon two adorable puppies and instinctively hold out my hand to them. They are mangy little girls, stray sisters of a similar labrador-like appearance, but one as black as night and the other like a sandy beach. I immediately want to take them with me: these are the two orphans who need me! I would have to drag them through several airports, trains, buses, and lodgings before we could settle down to be a happy family in Brazil. I shall have to leave them, trusting that they will survive with the tough genetic stock inherited from their mangy mutt forefathers. I play with them awhile, but eventually they amble off in search of food again. How wonderful it felt to pet them. I suddenly think of my friends that I shall see soon in the States. A happy thought sneaks up on me: I am really leaving this painful part of my life, and will soon see warm and happy people.

It is so peaceful by the lagoon, and the warmth and the breeze are just perfect today. This is really the last time. In a few minutes I must take the final climb up the seventy-seven steps, into the *delfinário*. I must say goodbye. I think I can do it without crying.

The dolphins look positively ecstatic before the show-- chasing each other around, leaping high into the air for the sheer joy of it, crashing purposefully backwards into the water to make larger splashes and more noise. They are in captivity but have found a way to be happy.

Berenice comes out to the audience again because there is still no electricity for the microphone. I am enjoying it nonetheless, and I know all the songs by heart, anyway, and can hear them in my mind. Halfway through the show, the electricity comes back on, and Berenice takes to the microphone. She quickly reverts into the real narration, the one replete with all the extraneous comments, witty remarks, and sarcastic jokes that were all too much trouble when she had to project her voice. I see a few of the tricks complete with their musical accompaniment before the electricity dies again. Since she is way back on the stage now, Berenice must shout the final few lines of the show.

Afterwards, the guards are more vigilant than ever (do they suspect Zapatista rebels are behind these electrical problems?!), and they will not let me pass until one comes by who recognizes me. I am finally allowed to head backstage with my parting gift for Berenice-- the enlarged photograph of her, António, and Alejandro, all "shaking hands" with the dolphins. I tell her I am leaving Mexico and would like to give her the photo to thank her for being the first to invite me down to the pool to see the dolphins up close.

She is stunned, and cannot stop thanking me even though I am trying to thank her. Finally, I say goodbye and leave, but a few minutes later she has cornered me in the ladies room. Now I am stunned as she tells me how she came running after me with her pen so that I could dedicate this very special gift to her. She asks when I will return, and I say I do not know because I am going to Brazil. I ask her how long she will work here, and she says she is not sure-- she loves animals and has started working with a veterinarian. We wish each other good fortune in the future.

When we part for good, the sobs start my chest heaving, and it kills me to think I will never see her again, never find out if she becomes a veterinarian. I will never find out what happens to any of them: they are another part of my life that is getting pruned incidentally because of proximity to the thing I really need to prune. No clean breaks.

Chapter 16

This is it: I dust off my suitcases and start packing up the remainder of my Mexican life. I hate packing. I am slow, methodical, and anxious about liquids spilling and knicknacks breaking. As usual, I run out of space and realize I will have to go for three carry-ons, hoping they are small enough not to be a problem with the airline. It takes hours and hours before my stomach starts settling down and I am sure I will not have to leave behind too many possessions.

I have been thinking about our former grocery clerk, the latest employee to pour his heart out to me last night. He is so unhappy already, and I have given him as much emotional support as I can, but I think he will have a hard time fitting in here. I hope he survives unscathed: it is rare to find a teenage guy so sweet. Yet I know he only had the courage to open up to me because he knows I'm leaving.

I take a break to watch the end of the Atlantic Coast Conference Basketball Championship. My two alma maters are battling it out, and I am ecstatic to see North Carolina win over Virginia--happy memories over unhappy memories. I may even get to watch the tournament with friends in Carolina. I suddenly realize I am actually looking forward to some fun in my life. I think, if the end of my packing goes smoothly, I may start feeling pretty darn good.

In the evening I take another break to watch Subcomandante Marcos interviewed on "60 Minutes". The interview is very surreal: I know that the U.S. audience is not going to get a clear picture from this. They cover the basics--the desperate poverty, the meaningless promises from the government, the negotiations process--but they never cover the issue of violence. How does he justify the violence? They ask Marcos how he feels to have brought back "romanticism" to Mexico, and he laughs. Anyone who reads enough *Playboy* and *Penthouse* to learn English must enjoy being a sex symbol. He is a perverse Robin Hood, not a gentleman, and he cannot be my hero. Yet, he is probably the closest thing to a hero Mexico has right now, and I hope they get their righteous demands.

I finally finish packing, hoping the airport authorities will not notice I have three "purses"--which was unavoidably necessary to squeeze in the last few possessions. I go eat supper, and my favorite cook tells me that, if I want to come back to visit, I can stay at her house. I know that she knows I will never want to come back to the Prophet's turf.

I am surprised by a member of the ecology committee who shows up at Casa Dolores with chocolate-covered cherries and well wishes. I pass the rest of the evening with the office manager and the two newest staff members. The teenage clerk plugs his guitar into our archaic sound system and plays sweetly for me for a couple hours. It is the perfect sendoff. Why couldn't every night be like that?

When we hug goodbye, the teenager tells me he is not sure to whom he can talk after I leave. My heart aches for him, but I know I could not have handled getting any closer to him: knowing he was ten years younger than I and had a serious girlfriend somewhere else was already driving me crazy. I am an emotional wreck and could have fallen really hard, and really stupidly, for this young sweet thing. I squeeze him tightly, then hug everyone else goodbye, and it hits me like a shock--I **will** be in the frigid industrial north of the U.S.A. tomorrow night, rolling the dice one more time.

When the alarm goes off in the wee hours, I am having bizarre pop music dreams, and am totally bleary-eyed. It is very early, and only Chillona is up to see me leave. I try to tell her goodbye, knowing it is useless. I manage to get my things out the door almost on schedule, but the cab I had called to take me to the bus station has not shown. I panic momentarily, but finally flag a taxi.

The bus ride to Mexico City is horrible--the air conditioning must be cranked down to fifty degrees. I huddle under my coat, trying unsuccessfully to sleep. My eyes are too tired to watch the gorgeous mountains we pass during the climb up to Mexico City. I am too sleepy to think about anything.

I change my money at the airport, use my residual pesos for a chocolate bunny, then sit down to scrutinize my U.S. declarations form. What address? I declare myself not to be residing permanently in the U.S. I declare I am going to the U.S. for business and will be there three weeks. I declare I have bought less than $50 of goods in Mexico. I declare I may never come back.

I am told to check the monitor in an hour to find out my gate number. The flight never shows up on the monitor. I go up and down the hallways, looking for a clue, my arms breaking from the strain of my two carry-ons and three shoulder bags. I finally conclude that I had better return to the airline ticket counter for the information, and I then race off to the faraway gate. When I get there, everyone else has already boarded, and the attendants address me by name! I try to explain it is not my fault--the monitors!–but they are not interested in my explanations. They just want me to get on the plane--**now**! I am the last one to get on the plane, and we fly away.

Part II

Violations of Parole

Chapter 17

The next few days are a blur. After dozens of forms and signatures, I am a University employee. I trudge around campus for photos and meetings and medical appointments, wearing layers and layers of the clothing I have, but I am freezing in the rain and snow and sub-zero wind chill of this late winter cold front. None of the staff have thought to offer me a spare winter coat while I am here, and I am too bent on making a good impression to beg for one. I open a bank account and learn what our team mascot is. I meet some Brazilian researchers and learn about my new laptop computer. I put together another shipment to Brazil–new computer manuals, summer clothes, fly swatter, sunscreen, sandals–so that I will be able to cope with hand-carrying the half-ton "laptop", as they insist I must.

I fly to Washington to meet representatives of the federal agency funding my new, interdisciplinary, cutting edge, super-deluxe program. It is all very boring, but they give me some papers which might prove useful. Exhausted, I nevertheless spend the weekend crossing the Potomac River back and forth, visiting friends in D.C., Maryland, and Virginia.

When I see my sister, I am too numb to connect with her. Somehow she understands and sticks to small talk--look how much Adams Morgan has changed! I meet Peter and am pleased at how sweet he is with her. When it is time to go, she asks me if I have contacted Michael yet. No, I just have not had the time or energy to do that, but I will. She says he may get paroled by summer.

On Monday, I pack my bags again, ready to head down to North Carolina. I feel like a rolling stone more than ever after seeing two of my D.C. friends ensconced in new houses. I can barely remember what I have stored in North Carolina, but I would be surprised if I even own my own lamp right now, let alone a stick of furniture. I never really dreamt of owning my own house, yet there is an ounce of jealousy in me: I want somebody to want to make a home for me...with me....

I get on the Amtrak across the street from the ominous Masonic Temple, home of the WASP mafia probably bankrolling the Senate campaign of that lying crook, Oliver North. It feels good to get out of suburban Virginia. I am happily looking forward to North Carolina. UNC has already been knocked out of the national basketball tournament, but nothing could mar my joy. The weather will be warmer, the traffic will be lighter, the scenery will be prettier, the grass will be greener, and my heart will be cheerier.

It is a long, rainy train ride, but I do not mind. We race by what seems an infinity of trees–not real forest, but replanted, fast-growing pines. Occasionally I see clear cuts with tiny baby pines dotting the barren landscape, but mostly I see woods and streams and small towns, then, later, farms and horses and deer. I will still be living out of suitcases for the next couple of weeks, but I feel as if I **am** going home.

Another friend, another home, another new person to meet in somebody else's life--this time, a baby. My tangible life takes up only nine square feet of her garage, and I sort through my boxes to figure out what I should take and what I should leave this time. I end up with two more boxes of books and clothing to ship, and I am thrilled to see that my careful storage techniques have, in fact, guarded my paltry possessions from mold and dust and pests. My residual stuff will survive in her garage during my two years in Brazil.

A week and half away from Mexico, and I suddenly realize I am no longer waking up with horrible stomach aches everyday. I have calmed down. My mind is occupied by the myriad of logistical details necessary to get to this new job, and my soul is soothed by the myriad of familiar faces and voices. Tomorrow my friend will drive me to Chapel Hill, and I cannot wait to be there again.

I get a surprising phone call: have I seen the news? A presidential candidate has been assassinated in Mexico. I flip the TV dials until I find the news: it is not **A** candidate, it is **THE** candidate. The ruling party, the "institutionalized" party of the revolution, has lost its designated future president to a killer's bullet. I am sure instinctively that it is not the Zapatistas, but they are morally responsible: it is they who announced to all of Mexico that violence is the only way to get rid of the status quo. Is it possible that Mexico will really slide into civil war again? So much hatred. So much violence. So many angry men. I wish someone would put the women of Mexico in charge--calm, patient, sacrificing, compassionate, faithful. I am relieved to be out of there, though I know I am a fool to expect much better from Brazil.

***

The day begins inauspiciously: the baby has been crying off and on all night, and I am tired. It is cooler, and rainy too. I pack up my stuff, fix a meal for my exhausted working-mom friend, and make my daily quota of phone calls. The good news from the University is that the Brazilian consulate has finally decided to be reasonable and I should get the proper visa soon. The bad news from the University is that the U.S. Postal Service has sent me a letter explaining that they are not responsible for forwarding mail addressed to a "private company", e.g., the San Diego courier service that had been bringing U.S. mail to us in Cuahtemoc. I am near tears--my mail! I cannot live without my mail! It will be so slow and unbearable, waiting for my mail to be taken from San Diego to the Center, then forwarded from the Center back to the U.S., to the University, then from the University to Brazil. I am so tired of living in limbo. I pull myself together and finish packing my bags.

When, at last, I am dropped off at my old apartment in Chapel Hill, I marvel at how gigantic it seems compared to my memory of it. The very large German shepherd looks like a pony compared to the

83

Mexican street mongrels! I have to sleep on the couch now, but it feels so nice and familiar to be here. The next few days fly by in a whirlwind of banking and errands and friends–visiting people I studied with, worked with, played with, churched with.

The town is beginning its spring ascent into Eden–pink cherry blossoms and white pear blossoms in the cultivated places, pink redbud and white dogwood in the wild ones. Pansies, daffodils, and tulips decorate the gardens, and clover and violets sparkle in the meadows. The weather fluctuates wildly between sixty and eighty degrees, between windy rain and gentle sunshine. I even see an early-blooming magnolia tree, my favorite--so wide and tall, flowering into hundreds of giant white flowers big enough to bury your face in that sweetest of fragrances. Michael and I used to joke about which Chapel Hill mansion we would buy for our retirement, and which of their giant magnolia trees would shade us as we whiled away the hot summer days on our Franklin Street lawn.

After days of embraces and warm words, it is time to tear myself away from the Southern Part of Heaven. I finish my final flurry of business and personal phone calls only to discover that now there is no longer any rush: my Brazilian visa will not be ready for another week. I book a flight to Chicago to see my family for Easter for the first time in over a decade. My mom jokes that she still has my Easter basket to put out for the Easter Bunny's visit.

Waiting for my plane, I am finally relaxed enough to call Michael at the prison. When he calls me back, he says he was thrilled to get the letter about my new job, and will come visit me as soon as he can. He sounds very tired, but eager for the news about Chapel Hill. I tell him random bits, trying to paint a picture of a place so special and so hard to describe: the Cat's Cradle had to move from yuppifying Chapel Hill to hippier Carrboro, one of my former coworkers had an adorable little baby girl, the burned-down Intimate Bookshop has been rebuilt, the public library will soon be in its new building, and UNC is at its glorious best for the university's bicentennial celebration. Life went on here without us.

I ask him if Stephanie was right about his pending parole: yes, actually, he just got approved for an early release! He will probably be out by May 1st. He plans to crash with Stephanie until he gets a job in Washington, and visit me in Brazil next year. I fight off a yearning impulse to beg him to come with me right away, at my own expense. I know I could afford it financially, but not emotionally: falling in love with him again would bankrupt me. He sounds depressed, though, and I ask him why he is not thrilled about his upcoming, inexplicably early release. "I'm just tired," is all he says. I force myself to stop thinking about him.

Chapter 18

I fly to Chicago on Holy Thursday. Lent will soon be over, and I will soon be reborn in Brazil. In between visits with family and friends, I file my tax returns and try to organize my new banking, insurance, and job papers–why is this paperwork so endless?

I am distracted by a TV special on dolphins, shocked to learn that eleven percent of captured dolphins die within two years, compared to a conjectured life span of forty-five years in the wild. Some of the trainers interviewed claim that most sea shows now breed dolphins in captivity, and that those dolphins are happy and healthy. Other experts disagree: not only does captivity prevent a dolphin from swimming a typical forty miles per day, it forces a sonar-sensed creature into a concrete box of sensory deprivation. Their anatomically permanent smile is a cruel joke that fools visitors into thinking a dolphin is having a great time.

One former trainer now takes boats out into the ocean to let people interact with the dolphins on their own terms. The dolphins freely approach the boats and humans, especially when music is played underwater. I am mesmerized by a videotape of the dolphins and humans swimming side-by-side to a Strauss waltz. *I am a wallflower.*

Now to another aspect of the debate: dolphins have been used with extraordinary success in recreational therapy programs for autistic children. The completely spontaneous and creative play of a dolphin can bring an autistic child right out of his shell. *Was I autistic in Mexico?* Some dolphin researchers actually believe that dolphins are psychic, which sounds like a marvelous field of research until the show reports on military experiments with dolphins. My mind is reeling from the pros and cons of dolphins in captivity, and I am chastised by one trainer's comment that people would not even care about dolphins unless they had seen them up close, in captivity. *I did care about dolphins from afar, but I was not madly in love with them until I saw them in captivity. I was autistic! I needed them!* They rescued my sanity and I cannot bear to think of their having suffered to do so.

On Sunday, I go to Easter mass with my family. It is a good sermon--slightly better than average--but I sense no response from the people. What is in their hearts? Have they been reborn? Because of the huge crowd, we are seated in the choir loft, and nobody seems certain about the order in which we should line up for communion. Eyes turn one way and another, anxiously searching for a signal as to how to proceed. Many people actually seem to be panicking, as if they truly fear that the body of Christ might run out before they have had their turn. Some of these same panicky people leave the church immediately after communion, unable or unwilling to await the priest's final blessing and the choir's final song. I leave sad.

In the evening I get a call from an old friend from Pax Christi: he is thrilled about my upcoming work and hopes that I will write articles on the experience, maybe even lecture in the future. He reminds me that military recruiters are combing the high schools for recruits, and that peacemakers must get out there too, talk about other career paths, talk about ways to change the world that do not involve bullets and napalm and nukes. Sure thing–I'll let you know when I figure it out, when I've changed the world, etc., etc.

The next day is, for a Chicago Cubs fan, the true first day of spring--Opening Day at Wrigley Field. I can get excited about basketball and football champions, but only baseball can get me ecstatic even when losers play. Baseball, the performance art, beautiful win or lose, is pure zen: balance, action, reaction, reestablishment of balance. Ying/yang, nirvana. Every at-bat is a brand new opportunity, and there is no ticking clock.

The arch enemy New York Mets fall 1-2-3 in the first, and the Cubs' leadoff batter belts out a homerun! It is a mind-boggling, stratospherically fantastic start to the new season, and the game continues on in a wild and woolly battle of risky running, crazy fielding, and ferocious batting. The lead-off hitter hits another homerun in his second at-bat, and still another homer his third time out. The fans are going wild! He is the first major league player ever to have homered in his first three at-bats of the season; even his teammates are bowing in homage to him. For his fourth at-bat, the pitcher is pulled, and the replacement manages to get away with walking him.

The First Lady helps Harry Caray sing "Take Me Out to the Ballgame" during the seventh-inning stretch, but things are starting to look bleak. The Cubs have scored seven, but are still losing. I know how that feels. They rally slightly in the bottom of the ninth, but end up losing 12-8. How can you score so many, but still lose? No matter--I am happy with the impressive display I saw, and I know they did their best.

Tuesday I wake up with a dreadful cold: the weather has snapped back to winter, and my body is protesting vehemently. I drink cup after cup of decaffeinated tea, trying to soothe my raw throat. By afternoon, I am in a daze, and end up weeping excessively over a sentimental midlife-crisis movie on TV. I am not even old enough for a midlife crisis! I think I took a wrong turn somewhere, but I cannot figure it out precisely enough to regret it.

In the evening, I head over to an old friend's house. Her beloved guinea pig--my "godson"--has died, and she cradles his stiff rodent body in her bosom. She is crying her eyes out. I am ashamed of myself: I just finished crying over fictional characters on TV, but I cannot feel this real loss at all. I put my arm around her, but I can think of nothing to say. She takes me home.

By bedtime, I can scarcely breathe through my stuffed-up nose and, panicky, take a near overdose of decongestants. I pile my pillows high and recline gingerly, like the elephant man. My breathing slowly eases, but I cannot sleep because "exceeding the recommended dosage can cause sleeplessness". I drift in and out of some sort of unconsciousness, too awake to sleep and too sleepy to think. I am alive, I am breathing, I must not complain.

On Wednesday, my two-year "cultural" visa for Brazil finally arrives! A couple more phone calls, and I am booked to fly out on Sunday. I can scarcely believe it...Brazil looms, at long last. I will arrive in Brazil *three months* after the possibility of going there was first mentioned to me. I will fly out of the U.S. exactly four weeks after I flew in.

In the evening my grieving friend picks me up for our dinner raindate. She tells me about the burial of the beloved guinea pig, but the thought of his stiff corpse keeps reminding me of the rat in my room last September and how it looked on the lawn after Rutilio had beaten it to death. I had discovered it on my toiletries shelf, of all places, and the thought of it nosing around my lotions and manicure set and toothbrush (!) had been unbearable. I had washed or thrown out everything, but the thought of it still makes my skin crawl.

What distinguished the wild rodent from the domesticated one? Was it only the fear of typhoid germs that led to beating to death that creature, whereas its Yankee cousin got antibiotics and tender loving care in his final days on this planet? I listen to her tell me about the little private funeral ceremony she and her husband had for, in effect, their first child, and she shows me some pictures and reminisces. They will get another pet soon, she says, and I know she will be OK.

At bedtime, I take another foray into my mother's ample medicine cabinets and emerge with something much better--a twelve-hour decongestant cold pill. I settle in for a much better night, awaking three times but managing some eight hours of sleep off and on. When I finally get up, Federal Express has already dumped on the doorstep the envelope containing my airline tickets. This is it, this is real, this is in my hand. Finally, out of the fog enveloping my mind, emerges the deep-seated relief and gratitude: I am really going to Brazil!

I set myself up with water and tissues and cough drops to watch the Cubs / White Sox Crosstown Classic. Michael Jordan--the best basketball player in the world, the player who led the Chicago Bulls to three straight championships, the player that grew up in a beautiful Carolina beach town and helped my beloved UNC win a college championship--is making his first and possibly only appearance in a Major League ballpark. After the brutal murder of his father last year, he had retired from basketball and later decided to return to his childhood love of baseball. So far he has not shown much promise, and is, in fact, only going to play in the minor, minor league, but he has been invited to don the White Sox uniform for this charity game.

After some initially poor fielding and batting, he takes charge of his right field perch and manages an RBI single and an RBI double. The fans are going wild! By the end of the game, he has received some ten standing ovations. He is a baseball star, if only for today. He says he has played basketball enough, and I admire this multimillionaire who was not ready to retire at age thirty, who was willing to risk complete humiliation, who would trade in something finely honed for a new and rawer challenge. This is far more inspirational than seeing him stay in basketball.

I am cheered by the game, but I still feel like hell. For a second day in a row, I anxiously shine a flashlight down my throat and search the mirror for signs of infection--no, just raw and scratched. I return to the couch and read my travel guide to Brazil. It is hard to picture the dangers of malaria while huddled under an afghan in Illinois with your nose running like a faucet. After going out to dinner with my parents, I try again for a better night's sleep.

In the morning, I am actually ever-so-slightly better. I am still an ENT specialist's worst nightmare, but I muster the strength and willpower to do a load of laundry. Finally done with the logistical headaches of planning this move, I force myself to read my long-neglected pile of papers on Brazil and the Amazon, simultaneously channel-surfing because I am too tired to focus on academic abstraction alone.

90

I have scarcely put down an article on how the massive TV proliferation in Brazil is expanding social consciousness to remote people and places when I hear on MTV that the lead singer of a popular rock group has killed himself with a shotgun. God. Not another one. Not another person who reached the zenith of his profession and then realized it was not enough, who decided he did not have enough reason to get out of bed the next day, who could not find something to justify his existence or eradicate his pains or simplify his problems. I am shaken by this stranger's suicide two-thousand miles away, through the power of TV telling me about it, just as this research paper on Brazil says. If I had witnessed the guinea pig's funeral on TV, it would have hit me harder.

***

Saturday arrives--my last weekend in the U.S.A. I am not just going south of the border this time: I am going south of the equator. This is really, really far away. I could die before I come back. Walker Percy died while I was in Costa Rica, and I am still mad about that: how could I leave the country for only a month and not have my favorite author alive when I returned? Somebody will die while I am gone: I am sure of it. In the evening, I go see "Philadelphia" with an old Chicago friend and cry over the actor's AIDS death.

On Sunday I say goodbye to my folks and fly to New York city to spend the night at an airport hotel in order to catch an early morning direct flight to Brasília. I have never been to NYC, and I open my hotel room curtains expectantly, but can barely see the famed Manhattan skyline. I settle for "Geronimo" on the pay-per-view and watch Hollywood take a revisionist look at the notorious Apache leader. I cannot stand the violence--another desperate struggle for land and resources. After years of studying economic development and environmental management, I am still not sure how mankind will ever rise above its fears and anxieties and suspicions to see that cooperation, not competition, is our only hope.

Monday morning I buy a New York postcard, even though I have seen nothing. It is a startlingly beautiful photograph of Central Park. I get on the plane, listening to the beautiful music of the

Brazilian Portuguese spoken by passengers and crew members around me. I am finally entering my new world.

Chapter 19

The plane ride goes on and on and on. Outrageous graphics light up the screen with a cartoon-like representation of our plane's trajectory out of New York and into the clear blue of the Atlantic Ocean. Detailed data on altitude, longitude, latitude, speed, time elapsed, and outside temperatures (-40 degrees Celsius!) are flashed periodically. This is followed by a Brazilian news program, which quickly puts me to sleep.

When I wake up, the first of three American feature films is showing. They are all very involved, and I am thankful they have been subtitled and not dubbed. By the end of the third, I am reeling from the excess of characters (was there a "Frank" in each film?!) and excess of themes crowding my brain. When the video graphics return, our cartoon plane is suddenly soaring above Amazonian Brazil. This is an excellent thing to know, in case we crash. Brazil dominates the screen, crowding out all those puny Spanish-speaking countries that were so much more important to me when I studied Spanish and prepared for a career anywhere in Latin America **but** Brazil.

We touch down quietly, some eight and a half hours after we took off. We have no terminal gate, so I descend the runway staircase with trepidation, trying to hold onto my life's most valuable papers and the 1,000-pound laptop computer. We board a shuttle bus to the immigration area, and I am pleasantly surprised at how fast, easy, and simple everything is. When I emerge, an English-speaking coworker is awaiting me, and she whisks me into the post-modern world of Brasília.

Intersections are not good enough for such a mod city, and I see scarcely a stoplight as we swirl around in a dizzying configuration of cloverleafs. One gigantic skyscraper after another looms forbiddingly in the darkness. There seem to be hundreds of them, and yet they do not light up the skyline, because there is no skyline. There is no skyline because there are still so many empty lots and, perhaps, planned green spaces between the skyscrapers. The ultra-planned city looks haphazard, accidental, and odd.

At last we arrive at the hotel room *cum* apartment that has been reserved for me: it seems I will have the tininess of a hotel room without the perks hotels normally give, but I take it because it is a bargain. It is one-tenth the price of the New York hotel room! We have to go find a convenience store, however, because it seems I need to provide my own soap and drinking water. How can such a new city have bad water already?

After my coworker leaves, I rearrange the furniture, trying to make enough space to open the suitcases without blocking the wardrobe doors. I turn on the TV, but there are no English-speaking voices to dispel the loneliness that has besieged me so quickly. I leave it on anyway, hoping to absorb the Portuguese by osmosis. Am I too old for this? French in high school, Spanish in college, Italian through ethnic proximity--the nuances and inflections of them all seem to be colliding in this Portuguese. At times I hear dead ringers for French ("garçon", "bonbons"?), then I hear exact Spanish ("desculpe", "de nada"?), then I am sure I am hearing Italian ("agora mesmo"?). How will I ever get a handle on this? It sounds like Italians taking Spanish lessons from the French!

The altitude experienced today by my debilitated sinuses and ear canals has wreaked havoc with the recovery from my cold. My nose is once again running like a faucet, and, when I finish unpacking and rearranging, I sink into bed with dizzy exhaustion. I get up momentarily to lock the sliding balcony door so that I will not sleepwalk to my death ten stories below. I return to bed, but am too uncomfortable to sleep. My old friend, the panic attack, is knocking at the door. I plug my ears and finally fall asleep sometime after three a.m., only to be awakened by a wrong-number phone call at 9:15, and I am very pissed. At 10:00 the phone wakes me again, but this time I ignore it. It rings again at 10:45, so I pick it up: it is the office, even though I was not supposed to be picked up for lunch until noon. I am too groggy to talk to them, in any language.

I cannot fall back to sleep, so I finally open the curtain to see how Brasília looks by day. I am dazzled by the seemingly endless horizon of puffy white clouds underlining an enormous expanse of blue sky. Across the street is a huge field of red clay, a comforting reminder of my beloved Carolina. Many buildings are still under construction, but the ones already standing look much better in the daylight. I can also see grass and trees and flowers and a finger of the manmade lake. This city has some potential.

***

Tuesday and Wednesday are full of dozens of irritating logistical details requiring my attention. My insane hope for immediate professional fulfillment has quickly been dissipated with headaches over currency exchanges, hotel arrangements, transportation problems, and communication breakdowns. I am thankful whenever I find someone who understands English, because the assurance that Brazilians can understand Spanish-speakers proves to be a gross exaggeration.

To make matters worse, my health is becoming a worry. My nose will not stop running, which either means I have the cold-that-would-not-die, or this place is going to be an allergy nightmare. I have already gotten some peculiar insect bite which itches and hurts and worries me despite having been told by a Brazilian it is of no concern. I have been completely unsuccessful in sticking to vegetarian eating here, getting ham in my mixed salad, my grilled cheese, and my scrambled eggs.

I am a vegetarian mostly for ecological reasons, but now I am simply panicking at the salt and fat and nitrates, and what if I get those horrible pork parasites? And why does everything I order come on a platter large enough to feed a family of four? I have been given a four-cup bowl of pea soup, a fruit plate that could have been

95

gift-wrapped for Christmas, enough salad to fill a refrigerator crisper, a pound of spaghetti, a potful of rice, and (could it be possible!?) a dozen scrambled eggs! I have yet to see beans on any menu anywhere.

Four of my six boxes have been delivered safely to the office, and this is something in which to delight. My things! I can rehang my calendar, repin my posters, redon my clothes, reshelve my books, refile my papers, and reprepare myself for sun (hat and sunscreen), rain (poncho and boots), illness or injury (first aid kit). I may move from town to town, country to country, but at least "my room" and "my office" can go with me--my cocoons, my islands of me-ness. Here it is, and here I am.

I settle into the office and struggle through Portuguese reports on natural resources, public administration, studies, surveys, and trips. The people at the Institute work so hard, and I admire their operation tremendously. I desperately hope and pray that I can do something good here--some small effort to reharmonize God's children with God's creation, to help the poor and suffering in Brazil. If Brazilians do not need me, I fear that nobody ever will.

***

By Thursday, I can start the day with my morning routine of breakfast cereal and milk: having finally made it to a grocery store, I can awaken leisurely to breakfast in my own room, rather than struggling with the sumo-wrestler meat-laden fare of the hotel dining room. This is a city without much of a central downtown, and I reflect bemusedly and guiltily on how much I actually enjoyed my trip to the shopping mall--a place full of people and color and music and aromas, a vibrant place, a comforting place.

Today will be a hard day: I need to figure out how to buy a car in a land where salesmen barely understand me, automatic transmissions are rare, and money is messy. This takes up my entire day, with little progress, then I return to the shopping mall to search for what I could not find yesterday. After the cereal, my next gigantic step toward normalcy is the purchase of an AC adaptor: upon returning to the hotel, I ecstatically plug in my clock radio. Music!

Music to dine by, music to dress by, music to brush teeth by--I really need this.

As I spin the dial, I associate the voices I hear with the beautiful men I saw at the mall and everywhere else--Amerindians, Africans, Portuguese, and Brazil's other immigrants have become an extraordinary melting pot of multiracial people whose accidental features blend together in one mysteriously enchanting face after another. This may be a tough place to stop thinking about my beloved half-breed. I wonder how Michael would feel--really feel-- living in this country. I set my clock radio alarm for the first time in a long time, and I close my eyes to the familiar glow of the red digits.

By Friday, I can detect actual progress on many fronts. Although I feel like an actress faking Italian and purposefully mumbling my half-forgotten lines, more people are understanding my "Portuguese". My nose is merely jogging now. I have even found a couple places that serve beans, fresh vegetables, and humus to eat. I am now recognizing many buildings during my taxi rides and have found an excellent tourist map. Though I am still fighting off that expensive yen to telephone a familiar voice, I have set a goal of making it through another week before calling to the U.S. I feel very alone at night, but that old acquaintance, the panic attack, is no longer on the doorstep.

Still, my heart trembles when I suddenly notice an adorable dog during a lunchtime car hunt. I suddenly realize that this dog-- hanging out its owner's front car window--is the first dog I have seen in Brazil. Brasília seems to have no street dogs! Dogs are the main reason I want to get an apartment soon: I want happy faces greeting me at the end of the day--somebody that needs me, somebody to love.

Before I leave work, I run the diagnostics on my laptop to see if it has survived my lugging it around for three weeks. I already resent it for my shoulder strain and wrist tendinitis, but I know it will take up most of my days down the road, and had better be functioning properly. I still am not sure how I will fit in here. My supervisor has been out of the country all week, and I wonder if he

97

will quickly pile on work when he returns, or hold back while I get settled in. How can I think about researching the natural resources of Brazil while my desk calendar is cluttered with notes about cars, banking, Portuguese lessons, and shopping lists? I need a personal valet.

For the first Friday night since leaving Mexico, I have no social plans for an entire weekend. I saw most of my friends and family in the previous four weeks, so this seems even odder. Mexico seems so far away. I gaze longingly at the photograph of myself, Alejandro, António, and the dolphins: I miss them most of all. I hope I will have the time and means to get to a park here soon.

On Saturday, I lie in bed until eleven, and it feels wonderful. Unfortunately, by the time I get out the door, it is too late to find a driving school still open, and I will have to master the stickshift another day–or somehow find an automatic to buy. I head back to the shopping mall to try another round of looking for needles in haystacks. Even though this is a diplomat's town, I may have to pretend I am out in the bush and resign myself to a paucity of certain personal care products. This trip does turn up a couple successes, including my discovery of a cinema in the mall. I am disheartened by the ugliness of the postcards: does my new city really look this bad? It seems I will have to live near the Dom Bosco Sanctuary or the Justice Palace if I want any architectural inspiration.

On Sunday, I really want to go to the zoo, but I fear the long taxi rides and uncertain admission price could be problems for my dwindling cash–which cannot, apparently, be augmented by any ATM in Brasília. I walk instead to the television tower plaza--an unusual tourist spot, but it really is surrounded by rows of artisans and flea market wares. One of the big sellers seems to be kites: yes, this is a city of wide-open spaces! I could not even imagine a kite in crowded urban Mexico.

Although my tourist map claims the television tower has an observation deck and a panoramic restaurant on top, they are both closed for renovations. I am incredulous when the guards tell me the observation deck will not be open for another seven months, and I rephrase my question several times to be sure I am not misunderstanding them. Suddenly, one of the guards whispers in English that he will take me up for ten dollars. Disgusted, I walk away--a cheap bribe, to be sure, but the principle! He probably would have molested me up there anyway: I have to be careful.

No sooner have I parked myself on a fountainside bench to study my Portuguese grammar book, then cold gusts of air start blowing in. After five minutes, it is clear from the darkening sky that the rainy season is not quite over, after all. I, along with hundreds of other people, head for the sheltering overhangs of the tower as the sky rips open.

There is a band playing live music beside the tower, and a young girl excitedly waves the group's cassette in the air to the enormous captive audience. They are actually quite good, crooning an amazing mixture of Jewish folk songs and American ballads. They seem to be a family: the mother looks Jewish, the father could be Portuguese, and the children resemble many dark-haired, olive-skinned, hybrid Brazilians. The crowd loves them--these Jewish Osmonds, these Brazilian Von Trapps--and I am amazed to see African-Brazilians dancing excitely to a Jewish wedding song. After having seen a Brazilian country music show on TV (Billy Ray Cyrus translated into Portuguese), I should not be so surprised: this is clearly a music-loving people.

When the rain lets up, I head to the mall for dinner. The best places are closed: in fact, everything is closed except the cinema and some fast food places. I settle for mediocre pizza and mango juice, and try earnestly to discern the intentions of the Egyptian embassy employee chatting me up. Undecided, I give him my business card, and hope he will not call me anytime soon. I head back to the hotel alone.

I have already abandoned my resolution not to call the U.S. for another week, but the mall has no phone that will take my "global" calling card. This plastic problem is getting on my nerves: this is the national capital of a gigantic country, not some Saharan outpost! I wish Chillona were here to sit on my lap. I hope she does not miss me too much. I suddenly realize I have only seen one cat in Brasília! Tired and frustrated, I try to force myself to study some Portuguese before bedtime. I must learn it--the sooner, the better. I have no one to talk to.

Chapter 20

It is my first Monday morning in Brazil, my first Monday morning at the Institute. I am immediately whisked off to an important conference on mining. I struggle to focus, but it is hopeless: a discussion of cost/benefit analysis, environmental impact, and technological innovation is not a good starting point for total immersion in a foreign language. It takes all the willpower I have to keep my eyes open; I know I will be working with many of these people in the future and should try not to look like a moron.

On Tuesday, I pay a courtesy visit to the U.S. embassy to meet some contacts there. The security guards do an annoyingly long search of my bags and still miss several places I could have hidden a plastic explosive. I meet one person who seems wildly excited about her program here, and another who spends over an hour complaining about the bureaucracy surrounding him. I am in no mood to think about the pros and cons of the U.S. presence in Brazil, or anywhere else, for that matter.

I return to the mining conference for appearance's sake, but spend most of the afternoon daydreaming. After a couple more hours of Portuguese inundation, I am hit with a linguistic brainstorm--Russian! I am hearing Russian! Am I nuts? No...no...this **does** sound like my college Russian. "Poleetchka", "oijay", "rougeka"--these could be Russian words, whatever they are! Where on Earth did Portuguese come from?

I must be losing it: boredom, freezing cold air conditioning, and cigarette smoke are taking their toll on me. I hold my water glass over my nose and mouth to breathe clearly for a couple minutes. Boy, I must look ridiculous now. I have been told by three people in the last week that I look a half decade younger than I am, and now I am doing my best to look like a weirdo, too. When I discover the run in my nylons, I resign myself to making a horrible impression at this conference.

When I return to the hotel, I am horrified to hear that the Egyptian has been hanging around the lobby waiting for me to show up! I gave him my office phone number, and this is what he does-- home invasion?! I am really steamed. I decide to indulge in the hotel's $10 massage. As the masseuse caresses my tense muscles, I think the same thing I always think during a massage: no human being should have to pay another to be touched. Animals instinctively jostle and cuddle and groom one another: what is the matter with us? Why am I shunning this Egyptian, then paying somebody else to touch me?

At night I dream that I am trying to stave off a tidal wave disaster: I am insanely trying to save a coastal town from the cresting ocean by shoveling water as far back into the ocean as I can hurl it. When I realize this will not work, I try to install pre- fabricated doors in the gaps of the bizarre sea wall lining the beach. I wake up exhausted, mentally yelling at myself, "Sandbags, you idiot!".

On Wednesday, I finally see the end of the conference and rejoice. In the afternoon, I slowly get back to my immediate concerns--how to whip my computer into shape, how to set up a bank account, how to get my boxes out of customs without paying these absurd levies. I am still getting tons of advice on cars, but nobody has yet had the time to teach me the manual transmission, so I may never be able to do any test drives.

The Institute President asks me how the conference was. I broach to him my Russian hallucination, and he actually confirms it: yes, indeed, there is a strong resemblance--not in the etymology, but in the phonetics. In fact, he informs me, Russians themselves say that Portuguese sounds somewhat like Russian! I am relieved not to be crazy.

I go home exhausted, wildly thrilled that tomorrow is actually a federal holiday and I can sleep in again. After supper, the Egyptian calls, and is pushier than ever. After having developed the habit of making allowances for a certain level of Mexican *machismo*, I do not immediately recognize this, but suddenly it occurs to me that he might be the genuine article--a true male chauvinist pig! He does not listen, he presumes, he assumes, he acts as if whatever he wants I will agree to without any thought to the contrary. The problem is that I am too tired to figure out how to handle this guy. After I have hung up, I am still not sure if I have avoided making a date, or actually made a date for which he will be pissed if I do not show. I do not want to spend my first Brazilian holiday with this arrogant man.

I sleep like a rock and still wake up tired: I must have an intestinal bug, since a queasy stomach and occasional cramping seem to be my only other symptoms. I take a taxi down to see the government buildings--the heart of Brasília. They all seem to be closed for the holiday, but I get a couple of guards to explain some of the structures. I am disappointed that the justice waterfalls are not turned on as I have seen in so many postcards: apparently, the pouring out of justice is also on holiday.

I drag myself down the sunny-hot esplanade--so much grass and so few trees. The ministry buildings are lined up like gigantic dominos. At the end of the northern flank, I finally reach the space-age cathedral, which looks like a teepee made of giant curved toothpicks. Upon entering, I am struck by the odd juxtaposition of breathtaking stained glass curving all around me to encompass...plastic chairs. Were the people who would be attending services here just an afterthought? Enormous angels hang precariously from the ceiling by giant cables, directly over the seats. Surely they would not hang...**stone?**...angels directly overhead? I sit down apprehensively, wondering if the angels are heavy enough to crush me if the cables break.

I am hot and exhausted. Ten years ago I entered another church in another city in another country, and I remember it like it was yesterday: Sacre Coeur, Paris, France. I had climbed the big hill of Montmartre in the heat of a Paris August, and had sunk into the pews of Sacre Coeur in a fatigued gratitude. I could not get up for over an hour--so tired that I had sunk into a mystical meditation on the beauty and inspiration put into that holy place. Today, my fatigue is equal, but I find it completely impossible to meditate in a plastic chair.

My eyes follow the paintings around the room, then freeze at the sight of the most unlikely of sculptures--Michelangelo's "Pietà". This is something I truly adore, and I walk over to revel in this surprising resident of such an ultra-modern church. It is an excellent replica, and my heart feels the warmth of Mary's arms and legs stretching to hold aloft her crucified Son. Pilgrims have left money and other objects in one of the folds of her gown. This is the Third World.

I walk downstairs to the chapel under the altar. I immediately smell the mustiness of old wood in a cool place: **now** it seems like a European cathedral. It looks like one, too, with dark pews lined up in front of the Host. I try to meditate here, but I still cannot. I go outside and buy a bottle of pop to drink in the presence of the giant statues of the four Evangelists, learning some more Portuguese along the way--Mateus, Marcos, Lucas, and João. The vendor here has the cheapest postcards in the city, and I buy a bunch.

I can see my shopping mall a little ways off, and resume the hot afternoon trek. The pop was not enough: I suddenly realize that Brasília has a very serious sun, and I am terribly dehydrated. Huge skyscrapers loom all around me, but I feel I am in the middle of the Serengeti Plain. The sun beats down relentlessly as I cut diagonally across huge fields of grass. Why are the trees only planted along the sidewalks? Perhaps they are alien, and need constant fertilizing or other inputs, and are thus planted only where it is easy to service them. After an eternity, I finally drag my throbbing head and aching body into the comforting coolness of the mall. Not many African safaris end in that.... I buy the first ice cream cone I can find.

Today I am determined to master this place. I study the mall map furiously, determined to get my bearings once and for all and

104

not have to go up and down and all around to find everything. I proceed to buy a newspaper and find a proven restaurant for lunch. I leisurely pick at my buffet plate, making my first stab at reading a Brazilian newspaper. I understand plenty of the grammar, but most of the Brazilian topics elude me. The news from the U.S. is slim: Robert F. Kennedy, Jr., got married to his pregnant girlfriend, while the man his assassinated father could have kept from the Presidency in 1968, Richard M. Nixon, was hospitalized in critical condition after suffering a severe stroke. Birth and death can sneak up on even the most mythic of figures.

My shopping complete, I am not yet ready to return to the hotel. I dread the phone call asking why I did not stop by the Egyptian diplomat's hotel. It did not take too much sleep-refreshed thinking to realize that there are a dozen things I did not like about this guy in the one hour he shanghaied me into eating pizza with him at the mall, and I am prepared to iterate them if he calls me again. Why did he pooh-pooh my attempts to speak in Portuguese and insist we speak in English? Why would he never let me speak for myself to clerks and mall personnel? How dare he try to take hold of my arm so quickly after meeting me! And what about all that bragging about all the languages he could speak? And how could I have been too tired to realize what a creep he was from the start?

I find a promising-looking salon and stumble through my Portuguese to arrange a soothing shampoo and much-needed haircut. I struggle with my dictionaries to tell her important details about my pitiful hair, but she is a natural: she figures it all out on her own, and even chastises me for going so long without a trim. "It is very fine! You need to keep it trimmed!" I ask for her name, and she hands me her card--"Divina". Indeed! She is welcome to be the goddess of my hair: I have not had such a good haircut since I lived in North Carolina.

I buy another bottle of water to survive the ten-minute walk back to the hotel. It is no use: I take a pain reliever as soon as I get there because my dehydration headache will not go away. I lie down until the throbbing stops, then get up to work on my postcards and look at the car ads in the newspaper. I am exhausted: am I actually living **on** the equator? It takes me five minutes to pick the sticky/prickly Serengeti grasses off of my socks and shoes.

I return to work on Friday: all I need to do to make it to the weekend is change some more dollars and review an article for the Institute President. My intestines are still giving me occasional twinges necessitating prompt trips to the bathroom, and I am irritated by noisy repairmen and cigarette smoke in the office. I spend the afternoon reading papers and an American news magazine--more Kennedy news. John F. Kennedy's widow Jackie is in the hospital, and Robert F. Kennedy's daughter Courtney has seen her Irish husband, Paul Hill, finally win his lawsuit against the British government for imprisoning him based on a torture-induced confession.

I head back to the hotel, more relaxed about spending a weekend alone than I was last Friday. I even venture out of the hotel to try a non-hotel, non-mall restaurant, and am rewarded with savory stir-fried vegetables. I can only charge the University for my meals for a couple more days: after I finish those expense reports, will I still feel as if I work for the distant "subcontractor"? My immediate supervisor is finally arriving this weekend: he is the suitor who got me to come, and he is the one who will really dominate my life in Brazil. I head back to my room, eager to meet the man who may actually give me the worthwhile work I have been seeking for so long...the man of my dreams, the man who will fulfill me.

Chapter 21

I wake up quite hot, and when I open the balcony door, gusty warmth greets me--a Saturday in shorts and t-shirt! I splurge for a taxi ride to the mall on the other side of town in order to catch the only attractive movie playing in Brasília that I have not already seen. Daniel Day-Lewis is spitting fire from the get-go as Gerry Conlon in "In the Name of the Father"--screaming, swearing, throwing things physically or hurling daggers with his eyes. His character is a jerk and a petty criminal, but he does not deserve to be imprisoned for an Irish Republican Army bombing he did not do. It is shocking enough to think that scarcely ten years ago an English jury would convict based on torture-induced confessions and forensic bomb nonsense, but it is incomprehensible to realize that the English authorities suppressed his alibi witness and would not free any of the convicts after the real criminal later confessed.

As Conlon fights fruitlessly to stop his father from dying in prison, I think about Michael and wonder if he will get out of there sane. The Guildford convictions were not overturned until fifteen years later! I cry when Gerry Conlon storms exultantly out of the courthouse, a free man. I cry when Paul Hill pushes the police away from him and declares, "I'm walking out the front door, with Gerry!" I cry when I see the faces of the others--now aged a lifetime of despair in fifteen years--react one by one to the dismissal of their cases. I cry thinking about how many other innocents have been imprisoned because of the stubbornness and paranoia and violent mindset of the world's governing bodies.

I walk out into the mall, dazed. I am in Brazil, and I know there have been untold numbers of political prisoners in Brazil, but I am surrounded by apparent affluence and nonchalance. Politics seem a million miles away from this mall. Uncle Sam's presence is certainly quite innocuous here--not tanks and helicopters, but cutesy appropriated Yankee English names on the stores--"Coral Gables", "Bill Brothers", "Sweet Factory", "Body for Sure", "The Good Guys", "Baby Dreams", and--most improbably of all--"Siberian Husky". I am suddenly dying of thirst and hunger, and head for another unfamiliar restaurant zone.

I have grown more sure of my Portuguese and order without consulting my dictionaries. Though I have succeeded in getting the beans, rice, eggs, and fried bananas I had expected, I am surprised to receive two sinister looking sausages and three (!) slabs of steak as well. Egads! If I do not eat them, I will feel guiltier than if I do eat them: I cannot just throw protein in the garbage in a land with so many hungry people. I think about ranchers burning down the rainforest with every funny-tasting bite I take, and force myself to swallow the meat to which I have become unaccustomed. I will not order steak again, even if I have to carry my dictionary into every restaurant I enter for the next two years.

As I taxi away from the mall, I watch a brilliant orange sun setting over the Serengeti plains--the real plains, the undeveloped rolling landscape dotted with scrubby trees. A full moon is already lighting up the other side of the sky, but it is the rosy pink side of the sky that mesmerizes me.

When I get back to the hotel, I have a message that "Estefany" has called. Stephanie! I hurry to my room to wait for her to call back. When she does, it is fantastic news: Michael is being paroled on May first! His parents will pick him up and drive him down to North Carolina for a few weeks, and then he will head up to D.C. to stay with Stephanie. I ask her what the conditions of his parole are. "Only two--he can never participate in any action criticizing the U.S. military or counsel conscientious objectors."

"They can't do that!"

108

"They did."

"There is no way they can do that! Freedom of speech! The Constitution!"

"Well, he's getting out: isn't that what matters?!"

"Yeah, but...that's...unbelievable." Isn't it? "Look, can you ask Peter to check on that?"

"He's not a constitutional lawyer--he's not even a criminal lawyer!"

"Just ask him! Geez, Stephanie, I mean, please, just ask him."

"Michael's already signed the conditions of parole. It all happened really fast. A friend of Peter's was already counseling Michael on this, but the offer of parole came up very suddenly, and Michael just signed it without even calling us. He just wanted to get out of there. I mean, he got some of the other things we were pushing for...."

"What other things?"

"Well...it's a long story--the important thing is that he's getting out--just be happy for him!"

We chat for a few minutes about Brazil, but I quickly feel compelled to remind her about the telephone bill: it will be much more expensive than calling Mexico was.

"Don't worry about that! You're my sister!"

"Well, you have to watch your pennies now: you'll have an ex-con freeloader in your townhouse soon!"

"Oh, I'm sure he'll get a job fast." Yeah, Washington is always looking for a few good men: half-breed, treasonous deserters. "Look," I can hear the concern in her voice now--she knows I will never stop worrying about Michael, "it's gonna be OK. We've got enough money to manage."

"'We?' Peter's going to help foot Michael's bills?! Geez, he **must** really love you!"

109

A moment of silence. "Yeah...yeah, he does." She says it as if she is believing it for the first time. "He does," she says again. What an idiot I am! Why was I so certain that she knew he loved her? Just because I could see it with my own two eyes does not mean she could, not after the emotional coma she went into after Fernando left her. Will Michael chafe her? Will he just be a constant reminder to her that we can lose the ones we love, in more ways than one...?

"Steph...I really miss you....I hope everything...everything works out OK."

"It will!" She sounds convincing! "Take care--I love you!"

"I love you, too."

A couple hours later, the phone rings again--the Egyptian, this time. I cannot believe it! I thought he would have given up on me after I did not take him up on his invitation to visit him on that holiday. He asks why I did not show up for lunch **today**, as I promised! Today?! I never made a lunch date with him for **today**! His English comprehension is either worse than he thinks, or he is some sort of an obsessed lunatic. He angrily tells me how he came by at noon for me. Thank God I left the hotel at eleven! He tells me how he had his hotel chef prepare a special brunch for two, and how he is quite upset that I never showed up! I tell him I never made this supposed appointment with him, but he will have none of it. Then, even more surprising, he asks me out again! Now I am really horrified: will I have to keep my hotel name a secret from every guy I meet, lest I live in fear of some crazy waiting for me in the lobby every evening, every weekend?

I tell him he is acting in a very disturbing manner, and I do not appreciate his ordering me around, constantly telling me what to do. "Well, we are both foreigners here, and for that, I wish you good luck in Brazil." Give me a break! You work in an embassy, pal: you are surrounded by your countrymen everyday, so do not try this lonely foreigner crap on me! I thank him, and he finally says goodbye. I wonder if he will show up at the hotel one day and mow everybody down with a machine gun.

110

I sit in a fitful mood, listening to my cassettes from Mexico. The Spanish lyrics soothe me: I can understand the words. It takes me hours to fall asleep: I am still seething about innocent people in prison. Every time I see a movie that gets me this riled up, I wonder why the movie has not inspired enough people to do something so that it never happens again. Why do only a handful of people ever take these messages out into the real world? Where are the inspiring people outside the theaters?

***

On Sunday, I take a taxi to the Brasília zoo. It does not look like any zoo I have ever seen: it looks like some sort of zoofari through which you drive a land rover. Indeed, I see people driving around the park, stopping their cars only near the animals they wish to see, but the majority of us take it on foot. Again, I am amazed at how many unshaded stretches of grass I have to traverse to get from one animal site to another. Why not give the **animals** all the extra space--expand their tiny habitats and reduce our dull commuting!

I am quickly fatigued, dehydrated, and sick of walking--in sharp contrast to the ostrich I see pacing back and forth, back and forth, along the edge of its confines. It has worn down the grass to red clay in that section, and my heart breaks for it, taken so far away from home. The red clay tread mill says it all.

The monkeys seem happy enough, and the hippos and alligators doze dreamily in their cool waters. The zoo has a score of aviaries, and I marvel at the diversity of the tropical birds. I examine a toucan's beak up close: it looks longer than my foot, and deadly, yet brightly colored like a Mardi Gras mask. The birds here do so much sitting and so little flying.... I cannot tell if the birds have enough space or not, but I notice that the trees in the aviaries do not: they have already outgrown the confines, pushing their branches through the fence holes, out into the open space.

The big cats seem saddest of all. They are absolutely stunning--black panther, spotted puma, Bengal tiger, African lion-- but they have nothing to do but lie around in the shade, waiting for the next feeding time. Unable to follow the strongest instinct they

111

have--the need to hunt--they have no reason to climb or run or leap. I see one leopard chewing grass, like a sick dog. Their habitats are far bigger than some of the pathetic cat cages I used to see in my youthful zoo outings in Chicago, but they still seem way too small to offer a decent life to these grandiose beings. I want so desperately to climb the fence, to go in to comfort and pet them: would they tear me limb from limb, or have they forgotten all that? Why do I feel that something so beautiful should not have to be so vicious to survive? I think about the animals dying in the Sarajevo zoo because snipers will not allow the zookeepers to feed them. If there is a heaven for animals, those innocent victims deserve to go there, deserve another chance for a real life, a free life, an untortured life.

I return to the hotel early to eat leftovers and work on more postcards. I should study my Portuguese, but I am sick of studying: I just want it to snap into place already! I flip around the TV channels--soccer, more soccer, some very old black and white movie, some bizarre game show called "Game of Seduction" (no tame "Dating Game" here!), and..."Living Free" dubbed into Portuguese! Right after my trip to the zoo--I cannot believe it! I once again watch the famed cat-crazy Brits say goodbye to the lions they have raised since orphaned, and I choke up, knowing it was the right thing to do, but at such a high cost. That is the real Serengeti Plain.

As the sun slowly sinks westward, I suddenly realize that I am not dreading the end of the weekend: I am not dreading Monday morning! What an astonishing feeling this is. Was it really only a couple months ago that I used to awaken to the same instantaneous thought every morning: "God, I hate my life..."? I drag the chair out onto the balcony, pull on my headphones, and sing to the setting sun.

Chapter 22

I wake up in pain: my left ear has been crushed for hours. I gingerly roll over in agony, waiting for the blood to return to the scene of the accident. My dreams are always so restless that I am mystified as to why I systematically roll into the same sleep position every night. I cannot remember a time when I did not awaken on my stomach, one knee bent outwards, one arm shielding the exposed part of my face, the other arm hanging limply by the straight leg. I have never been able to fall asleep in this position, but my subconscious always demands and gets it. If it demands the position very early in the night, I wake up with a crushed ear.

I lie in bed, trying to reenter my dream. I love that magical place where there is always something new happening to me, where I hardly ever have to make decisions, where I meet interesting people without even trying. The telephone rings. Aargh! It is way too early. Either the Egyptian has flipped out or--"*Alló?*"--just as I figured, a wrong number. I am rudely brought back to full consciousness. I guess I will get out of bed: after all, I have already forgotten the dream place, and I do not hate my job or my life right now.

When I return from lunch Monday afternoon, my mysterious suitor and now boss has finally arrived from New York. I am shepherded into his office to shake his hand. After a quick "nice to meet you" and "how ya doin", he is interrupted by a phone call. I exit his office, and he does not seek me out the rest of the day. I can understand how busy he must be after being away for so many weeks, but I cannot help feeling disappointed. He courted me, and I came, but he does not seem to care. I know this is not true, but my insecurity flares up like incurable rheumatism.

In the morning, the Institute President wishes to see me. What have I done wrong?! I go to his office as quickly as I can, before my stomach has time to get sick. What a pleasant surprise it is: he is quite happy with my first project for him. Thank God! Will I ever get used to a warm, supportive, appreciative environment? They happen so rarely in my life. He asks if my boss has had time to talk to me, and when I say no, he explains why my boss is overwhelmingly busy. It seems my suitor is truly stretched to the limit, so I must forgive him.

The President also comments that I seem sad. Sad? I struggle for a response, shocked at such sensitivity and sympathy from so lofty a managerial level. "No, I am just frustrated," I explain. "I still don't have a bank account, a Portuguese tutor, a car, or a computer network linkup. I guess I should just relax about all that." He agrees, and adds that I would be getting more help from the staff if they were not dealing with the severe exigencies of work right now. As I leave his office, I wonder if I am actually sad. In comparison to Mexico, I should be jubilant right now. I am lonely, but not sad, I suppose.

At night I make my third pilgrimage in search of peanut butter--this time, armed with more vocabulary and helpful hints from the receptionist. It is no use: the supermarket manager explains that they never stock much of it, and right now they are sold out. I can scarcely conceive of a world without peanut butter: this could be the culinary calamity of my life! I settle for a tub of expensive cashews.

When I return home, the local TV news is on, and I am shocked to learn that the cinema I just visited on Saturday was shut down by inspectors today! I struggle to understand the Portuguese: at first it sounds like "financial irregularities", but then they are talking about filthy bathrooms and rugs that are completely...what? Dirty? Wet? Torn? I never noticed anything wrong there, although I did not use the bathroom. I have certainly been in much filthier cinemas in the U.S. I wish they would raid the zoo bathrooms: now

those are a sanitation felony. I am thankful I saw my movie before the raid: had I spent that much money on the taxi ride across town to no avail, I would have cried.

The next day, I finally succeed in getting a Portuguese tutor to come to my office. He quickly makes it clear he will not let me cheat with any more Spanish or French mumblings. "Forget that! You must only think in Portuguese now!" No, please, no! I am too old to learn a brand-new language, too old to learn how to talk all over again!

Before I leave work, I read in the newspaper that a day of mourning has been declared for the funeral of ex-President Nixon. Even the New York Stock Exchange will close down! I had not been aware of his death days ago. Is he really mourned, or just lamented? The first faraway death has already occurred, and I am not even speaking Portuguese yet.

***

On Thursday I go to customs to pick up my final boxes. They have arrived intact! My life has been transplanted successfully to the South American continent! In the afternoon, some of my coworkers have time to talk to me about cars and apartments. Will I actually be able to get settled in the next couple of weeks? In the evening I try the only vegetarian restaurant I have seen so far. Unfortunately, they specialize in breakfast, and evening fare is just a soup and pizza buffet. I find myself doing something extremely surprising: reminiscing about something in Mexico--my special vegetarian restaurant there. The owner was a delightful man--a former cruiseship singer who loved to serenade his clientele while they ate. He had a lifetime's worth of photos, posters, and paintings on the walls, from all over the world. It suddenly occurs to me that this man, somehow, after seeing the whole (?) world settled down in the one place I never wish to see again. Soon, there may be nobody left there that I would wish to see even if I could face Cuahtemoc again: I have just received a postcard from the Center's office manager, and she will probably be heading onto a new job in southern Mexico soon.

115

Friday is tremendous! I finally figure out how to establish computer contact with the U.S.! By lunchtime, I am able to send some email, and after lunch, I scan the on-line news items: the Tiajuana chief of police was ambushed and gunned down less than five weeks after that Mexican presidential candidate had been assassinated in Tiajuana, and Pope John Paul II fell down in his bathroom and broke his leg. Why do I feel better reading this stuff? There are people living in the Amazon who do not need such news, but I need it. I need every possible clue about what is going on. I am too much like that Brazilian at the café who ate lunch with a cellular phone pressed to his ear, far removed from the existence of the little boy circling the café with his shoeshine box.

When I get email replies back from the U.S., I am jubilant. I become even more jubilant when I am invited out for drinks after work--human contact! I make a valiant effort at rum, but my empty stomach implodes into a fiery ball. Embarrassed, I have to order bread and cheese to calm it down, absorb the poison. So many years have passed since that doctor told me not to partake of alcohol, caffeine, aspirin.... Not a day goes by without my knowing I cannot eat or drink whatever I want...not without consequences. I cannot even succeed at being a social drinker, but tonight I am in a great mood and have no problem acting drunk and playing along. I am insanely jealous over all the platonic kissing going on, and wish they would start feeling that friendly with me. Yet, I cannot complain: I have two engagements this weekend, and my overeager heart is ready and willing for my social life in Brazil to take off.

Chapter 23

Another beautiful, sunny Saturday dawns in Brasília. As I putter around my room, I am surprised by a familiar voice on the radio singing a seemingly Brazilian song. Yes! James Taylor! Yet another pop singer from the North has created a duet with Milton Nascimento. JT sings about the samba and the Portuguese, hungry children and the holy southern cross, as naturally as if he were singing about his beloved North Carolina. "...only a dream in Rio...." I remember back to how I had awoken to Taylor's "Mexico" the morning after I accepted the job in Mexico, and how I had thought it was a good sign. I hesitate to believe in signs anymore, but this Carolina voice singing with Milton makes me want to believe again.

On Sunday morning I wake up thinking about Michael. It is May first, and he will be free. I picture his parents, somber in their ancient Ford, driving away from Zanesville with Michael in the backseat, fidgeting. Did they ever really understand? His heart will feel an enormous weight lifted as he departs Ohio, and his heart will be singing by the time he reaches the Smoky Mountains of North Carolina. Why does he want to torture himself with Washington, D.C.? He deserves an early retirement from politics; he deserves a simple life in the lush bosom of Carolina. Maybe he will change his mind.

When I open my curtain, I am surprised to see a sky full of gray clouds: this is not the wide sea of bright blue with foaming waves of white to which I have grown accustomed. Yesterday was a frustrating day of shoe-shopping, apartment-hunting, and postponing of my stickshift lesson. Now, the phone rings, and it is postponed again. I look out at the dubious sky, wondering if my afternoon barbecue invitation will be canceled as well. Please, please, I do not want to spend more time alone.

I flip on the TV to the Sunday morning news. Nick Constantine--Britain's most reluctant pop star--has quietly purchased the largest cattle ranch in the Amazon. The acquisition was discovered by accident, it seems, but I cannot follow the Portuguese. Did he give all the cattle away? Is that what they are saying? Maybe I can get into the electronic news service tomorrow to figure this one out.

The barbecue is not canceled. My boss shows up promptly at noon and whisks me off to the other side of the lake. His girlfriend has an exquisite house with a swimming pool and a fantastic view of the city across the lake. It is the quietest place I have been in a long time. I listen in awe to the casual topics of the chattering guests--the World Bank, the Brazilian government, the NGO community. These people are insiders, they are experts, they are way beyond me and would be appalled if they knew that my last job included large chunks of time buying bread and washing dishes. It is hard enough to convince myself I am qualified to **work** with these people; I feel completely unqualified to **socialize** with them. They are so friendly, however, that I am somewhat at ease. One woman is so kind as to tell me she will bring back peanut butter for me when they return from their next trip to the U.S., and I am very touched. I return from this gorgeous house to my hotel room, sick of its tininess. I need some living space.

When Michael calls, I suddenly must fight back the tears. I could have guessed he would call, but I had not wanted to get my hopes up. He is at his parents' house, and I tell him how thrilled I am that he is out of jail. He does not want to talk about prison; he wants to hear about Brazil. I tell him all the good things. I do not tell him how much I am yearning for a house, a husband, two kids, and some puppies. I do not tell him anything bad at all: how can I ever complain to him about anything I have suffered, knowing what he has?

118

He jokingly asks me if I have already made plans to visit Nick Constantine's ranch; he knows how much I adore this man's music.

"Tell me about it! What's going on?"

"Well," he says, "I don't know all of it. It just came out in the news yesterday. He bought the biggest ranch in the Amazon. Nobody knew about it until some old girlfriend of the former owner showed up for an unexpected visit, not having any idea her old boyfriend had moved away! So she blabbed it to the press, said all the cattle were gone, and after the story broke, all sorts of schools and churches and squatter settlements reported that they had received anonymous donations of cows. He gave them all away! This afternoon, his spokesman confirmed all that, but would not say what Constantine's plans were or whether he would ever live on the ranch. So, are you going to check out the ranch?"

"Right! On my private plane! I can't believe you just got out today and you know all that already."

"Well, it was on the radio, driving back, and there was more in the newspaper. What do you think he bought it for?"

"He must have run out of ideas for what to do with his money. Geez--he's going to be overrun by tourists and fans and beggars now." Beggars. I suddenly remember how poor Michael's parents are. "You'd better get off the phone now: this is going to be very expensive."

"Don't you want to talk to me?"

"Of course I do! But it's so expensive!"

"It's OK: my parents even asked if I wanted to call you! I...I don't know.... Sometimes I can't even remember why we broke up.... I mean, I don't regret it, but...well, you're my best friend."

The tears roll hotly down my cheeks, and I put my hand over the receiver so he cannot hear my troubled breathing. I cannot remember why we broke up either. It is like trying to remember those physics equations from high school: I cannot remember the formulas, but there was definitely some sort of natural law at work that pulled us apart. Was it centripetal force? Centrifugal force? It does not matter which force it was: mastering the math would not have altered the force. I swallow hard and bite my cheek: I do not want him to hear me crying, not today. "You're my best friend, too." I think about you all the time, that is. "I'm so glad you're out." I wish you were here, though. "Look, if Washington doesn't work out, don't kill yourself there--just go back to North Carolina." Or come here...maybe the laws of physics work differently south of the equator....

"I spent twenty-seven years in North Carolina: don't you think that's enough?"

"No, but two years in Washington was more than enough for me! Just take care of yourself: don't let all that bad karma eat you alive."

"I'll be OK--I'll be with Stephanie."

"I know, but she doesn't really understand people like you and me: she won't understand the trials and tribulations of the nonprofit subculture there."

"She cares and she's helping me. I can't ask for more than that."

"When are you going up?"

"I'm not sure--I'll call you when I get up there."

"OK--take care, and congratulations!"

"Thanks! Send me some more postcards!"

When I hang up, the sobs erupt with a vengeance. I miss him so much. I am insanely jealous of Stephanie's getting to live with him--I never got to. I would love to awaken to his dimpled smile and his warm brown eyes every morning. I need to find somebody else. I hate that feeling because liberated women are not supposed to have that desperate feeling. It is not **need**, I tell myself, just longing--fight it! Be strong!

My thoughts wander back to Nick Constantine. I love his music. He writes songs as if he knows exactly what I am thinking. He can sing like a man or a woman, a peacock or a dove, a devil or an angel--but I always hear his voice deeper inside me than I can ever hear anything else. Will he write a song about the rainforest? I doubt it. No, he will leave that to people like Sting. What is he doing with that ranch? I pop in his latest cassette and put on the headphones to search for clues.... His soul is calling out to him.... He needs to leave the material world.... Maybe his spirit is leading him into the wilderness....

Chapter 24

I am surrounded by visions of death. Every TV channel I watch and every newspaper I see bear the words and photos of the auto-racing death of Ayrton Senna. I have never heard of this man, but Brazil has gone into public mourning for him. They were proud of him; they loved him; now he is gone. I am in a different society now, but I am not of it: I do not even know enough to mourn for this man. Why does he mean so much to them? I see his beautiful, smiling face in photo after photo; I read about his life; I turn away from the film of the car crash which they keep running over and over again. He is on the other side. He is with Kurt Cobain and Richard Nixon. He is with billions of souls now, souls who comprehend eternity. I want to comprehend it too...without dying.

My on-line computer news is full of rebirth: South Africa has elected a black president, and *apartheid* is history. Change is possible. Good change is possible.

In the evening, a coworker takes me to a quiet parking lot near the National Theater to give me manual transmission lessons. I feel like a fifteen-year-old again. I thought I knew how to drive--have I not been a driver all these years?--but I am moving my feet up and down on the pedals in bewilderment. "Push the clutch **all** the way down. No, third gear is like **this**...." We have not even circled the parking lot once when we are pulled over by traffic cops! There is not a single pedestrian or car in this deserted space, we are disturbing nobody, and we are only going about fifteen miles per hour.

I quickly realize from the smattering of Portuguese I know that this is pure harassment. My companion and I must produce our driving licenses, and the cop proceeds to chastise me for using a U.S. license, and her for teaching without an instructor's license. He berates her for ten minutes, and I begin crying in earnest, exasperated, convinced now that I will never get a car or an apartment, convinced that I will be stuck in that stupid hotel the entire two years I am here. When we leave, she tries to calm me, telling me they were just hoping for a bribe: they know this is the spot where people teach their kids how to drive, and they are usually trying to nab the teenagers who do not have any license, to get a bribe out of their parents. I am uncomforted.

I sup on luscious French bread toasted with smooth, mild cheese, and sip mango juice. When I return to my hotel room, I burst into tears again, watching the news report on the outpouring of grief over Senna's death. My own troubles are insignificant: this man has broken a billion hearts.

Wednesday morning I taxi to the Department of Transit. They will not accept my filing a harassment complaint without the automobile owner there, so I settle for getting instructions on how to use my U.S. driver's license to obtain a Brazilian license. They make it sound so simple....

On Thursday, I scour the special automobile section in search of automatics. The thought of attempting another stickshift lesson or of delaying getting a car one more week makes me want to scream. Surely that fiasco was a sign from God!? "You have enough changes to adjust to right now: don't torture yourself trying to relearn how to drive, too!" The automatics are few and far between, but I highlight a few promising ones and cart a couple savvy coworkers off car-hunting.

The first car we look at seems gigantic compared to my old Japanese compact, and it is painted that golden beige color that I have never seen on any other car except a Mercedes Benz. The shape is vaguely like a Benz, too. This car is like nothing I would have bought in the U.S., but after the test drive, I realize it will be perfect for me right now--good price, low mileage, strong motor, clean car. Can this be happening so easily? This is too easy. We race over to the bank to push my money through the dollar account, into the *cruzeiros-reais* account. There are problems, confusions galore, and we have to race against the clock to get it done by the close of the business day. Ninety minutes later, we zoom back to the dealership, I sign some papers, and the car belongs to me. It is a miracle! One of my companions drives it back to the hotel for me since I do not yet have a Brazilian license or insurance, and I leave it to sit quietly in the parking lot until I am ready for it. It is beautiful: it will probably be stolen tonight! It is even a cane alcohol car, less damaging to the environment.

In the evening, I am weary but immensely relieved--so much closer to having a normal life! I turn on the TV to the coverage of Ayrton Senna's funeral. The cameras pan across fancy motorcades, parading horses, floral arrangements, gun salutes. It seems so beautiful until they pan across face after face after anguished face of mourners. These people did not just come to pay their last respects: they are crying their eyes out. Children, women, and men alike are sobbing and sobbing and sobbing. Is this what the funeral of Elvis was like? Did they just say 100,000 people have filed past the casket? The real irony now hits me: I felt as if my life could not really begin here without a car, just to putt around in, but Senna could not live without the thrill of driving the fastest, best cars in the world. I will be the slowest, most cautious driver hitting the unfamiliar Brazilian roads, while Brazil's fastest, most courageous driver will never grace a road here with his presence again.

Chapter 25

On the weekend, my supervisor from the University arrives for a visit. My boss wines and dines him and drives him all around the city to see everything there is to see. I am invited along, but cannot help resenting the fact that I alone did not rate this treatment, that I alone did not deserve a tour of the city. Yet, it is good that this supervisor is here, because he pokes and prods and hints to my boss about what I should be doing while placed here. He is especially keen on not wanting me to sit behind a desk for two years, and for the first time, my new boss asks if I would be willing to go to the Amazon. "Sure!" Yes, a million times, yes! "But I don't want to wade through piranha waters or anything."

He laughs heartily, and, with great delight, describes all the creatures I would encounter swimming in the Amazon River system: electric eels, stingrays, chiggers, and, of course, piranhas. "But jumping into the river when you're all hot is the best part!" He also mentions porpoises.

"Porpoises?! In fresh water?"

"Yeah." He goes on to tell me some crazy story about the emergence of the Andes mountains a zillion years ago, and how the Andes reversed the flow of the Amazon River, and that is why many saltwater fish and mammals adapted to life in the Amazon River: they were trapped there. I do not understand, but I am thrilled anyway--dolphins in the Amazon! I can't wait.

Before we return to our hotels, we get a tour of one of the "satellite cities". This particular one was created when a spontaneous slum settlement was completely relocated to a more desirable location--more desirable from the government's viewpoint. It has grown rapidly, and is replete with its own stores, restaurants, services, and even its own newspaper. The place is hopping today: a carnival is in town! Indeed, it looks like a much more entertaining place to live than the staid hotel district. I force myself to look deeper into the house lots: they are not so entertaining looking. I know they have no indoor plumbing, and are surely lacking in a thousand other ways, too.

On Monday I find myself serving as my visiting supervisor's interpreter, improbably enough. He is my advocate on this visit, but I am overanxious to please, knowing he will ultimately be judging my performance. After work, we dine alone in a lovely continental restaurant. I am struggling to sound simultaneously intelligent and charming, serious and witty. Is he really my ally? Maybe I will never really trust any boss again.

On Tuesday he departs. He has left behind peanut butter and advice. My boss at the Institute moves quickly to respond--assigning me my first significant project since my arrival. I still do not feel ready, though. I have just completed days of paperwork and running around to get a Brazilian driver's license, and I am burning to use it: I want to shop for the black-eyed peas I discovered at lunch today, take my clothes to a laundromat bigger than my hotel bathroom sink, find a swim club, go horseback riding, and, most of all, search for an apartment.

In the evening, I take what I hope to be my last taxi ride back to the hotel. I enter to find a bare mattress on my bed: am I being evicted? I telephone for sheets, and a maid comes to make up the bed in that pristinely perfect way I will miss when I move out. I settle down to eat the scrumptious leftovers of last night's elegant meal.

When I reach into the fridge for an apple to top it off, I am startled by a cockroach scurrying amongst my provisions. No! This cannot be! They only come out in the dark! I am only supposed to see them if I suddenly switch on the light to make a midnight bathroom run! I could almost stand them when I knew they were polite enough to wait until I went to bed, but this!

I slowly start poking through my things, trying to find him. My food is all in plastic bags, which make unending rustling noises that cause me to jump over and over and over again as I move them around. I gingerly look into them, one by one--yes, "clean"--and tie them each up again, this time more tightly. Nearly everything is wrapped, but the aromas must be tempting the cockroaches anyway. I throw my toothbrush into the garbage, and move the cups and spoon into the bathroom to be washed and rehoused. I move my fridge-top "medicine cabinet" to the table item by item--bottles of allergy pills, vitamins, pain relievers, antacids. I am now almost ready to scrub down the fridge. I pick up the remaining two packets of pills--and quickly hurl them against the wall. Yuck! The roach was hiding right in between them! That sneaky devil. His reflexes are surprisingly slower than mine, and I quickly smash him with the fly swatter. I am shuddering all over.

I rub soapy suds all over the fridge, then begin to wipe off my bottles one by one. Just as I finally start feeling I have made progress in cleansing my environment, I scream at the sight of a huge roach scurrying on the wall above the fridge. I reach for the swatter again and send him plummeting four feet to his death. I am near convulsions. What kind of roach would be on the prowl with all the light and sound and commotion I am making? Have they no shame? I look around the room in shivering horror--dark brown blanket, siena carpeting, cocoa brown fridge, wood-paneled air conditioner, hardwood wardrobe, beige upholstered chairs--did they purposefully furnish this room to camouflage these damned assailants?! Their sneak attacks will give me a heart attack one day. I have to get out of here.

Later, after I have calmed down a bit, I reflect again on the satellite city. How many of them would probably swap places with me in a minute--hot showers, electric ventilation, nice furniture, color TV, clean linens daily--and not utter one word of complaint about being visited by a couple of cockroaches every night? I fight off the guilt trip; I remain determined to get out of here; I have been here exactly one month; I have been living out of suitcases for two months.

At night I dream that I and a group of people are fighting off the attempt by a Satanic disciple to take over our minds. Somehow, I trust the power of my prayers and I am not frightened--just determined.

In the morning I shell out money for another two weeks in the hotel: the shortest possible period that still has the "apartment hotel" rate. I head out to my car: this is the first day of the rest of my life in Brazil! I wipe the dirt off the fender and carefully apply my brand new Amnesty International bumper sticker. I slide into the driver's seat and gleefully turn the ignition. It grinds--nothing. I pump, I turn, I turn some more, I pump some more--nothing. It will not start. I have a dead car. I just bought a dead car.

The tears are already welling up as I head to the taxi stand. I fight an impulse to return to my room and dive back into my bed. When I get to work, I quickly shut my office door and stare out the window, trying to get a hold of myself. The tears slowly subside as I resign myself to partaking of the taxi life a little longer. I try to force the thought of my beautiful dead car out of my mind. I have lots of work to do now.

I check my email and end up getting disconnected six times during the course of the day. Over and over again I type the same messages, trying to send them before the next disconnection strikes. Inside, I am boiling. I spend half an hour on the phone to the U.S., trying to get a copy of my missing calling card bill. Today was the deadline to submit my expenses to the University, and I am pleading with the customer service representative to help me hold off garnishment of my wages. Will anything start going right? I struggle to put together some spreadsheets on my new system, silently cursing the University for not giving me software I already know: will I ever be able to accomplish anything here without some horrific learning curve?

At lunchtime, I go to the bank to withdraw money, and am told I cannot touch it: it is invested. "What!? Of course it is invested! If it were not, it would be losing value every day!" They calm me down, and tell me I just need to fill out one additional form; then the bank will automatically move money from the investment into my account. Good grief--I cannot even operate under the same banking concepts I have used all my life. I can take absolutely nothing for granted here. The afternoon drags, the finale being a depressing Portuguese class focusing on housing vocabulary. I learn how to repeat a dialogue about inviting a friend over to your big house for the weekend, because she lives in such a cramped place! Why is my tutor rubbing it in?

I leave work as early as I can. I think about the irony of trying to work for sustainable development for Brazilians, while I must be obsessed with protecting the value of my own money on a daily basis. I head off to the mall to engage in more consumer activity. It is embarrassingly soothing. It is slow, to be sure--it is still terribly difficult to find anything--but slowly I tick items off my list. I even find cute gifts for the people at work who helped me so much in my car hunt. Best of all, I discover a bookstore with an English-language section. Hallelujah! That this is truly, truly a miracle sent from above becomes indubitable when I come across a novel by a wonderful North Carolina author.

***

I pass the night without incident: the roaches seem to be in momentary retreat. Perhaps my strategy of spreading apart all my fridge-top items has been successful: they are too scared to roam from goody to goody, traversing the vulnerable open spaces. I start my book over breakfast...ahhhhh.... For a few minutes a day, I can be in the warm bosom of North Carolina.

I head to work considerably refreshed. I am determined to have a productive day, to see some benefits from these arduous learning curves! I spew out translations and spreadsheets right and left, intimidate the email into behaving, write a fast outline for examining female health issues in the Amazon, and march

129

confidently into the bank to withdraw more money. I am stunned by my own success. When the part-timers come in this afternoon and offer to jumpstart my battery, I am even calm about it.

With astonishment, followed rapidly by embarrassment, I hear my engine ignite--no jumpstart necessary. They explain to me that alcohol cars have a lot of trouble igniting when it is cold, and I need to pull out the "*fogador*" while I am cranking the engine. *Fogador*?! I am clueless. I thought that lever was the hood-release! They tell me it creates more heat to help with the initial ignition. They proceed to show me that the *fogador* is connected to a small gasoline tank, but that it is currently empty. I silently curse the previous owner for not leaving the auto manual in the car, but I cannot stay mad now: I am delighted! After getting the gas, I drive back to work. Has it been a whole year since I last drove to work?

Empowered, I pick up the newspaper to begin looking at apartment ads. I am greeted by page after page replete with photos and articles of yesterday's military occupation of Brasília! What are they talking about?! I struggle through the Portuguese: the army has come because the Federal Police have been on strike for almost two months, and they need to...to...to what? My boss walks by, glances over my shoulder, and just laughs about it. He thinks seeing tanks in the streets of Brasília is quite a hoot. The picture of tanks at the National Cathedral certainly is absurd. Apparently they have already staged some test runs of operations around the Presidential offices. (What does **that** mean?!) If the Federal Police are so important to our safety in the Federal District, why did the government move so slowly to get a replacement police force in here? And how is this being explained in the U.S. press? Will my mother see photos of tanks in the streets here and think there has been a coup d'état?

Satisfied that it is actually no big deal, I turn my attention to the classifieds. Most of the apartments are in obscure locations, and bear no price tags. The ones with price tags seem to be all really cheap or really expensive: maybe there really is no significant middle class in this society. I see some ads seeking roommates and wonder if I now know enough Portuguese to avoid getting a lunatic roommate...not that I have always done such a great job at sizing up potential roommates in English.... Is the request for "nonsmoker" enough indication of compatibility? Does the request for an "evangelical" prove moral uprightness? Do the words "excellent references required" indicate especially discriminating taste? I am hesitant--better to look at small apartments and see if I can afford something on my own. I will start in earnest on the weekend.

I head gleefully out to my awaiting car. The only thing proving "autumn" here is that it gets darker faster every night, and I regret the fact that my first car ride back from work will be in the dark. I slowly and methodically adjust the mirrors, the lights, the fan, the radio--OK! I back out--whoa! This is a big car! I hope I do not start sideswiping things. I pull out like a little old lady, and drive back to the hotel with acute concentration. I made it! I am in business! I could now eat dinner anywhere in this town, but I will not push it: I settle for a toasted cheesy baguette at the hotel, then return to my room for an apple. My book, my car keys, and a successful day's work are my comforts tonight.

In the morning I call the headquarters of the Federal Police, to see if the occupying forces will do my "registration as a foreigner"; I explain that I was supposed to have done it by now, but the Federal Police have been on strike ever since I arrived, and now the deadline for registering myself is creeping up.... The receptionist transfers me, and the phone rings fifty times before I hang up and dial the number again. She transfers me again, and I count off the rings while I stare out the window trying to figure out the intent of the conversation of the birds in the eaves. They are so sweet, so beautiful. Fifty-five, fifty-six, fifty-seven, fifty-eight, somebody picks up: no, the army is not performing any of the internal functions of the striking Federal Police, and, no, I will not have any legal problems because of this. I hang up, mostly reassured, but feeling that I would not be surprised if I ended up deported, anyway.

In the evening, I am alone and lonely. All I have to look forward to this weekend is looking at expensive apartments. I go to the mall and try not to gaze too longingly, too obviously at the people.

131

Everybody has somebody: I am the only loner in the entire mall. I catch my breath over dinner at the sound of two American teenagers talking: maybe they will strike up a conversation with me! No, they pass by. Nobody guesses I am American here...or cares. I look at clothing. There seems to be no middle-class clothing. A blouse in one store is $5; in another, $50. The dress prices are frightful. I purposefully avoid the music store: I must save that for a day of heart-wrenching, agonizing depression. I leave with only a few drugstore items and the memory of the extraordinary discovery of a place that sells chocolate mousse.

The weekend is long and tedious. I only manage to see three apartments: two of them are small and icky, and one of them is gigantic and too good for me. I keep thinking about it, though. I do not **need** to spend that much money, but I **could**. I do not **need** to have three bedrooms, but it **would** be great for getting some puppies. I do not **need** an apartment right next to a small park, but it **would** be marvelous to spend my evenings there, walking the dogs. I cannot do it. The University is paying me more than most of my underpaid coworkers earn: how could I ever invite them over to my apartment, knowing they could not afford such a place?

When I return to my hotel room late Sunday afternoon, the maid has thrown out the newspaper I had left on the bed. Furious, I call to complain. They offer to retrieve it, and I tell them I do not want it after it has been mixed with the garbage. They did not even change the sheets: I have lost my paper to a mere tidying-up! I am exhausted and grumpy. I have lost my ability to cope. I hope desperately that this is just my mercurial hormones, and not the beginning of a long descent into culture shock. I need an apartment to reach out and embrace me, to tell me, "Come on in, this can be your home."

At night, the red rain finally begins. Tomorrow will be a tempest, but in a couple days, the sky inside my mind will finally be clear again. Clear for a couple weeks, or a couple months--I never know when my body will think it time to try again. It cannot read my psyche much better than I can, for I am too ambivalent about being a

132

woman. I have paid so many costs, seen so few benefits. Why does my body keep seeking out the wrong men, then punishing me when I fail to reproduce with them?

Chapter 26

I awake surprised that the lamp is not on. I have been leaving it on at night--the final recourse of a roachphobe--but I must have turned it off in my sleep. There are very few things I can do in my sleep. A subconscious too stupid to roll off of a paralyzed ear, too stupid to pull up more covers when cold, is surely too stupid to turn off a lamp? I have occasionally hurled pillows around, ripped jewelry off, and rattled garbage cans in my sleep...but I do not think I have ever turned off a lamp. What if the roaches did it? Maybe all these roach nightmares I have been having are not so subconscious after all....

I shudder, remembering when the rat invaded my old room in Mexico. When I spent the night in an empty guestroom, I had left the lights and radio on to discourage the rat from wreaking more havoc before the maintenance staff arrived the next day. In the morning, upon reentering my room to retrieve clean clothes, I nearly had a heart attack when I saw that the radio plug had been pulled right out of the outlet. If that rat was intelligent enough to do that....

In the afternoon, I am uncontrollably repulsed by a beautiful apartment because it has too much brown: I will not tolerate another camouflaged environment! My hormonal fever is gone, to be sure, and my emotions have calmed down, but even my fully rational mind never forgets or forgives those rough nights.

In the evening, I stop at the mall to buy a small nightlight: there are none to be found. I am directed to some electronic "district" in the south of the city. The largest mall in Brasília does not sell nightlights...or washcloths...or Borax...or...my shopping list continues to grow faster than I can handle it. I am determined to leave the mall only after finding some source of contentment, however, and so will buy at least one stupid little thing to make me happy. I try on dozens and dozens of sunglasses before indulging myself in the imported French model, realizing that Brazilian shades are not tinted enough for pale Northern eyes. I love these glasses--I really love them!

When I go back to the hotel, I find a huge alien roach-like creature in the bathroom. I smash him quickly, then examine him for clues. Will it just keep getting worse as the dry season progresses: will all the insects come in to look for water? When I flush him, I cannot see him go down, and, paranoid, wonder if he has bailed out under the toilet rim.

I lie in bed, exhausted, wishing I could sink back into that luscious sleepy state I was in this morning when the alarm went off. It always takes me so long to fall asleep, so long to wake up. I roll over, and my pest-intruder sixth sense tells me to open my eyes just as a roach is sauntering from the air conditioner over to the balcony door. I jump up and grab my swatter--too late! He has already disappeared into the brown camouflage. Was that the spot I saw in my nightmare--so close to my bed? Two nights ago, I would have broken down in hormonal tears, but tonight I can calmly resolve to talk to the desk clerk in the morning.

I pull the bed as far away from the scene of the crime as I can. Wait! I think I see it! Can that be a roach lying a scant three inches to the left of the swatter? I gingerly pick up the swatter and poke. Yes! He moves. Apparently, I **had** succeeded in knocking him down when I was probing the door frame for him--damn camouflage colors! I swat and swat and finally get him. No, I absolutely will not take an apartment in earth tones! I pop another allergy pill to help me fall asleep: the absurd adrenaline of the hunt-or-be-hunted is pumping raucously through my veins.

Forty minutes later, I am finally beginning to calm down. I get up to go to the bathroom again. Astonished, I see a huge bug floating in the toilet. Is that the one I "killed" four hours ago?! He

135

did bail out under the rim! I can scarcely believe my own eyes. Am I asleep and dreaming this? That was just paranoia, right? I pump the flush again, and vigilantly watch him go down this time. Maybe I have flipped: maybe I am imagining **all** these bugs, and soon I will be locked up in a little white room in a straightjacket to stop me from trying to kill all the bugs. Well, I **am** in the tropics, I suppose: if I were "seeing" all these bugs in the Arctic Circle, insanity would be a more likely culprit than it is here. I must not let the skyscrapers and six-lane freeways fool me into forgetting that I am in the Brazilian savannah, after all...and the bugs were here long before this hotel was.

***

I awaken still fatigued, the lamp still glowing this time. I talk to the desk clerk on my way out, and he tells me they will spray the room. Relieved, hopeful, and ashamed of my acquiescence to chemical warfare, I head to work. I am exhausted: this is not the "time of month" when I can afford to get so little sleep. After a couple hours of fruitless apartment phone calls, I am in tears: I will never get an apartment, never have another good night's sleep! As if to say "never say never", my missing long-distance phone bill shows up on the fax machine--finally! I only need one more fax to complete my expense reports for the University, and I can finally get **that** ugly pile of receipts and notes off my desk.

I try to master more spreadsheet skills, but I am way too tired. I pass the rest of the day reading the rules-of-the-road handbook for Brazil, until I learn from a coworker that advertised rental prices only reflect half the cost of apartment rentals, because there is also a huge condominium tax! I sink into complete apartment despair and make arrangements to hire an "assistant" to help me find an apartment: I will never be able to handle it alone. I return home, bleary-eyed. Please, please, please let there be no bugs tonight.... I want to sleep so badly.

Upon entering the hotel room, I can detect no smell of bug spray. Am I too congested from allergies, or has it wafted out through the balcony door already? Or did they not spray, after all? I

136

go down to the snackshop for a grilled cheese. They have to send someone out to get change for the bill I fork over, worth less than four U.S. dollars. I stop by the hotel counter to pay my weekly restaurant tab: they cannot give me change either, for a measly meal charge of six U.S. dollars. I blow a fuse.

"It is ridiculous for me to have to write a check for such a puny sum!" I have been waiting since last Friday to get more checks from the bank: why will they only give me twenty checks at a time, if everybody in Brazil supposedly uses checks for everything? If I were not using cash, I would be writing three or four checks a day! I do not understand, I do not understand, I am tired, I want to cry, I am ashamed at my lack of patience and tolerance, and I am so tired.

I retreat to my room and bury myself in my North Carolina novel, munching on cashews and an apple in between turning the pages. It was so funny before, but now I am in tears as I read about Meredith Copeland's return from Vietnam. He has nothing to look forward to but the expected departure of his wife, whom he is sure will not stay with a cripple. He looks to his sweet and adventurous Carolina past for comfort. I find myself crying again.

After my shower, a moth appears out of nowhere and divebombs right into my freshly toweled head! Is the whole insect community of Brazil now at war with me? My balcony door is not even open! I reach for the swatter again, hoping he is not a she that has already laid eggs in the few sweaters I have brought to Brazil. I am losing my enthusiasm to see the rainforest. The truth is, I would probably forgive Brazil all these things if I were having more fun. The truth is...the truth is...I am not having fun, I do not love my job, and I am lonely as hell. Swat-smash.

Around two a.m., I turn off the alarm clock because I cannot face it. I finally fall asleep sometime before three. My internal clock wakes me up three minutes before my alarm normally goes off. And my body wonders why I hate it so: whose side are you on, anyway?!

I head to work pessimistic, expecting to be a physical wreck, but I am not. My blood level and hormones are returning to normal, and my energy level is higher than I had expected. **Good** body! In the morning, I get the final bill I need to complete my expense reports for the University's sending me down here, and it makes me ecstatic. When a real estate agent telephones about showing me a two-bedroom furnished apartment, I am beside myself.

It is nice; no, it is pretty darn wonderful. I, myself, would not have chosen black vinyl sofas, and the carpeting sucks, but the kitchen is the best I have seen in a small apartment. The bedrooms are small, but with two, I can divide them into a sleeping space and an everything-else space. I check everything over and over again. The price sounds too good--I take great pains to be sure I understand the cost of the condominium fees, and it still seems quite cheap. Nice neighborhood--a long commute by Brasília standards, but less than a half-hour. I should take this place.

I hold back--patience! I am always so impatient. I will wait to see how my apartment-hunting assistant does tomorrow, and then decide. If it is snapped up that fast, so be it. I return to work energized enough to delve into the Atlas of Brazil for my demographics project.

When I return to the hotel, my nose and eyes sting from the chemicals the moment I enter my room. Oh, happy acridity! Will I finish my days here in peace? The more I think about the apartment, the more I want it.

***

I sleep a little better, and again wake up three minutes before my alarm goes off. I head straight to my appointment with an allergist. I show him my list of allergies, but he says none of them but the dust exist here! He quizzes me about my symptoms and schedules me for a sensitivity test to local allergens. I will have to stop taking antihistamines for five days prior to the test. "I won't survive!" He prescribes two nasal sprays to get me through it, and counsels me to take cold showers only: cold showers pump up your adrenaline, and adrenaline is the body's natural cure to allergies! Oh, joy. Now I have to choose between cold adrenaline or hot comfort for my backaches, my surgery scars, my constant muscular tension. If I am a nervous wreck, do I really need cold showers to pump up my adrenaline?! It is bad enough that he wants to put me on shots and take away my drugs, but cold showers too?!

I head to work, hating my body again. I cannot take the apartment I want because the allergist emphatically instructed me not to take an apartment with carpeting. My body, sensing my enmity, counterstrikes with the mother of all cramps. Hell!!! It is spreading quickly from its uterine epicenter down the walls of my intestines and into my groin. I massage frantically at every stoplight, to no avail. When I finally get to the office, I dash into the ladies' room, expecting a baby to pop out when I pull down my pants. No, just blood--the reproductive sponge has now officially been squeezed completely dry by the sadistic hormonal hands inside me. All gone! Better luck with your next egg, dearie! If men had to go through this, a cure would have been discovered centuries ago.

I retreat to my office, alternating between frantic pacing and bizarre stretches that involve wrapping my body around my chair in as many permutations as I can think of. I pop two more pain relievers, even though I know I took some a scant two hours ago. Slowly, my throbbing muscles begin to calm down.

My apartment-hunting assistant has not called or shown up, and I must face the classifieds alone, again. I am determined to find something, even if I have to neglect my work to struggle with the road map all day long. The first one I see is a real lemon. The second is a real peach--too much of a peach, actually. I could probably afford it, but I do not want to pour all my money into an apartment: I want fun money in my budget. Midway through the afternoon, a torrential downpour erupts: if this is the dry season, what on earth does the rainy season look like? As I approach my third apartment building of the day, I see a beautiful rainbow stretching across the big Brazilian sky. Please let this be a good omen!

I love it. I love this apartment. From the moment she opens the living room window and I see the unbelievably gorgeous view of the lake that has been my desperate dream, I am in love with this apartment. I love its parquet floors, its closet space, its bathroom tiles and bidet, its unusual kitchen, its view of the tree-lined lake from every room. Within five minutes, I am telling her I want it.

She bursts my bubble: I will have to wait until morning because she promised two earlier viewers that they could have until tomorrow to decide. What?! I am forlorn, panicked. I want to beg with her, plead with her, offer her six months' rent paid upfront--but I fear offending her, so I just tell her earnestly how much I love the apartment, how I am sure it is perfect for me. (How could I find another like this one?)

In the evening, I enter the bathroom ambivalent. My scar tissues, my spine, and my postpartum-like abdomen are crying out for a hot bath. What could a cold bath accomplish here, anyway? I will be inhaling dust from dirty curtains, thick carpeting, and old cushions all night. I turn on the hot water, and it comes out hotter than it has ever come out in this hotel before: how can I refuse? I sink into the hottest bath I have had since I was in the U.S., and it feels wonderful.

I fall asleep late and wake up way too early, unable to stop thinking about my dream apartment and all the cute little things I could buy to make living there a joy. I get up queasy. I eat some chocolate--the only thing that can wake me up without making me sicker--and slowly and carefully start on some breakfast cereal, reading my Pax Christi mailing. Nobody is faster in catching up with new addresses than the nuns of Erie, Pennsylvania.

Out of the corner of my left eye, I see a sudden movement, look down at a roach crawling on the wall six inches to my left, and leap away from the table, banging my knee wickedly on the table in the process. Cursing vehemently, I reach for the swatter and knock him off the wall. It takes me five minutes to find him in the camouflage carpet and finish him off. I am shaking. Morning! Daylight! Radio on! Two days after spraying! I have to get out of this place.

The minute I walk into the office, the receptionist tells me the landlady is on the phone! It is mine! I get instructions to go to her lawyer's office in the afternoon and to bring certain proofs of identity and salary. Is this really happening? I am half-relieved, still afraid it will fall through somehow.

I rush into a meeting with the Norwegian ambassador late. It probably does not matter in the least if I am there or not, but I want to go: I have never met an ambassador! This **is** a great job.

After that, I sit down with a calculator to look at my finances, which have grown ridiculously complicated--one savings account and two checking accounts in the U.S., one dollar account and two *cruzeiro* accounts in Brazil. How much do I have, and how do I need to move it around? It all depends on how many months she wants up front.

I head to the lawyer's office with all the papers I need, only to learn that he will **now** write up the contract: I cannot sign it until tomorrow or Monday! I try not to worry: what could possibly happen now? Some long-lost friend or relative of the landlady's could show up unexpectedly and get it, that's what. Will it really be mine? I already love it too much.

By late afternoon, I am exhausted and can scarcely keep my eyes open. I desperately need more sleep. How many days will it take to get my apartment ready? I need to buy everything: I will not even have a working telephone or drinkable water in this place. My Portuguese tutor offers to help me shop this weekend. Hallelujah! I will take him up on it--more for the social company than anything else. I can shop for pots and towels without much help, and I cannot get the big things until I have a place to store them.

Before I go home, I check the news online. Jacqueline Kennedy Onassis has died of cancer. The most famous widow in America is gone, thirty years after she became the most famous widow in America. She died at home, as gracefully as she had lived. While I was pondering the impending acquisition of real estate and personal possessions, she was pondering her impending departure from the material world into the spiritual. The Brazilian newspaper tactlessly headlines her net worth of one-hundred million dollars. She cannot take it with her. She does not need to take it with her. Someday, I too can stop thinking about all the things I need or think I need to survive, but tomorrow morning, I must draw up a list of what

141

I need to buy for my new home.

I lie in bed for twelve hours on Friday night, but can only sleep six of them. I finally get up, headachy and weary. It was incredibly difficult to resist those drowsiness-inducing antihistamines last night, but I want to clear my system for the allergy test coming up. My mind will not shut off its worrying. How quickly can I furnish this apartment? Will I dry up my savings account if I buy everything in a hurry? Will I ever actually be able to put in a real eight-hour workday, or are they going to catch onto the fact that I spend most of my time on personal things? Do they expect that? Do they know how complicated and time-consuming all this is? Maybe I should just ask for a couple days away from the office this week, instead of trying to do it in bits and drabs.

Can I get my act together in time to take a couple of the puppies from the upcoming litter of my Portuguese tutor's dog? Will the roach population of my room keep increasing exponentially until they are swarming over every square inch? I feel paralyzed with worries, and see that old burglar the Panic Attack lurking around my back door, trying to sneak in again.

***

When I call my Portuguese tutor, I am told he is not at home and will not return until evening. I scour the classified ads for moving sales, and, after several phone calls, can only locate one. I get directions from the hotel desk clerk and head off. Somewhere along the way, at one of those intersections which have no explanation until your car is at the point where an instantaneous decision is required, I make a wrong turn. I am heading out of town to some distant suburb. I do not panic until ten minutes have gone by with no turnoff. What if this suburb is fifty miles away and I cannot turn around before then? I look at the Serengeti plain stretching around me and begin to cry. I am not ready for a safari to Africa. I do not even have a water bottle with me.

The first turnoff appears so suddenly that I miss it; now I am really crying. I finally find an exit where I can turn around. An hour has passed by the time I find the neighborhood with the moving sale.

142

It looks like a hybrid of warehouses and shanties, and, after all the effort, I skip it, nervous.

I stop at the enormous grocery store down the road, in desperate hope they will have peanut butter to expand my dwindling inventory. I start browsing household goods, and immediately begin panicking about the prices. One innocent box of dinner plates multiplies into five-hundred similar purchases in my mind, and I am sure I will spend every penny I have to set up this apartment. I think about my boxes and boxes of things stored in North Carolina.

Fatigue, thirst, and hunger are settling in rapidly. I slowly accumulate a few items with reasonable price tags, then search the import section. There are 5,000 bottles of booze, but only one kind of peanut butter--the kind with grape jelly already swirled into it. Kid's stuff. I pass it by, though I suspect I will be back for it in some future moment of peanut butter despair.

I load my things into the car, then stop to eat, afraid I will pass out if I do not get something soon. I place my order, then sit down to attack a bottle of water. I watch three nuns eating ice cream cones; they look so content that I have an urge to go ask them to pray for me. When my corn soup comes, I tell the boy he has made a mistake, this is chicken soup. "Yes, chicken and corn soup."

"I'm a vegetarian!" I wail. One of the nuns looks at me funny, and I desperately wish there were a beggar nearby to whom I could pass the bowl of soup. I start spooning it down, looking suspiciously for bones and tendons. I begin squirting mustard recklessly on my bread--yum! Has it been that long since I have had mustard? I never craved mustard before.

I head off to find the "electronic sector", apparently the only place I can find a nightlight. I swirl around and go up and down the cloverleafs and highways for an eternity, then finally find the sector. It looks like a small riot is forming: hundreds of young people are hanging out in the streets, drinking and looking too cool for me. I see lots of black leather and spiked orange hair, circa London 1982. The show is great, but all the damned electronic shops have been closed since 1:00 p.m. It is 5:00 in the electronics district: too late to buy gadgets, but early enough to start serious Saturday night drinking. I wonder if the next mysterious sector to which I am sent will turn out to be the after-dark transvestite block.

I make one more stab at finding some household items, and after twenty minutes of looping around, I find the household goods store that has been recommended to me by the hotel desk clerk. After fifteen minutes in the towel section, I realize I will not be able to find any color I like in **both** bath and hand sizes. I settle for buying a new purse and checkbook/wallet to carry around my bourgeoning collection of financial instruments and IDs. As I unlatch my steering wheel lock for the upteenth time today, I break my jade bracelet from Mexico.

I return to the hotel exhausted and ponder whether or not to go to tonight's British embassy party that a coworker told me about. I want to meet people, but I am tired and woozy and could make a terrible impression on everybody, and have a terrible time. If I do not go, I will lie in bed tired, but probably not be able to fall asleep until the middle of the night. I guess I will go, but I will take a taxi: I cannot face the task of navigating one more time today.

The taxi driver has trouble finding the embassy, and the ride is expensive. It is a lovely place--swimming pool, tennis court, fruit trees, and parrots. Everybody is talking in English, mostly in the lovely Queen's version. The bartender calls me "luv", and I want to kiss him. I was expecting a hot, sweaty, indoors dance party, and I am not dressed to sit out on a patio in the chilly evening air. I eat and drink alone. Nobody talks to me, my coworker does not show up, and I quickly tire of seeing strapping young lads strolling around with pretty young things attached to their elbows. I wish Nick Constantine would show up. Maybe he **is** here...in disguise. I wish I were a child and could join the rollerbladers or hide-and-seekers. After an hour, I am cold, tired, and lonely, and I go back to the hotel. I have spent over twenty bucks on this fiasco. That could have been cooking pots or cleaning supplies.

I manage to sleep seven hours, on and off, though I dream about Nazi espionage and homosexual murder mysteries: is that what my subconscious associates British diplomats with? Too many movies. After breakfast and pain killers for my headache, I set out to attempt some more shopping. I go by the artisan market in search of a blanket, and end up instead with an exquisite, handmade skirt with matching jacket. How could I pass it by after that man told me how beautiful it was on me? I then head to the big bus stop flea market, where I buy a tape measure, and nothing else. I stop by another street flea market and buy some strange bowls and a set of cheap cutlery. Now I am getting somewhere! Flea markets!

On the way back, I stop in search of inspiration at the Dom Bosco Sanctuary, a breathtaking assemblage of marble and stained glass. I try to meditate, but cannot. It is beautiful, though, and I say some prayers. I have not been to mass since Easter, and I am feeling the absence. I pick up the church bulletin and read it over supper at the mall, a paltry excuse for a spiritual exercise. I go back to the hotel. I have probably spent almost $100 this weekend, and only a few of those bucks went to beggars. Please let me get settled in soon, so that I can start working hard at the Institute. How many times will I pray that I can do some good in the world before I actually do it?

Chapter 27

As Sunday night crawls along, nervous exhaustion builds up in my system. I try to figure out why. I am too tired to cope, for one thing, but it is more than that. I realize I am dreading the loneliness of my new apartment. I have never lived alone before. I am lonely at the hotel, but it is not the scary sort, for I am not alone here. I can get somebody to change a light bulb, call me a taxi, make me something to eat. I will really be on my own in this apartment. Nobody will care or notice if I come home at night or not. I may have to shell out $1,000 just to have a phone line so that I can get calls at night to break my isolation. Of course, if nobody ever calls me, I will just feel worse. I wonder when those puppies will be born.

I am scared to go to bed: I will cry if I cannot get to sleep. I will listen to music until I get a really big cry: I need it so badly. I need to get these tears out so they stop welling up at every incident and anxiety. I only manage to shed a few, but I have not seen a roach in forty-eight hours, and manage to fall asleep around midnight.

I am awakened early by hammering. I know by the time I figure out from where it is coming and which words I need from my Portuguese dictionary to complain about it to the front desk that I will be wide awake, so I just get up. I am dizzy and nauseous. Will I understand the contract I am signing today?

The landlady brings the contract to the Institute at 11:30. I have woken up enough to read the contract, but I do not feel confident until my boss reads it, too. It is much more confusing than anything I ever rented in the U.S.: their condominium system is quite baffling. I am finally ready to go to the bank to withdraw the money:

a check in Brazilian currency is OK with the landlord, but the lawyer's fee is to be paid in American cash.

The landlady returns early in the afternoon to collect the money, but has forgotten to bring me the keys. Typical. She points out that some workmen need to get in there for the final touch-ups today, anyway. I have already paid for today and I want the keys: how can she immediately rip me off for a day's rent? I need to get in there to take some measurements and visual notes, but it will have to wait until tomorrow; I do not want to make a bid deal out of it.

I have a Portuguese class and do a little more shopping-- kitchen utensils, paper towels. I take notes on prices of other things. I am getting woozier every hour. I have been in the bathroom heeding my unhappy digestive tract half a dozen times today. I finally call it quits around 6:00, head back to the hotel, and call for a hotel masseuse. As I lie on the massage table, I mentally tell her "no, wait, more here, more **here**!" as she passes too quickly over the tightest spots. She treats all the muscles equally, even though some of them are fine while others are hard as rocks. I leave fifty percent better. Tonight, the biggest goal in my life is to get eight hours of sleep. Nothing else matters.

I fall asleep before midnight but am rudely awakened by neighbors before I make it to eight hours. I roll over, trying to reenter unconsciousness, but my intestines are groaning, and I have to get up. I move slowly.

I return to the allergist's office for my allergy tests. I have been off the antihistamines for five days, and have done pretty well with just the nose sprays, aside from the fact I missed out on the sleeping-pill side effect I had grown accustomed to. He squirts offensive substances all over my arm, then scratches each application to see which ones my body despises. Dark red splotches start appearing within a minute, and the itchiness commences another minute later. He abandons me for fifteen minutes, and I helplessly watch the welts start popping up, prohibited from scratching them.

After an eternity, he returns and pronounces me allergic to dust, dust mites, and fungus. He prepares a vaccination and instructs

147

me on how to use it. If I still have problems, I can use a little nasal spray, but I am absolutely not to take the antihistamines: they have too many side effects, and I have been on them too long. I tell him I have never suffered from side effects.

He eyes me over his bifocals and declares, "They make you fat!"

Chagrined, I sheepishly tell him that chocolate is a more likely culprit.

"No, these drugs increase your appetite!" Well, that would be a convenient excuse. If I have to jab a needle in my arm once a week, shedding some pounds would be a nice reward. I pay my bill and head out, left arm sore from the shot, right arm still itchy and covered in neat rows of rosy welts. I stop at the hotel to stick the vaccine in the refrigerator and call my landlord about the keys. Just as I expected, she is not home--has probably taken the money and run off.

I head back to the mall to work on some of the smaller purchases that do not depend on my measuring the apartment, then telephone her later in the day, but she is still not there. I finally find some really cheap kitchenware, and my financial confidence starts rising. After all, I am a Brazilian "millionaire"! My calculator cannot even show all the digits in my *cruzeiro* account. The household goods will add up, but not to a catastrophic level. The tougher decision will be whether to shell out over 1,000 bucks for a phone line, or to rent one.

I call the landlord again mid-afternoon, and I finally turn my key in the lock of my new apartment at 4:00 p.m. I cannot be cross with her: she is so friendly that she has already invited me to spend a holiday at her beach home in Santa Catarina. I waltz around my apartment, mesmerized. I write down colors and measurements, details about nail holes and hooks in the walls, sketches of cabinetry and bathroom fixtures. I unpack the things I have already brought, and make a mental note of what needs to be cleaned after the workmen finish the final touches. I smile at the piece of candy, rubber band, and half-dozen paper clips the previous tenant has left

148

me. I smile at my trees, my grass, my lake, my sky.

I stop to chat with one of the condo employees to try to figure out how the finances and obligations work here. I drive off around 6:00, driving in the opposite direction of the rush-hour traffic: will I have to contend with **that** every night? I clock my approximate commute to work at ten to fifteen minutes, without traffic. I smile at the beautiful full moon shining down on the lake, the lake that now feels like mine.

I stop by the mall for supper and some more shopping, but the store on my itinerary is closed for inventory. I settle for some preliminary examinations of furniture and appliances, which I will start considering after I get more sleep. I will not set the alarm tonight. I do not want to rise tomorrow until I am ready to face the world.

I wake up a couple times, paralyzed by anxieties--I will never get this apartment ready, I will never return to work--but wrestle myself back to sleep, finally squeezing out eight hours for the first time in a very, very long time. My stomach is still queasy, but my head feels clearer. I map out my long and difficult day of consumerism.

I run around like a maniac. It is all a blur. At the end of the day, I try to figure out what I have bought and what I still need, how much I have spent and how much I have left to spend. Tomorrow will be more of the same. Exhausted, I am thankful that, after the initial flurry of refugees, the roach population has apparently died out in my hotel room. Now, I am truly thankful for this room, remembering the colossal cockroach I saw in one of the furniture showrooms today. When one salesclerk swiped at it, he inadvertently flung it into the bosom of the other salesclerk. She screamed, but not nearly as loudly as I would have. That one was a real monster--as huge as the ones I have seen in Mexico and Costa Rica. I was hoping roaches **that** big did not exist here.

I am happy I have such a nice apartment. Living there almost seems within my grasp now. I wish I did not feel so much anger at all the married people of the world, who never have to face these

149

challenges, do these things, alone.

***

My whirlwind tour of Brasília marches on, with no apparent end in sight. Some places I find easily, some places I find after much effort, and some places I never find. Most are complete dead ends. After so much shopping, it is very depressing to have a million things left on my list. My apartment remains unfurnished.

I collapse in my hotel room, exhausted, on my last prepaid cheap night. If I do not check out tomorrow, I have to prepay another two weeks, or start paying at the expensive daily hotel rate. Why has every move I ever made come down to the wire? I toy with the idea of staying an extra night. It is not just the expense holding me back, but the guilt of being away from work so long. I have not yet figured out how to use my water filter, my dining room chairs are unassembled, my kitchen cabinets are dirty, and I will have to sleep on the floor, but I resolve to move tomorrow.

I start packing up my things, yet again. I eye my new purchases suspiciously, aggravated that I have bought them so quickly, based more on price than on whether I will be satisfied with them for two years. I will miss the friendly people at the hotel. I wonder if Brazilians are neighborly. Midway through brushing my teeth I remember that I already brushed them. Boy, am I tired. I look at my finances again. I am lonely for my coworkers.

My possessions have already multiplied dramatically. Packing and moving out of the hotel takes two hours. I have so many things to clean and sort out at the apartment that I hardly know where to start. I quietly see, with frustration, where **not** to start--the bathroom, bedroom, **or** kitchen, all of which are still awaiting repairs. I sort out a few things, then head back to the bank.

On the way there, the traffic is vicious and I nearly get rammed by a driver who did not apparently notice that I was already in an intersection. I drive off horribly shaken, trying to hold back the tears that will ruin my already nervous vision. I cry for several minutes in the parking lot, then go into the bank, blotchy-faced. I

150

keep expecting someone to ask me why personal banking makes me weepy, but nobody notices. I head off to work, or, more accurately, to the office, to check my mail and messages and use a phone. I call the landlord, who assures me that the bathroom job will be done this afternoon, and the carpentry work tomorrow. I get some advice on my water filter and fridge, then head off to the mall to pick up some food for my camping trip to the apartment.

When I reenter, the bathroom job is done. There are scraps and nails all over the floor, and I am not sure if these were left out of laziness, or have already fallen out. I get my TV hooked up exactly two minutes before my soap opera comes on. The reception is terrible. Afterwards, I do some more cleaning and spread out a new comforter on the floor. I think I will be tired enough to sleep OK. Soon, I believe I will start feeling very good. For now, I keep thinking about that car that could have squashed me, and I want to cry, I want to scream, "I need help! Please, somebody help me! I'm scared...."

I sink sweetly and easily into my floor bedding and fall asleep instantaneously and deeply...but awaken way too early to the sound of Saturday morning child's play. The same lack of carpets that makes this an allergy-avoidance zone also makes it a floor-clattering echo chamber.

It feels good to wake up here, though--MY PLACE. I have never ever had my very own place, and I like that feeling, in spite of the loneliness. It is not lonely for long, as workmen and condo people start making appearances.

I finally make it out the door at 1:00, just as the heavens are opening up for a torrential downpour. I have to pull off to the side of the road as visibility plummets. Few Brazilian drivers use headlights in the rain: how do they see each other? By the time I manage to check out some household furnishings, drop off my clothes at a laundromat, and get my car lubed, it is already too late to go into the office. I head back to the apartment to wait for the carpenter coming at 5:00. I wait until 6:30, then return to the mall, ticked off. No stores will be open tomorrow, and I have wasted precious shopping time.

151

I return a few hours later, totally spent, near delirium. I flip on my grossly out-of-focus *telenovela*--must not miss a day of this Portuguese conversation learning tool!--and put away my camping groceries. I still have not found a can opener anywhere, have no stove gas with which to cook frozen or raw foods.... I practically pass out at midnight, and sleep straight through for a blessed eight hours, dreaming of old roommates, my perplexing water filter, and intestinal parasites.

On Sunday, I go to the weekend artisan fair to order a custom-made bed to fit my small bedroom. The size of the bed is called "widow's size"--ha, ha. I will have to sleep on the floor another week to wait for it. I will need to order a custom mattress to fit it.

I go to the office Sunday afternoon to work a few hours, finally. My boss is there, too, so at least I score some brownie points. I am burnt out after four hours and head to the mall to unwind with a movie, knowing I can finish unpacking tomorrow, when I have to sit and wait for a delivery, anyway. The movie is good, but not what I need to see right now--depressing homelessness, mental illness, and violence. I am living like a queen, with my comforter on the floor. I am lucky. When I leave, I give the parking lot "car guard" a bigger tip than usual. Maybe he is homeless. That is why I am in the Third World, right? To help fight poverty? My suffering is so puny here.

On the way home, I throw my back out blowing my nose. Well, this is a first. Damned allergies. My spine must have been screwed up by the arctic air conditioning at the cinema. I lie down on top of a heating pad, but it does not help at all. I take some pain killers and wonder how long it would take my new fridge to make ice. I hate ice. I do not even know where I would put an ice pack, because every part of my back hurts. I stretch and strain and twist and massage to no avail. I will just have to give it time.

I wake up after a night of tossing and turning. Have I even slept five or six hours? This is a Monday morning catastrophe. There is a conspiracy against me. Who has plotted it? Will I ever relax again?

The Federal Police have ended their strike, and I now must register as a foreigner without delay. I drive for half an hour to the other end of town, and they send me off to get some stupid payment form at "any bookstore" because they are too cheap or too lazy to provide their own receipts! Unbelievable. Are these people insane? Have they **ever** heard of the concept of efficiency? Keep the lousy form in your office and charge people for it! Is that so hard to figure out?!

I arrive at the office very late in the morning. I call my landlady about the repairman that never showed on Saturday, but she is not home. I try to order a mattress over the phone, but they insist I have to come back to the store in person. I call the appliance store to verify that they will deliver the missing chair parts and gas can for the stove--no dice, more complications. I have one assembled chair, an unfueled stove, no bed, and again I burst into tears. I cannot cope much longer. I am falling apart. By the time I figure out how to live in Brazil, I will be dead.

I shut my office door until my tears are under control. I salvage the afternoon with co-worker advice on the Federal Police registration process, installation of a better word processing program on my laptop, and a Portuguese class. My teacher never did help me shop, and has not been around at all in over a week, but offers to help now. I drag him off at 5:00 to search for gas cans and get my car headlights repaired.

We find no gas cans, but he does help me find a mechanic who quickly fixes my electrical wiring, free of charge. I thank my tutor profusely, trying to express my gratitude for saving me so much time and money on the car repair, but I am not sure he understands. He tells me in his adorable English, "you are very courage." What?! "You come here alone, get a car, get an apartment." He is **impressed** by this?! I just shake my head at him: no, I am **failing** to accomplish these things, but I do not know how to explain that to him.

We stop at the mattress place, and I am ready to place an order when I am shocked to hear a quote ranging from 12-28 days. "What??!! I was told by the other clerk that I could get a mattress made in five days!" I **know** my Portuguese was not at fault here: "five" is the same in Portuguese as in Spanish.

The other clerk is not around now, of course, and when they finally locate him on the phone, he claims he told me "5-12 days".

"I never would have ordered a special bed if he had originally told me it would take that long to get a special mattress!" I storm out, furious. I cannot even remember the last time I had a good day in Brazil. Somewhere, somehow, I have made another wrong turn.

When I get home, I test the key copies I have just gotten made for my apartment, and two of them do not work. I unpack some more clothes while I listen to my *telenovela*. I crash and, with my spine starting to loosen up again, sleep on and off over nine hours. I go to work actually feeling refreshed.

No dice. It is another day of frustrations, culminating with my bursting into tears at the office of the Federal Police when they tell me that stupid form I had to obtain was supposed to have been brought to a bank for payment **prior** to returning to the Federal Police. "Calma, calma!" The official tries to calm me down, telling me he will process it anyway, and that I can send the payment receipt by later. I know he does not know why I am having a nervous breakdown over such a trivial matter, but he has responded to my tears with kindness and pity. How can I explain to him that I feel I will never get any work done here, that I will spend every day of my Brazilian life in some sort of existentialist treadmill of lists of things to do, lists that never seem to get smaller no matter how many items I cross off?

I head out. I was **really** crying in there. People stare in amazement at my red, blotchy face. They probably think I have been tortured in police detention. I head off with my map and a tip on where I might be able to buy a stove gas container. I end up in a colossal warehouse of a store with zillions of household goods and appliances and bulk food items: hallelujah! I pull my colossal-sized cart slowly up and down the aisles, picking up item after item to cross off my list. My heart skips a beat when I actually find the holy grail itself--a can opener!!!!!! In my shopping delirium, I almost forget to pick up the gas can, but swing around again to get it before checking out. It is frightful-looking. I do not want to go to the gas station to fill it up. I am terrified it will explode and kill me. I will have to ask for help at work, I decide. I will not try to handle this explosive device independently.

I barely drag my trunkful of new belongings into the apartment in time to watch my soap. Either my Portuguese has improved dramatically, or this *telenovela* that used to be such a torturous way to learn conversational Portuguese is actually starting to get interesting. I wearily sort out my finances and shopping lists again, test my remade keys, and prepare to inject myself with allergy serum since it is way too late tonight to go to a pharmacist.

I take a shower, then get out the syringe. Oh, I do not want to do this.... I do not have to: I cannot get the serum bottle open! I do not believe this. Is this all turning into some sort of joke? I cannot do one damned thing in this country right! I fight back the tears and make myself go to my comforter on the floor. This will be my last night sleeping on the floor, since the sofabed I ordered on my lunch hour will arrive tomorrow. It is two-thirds the price of the special mattress which will not arrive for another two weeks, and will be here within twenty-four hours of purchase.

I sleep better than expected--quite soundly, actually, until the alarm rudely awakens me. It is a completely abnormal day: I cross off fourteen of the fifteen items on today's to-do list, **and** finish before 7:30 p.m. It is a miracle: yes, yes, this was a **good** day!! I finish off the day wandering around the cute little shops in my neighborhood--health food store, imports, health club, dance studio, pizzaria, two drugstores, minimarket, video store, fruits and vegetables.... I think I will really like this neighborhood.

I pile my retrieved laundry on the new sofabed, which has lit up my salon and my life. Only four dollars for these neatly folded, sweet-smelling things? Hell if I am ever going to shell out half a grand for a stupid washing machine! I am clean and dry, safe and warm, and life **is** going to be sweet here: I am determined! Life **will** be sweet, I **will** be happy, and I **will** make a positive contribution to

Brazil! I can even laugh at my sore arm: the pharmacist told me I am not supposed to **open** the serum bottle, just stick the needle **into** it through the cap. If only everything had such a simple explanation. If only anything could be explained in advance.

Chapter 28

On Thursday, I arrive at the office to find only a couple people working: it is a holiday, but my boss did not decide we would honor it until after I had left yesterday. I would have come into the office anyway, but I certainly would not have set the alarm. I am really pissed: that alarm woke me up during a really nice dream about Nick Constantine! It is a productive workday, though. I feel quite good about the amount I get done before heading off to shop some more. As I leave my final store of the evening, I pause to marvel at the store's wall-to-wall TV screens presenting a video of Duran Duran and Milton Nascimento singing about the romantic, mystical, beautiful Brazil that I still have not seen.

Friday I get another large chunk of office work done. It is an extraordinary feeling, and almost makes up for the three and a half hours I spend in the afternoon getting my car registered. I go home bone tired, thrilled to death I do not have to set my alarm clock tonight. Tomorrow I will clean my apartment and receive my custom-made bed frame and shop and be glad. On Sunday I will go back to work. I am very tired, but I do not hate my job. For the first time in a long time, I think equilibrium is in sight for my life.

It is a lonely Friday night. I watch my soap opera antagonist mystically produce a breathtaking *aurora borealis* and listen to a neighbor play beautiful guitar music and wish for somebody magical in my life.... Not Michael, but I do wish Michael would write. I wonder why he has not made it to Washington yet. I still have no home phone, so I cannot be tempted to call him or Stephanie.

No doubt he is finding it hard to leave North Carolina in full bloom. By the wilting heat of mid-June, he will be ready, one year after I left North Carolina for a quest as elusive as his. Someday, maybe we will be sitting in rocking chairs, inhaling the sweet fragrance of spring honeysuckle while we watch the sunset over the tall Carolina pines, talk about azaleas and how big the magnolia tree has gotten, and laugh about the wild goose chases of our youth. Save the world, save ourselves...save something, save anything.

***

Is this what they mean by falling asleep as soon as your head hits the pillow? I am out like a light, and sleep straight for over eight hours--still not enough. Today my bed frame is coming at 2:00 p.m., so I spend the morning catching up on my cleaning, sorting, arranging, and reading my Greenpeace guide to fighting indoor insects without toxics. I am pissed off at the ants attacking my breakfast cereal--not as bad as roaches, to be sure, but I do not want ants, either.

The bed guys actually arrive at 2:30, and I am pleasantly shocked...though slightly disappointed that it takes them an entire hour to assemble the bed. They got the measurements right, but the built-in bookshelf is proportioned pretty badly. Oh, well: it is pretty close, considering the guy was going on my broken Portuguese and crude sketch. I just hope it is not too difficult to resell, as unusual as it is.

I head off to one more import store, on a tip. It is gigantic, but they still do not have peanut butter. I am devastated. The trip is not a total bust: I find a couple other things that have been eluding me. I head off to the mall to try to finish off the last few odds and ends of shopping, and do a serious grocery run, too. I drive home, exhausted but feeling slightly better: I am now only missing a few things, and my apartment will be nicely livable soon.

When I turn on the living room light, sparks fly, and I promptly turn it back off. I try other light switches, and quickly realize it is the circuit, not the bulb. I flip the circuit breaker, and hear more sparks. I call the building personnel on the intercom, and

158

one of the condo employees comes to check it out. I hold the flashlight and help as best I can, but I am stupid about these things. I picture bugs and rodents inside the walls, chomping away on my wires. An hour and a half later, he has gotten everything working right again.

I will truly collapse tonight: I cannot face the thought of working tomorrow. I will go in very late and leave very early. I poke through my purchases, trying to get the thrill of consumption. This is great, that is perfect, whoops--I bought scissors in two different stores. I am way too tired. This is getting scary. I need some rest...lots and lots and lots of rest....

I pass out again, but wake up too soon, thinking about my endless list of things to do. I look over my bank accounts: my money is moving faster than the naked eye can follow. I am nearly at the end, except for the decision whether to shell out a thousand dollars for a phone line or start renting one. I can procrastinate that for awhile. Any Brazilian calling me is calling during office hours...for business purposes only.

I try to catch up on my cleaning, and attack the kitchen ant problem. Greenpeace instructs me to "locate point of entry". I look around the kitchen in bewilderment: there are dozens of cracks and nail holes between the wall tiles, and they might also be entering through the back door frame. I rub chalk on the wood surfaces and lemon juice on the tiles, and stick lemon rinds in the large holes and crevices.

I spend fifteen minutes preparing for my stove's baptism: I am determined to make scrambled eggs today. I read the instructions for the gas tank, the lighting device, and the stove. I flip this on, I flip that on, and I pray that the whole thing does not blow up in my face. The air starts filling up with the intoxicating smell of gas fumes, but I can produce no fire. I turn it all off, open the windows for half an hour, reread the instructions, then try it again. No dice. I am trying to remember why I did not just buy a microwave....

159

Pissed, I settle for the same camping meal I have had a dozen times in the past week--buttered bread, cashews, fruits and vegetables. I write some birthday cards and letters back to the U.S., wishing I could have these people here to comfort me. I am pathetic. I go to the office at 4:30 and manage two hours of work before returning home.

I put away the dry dishes and wash another load of utensils, unpack some more, and fight off my looming anxiety attack. I do not want to eat--the thought of the ants, the thought of the stupid repetitive food. I finally force down a slab of bread with margarine and jam--a Linus jelly bread sandwich. I soak some black beans, optimistic that somebody will light my stove someday. I finish my urgent correspondence, and go to my sofabed to pass out for eight hours.

Morning: I open my plastic container in the bathroom to deposit my "specimen" for the lab. I have developed a conviction that my constantly cramped lower intestine is harboring five-inch long worms. I wash my face, head into the kitchen for breakfast, and find ants in a new spot. Hmm...maybe they detoured around the chalk! I trace their path back to...the back door.... Damn it! They are marching **right over** the lemon rinds! Maybe rinds do not work after they dry out...or maybe they do not work at all. Another stupid home remedy that has been repeated for ten-thousand years without ever having been verified.

I pull out the chalk, and try to apply it to the edge of the door frame. I see an ant seemingly "retreat" from it, and maliciously draw a circle around him: it works! He is trapped in the circle--cannot, will not cross the olfactory-stumping chalk. How can I possibly chalk the entire kitchen? I try to eat breakfast, knowing if I see an ant jump into my cereal, I will barf for sure. I thought I had left behind my ant-infested days when I left Mexico. I repeat my mantra: not as bad as roaches, not as bad as roaches, be thankful for electricity and running water, be thankful....

It takes me a scant fifteen minutes to get to the vicinity of the medical lab, but another fifteen minutes to figure out which road actually leads to it. I start crying again. What kind of a crybaby am I turning into?! I am circling for so long that my car starts reeking of my excrement cooking in the light of the sun. I finally drop off the offensive substance and head to work.

It is a number-crunching day, and I am way too tired for it. I read with horror the AP online news report about Oliver North capturing the Republican nomination to run for the Senate. If he wins, I cannot return to Virginia. Even if he does not win, I will be afraid to live in a place with that many voters who have completely lost their political minds. I am relieved to see that the standing Republican Senator from Virginia will not support this monster who lied to Congress about his violating the Constitution. I believe he is telling the truth **now**--that Reagan made him do it--but he should be doing public penance, not trying to build a political career on the graves of so many Nicaraguans.

I head off to the doctor's office for the consultation. He speaks fluent English--a product of American medical schools--and I reply carefully to question after question. He pokes and probes my belly, and then recommends another lab test tomorrow. I head home, and manage to get one of the building employees to come look at my stove. He tries and tries--no dice. He eyes my new-fangled ignition appliance with suspicion, and pulls out his cigarette lighter--bingo! Fire! There is nothing wrong with the stove or the gas. We fidget with the high-tech lighter and finally get **it** to work, too.

I make scrambled eggs, and my heart soars. I scrounge to find my new pepper and new salt. I have some lemons leftover from the ant war, and squeeze some of that on, and it is a culinary masterpiece. I wolf them down: I have never enjoyed cooking anything as much as I enjoyed cooking this.

I take one last stab at sealing off my cabinets, methodically drawing chalk on all the edges, and all around the door frame, too. The lemons were definitely a bust, but I can plainly see the ants retreating from the chalk. I am jubilant: even if I have to reapply it every week, it will only take ten or fifteen minutes, and chalk is cheap. Bone weary, I get ready for bed. Not bad, for a Monday.

161

I picture Michael laughing his head off if he could have seen me with the chalk clenched in my hand. "Let them be," he would have said. "They're just scavengers on the Earth. They aren't threatening your existence." So logical. So rational. Maybe that was why he could never get a handle on what happened in Panama.... It was all so...irrational.

I awake tired again and get out of bed to produce another "sample". I feel faint while driving. Is this just exhaustion? I stop at the bank and get to work quite late--no matter, my boss is not there. I need to get some information from him before I can proceed on my project, so I spend most of the day doing odds and ends.

Late in the afternoon I get a phone call from Stephanie. "Steph! Geez, I've been waiting forever for you to call."

"Well, I kept waiting for Michael to show up, and he kept putting it off. He finally got to D.C. last weekend--hitched a ride with a guy he knew in the Army."

"He still has friends in the Army?!"

"Yeah! Hard to believe! I got your letter about the apartment: are you all settled in now?"

"Ha!"

"Why not?"

"I don't know. Everything is a colossal hassle here."

"What's your phone number?" I explain about the phone lines. "Look, you have to get a phone so we can call you on the weekends! I can't keep sneaking Michael into my office to call you at work!"

"He's there?"

"Of course he's here! Here...."

My heart sighs. "Hey!" His voice is so sweet....

"How was Carolina?"

"Great! The weather was perfect--it was an incredible spring, just gorgeous. How are you doing?"

162

"I'm fine," I lie. "Tell me all about Carolina!"

He tells me who he saw, where he went, what was happening in the mountains and in Chapel Hill. "I miss it already, but Washington's really exciting." Yes, no shortage of adrenaline there.

"How's the job hunt going?"

"Slow! Actually, I'm painting an apartment in Stephanie's building right now, which is great, because I will be able to take time off for interviews."

"Great! Are you getting along OK with Peter?"

"Sure--he's great. I just avoid talking politics with him." I hear a snort in the background: Stephanie is laughing. "So, how's Brazil? You got an apartment now?"

I tell him how great the apartment is, how great the job is, how great everything is. I do not want to lean on him. It is enough just to know he still cares, but I do not want to burden him with anything. And there **are** good things to report, so I talk about those, and omit the frustrations, the dozens of times I have burst into tears. Stephanie gets back on for a few minutes, then they hang up.

I go home, lonely. I enter the kitchen for the post-chalk inspection--quiet...still... no movement...NO ANTS! I am victorious-- for now, anyway. Someday this apartment **will** be a tranquil haven. I walk out to the local shops to get my laundry and allergy shot. I stroll around slowly, making mental notes about my neighborhood. I stop for supper at an Italian restaurant, and it is exquisitely delicious.

I head out, closer to contentment. I stop dead cold. Fernando is coming into the restaurant. He stops dead cold. We stare at each other. He finally moves his mouth to speak, no doubt worried about what his female companion is conjecturing about the way we are staring at each other. "I can't believe you are in Brazil! What is this? What are you doing here?"

I tell him briefly about my job, and he congratulates me. He then introduces me to his companion, in Portuguese. "This is a...this is the sister of a friend I knew in Washington." She looks

163

unconvinced, but shakes my hand and declares it a pleasure. "How is Stephanie?" He has a pained expression on his face: he knows he hurt her terribly.

"Fine! I just saw her in March, actually, shortly before I came down here."

"Good! Good." He looks at his companion. I have no idea if she can understand our conversation in English or not. "Leticia is very hungry. Why don't you give me your phone number, and I will call you for lunch?" I hand him my business card, which he duly admires. "Até logo!"

"Tchau." I walk home, sure he will never call me. Then again, he might. He probably would have questioned me more about Stephanie if he had not been on a date. People are always curious about the wrecks they have left behind, wondering if the victim actually **did** manage to walk away from the crash. Steph did. Sometimes, I think I did; sometimes, I think I will always be trapped in the debris--that those moments when I thought I had gotten away were just the fleeting hallucinations of a dying woman pinned in the wreckage. I do not set the alarm clock. I want so desperately to sleep.

Chapter 29

Something mysterious awakens me early, and I get to work on time, despite my exhaustion. I have caught up, anyway, and really need further input from my absent boss to proceed with my project. I settle for educational sessions with my Portuguese tutor and my computer.

My doctor calls to tell me I do not have intestinal parasites. He quizzes me some more, and when I tell him I can barely walk up stairs because my legs feel so weak, he finally has a brainstorm: I may be deficient in potassium. He tells me some fruits to eat, and asks me to call him back in a few days. Potassium?! Can it be that simple? I suddenly remember how horrendous my last period was: potassium has something to do with that, I think.... Potassium? Is it because I have been deprived of my peanut butter? Does peanut butter have potassium? Maybe I am losing potassium from crying too much.

I finish the afternoon by going to a mechanic for a thorough car inspection. It is in pretty sad shape, just as I had begun to suspect. He will call tomorrow with the cost estimate. I will try not to cry: I need to guard my potassium. It is nice to go home to a seventy-five percent livable apartment, putter around in the kitchen, and sing to the radio. I will not give up.

I go to work feeling, yes, pretty decent. Potassium! My legs were shaking a little last night, but the cramps seem to have disappeared now. I work like a dog on computer graphics all day, and finally attain my goal at 6:00. I pause to read the online news. I did not have the shakes last night: Brasília did! An earthquake in Bolivia reverberated all the way over here! What next.

I go home and cook my first of many batches of delectable black beans in olive oil and garlic salt, pack a lunch, then sit down to face my first checking account bank statement. It is frightful--forty-three checks, half a dozen deposits, and some mysterious debits. I miss sticking one-hundred dollars in my wallet for the week and having an easy bank statement at the end of the month. And these dizzying numbers that go on for so many digits! I find one slight mathematical error, and must carry over the correction twenty times. Where is my interest payment? Where is my forty percent interest payment?! I start panicking, rereading the statement from top to bottom. This money has already devalued tremendously.... Where is my forty percent interest payment to make up for that?! An hour has gone by, and I still can find no interest payment. Oh, my God, what have I done to my money?

I wake the next morning without cramps--this is great! A few choice fruits and my body is completely renewed! If only everything were so easily solved. As soon as I get to the office, I telephone the bank. Within minutes, I am in tears. It is a horrible mistake, my money was never put in an inflation-hedging account, and I am out megabucks from the currency devaluation. I try fruitlessly to argue with my "personal banker"--who obviously speaks English a lot better than she comprehends it--that I **had** asked to open the inflation-hedging account, but she insists I **never** requested it! She remembers my **asking** about those types of accounts, but insists I did not actually **request** one!

This is preposterous! I am outraged! What the hell does she think? That I purposefully inquired about inflation-hedging accounts, then deliberately chose the one where I stood to lose tons of money to hyper-inflation?! To add insult to injury, she tells me that all those mysterious debits were weekly government taxes on all my financial transactions! I would have **more** money right now if I had put my millions of *cruzeiros* in a suitcase!

I pull out the calculator, but I cannot muster the courage to figure out my actual losses. I just do not want to know. I think it would make me hysterical, and it is too late to do anything about it. Could be hundreds...or worse.... I sob and sob and sob for an hour, then collect myself to head over to the bank.

I stop at the other international bank in town to see what they have to offer. I have already decided to pull my money out of my bank: I will never forgive them this blunder, this preposterous and insulting treatment, this obvious exploitation of my unfamiliarity with Brazilian banking policies. I pick up some banking brochures to read over the weekend, then head over to my own bank.

I can barely muster a civil "hello" to the idiot who set up my account. I speak instead with somebody else, vent my grievances, get no redress, and refuse to leave until they hand me **all** the rules of my account **in writing**. I sign the damned document necessary to "invest" my funds so they will not be annihilated by inflation anymore. I drive back to work, thinking about the millions of Brazilians living much closer to the edge than I am...the ones who **really** suffer when the currency snowballs out of control....

I attend a couple afternoon meetings, then collect some number-crunching to do at home this weekend. My boss is back in town and ready to meet with me again, so I share with him the non-stop resettlement difficulties I have been experiencing. He gives me some advice on the banking and a few other things, and then encourages me to ask people in the office for more assistance. I tell him that it seems I impose on people here too much. He tells me that, to the contrary, it has been remarked that I do not ask for assistance very often.

Oh, really? I fume at the absurdity of that statement, which should be put more accurately as: "Most of the time when she asks for help, we simply forget that she has asked, or avoid her until the end of the day when we can sneak off before she looks for us again!" The things that I **have** gotten help on were things that I pestered coworkers about over and over and over again, like getting the car. Nobody helped me get a Portuguese tutor, nobody showed me how to drive around the advanced space-age intersection system, nobody helped me look at apartments, nobody helped me move, nobody told

167

me about utilities, nobody is helping me furnish or fix up the apartment, and this morning three people saw me crying my eyes out and heard about my banking calamity without bothering to ask me if I needed help straightening it out.

And the most frustrating thing is that I know they are all too overworked to give me much assistance, and that is why I have stopped asking, and I desperately want to beg my boss to liberate somebody from their official duties and just let them help me get resettled, please.... Should I point out to him that it is inefficient for me to be spending weeks and weeks trying to figure these things out by myself, rather than let a Brasília insider or two spend a few days showing me the ropes? How does he expect the office staff to feel when they see me contributing so little work, coming in late and leaving early, and constantly stealing bits of their time with endless questions and worries?

I cannot figure out a way to express that without sounding like a whining crybaby, so I do not. He asks if things are under control now. "No!" This I will attempt to answer: "It never ends!" I explain my worries about my car, my money, my messy apartment full of broken things and unpacked bags and a decided lack of furnishings....

He peers at me over his spectacles and declares "don't feel pressure" in the firm, steady voice one would use to tell a bouncy dog to sit. I optimistically interpret the remark as meaning I should not feel overwhelmed by office work, since he does not seem to be offering a comprehensive psychotherapeutic assessment of my entire life situation.

I prepare to depart the office, pausing to browse the phone book for additional Chevy mechanics and to telephone another import shop to see if they have peanut butter. They only have the grape-glopped stuff, but he adds another comment which I cannot quite understand at first, but after a couple more questions, finally understand to be a clarification that normally they **do** stock plain imported peanut butter, but are momentarily sold out. I carefully tuck away the address and phone number: I will call every week

168

until they have it, then race over to buy twenty pounds of it.

I go home, brooding about my financial setback. My next paycheck--twenty days hence!--is already spent. I really may have to deplete my savings fixing up this apartment and fixing up the car...and getting a telephone line...and.... I will put off the phone until the next paycheck, I guess, and a few other purchases. Linens are terribly expensive here...utility bills are coming up...health insurance reimbursement will be slow for sure...imported peanut butter fetish...the unknown terrain of car repairs. I have not worried this much about money since I was in graduate school. I know the first few months of a move are the most expensive.... The problem is, I have a terrible feeling that I am nowhere near the top of the hump I need to get over here.

It is Friday night, and I am sure the weekend will be bleak and tedious. Everybody in Brazil is celebrating the "Day of Sweethearts", and I am sick to death of hearing about it. Feminist independence is a glorious intellectual endeavor in the First World, but it just sucks here. *C'mon, sweetheart, I'll take you to my bank tomorrow morning and set you up a good account. And I know a real good Chevy mechanic--he'll check it all out, figure out what's wrong with it, and not charge too much money. C'mon, baby, I'll show you where to get good used furniture, and cheap linens. Call me if you have any more electrical problems, OK? Call me the next time you feel bad: I'll take you to the doctor, OK? Guess what I got behind my back? Flowers...and peanut butter!*

Well, it would not necessarily have to be a **man**.... It could just be a personal slave...or a robot...or a well-trained chimpanzee, maybe. I mean, kisses and caresses would just be icing on the cake, really. I do not need a man, per se, I just **need**.... Well, at least I can sleep in tomorrow.

Something makes me wake up too early again. I toss and turn for another seventy-five minutes, then get up. I walk over to the neighborhood laundromat to exchange dirty clothes for clean ones, then drive off to the mechanic strip. What kind of idiot am I? They are all getting ready to close by noon, of course. The car will have to wait until Monday.

I head to the mall. I feel as if I am at the mall every day, but my shopping list continues to grow. I must buy winter pajamas (much to my surprise), an iron, a toilet brush, light bulbs. It is a fairly good afternoon of shopping, and it becomes a blessed afternoon of shopping when I actually find that peanut butter has arrived at the grocery store! It is a Brazilian brand, and I hesitate over how much to buy. What if it is horrible? How horrible could it be? It is a pretty simple recipe.... I decide to buy $4.00 worth, as much as I am willing to blow if it is inedible.

When I get home, I have another happy surprise: my custom-made mattress has arrived a week ahead of schedule! One of the condo employees lugs it up to my apartment: boy, the guys who work here are real sweethearts! It fits the frame perfectly! It has a gorgeous design and looks beautiful just sitting there. I stretch out on it--ahhhhhhhhhhh. I have been taking my time comparison shopping for sheets and blankets, shocked at the prices, and still have not bought any. I leave the plastic on the mattress and cart the comforter-*cum*-sleeping bag in from the living roof sofa bed. I will sleep like a queen tonight!

I putter around the living room. Now that the sofa bed is set up as a sofa, it finally looks like a living room. I try to consolidate and neaten the remaining suitcases and boxes, but cannot finish unpacking them because the landlady still has not found a carpenter to repair the wardrobe. What the hell is her problem?

I iron and cook and scrub the toilet and feel very domestic. It **is** getting there, right? Maybe it will take two more months, but this apartment **will** be a cozy home. I may be broke, but I will be cozy! I snap some photos of the lake at sunset, then shut the window. It is starting to get very cold at night. I really need to get those winter PJs within a week or two.

Saturday night I stretch out on my brand new mattress as I could never stretch out on the narrow sofa bed. Truly marvelous. Luscious. I have shut the door, and my tiny bedroom is a warm cocoon. I drift off and sleep well. Sunday morning I clean some

170

more--kitchen shelves, new utensils, dirty dishes, hand wash, the floor. Prepping this apartment has turned my skin to sand paper.

After the washing, I sit down to analyze banking literature. I have been in Brazil two months, and I am still trying to figure out how to manage my money! There are too many legalistic clauses in these brochures, and I will have to get translation help before I can narrow down my decision.

I make lunch, then head out to the artisan's market. This is my absolute last attempt to find a beautiful Indian blanket for the bed: if I strike out again, I will have to buy an ugly and more expensive manufactured one at the mall. I browse a few and finally settle on a blue, green, and white design. It is terribly plain compared to the spectacular blankets I have seen from Mexico and Guatemala, but at least the colors are bright. It is much, much cheaper than the prettiest blanket I saw at the mall.

I glance at living room odds and ends. Maybe if my car repairs are not a catastrophe, next weekend I can come back for such things. For now, I will keep living in a half-empty apartment. (How can an apartment this small still be half empty after a thousand shopping trips? I must have a hundred plastic bags collected already.)

I head back, do some more cleaning, and write a long-postponed letter to the office manager at the educational center in Cuahtemoc. She has already written me again with news of more staff turnovers, including her own: she is heading down to Chiapas in August. I am thrilled at the opportunity she has to work at the grassroots there. I can already picture her there, blossoming. By the time I finish the letter and make dinner, it is too late to do the number-crunching I had brought home from the office. "Don't feel pressure. Don't feel pressure." This is my mantra. My calendar for the upcoming week already has dozens of memos scribbled all over it. I will never be able to goof off again, and thank God for potassium.

Chapter 30

I sleep until I wake up naturally, of my own subconscious volition, and it is marvelous! I will take my car mechanic-shopping this morning, and I will take my time. Don't feel pressure. Go to work late. As I begin breakfasting at 9:00 a.m., the intercom rings: my landlady is downstairs with a carpenter to fix my broken shelving and cupboard. I tell her they will have to wait until I eat and get dressed. She pleads with me--five minutes? "No!" I **will not** start a Monday morning running around like a chicken with my head cut off. I try to tell her in a non-pissed-off voice that it cannot be helped, that I did not know they were coming, and therefore that I am not ready, even though what I really want to scream is, "I waited three weeks for the carpenter: you and the carpenter can wait thirty friggin' minutes for me!" The carpenter insists he cannot wait more than five minutes, so she has to bring him back later! I thought people in this country were accustomed to waiting.

I head off to the auto repair strip, and stop at the first promising one I see. A friendly, somewhat-English-speaking mechanic greets me, checks it out, tells me what he can fix and what needs to be taken elsewhere, and gives me a reasonable estimate. I try to accept calmly the news that I have been driving around on a wheel that could have flown off at a high speed. This heroic savior mechanic drives me to the office, and I put my faith in him.

I do a scant amount of work, and spend the rest of the day preparing health insurance claims--$170 worth already!--frantic to start building up my financial reserves again. I then review the banking brochures again. I finally start getting the picture: the big international banks in Brazil have steep minimums, costly fees, and difficult rules in order to attract only wealthy clients. My bank was a **very** big mistake. The Brazilian banks do not have minimums, and their rules and fees are reasonable, except that I will have to master their details in Portuguese.

At 5:30, I call the mechanic: it is taking longer than expected, and the car will not be ready until tomorrow. He makes up for it by picking me up at the office and driving me home! Wow!

I find my kitchen shelving and bedroom wardrobe repaired--jubilation! After dinner, I set to work wiping up wood shavings and scrubbing grimy shelves and drawers. I can now rearrange all my kitchen things in a rational manner. I can now empty my final suitcase and relocate the clothes draped all over the dining room chairs. Oh, this **is** exciting! This should all have been possible weeks ago, and it is a huge relief. It is scarcely comprehensible that I could have been living out of suitcases for three months, but I was.... My apartment will look completely normal very soon...very soon, I think, as I go to bed weary, weary, weary. Maybe this weekend I can actually just go to a park or something. What a luxury that would be.

I wake up too early, again, and lie in bed without being able to fall back to sleep. I finally get up at 8:30, do a little paperwork I brought home, clean and put away my suitcases, then catch a taxi to the auto mechanic. Far from being "definitely ready at 11:00 a.m.", it will not be ready for several more hours because they have encountered complications which will, in fact, double the cost and time. The mechanic drives me to the office again. I am despondent, I must stop thinking about individual things costing me too much money, and file it all mentally under "relocation costs to Brasília"--one big, enormous, horrible, and still mounting expense. I stop at the Brazilian bank next door to open a checking account.

I scarcely arrive at work before lunchtime, but manage a few hours of work before the mechanic comes to get me again. He is a nice guy, and I fork over the money. I have drained my stinky bank's accounts to a scant forty U.S. dollars and maybe forty more worth of Brazilian currency: maybe these accounts will just dry up naturally, and I will not even have to transfer the money elsewhere. I can't believe I already need to pull more dollars out of the States.

Before heading home, I stop at a huge furniture store across the street from the mechanic. The stuff looks wonderful, but the prices throw me for a loop--some very high, some shockingly low. I find an outrageously comfortable recliner on sale for a decent price, and living room shelving on sale for a shockingly low price. What's the catch? Apparently the chair is the last in its line, and the shelving was a display model, or something like that. I push and probe and test, and then visualize my living room space. They are not ideal colors, but they will work very well for such good prices. I will have to return later unless they will accept a U.S. credit card–they do! It is a Godsend! I will not have to pay the bill for a month or so, and they are not even jacking up the price for the privilege of using the plastic. Surely this makes up for the car expenses? Well, maybe ...but I am not finished yet.

I drive home in the surprising rain, feeling fifty percent safer in my car. I have never before felt it so difficult to prioritize. I have never before put my job so low on my list of priorities. I need to get out of this groove...but not this week. This week is already shot. I think about Fernando, even though I know he will never call me.

I wake up too early, again. I am going to have to leave a note asking my upstairs neighbor to stop the early morning bowling, or whatever it is that causes thirty-pound objects to bounce on the ceiling right above my bed. This time I manage to fall back to sleep but have stressful dreams about my apartment: waters flood in, and my Indian blanket is ruined. I do not know what it means, but I awaken feeling groggy, drugged. I walk up to do my laundry exchange and allergy shot which I could not do last night because I got home too late. By the time I find the right mechanic to do the next important job on my car, he says it is too late in the day, and I need to return tomorrow morning, "early". He directs me, however, to another shop for the electronic repairs.

I sit in a café, drinking mango juice and reading about governmental household surveys for over an hour, return to the shop to find they are lacking an important part, and have only done two-thirds of the job--the less important thirds. He says, however, he can bring the part over to the other mechanic's shop tomorrow morning.

I arrive at work at lunchtime again but manage to crunch an array of irritating numbers before I leave. I really want to finish this boring project and move onto other things. I send a couple urgent e-mail messages to the U.S., trying to find somebody to verify my U.S. checking account balance. Have my wages been directly deposited yet?

I head to the mall because I am out of vegetables and need sheets. I try unsuccessfully to find the right color for my weird Indian blanket at the cheap stores, and end up having to go to the expensive one. Geez! How can sheets cost this much?! I shell out more big bucks for a spice grinder, but pass up the facial moisturizer my skin is crying out for as the climate gets gradually drier and drier. I just do not think I can spend one or two hours of wages on a tiny jar of facial moisturizer: I will have to find something else. Maybe I should just start boiling chocolate and smearing cocoa butter all over my face. Organic! Natural! I grab some groceries and an ironing board, then head out, loaded to the gills again, pissed off that I could not find slippers anywhere. My feet are cold when I come out of the shower.

I hate shopping. I have always hated shopping. I just do not know how much more of this I can stand. I get home late, missing half my soap opera, which completely pisses me off. My left shoulder feels dislocated from the strain of so much toting--day in and day out, starting with that 1,000 pound laptop computer I brought into the country. As I am getting ready to go to bed, the electricity in the building goes out. I do not think I can cope with this right now. I am going to flip out. I do not want to go to bed all sweaty. I do not want to take a cold shower in the dark. I am sick and tired of being tired and frustrated and grumpy.

I go out in the hallway to watch the undramatic rescue of a neighbor trapped in the elevator. She is so calm! If that had been me, I would have flipped out. I would have been screaming hysterically, sure that I would be trapped in there for days. No emergency lighting, no nothing--just a box hanging in the air. She emerges cool as a cucumber. I am stunned by her composure. After inquiries, I learn that the entire neighborhood is blacked out--no telling when it will return. I am exhausted. I will just have to brush my teeth and go to bed. Thank God I bought a flashlight already. I have spent so much money already, I should probably just splurge for candles, too. They are probably two hours' wages, too.

I clean my face, moisturize my tired skin, and get undressed, then the lights return just as I am heading for bed. Maybe I can procrastinate buying candles. I return to the bathroom for a warm shower, glad I do not have to go to bed soaked in sweat.

I sleep well and take my car back to the mechanic in the morning. This should be the last day of repairs, and his estimate is much lower than I feared. Car parts: they all look like lumps of steel, rubber, or plastic, and I have no clue why some are ten times or twenty times as expensive as others. It is a good work day, and I accomplish a lot.

I have not cried in days, but I burst into tears at lunchtime over an unlikely subject--a hot dog vendor. A vendor has shown up in front of our office building to cater to the lunchtime crowd--his cart full of hot dogs, catsup, mustard, and pop bottles. What makes the tears come to my eyes is his lone folding table with two chairs, neatly set up for potential customers. The other restaurants have scores and scores of tables, but he only has the one--a minuscule capital investment set out like a small beacon of hope which tugs at my heartstrings. I suppose he sells most of his hot dogs to people on the run, but I cannot help wondering how many customers he could possibly serve with just one table. Is my struggle anything compared to his? I wish I wanted a hot dog, were not afraid of hot dogs. Maybe he sells french fries.

My car is ready early, and as I sit in the mechanic's office writing my check, I look up at another smiling picture of Ayrton Senna. I have seen his face in every mechanic's shop I entered this week. He is, apparently, the patron saint of Brazilian automobile repair. Perhaps it is his angelic spirit that has protected me from the five-hundred accidents that might have been, from the dangerous traffic mistakes I might have made, from the mechanical failures I could very well have had, from the Brazilian drivers and pedestrians alike who give only a minuscule amount of attention to tons of steel bearing down at eighty kilometers an hour. Perhaps it is Senna who held my corroded rubbers on when I had to brake fast and my left wheel groaned and threatened to jump ship. Perhaps it is Senna who enhanced my vision to see the blurs of pedestrians running recklessly across the roads in the darkness. Perhaps Senna has even guided me to good, effective, honest mechanics. I leave, scarcely believing I have actually resolved my car problems: I have scratched one, **huge** item off my list!

By nightfall, dizziness and cramps have returned, but I suspect this is now the hormonal variety. Whose side are you on?! I am obviously in no condition to be contemplating motherhood right now!! Just leave me alone!! I lie down and pass out. I wake up feeling a little better: it is Friday, after all. I get up so early that I have time to mop the kitchen floor before I leave.

Midway through the morning, I do the thing I have been dreading for weeks: I lose my faithful office assistant, the calculator. I have long suspected the over-used batteries to give out any day now, but, instead, I simply drop my trusted assistant on the floor of the Institute library, and it is a goner. I borrow my boss's calculator and continue crunching numbers. I will not be able to balance my zillion-digit checkbook balances and budget until I buy another one, or go through the hassle of trying to get it repaired. Ha! I only reflect on that for two seconds before knowing I would be insane to try to get it repaired--I do not know where to go, who to ask--just buy another one. What the hell: my finances are already a catastrophe, I might as well just buy my way out of every hassle I can. My time, my life, are going down the drain faster than the money is.

In the afternoon, I head over to my new bank to see if my checks are ready. I see the hot dog vendor sitting in one of his folding chairs with his headphones on. It is way past lunchtime, but he is holding out for afternoon stragglers, I guess. I want to tell him, "Don't while away your time: read a book, study something so you do not have to sell hot dogs all your life!" But who am I to say that? I, who have studied so much and come a zillion miles just to spend all my time wearing out my calculator on consumer spending and pointless demographic calculations. At least this vendor is giving cheap food to the hungry masses. What am I giving?

In the evening, I walk up to my neighborhood shops with a list of things to buy, and tick them all off my list: oh, I **love** that! What a great neighborhood! I eat some pizza before heading back with the prized possession--my freshly laundered, brand new woven Indian blanket. I pull out my new sheets--100 times as expensive as a bag of oranges--and serenely "make" my bed for the first time. I frown at the result. No, this blanket will not win any folk art awards. It does not look particularly folksy--was this really the best one I saw? Maybe I should have just gone the conventional route. Still, this did save me a bunch of money. I am still reeling from the calculation I made today that I have already spent $1,000 on my car **since** I bought it. Insurance, registration, repairs--$1,000--whoosh. I get ready for bed. It has been over a year since I slept in sheets that I owned. I lay myself out spread-eagle. It feels perfect, and I pass out.

Chapter 31

I awaken at dawn, my stomach screaming. I know I did not eat my potassium fruits yesterday, but this is too much. I take some antacid and go back to sleep until upstairs neighbors awaken me with loud music--8:15 a.m.? What is the matter with these people? Are they deaf? Does it never occur to them that some people like to sleep late on Saturdays?

I put on my robe and walk up two (!) flights to find the offenders. One is the same guy as last time; the other, a first-time offender. They both acquiesce amiably to lowering their volumes. No grumbling, no whining, no dirty looks--much better penitents than gringos would be.

I cannot fall back to sleep, though, and finally get up. I am determined to get the boxes and bags of stuff out of the living room this morning. I sort and clean and put away, pausing twice to heed my cramp calls and visit the toilet. After the second gut-wrenching experience, I take the straight potassium supplement pill for the first time--**bleh**! Worse than drinking salt water. I have been nauseous all morning, and can barely hold my breakfast down after the foul brew. I am unsure about my body now--hormones or minerals?

I bring my wooden stool into the bedroom to reach up and examine the non-working pulley on my window shade, dismayed that I have mooned the outside world every evening this week because I was too tired to deal with it. Using my fingers, a knife, and a carrot peeler, I finally free the trapped rope, and the blinds start hurtling downward. I open and tighten them several times to be sure, then get down. Tomorrow I will clean and rearrange the living

179

room area in preparation for my final big furniture deliveries. By next weekend, I hope to have all my pictures and posters up, four weeks after I moved in.

I head off to the mall across town to treat myself to a movie I have been meaning to see--Isabel Allende's "House of Spirits". It is a simultaneously brutal and beautiful examination of people torn apart and put back together again, over and over. Hatreds, rapes, tortures, grisly accidents and gruesome assaults: yet the peaceful spiritual world reclaims these suffering people over and over again. I cry for their suffering, and I cry because I want to see those calming angels, too. I guess I have not yet suffered enough to get my own angelic visitation.

I stop at the grocery store. Now that I am stocked up on the basics, I want to browse every square inch of the store to see what is and what is not possible to eat in Brazil. I simply must know. I find pickles and maple syrup. The soups and frozen foods are all a vegetarian bust: I will be cooking a pot of beans every week of my life here. I hate cooking. I pick up some corn meal and return to the produce section to buy green tomatoes. If Idgie can make "Fried Green Tomatoes", surely I can, too.

I head home, duly noting the piece of paper I have stuck to the dash lights--"get gas!". I am on the road five minutes, and my car completely dies. I become hysterical, truly and completely hysterical. I have spent $600 on this car in the past week: how could it die on me?! HOW COULD IT?! HOW COULD IT?! I am flying through the tissue box, crying uncontrollably, watching the rear-view mirror in vain for signs of a police car or Good Samaritan stopping to help me. I am in the city, but I am in one of those no-man's-land highways, and I have no idea where the closest gas station might be. It is very dark out, and somebody could easily attack me. The cars whizzing by are going too fast to notice me struggling...screaming....

I implore God to help, but God has already heard the unspoken blasphemous curses I am hurling as well. Six-hundred dollars on this car in one week--I will **kill** that mechanic!! Why did You bring me to Brazil?! All I do is suffer, suffer, suffer! I am not even suffering to help the poor: I am not helping anybody! I am just suffering and falling apart!

I cannot stop crying, terrified I will be robbed, raped, and killed if I get out of the car. I am also terrified these things will happen if I stay **in** the car. The "desert winter night" has already descended, and it is getting colder by the minute. I am crying out every last drop of water and ounce of potassium I have in my body: I have not had a drink since the movie pop three hours ago, and no water for six hours, and will surely die. Nobody will help me.

After thirty minutes of hysterical crying with no rescue, I get my bearings and depart my car. I clutch the car key grimly between my knuckles, prepared to stab any assailant in the eye. I am supposed to be a nonviolent person. I soon see I will have to cross two four-lane highways to get to some civilization. I watch the cars hurling past and ask God if this is really it: will I die right now, squashed like a grape? I run across one, then the other. I continue another five minutes and realize I am at some sort of bus station, full of people. Thank God. No, no, I am still mad at God.

I find a phone and start going through the phone numbers I have in my purse--not home, not home, not home. Yes, my coworkers all have nice social lives and do not spend their Saturday nights waiting by the phone for me to call with my asinine problems. I only have one phone number left, and so I have to call the President of the Institute, mortified with embarrassment. I know he is a great guy, but this is too much. After several questions, he can finally understand from my perplexed comments where I am, and tells me he will be right over.

I head back to my car to await him. I sit in silence, my tears finally abated. I think if I had not resolved to get out of the car, I could have cried for three straight hours and died of dehydration. I watch the rear-view mirror fretfully. I have seen many cars go by, yet nobody stops. Wait.... This one seems to be in my shoulder lane.... It must be him. He does not seem to be slowing down much.... Oh, my God! He's going to hit me!! I stare in horrified shock at the rear-view mirror as the car suddenly swerves around me at the very last minute, and I am incredulous. I check again to make sure my emergency blinkers were on--yes! I close my eyes: if I am going to get creamed, I do not want to see it coming. I open them again to fasten my seat belt, then close them once again and try to prepare for sudden death.

At long last he comes. I am the queen of all idiots: he quickly ascertains that my fuel tank is empty! I cannot believe it! There is a quarter-inch between the "empty" sign and the gauge marker! God-damned car! I miss my logical Japanese car. And no low-fuel warning light?! I am mortified, deathly embarrassed, trying to tell him I have never run out of gas in my entire life. He is kind and sympathetic, and heads off to a gas station to get some engine alcohol. What is wrong with me? Am I really incapable of being on my own in this country?

As I drive home, I hear Nick Constantine's voice on the radio, asking how he can help me, how he can heal my inner pain. Will there ever be a man like that in my life, if I live to be one-hundred years old? I doubt it. I am slowly dying inside. Shivering, I turn on the car heat. When I get home, I eat a peanut butter and banana sandwich and gulp down glass after glass of water. No puppy. No bathtub. No answering machine. No liquor. Nothing, nobody to comfort me.

At night, I dream I am back in Mexico, visiting my enchanted park. Toto, the giant sea lion who kissed me so many moons ago, sidles up to me and pins me affectionately to the wall, just as a former roommate's German shepherd used to do. He is wet, but warm and strong. He could crush me against this wall, but I know he will not: I trust him. António comes over, and I expect a scolding for playing with Toto unattended. Instead, he gives me some advice about where to buy a good used car. Suddenly, I am back at my old job. No! No! It is horrible. The place is chaotic--teeming with students and guests. I do not want to wash all these dishes! Why is the kitchen so messy?

I wake up--phew--just a dream. That is all far away. I knew I would have nightmares of that place for years to come. Yet, I miss

182

Toto and Blondie and the dolphins. I wonder how they are doing. Gypsy must be nearly grown up now. I remember how she used to do unbeckoned tricks, following and imitating the other dolphins making their rounds. I never knew if she did it out of instinct, out of fun, out of peer pressure, out of a love of learning, or out of desire for the fishy rewards she saw her older buddies were receiving. I used to be a fast learner. Have I slowed down that much, or am I just overwhelmed with too many new tricks at one time?

I get up, still tired, go to the bathroom and see the truth of the matter. Bleh. Hormones. Why else would running out of gas have seemed like the end of the world?! I struggle with my first assignment of the day--rearranging the living room / dining room space for my upcoming furniture arrivals. I sketch one layout after another, but they all come up deficient. This is a pretty small room, and the TV antenna must go **there**, and the phone can only go **here**.... I puzzle over the sketches for more than an hour. I cannot make any decisions if my hormones do not wish to. I finally pick a plan, rearrange, and mop the floor. It is going to look a little strange, but I think it will work. I usually set up rooms perfectly the first time and never change my mind, but these awkward outlets and off-center window are interfering with my spatial sensibilities. This will never be perfect, and it is really bothering me.

I finally go to the office late Sunday afternoon. I do a good three-hour chunk, then catch up on electronic and postal correspondence. I get home at 10:00 p.m. and take my nauseous stomach and cramped womb to my sweet bed.

Monday is the day to which all the Brazilians have been counting down--Brazil's first soccer match in the World Cup. In the past week I have seen the proliferation of t-shirts, flags, banners, and green/gold/blue paint on streets, curbs, sign posts, and walls. The office is all abuzz: we will be let out at 3:00! I have other things on my mind: today is the day I have all the paperwork ready to change bank accounts.

My new branch bank cannot take a dollar check for deposit, so an office assistant takes me to the central bank to do it. We wait in line for an hour, then are told it would be a 30-45 day wait for my U.S. check to clear, before I could draw on it. I am at the end of my rope now. We head to the "other" (?!) central bank just to make sure, and are told the same thing. We get back to the office a half-hour before "quitting" time. I do not know what else to do except go back to relying on the Institute to change checks for me. I do not think it is right to burden them with my personal banking, but I do not want to keep interest-less, inflation-killing minimum balances just to be able to change checks, either. The accountant has an idea of another bank that might work, and she will call them in the morning on my behalf.

To my surprise, I discover we have all been invited to a co-worker's house to watch the soccer game. I am told this as everybody is heading out. I am not dressed for a party and do not trust my cramps to stay in abatement, but I must go because I need so desperately to make friends. I try hard to get into the excitement, but, it is hard for me to stay awake watching a game with hardly any points scored. After the victory, before I quite understand it, I have been drafted into helping drive our jubilant crowd down to some neighborhood for a street celebration. I really am not up for this, but I cannot afford to pass up social events.

It turns out to be the electronics sector: the sector where I saw those punks is apparently the official party zone of the city. The throngs of people are intense, just as they were when the Tar Heels won the basketball championship, but it is a sea of green and gold here, not blue and white. Most of them are so young, too young to remember Pelé's victorious teams over two decades ago. I remember, even though I was just a tot. Soccer formed my first thoughts about Brazil, long ago.

The music is great, and the crowd is fun, but I feel hopelessly alienated from it all. For one thing, it is just the first match, and it is a long road to a World Cup championship: I simply cannot understand their getting so excited so quickly. For another, I do not really feel I am with friends. I feel unconnected to these people, and I do not know how to connect. I am dehydrated, cramped, dizzy. I finally tell my passengers that I need to leave at 10:30 p.m., and they cheerfully oblige. Somehow, I make it home, and am quite ready to pass out by the time I crawl into bed. I am still optimistic about this job--it could be the best I have ever had--but I fear my loneliness will only continue to grow.

Chapter 32

I head to work late, after sleeping in a bit, but I still have to rub my eyes all day long. I need some serious rest. By the end of the day, my banking is still not resolved, and I get the annoying news that I will have to move out of my office by month's end to make room for a returning professor. My boss is surprised that I am surprised: he thought I always knew my office was temporary. No, I would not have hung maps and posters all over the walls and arranged books and papers all over the shelves if I had known it would be temporary, now, would I?! I just shake my head, "no, I did not know." No, I did not know that I would have to pack up more boxes and move on again. I never would have unpacked them, not for that short a period. I want to stare at the same four walls every day.

Before I leave, I read the online news. Nick Constantine has lost his contract dispute with Swiny Music Corporation. He no longer wants to work for an organization that considers his songwriting abilities less important than his celebrated sex appeal. He wants to leave his sex symbol days behind him, in his youth. He wants to be recognized as an artist. Swiny wants six more albums out of him, with dozens of hip-swiveling videos to sell them. He does not want to market his ass anymore: he wants to market his music. His music has matured, and his lyrics have grown up. He could become the best songwriter of my generation if he could break away from his own youthful legacy.

He told interviewers that he will appeal. It is estimated that he has already racked up over 4.5 billion dollars in legal fees, trying to escape "professional slavery". Asked if he bought the Brazilian

186

ranch as a tax haven, he laughed and said, "no, it's just a ranch." *(Why did you give away the cows if you wanted a ranch?)* "It really has nothing to do with this," he pleaded. *(What about the vagrants invading the ranch?)* "I have asked the police to leave them alone. I really don't have anything else to say about it." *(Is it true you have secretly bought other ranches in the Amazon?)* "I called this press conference to answer questions about my lawsuit with Swiny-- nothing else."

After I get home, I walk up to get my laundry and allergy shot, but one of my neighborhood drugstores is closed, and the other is out of syringes. I have to choose between going back for my car to drive somewhere else, or taking a long walk to the next neighborhood. I decide on walking, but quickly regret it when I realize how hard it is to cross four cloverleaf ramps at rush hour. I must alternate between racing for my life across the ramps and walking along the edges of the dark underpasses. My legs are so weak I can barely run across the ramps. I ate my damned banana and orange today! How much more potassium do you need?! Stupid hormones. Stupid everything. I buy five needles. I should really just learn to do it myself. I quickly reconsider: a person incapable of using eye drops is hardly going to be capable of jabbing needles into her arm.

I walk home, eat dinner, pack lunch, and finish washing the dishes at 9:00 p.m. Time flies when you're...whatever...stupid, incompetent. I want to invite Nick Constantine to come hide out from Swiny Records with me, write songs here, looking out on the lake or the pine tree near the window. He may have wagered his entire fortune on the elusive bluebird of professional fulfillment; I may have gambled away my entire youth.

I sleep very badly--six hours, maybe--and start the day off by slicing a worm in half when I cut into my orange. I want to go back to bed. When I get to work, there is a message waiting for me that my Portuguese tutor will not make it in today because his Doberman just had puppies. Oh, man, I want a puppy...but not a Doberman.

An American graduate student has shown up to do a couple weeks of research, and we pass the entire morning chatting. We have lived in and visited many of the same places, and we have many of the same professional interests and goals. This is an unexpected delight!

After work, I take her to the mall for dinner and shopping. I finally get another calculator, but the religious bookstore is closed again and I cannot pick up a missal. I need to go to mass badly, but I do not want to attempt it without a missal. I stop at the water filter store to ask why my water filter has slowed down so much. He tells me I have to clean it three times a week! I thought the instructions said once every three weeks. We stop at the grocery store, then head out. It is wonderful to have a companion, but I am too tired to enjoy this thoroughly. I still have more handwash and ironing waiting for me at home. She will be gone in a few weeks, and befriending her would be as pointless as befriending all the transient visitors at the educational center in Cuahtemoc was.

I go home and work on cleaning the water filter. I drop it on the floor, and part of the clay breaks off. I am ready to burst into tears, but I force myself to examine it and analyze it and decide it will still be OK. I do not want to spend more money on another water filter.

I sleep restlessly and wake up too soon, my intestines screaming. My life has slipped away from me and is now lost in a quicksand of broken objects, unpacking, repacking, cleaning, rearranging, shopping, and muscle cramps. After all this effort, my life is still a mess: electric sparks still fly out of my wall, I do not know if my water is safe, I know my money is **not** safe, my apartment remains a half-furnished wreck, my shoulder feels dislocated, and now I am seized with such a sharp chest pain that I have to hold my breath because it hurts to move my lungs. I know it is heartburn, but it scares the hell out of me. When will all these pains stop? I want my life back. I want to be like this young graduate student again--full of the promise and adventure of life. My life is measured in mouthfuls of liquid antacid.

I struggle through the day, trying to change my attitude. I am in some sort of detour. I must not give into the despair that it is a wrong turn: it is simply a detour! So many problems are plaguing me, and yet, in theory I must believe they will abate--not as soon as I would like, but sometime, surely. I am on the verge of tears all day, and I can no longer blame hormones or potassium. I am dying of loneliness, and feeling it more because I have so many obstacles to face without anyone by my side.

***

The days swirl by me, out of control now, one into another. Our visitor is a delight, a kindred spirit, yet I see in her myself half a decade ago, and I am in a constant state of mourning for my lost youth and idealism. She is me in Costa Rica four years ago. Will this trip just be a distant memory to her someday, too?

I watch Brazil win soccer match after soccer match, as the World Cup takes over a month of life here. In Cameroon there are riots and a threat of civil war sparked by poor soccer performances and related intrigues. After the goalie quit over unpaid wages and other grievances, his family home back in Cameroon was burnt to the ground. In Colombia, a player who made a grave mistake during the Cup was shot dead in cold blood by an irate gambler. Things could not get that bad here, could they? I am glad Brazil is still winning.

On July 1st, the new currency arrives. It is set up with the value of an American dollar. It is worth 2,750 of the old *cruzeiros*. I leave the bank with a fistful of "dollars". I am the only person in the office who seems excited by this. The Brazilians simply expect it to begin to devalue again, like all the other new currencies.

My Portuguese tutor shows up ninety minutes late. He has spent all day trying to figure out what happened to his week-old puppies, which disappeared in the night. His Doberman is not acting distraught at all, and the vet is suspicious that she killed them. I am horrified. Surely they were stolen?! He does not think so: he heard nothing in the night. They checked the yard for burial spots and felt her stomach for the pups, but they cannot ascertain that she has buried them or eaten them. Gone without a trace. How could she

189

give milk to them for a week, then reject them? It is preposterous! Surely they were stolen? I cannot stop cringing, picturing a puppy that could have been mine, a puppy I did not want because I knew it could grow into a vicious brute.

In the evening I take our visitor to a co-worker's apartment to look at slides of Brazil, jealous of her upcoming trip to the Amazon. I want so desperately to get away from all the headaches of my life here, the mental and physical clutter suffocating me.

At night I dream I am swimming in the Amazon river, surrounded by development and environment specialists. A World Bank official hands me a gun. "Now's our chance!" He wants me to shoot the man from the World Wildlife Fund. Everyone is frolicking and splashing playfully, except us. He repeats over and over again, "Now! Now! Now!"

I pull the trigger. The victim looks up, surprised. He has a bloody bullet hole in his shoulder. "Again! Now! Now!" I aim lower, and pull the trigger again. He is critically wounded but is taking it far better than I. I am in shock. My God! Why did I do that!? I want to rush over to him and apologize, but I know if I make any admission of guilt, I could end up in the slammer for life...or in the electric chair. I need to find a lawyer who will make the jury understand: it **was** temporary insanity!

We are all on the shore now, waiting for an ambulance. (An ambulance?! In the middle of Amazônia?!) I am staring into my victim's eyes. He seems to understand, but I do not understand. I think he will live. It is a miracle, a true miracle. Will I die for this?

I wake up, relieved beyond measure. If I am dreaming this crap, I am only half-crazy. Only **doing** it would prove I am **totally** crazy.

***

I spend the weekend trying to do fun things with the Institute's visitor. We have some fun, yes, a little: only half a dozen things interfere with our weekend itinerary, and I can see that she is far more charmed for life here than I.

190

On Monday we go to another office World Cup party. Brazil is playing the U.S. We root passionately for the underdog U.S. team, amidst a dozen Brazilian fans. I am the underdog Yank against the Brazilians, too. I have begun believing that I will die in Brazil--never see the U.S. again. I do not understand how to live here, but I think I could easily find a way to die here.

The U.S. team loses 1-0. We party in the streets, happy enough for Brazil and the good showing by the U.S. team, which put up a far better fight than I am managing. I am tired of fighting. I have signaled to Brazil my desire to forfeit, but they want to keep playing the match.

The next day, I take our visitor to the bus station to leave. She is off for research adventures in the interior, and I am heartbroken-- my only friend. How quickly I became terribly fond of her! I stop by my damned bank to close that account; at long last, now that the final check has cleared, they will let me close the checking account. I ask if I can get a refund for the expensive (dollar per check!) checkbook I never finished--**nope**. I protest vehemently. The woman asks, surprised, "weren't you advised of this fee before?" No, God damn it! You robbed me blind, right and left! Nobody ever told me any of this shit! I lost hundreds of dollars here, and nobody is going to jail, you God damned crooks!

I am screaming inside my head, and try to sum up all the rage in one coherent indignant remark. I simply do not have the strength to try to express **all** my anger, not in Portuguese, anyway. I go back to work for a few hours, then get ready to leave. The car will not start; it will not even roll over. Then I see it--the headlight. The man who washed the car this afternoon accidentally knocked on the headlight while he was cleaning the interior.

No. No. No. No. No. God!!! I cannot monitor every single thing every minute of every single day! God!!! **You** have to do **something** for **me**!!! I am desperate. This is the end of the line. I know now I will never have any peace in this country. It will be one headache after another, misery upon misery, with no rest for even one single day until I drop dead.

191

I return to the Institute for help. "Don't cry!" They do not understand. They think I am crying over a God damned battery. What is the matter with these people? How can they be too blind to see that every single day of my life here has dead batteries? I hide in an empty room to cry my eyes out until the "mechanic they know" shows up to do a jump-start. I cannot take it anymore. This time I really mean it, God! I cannot take it anymore! Do You think this is an empty threat?! Do You??

I wake up too early. I wanted to sleep ten hours, maybe fifteen or twenty. I stare at the clock, paralyzed--six and a half hours of sleep. I am too terrified to get up. I cannot tread water forever: soon I will collapse and drown. I stare at the posters and photos finally taped to the walls three days ago, four months after I took them off the walls in Mexico. Four months! I am crying before I have even gotten out of bed. I have nothing to look forward to but more calamities, with no solution in sight, and no comfort at all. Two hours later, I drag myself out of bed. I look in the mirror and try to wash my face, but the tears come faster than I can wash them off. I am afraid to drink my water, afraid to cut into another orange, afraid of everything.

By the time I steel myself to return to my belligerent car, it is almost 11:00 a.m. Well, at least the roads are relatively tranquil. A hauntingly beautiful piano piece begins streaming out of the car radio. I have never heard it before. I have never heard anything like it before. I steal a few glances at the lake shimmering an unusual turquoise color to my left, and I badly want to veer off the road straight over to it. I want to swim in it...or sail away into that sparkling turquoise.... I keep driving straight ahead, the piano melody slowly developing into an exquisite song.

Then the voice. Oh, my God. It is Nick Constantine. He has definitely left this world, his voice so angelic I am knocked out of my senses. Am I dreaming this? He swore he would never record for Swiny again. Where did this heavenly creation come from? Have I lost my mind, or are miracles still possible in this world? He is

192

begging his angry lover to cool down, and let him give comfort to the one whom he would love to see smile. Who would refuse it? Not I.

Chapter 33

It is a grueling day at work, short as it is. Finally, the receptionist sees how badly I am doing and takes me to a little bakery/café after work. My heart melts--human kindness! We chat at length about the Institute and things. If only I could multiply her. I know she is working full-time at the Institute and attending college at night, and has no time to be my permanent hand-holder.

The next day, after a week of trying, I finally get the warranty repair shop pinned down on a time to come inspect my non-functioning oven. After a month of boiling and frying, a change would be nice. I frantically try to make the best of a couple more hours in the office before I need to head home to wait for their 1:00 p.m. appointment. The computer whiz informs me that days and days of my work will have to be redone because the data he had given me has now been readjusted. I am beside myself. No, no, no, no. I retreat to my office, shut the door, and let the tears flow again. Soon I will not even have an office door to shut: I will be crying openly in the large, impersonal consultant suite. There is a knock on the door, and a postcard is handed to me. Does she see my tears? There is another knock on the door, and a currency exchange memo is handed to me. Does he see my tears?

I look at my "to buy" list and try to decide if I want these things badly enough to change one or two thousand dollars at the absurd exchange rate being offered. It would cost me a thousand dollars to buy the telephone line, which was only eight hundred dollars before the new currency came in. I am crying harder now. I can procrastinate on the rest of the furniture, but I want my telephone line so desperately. And other things. I cut myself down to a small shopping list and leave only a $600 check to be changed, then go home.

I make lunch, then set to work taking advantage of my waiting time. I catch up on correspondence, filing, unpacking, and cleaning. I blow through the apartment like a white tornado, full of that special mid-day, mid-week energy that is always dissipated by the time I usually get to these tasks on weekends or evenings after work. By dusk, the apartment is in wonderful shape, but the oven repairman has not shown. Without a phone line, I cannot call them to ask why.

I decide to take a walk down to the lake to relax. I have not walked down to this--the driving force behind my taking this particular apartment--the entire six weeks I have been here. Six weeks! I quietly realize what a semi-tropical lakefront is like at dusk as I walk smack into a million swarming mosquitoes. I am fully clothed, though, and so battle on. I pass an implausible Siberian husky out walking two Brazilian men, I cross two roads, I see a squatter hut nestled in the trees near the water, then I arrive at the shore.

I peer at the dark body of life in front of me, pulsing with unseen creatures popping up to the surface, then quickly slipping under it again. Water is the only thing that unequivocally proves God's existence to me. Immense, huge, mysterious, powerful, and beautiful, yet soft and gentle enough to touch, to enter, to feel. It is safe and caressing and exhilarating if you stay close to the edge, if you stay content with only accepting what it reaches out to give. I gaze for a few minutes through the filter of mosquitoes, then turn back.

I stop by the *porteiro* to chat with him about the non-appearance of my stove repairman this afternoon. He comes up to look at my stove and confirms my analysis: yes, a piece of it is missing. Hallelujah! I actually figured something out! I am not too stupid to work the oven!

195

I get out the frying pan again to make my supper. In the middle of eating, the intercom rings. I cannot understand what the *porteiro* is saying about the stove, so I go downstairs with my dictionary. The condo manager is there, very concerned. After a few minutes, I realize they are telling me that the missing piece was letting a dangerous amount of gas leak into the air, and I could have an explosion at any minute!!!! He wants to call the vendor first thing in the morning and demand immediate correction of the problem because the lives and apartments of hundreds of people are at risk!!!! I can scarcely believe my own ears. I return to my apartment with a different *porteiro*, one who knows more about this sort of thing. He looks it over carefully and decides it is OK as long as I do not try to turn on the oven. Slim comfort.

I clean up dinner in a daze. Should I cry? Should I laugh? Did I come close to death, or is it really no big deal? Was my paranoia about this crazy gas stove well-founded after all? It will never end. There is no limit to the number of things that can go wrong here, and no limit to how ignorant I can be in responding to them. Am I cursed? Should I find a priest and get an exorcism? I fight back the tears but cannot hold back the fever that is now raging in my head. I want to lie down and not get up for a year.

In the morning, I leave the keys with the *porteiro* and head to the office, late, hoping my oven will be miraculously repaired in my absence. I have three phone messages waiting for me from the University in response to my puzzled inquiry about an odd notation in my stateside bank account: the $7,000 car loan was, indeed, pulled back out of the account three weeks after it had been deposited! I am stunned. My God! This stupid U.S. bank has completely trumped all the stupid banks of Brasília combined! The University will wire transfer the money back in, and stop payment on the $7,000 check--which was deposited, then undeposited, then put in an airmail envelope to wing its way to me in Brasília, an envelope which was probably mistakenly addressed to "Bermuda" like my first bank statement was. It is a miracle I have bounced no checks yet. I am in shock. Seven-thousand dollars! Here and gone! My money is not safe anywhere, it seems, except in my little state credit union in

North Carolina.

The Friday afternoon winds down slowly. The computer whiz has rechecked the data one more time, and it turns out I will only have to redo a couple hours of work, not a couple days, with his new figures. Hallelujah! I will **not** come into the office this weekend! I close the afternoon with a long meeting about the project, which now appears to be ninety percent finished. As the meeting progresses, my heart sinks lower and lower: my boss is adding more and more and more dimensions to this project. It will never end. I will never get to move onto something more interesting. I will be crunching numbers my entire two years here.

I face another weekend alone--no World Cup party invitations and no stateside visitor. I am determined to buy some fun stuff this weekend. After a couple days of shopping, I gather a cassette player, a gymnastics mat, and several price notations on roller skates and electronic keyboards. I am going to have fun come hell or highwater!

I watch Brazil win another soccer match, and listen half-despondently to the revelry outside. I am not Brazilian, and I have no reason to believe I ever will be. I put a saucepan on the range--unbakeable dinner for one, again. If things ever come together here, I will drop dead of shock.

***

The week drags on. The nights defy my expectations, dipping colder and colder. I am already sleeping in heavy pajamas, with an Indian blanket and a comforter! Will I have to buy a third blanket for this winter that will probably be over within a month?! By week's end I have caught the cold making the rounds at the office, and cannot believe my immune system has not already totally collapsed.

Alone again, I pass the weekend trying to find the odds and ends I am still lacking. Why is this lamp so cheap? Why are the toasters nearly as expensive as the microwaves? I need a vacation from the malls.

By Saturday night, I am raging with fever, with aspiring vomit churning in my stomach. I hold the body surrounding the agitated stomach very still, trying to focus on the grand finale of the second soap opera I began watching to learn Portuguese conversation. It is a true *denouement*, and the loose ends of one life after another are neatly scooped up by the director and poetically tied into artistic and unbreakable bows. Comedy, drama, romance, religion--they all come together, and the puzzle pieces finally fit. It is the most outrageous and unreal depiction of Brazilian society I can imagine I will ever see, but I love it and its homage to idealism. Well, at least I learned a lot of Portuguese watching this nonsense.

On Sunday, I lean back in my recliner for the hour the Brazilians have been marching toward inexorably since long before I set foot on Brazilian soil--the championship game of the World Cup. My head is swimmingly hot, and I suffer through a long, long game with no scoring. What has dragged on for so long has improbably come down to a showdown of penalty kicks. In a matter of minutes, Brazil has won an unprecedented fourth World Cup.

I gaze longingly out the window, tears in my eyes. I know I can join up with some co-workers to head to the carnival celebration, but I am weak and feverish and nauseous. I will miss the biggest party this city may ever throw. I listen to the symphony of honks and fireworks that are only just beginning to approach full volume, and I watch the steady stream of car lights crossing the bridge over the lake and into the city, heading downtown for the exaltation.

I settle for watching the continued television coverage-- poetic replays, emotional interviews, jubilant crowds throughout Brazil. I see the banners proclaiming that the Cup belongs to Senna. There is a spelling mistake in the banner. I wonder how many of the team members came from Brazilian slums, where learning soccer was a better career option than learning to spell. I listen to one of the team's stars say he hopes Brazil will keep on moving upward, upward, for all its people. Yes, yes, yes--that is why I came here. Why do I keep losing sight of that? If only I knew how my months of tedious arithmetic at the Institute were going to accomplish something. I just do not see it.

Chapter 34

Slowly, my project progresses, but I do not. Half the population of Rwanda has fled its civil war, mostly to encounter the alternative of death by cholera in the refugee camps which were too quickly overcome with the avalanche of misery. Was there no one who saw this coming? An African statesman declares the Apocalypse is upon us.

For the first time since my arrival, I leave work early. I have come to work late on many occasions, and I have departed for necessary appointments, but I have never simply resolved to leave early. I am sick and say I am sick and go home. What home? There is nobody waiting to boil water for my tea, measure out the spoonfuls of medicine that I require, turn the television channels to divert me from my suffering. After eight-hundred milligrams of ibuprofen, my head is still exploding; after two days of dimethicone, my stomach is still exploding, too. I writhe in agony, trying to sleep to no avail.

It suddenly occurs to me that my newly prescribed anti-inflammatory might be doing this. I read the insert: possible nausea, abdominal pains, headaches, inability to concentrate. Oh, God, must I endure this for ten days just to mend my mutilated shoulder? I think of the walking wounded I have seen at the orthopedic clinic. I think of the x rays, heat rays, sonic rays, pillows, bars, bungee cords, knobs, levers, pulleys. So many people screaming silently their pain, trying desperately to get their limbs back. Fleeing Rwanda, the stronger limbs trampled the weaker ones. If I stay unhealthy and unsound, I too can be a victim.... I can be innocent. Will I ever be strong enough

200

again to make a moral choice? How is it that I am still strong enough to care?

***

I decide to rewrite my will. I am in a different place now, surrounded by different people, in ownership of different things. I now spend much of my time thinking I will die here--obliterated by kamikaze drivers or executed by some stealthy virus. I pull out my old will, and a shiver runs up my spine when I see that it has been exactly one year since I wrote the last one. A will anniversary. I should be happy to observe it--still alive!--but it freaks me out. **Hell** of a coincidence. I do not think I will see another will anniversary. I cannot take care of myself anymore. I have dragged myself in and out of physical therapy, and my shoulder only seems to fall further out of its socket. If I die in my apartment from a drug reaction, will they break down the door a week later to find my body covered in ants?

The ants will not leave me alone. I have cut off their highways and byways as fast as I have seen them lay down the new routes. My kitchen is crosshatched with orange and blue lines of chalk everywhere I look. Stubborn bastards. I mix up some plaster and start filling in cracks and drilled holes in the tile walls. I start out spooning on the mixture daintily, delineating it neatly with my finger, but as the number of holes and cracks looms more and more ominously in front of me, I accelerate my actions, slapping globs of plaster right and left.

When I head out to shop, I find one of the *porteiros* hacking apart a flowering bush. I ask him why he is killing the tree, and he tells me he is looking for a cobra!! I recoil in shock and terror, asking several more questions to be certain I am understanding the Portuguese right. Three kids are scampering about, eager to see the cobra hunted down and destroyed. "We have to kill the cobra so he won't eat us!" I have been upstairs fighting with speck-sized insects while these people have been trying to defend our condo from a venomous assassin.

201

I head out, determined to finish furnishing my apartment now, this weekend, before I pay a third rent on it. I have one more tidbit of information on a possible place to get some living room furniture. It takes me awhile to find it, and when I do, I celebrate it and curse it simultaneously. Two-dozen furniture stores under one roof! **God Almighty, why did no one tell me about this place before?!?!** I nearly burst into tears thinking of all the kilometers and hours I have logged running around trying to find cheap furniture in stores all over the city. Two months of evenings and weekends! I could have furnished the whole apartment, room-to-room, right here, in one day, with dozens of price comparisons at my finger tips!

I walk by the gorgeous varieties of couches, desks, tables, and chairs with willful blinders on, zeroing in only on the couple of things I still lack. In the back of my mind, I can hear the curses. I could have actually ended up with things that **matched**. I could have done something else with a hundred hours of my life. I sign the papers, write the check, and walk out, wishing I could be angry at somebody about this, but I know that nobody was appointed to welcome me to Brasília and show me how a sensible person would furnish an apartment. I know that nobody was appointed to welcome me to Brasília, period.

I return home, exhausted out of my mind with the cold that is quickly taking me hostage. I check out the kitchen. Ha! I find a horde of ants in a state of panic, congregating near their sealed-off exit tunnel in the wall. I wipe them up with a paper towel. I search for more and wipe up some more. I see an ant moving on the floor ten feet away. I am obsessed. I am sick. I mop up the floor. When it dries, I return to make supper. I see some ants sneaking out a tile crack the size of a...well, an ant. My God! I cannot possibly plaster up all the cracks **that** small! I would have to plaster over every tile on the walls! I plaster over this one, wildly hoping the ants will give up long before they discover that there are other ant-sized holes waiting to be found. There is still a cobra out there somewhere, and I am still defending my home from ants. I am a complete lunatic.

Sunday evening, I sit down with some homework: the President of the Institute has asked me to critique his critique of the World Bank. I hold his paper reverentially in my hands. If this paper gets read by the right people, it could result in the redirection of billions of dollars of Third World loans and development projects. IF. I want to see that happen. The President of the Institute wants to see that happen. I am bursting with things I would love to say to the World Bank.

I pick up my pen gingerly. I do not want to say anything stupid. I do not want to wreck what he has already done. Yet...yet...my God! The chance to reshape Third World economics! It is...oh, my God, this is really a dream come true. This is what I have been hoping to do...for so long. I do some comma editing. Should I be bolder? Dare I throw in a word? A phrase? A sentence of my own opinion?

I cannot concentrate. I quickly set it aside. My head is swimming too much for this; my nose, running too much. I want to sleep--too tired even for dreams. I am not ready for this! I am too bogged down. I want my strength back.

I pop another pill and wish I had not run out of decaffeinated tea this morning. I am terrified of sore throats, scared to death that my throat will become too wounded to swallow, and I will somehow choke to death or suffocate.

I start thinking about all my fears, all my deep fears, and I suddenly realize something that scares me even more than any of them: I have never developed a major fear that I was later able to overcome. I have moved my body and belongings dozens of times, but my fears have always followed, uninvited. I do not know how to overcome fear. When do they teach that? Where was I when they were teaching that? Every year of my life, I have found new things to fear, even as my fear of old things continued and swelled. I have conquered none of them. None. Someday, I may wake up and realize that I am too afraid to live. Coldness, spiders, the first day of school, forgetting the number to my combination lock, asking a boy out, vaulting the vault, hurdling the hurdles, back dives, back somersaults, back bends, snakes, rats, insomnia, fire, guns, knives, murder, rape, war: when I learned what they were, I despised and feared them and could never, ever let go of my terror.

At the office the next day, I struggle with the World Bank critique. It is rich beyond measure. I want to make this man king of the world: he understands! He understands it all! He understands the **big** picture--what the World Bank has **really** wrought. I rearrange commas and phrases, adding scant comments; it would be easier for me to suggest alterations to *War and Peace* than to this philosophical, analytical brainstorm. It could change the world...without my help.

I pick up my keyboard on the way home from work: one cannot be a part-time sustainable developmentalist, but one **can** be a part-time musician. Music, music--my long lost love of piano can be resurrected at last. This is the crowning piece to my apartment. My new life is now officially furnished and equipped.

I set it down and head to the kitchen for the nightly inspection. The ants have launched an attack from a completely new flank, and have actually approached within inches of my food cabinets! I assess the situation quickly and reach for the plaster mix, sealing off their wall opening with quick globs of goo. They rapidly congregate in a tizzy near the sealed-off escape route. I wet paper towel after paper towel, wiping up ant after ant, raging with a burning fever, pausing only to blow my nose and grab more paper towels. An hour has gone by before I call it quits. My food is safe--for tonight.

I see a couple ants turn in a frenzy upon approaching a dead ant in their path. After months of seeing such carnage, surely some ant will go home and tell the others to give up on my apartment? There must be a thousand smeared ants in it now, or at least the scent of their spilt blood. Do they have blood? Go! Report the carnage! Retreat forevermore! I do not want to spill more blood.

I am in a Kafka nightmare. If I ever do succeed in safeguarding my kitchen, they will surely move onto the bathroom or bedroom, and my doom will be sealed. Will I wake up a giant cockroach one day, full of self-loathing? Or will I advance in my murderous tendencies, descend with Kurtz into *The Heart of Darkness*? Will I one day be leaving human heads around as warnings instead of smeared ants?

I retreat from the battleground, nauseous and exhausted. I want to sleep so desperately. I am too ill to try my new keyboard. I am too ill. I **am** ill, right? I cannot be this crazy. It must be delirium from fever.

My fever slowly recedes after a couple days. In a final stroke of feverish genius, I realize I could quickly seal off the mortar cracks with cellophane tape. I put the plaster aside and reach for my tape. Hope is returning to me: I may foil them yet.

***

The day finally comes for my last Portuguese lesson, for we have reached the University's monetary limit on language instruction. For my last class, he has brought me a wonderful mini-dictionary, English-to-Portuguese, arranged in the main categories of life--school, home, work, church, body, colors, and so forth. We chat about the future and look over some of the lists, too. I am in shock when I see that "*cobra*" is simply the Portuguese word for "snake"--generically, not in particular reference to the venomous, reared, hissing, Hollywood-monster variety! I cannot stop repeating "Oh, my God!" and "*Meu Deus*!", trying to explain to my tutor how terrified I had been that a "cobra" was stalking our condo! How am I going to understand what is going on without my tutor? Will he really keep in touch, as he says? Will he act strange if I call him up? I do not understand this culture, and now I have lost one of the few signposts I had. I have been in Brazil for four months and am still lost.

Chapter 35

One of my best friends just had a baby. At least, according to my calendar she did, halfway up the hemisphere, somewhere. For the first time, I will splurge and telephone stateside. I head out on Sunday to the neighborhood public telephone. Half an hour, four operators, and two bystander conversations later, I learn that the "red" payphone is only for Brazil; I need to find a "blue" payphone. Half an hour, one disconnection, and six operators later, I learn that my calling card company has no agreement with the payphone system of Brazil: I need to use a "private" line.

I bolt away from the cursed payphone, blaspheming Brazil through my fast, hot tears. Nothing, nothing, nothing, nothing. I will have to shell out the big K for a telephone. I cannot wait any longer for these mythologically portended price reductions while the damned phone lines just get more and more expensive every week. One-thousand dollars just to see if my friend has had her baby. I will call her from the office.

Stephanie still cannot get through to me, despite two months of attempting to connect her electronic mail system to mine. She has written me a letter to explain about the relay stations, the nodes, the incompatible routing formats; all I understand is that I miss her desperately. I miss being around people who give a damn about me. She was always the computer whiz. Why can't she figure this out? Is she really trying as hard as she can?

I sprinkle out the toxic, chlorinated cleanser liberally, scrubbing down the ant graveyards which are my cabinets, walls, and counters. They are having a terrible time of it now: I have sealed off hundreds of entry points. They seem to be finding new ones, though--the question being, can I discover their scouting parties fast enough? Will their desperation only make things worse for me? I can no longer walk into my kitchen without shivering, terrified of what new scene of invasion I may see: they have already crept into my expensive imported breakfast cereal, and have come within inches of my precious water filter. If I secure these areas, will their revenge be the stove? The fridge? The bathroom?

Back to work. I hear that a diplomatic incident has taken place over the weekend: Princess Helena and her two sons have been granted political asylum in Brazil, on the grounds that she is and forevermore shall be politically persecuted now that she has dumped her petulant philanderer of a husband, the dubiously future king of Great Britain. The Brazilian foreign ministry made the announcement themselves, and will not reveal where Helena and her sons are at the present moment, though the media was given a videotape of the three, calmly bidding a prepared farewell to the British public.

Helena stated in it that she cannot continue tolerating the ostracism and abuses of the royal family, nor permit her sons to be raised as political prisoners, nor accept a divorced political exile without the hope of seeing her sons again. Her sons embrace her warmly in the video, and say they just want to live like normal children, and see their mother happy.

The British government and public are in an uproar: sixty percent of the people polled feel that the British military should declare war on Brazil if the princess and young heirs do not return forthwith. The Brazilian government is standing firm, and has produced a cadre of international legal experts to buttress the argument that they have ruled rightly on this claim for political asylum. The prince, in his usual fashion, has denounced his wife as a silly cow, and feels nobody should do anything since she will come back as soon as she runs out of money or gets bored. The queen has refused to comment, other than to express her devotion and concern for her grandchildren. The Prime Minister and Parliament look to be arguing about the affair for weeks to come.

I picture her, sequestered comfortably in the private home of some old quasi-royal friends of hers, perhaps near a sparkling beach. Good for her. She **was** a political prisoner. I hope Brazil proves a good place for her to put her life back together. It is not so for everybody.

***

On Saturday, I join the American softball "league". I am surrounded by Americans, but feel a freak. The large cohort of Marines eye me suspiciously: they do not recognize me, and see no softball potential in my mediocre muscles, though I do appear to be an unattached female. They seem so American. Do they learn Portuguese, or just stand around the embassy with guns for a couple years, then move on? The rest seem to be embassy officials, spouses, and kids. They all know each other and completely ignore me. I know only one person, and barely, at that. He is not even American, and I suspect they let him on their team because of his tremendous athletic ability. I came to make friends, but I feel uneasy, looking around. I think I am the only person with that agenda.

I listen to one embassy wife complain how unbearable it was to have to use rented furniture for months while they waited for their own furnishings to be shipped here, and I just want to slap her. She does not even know how lucky she is. I know. I know these embassy people have houses waiting for them, maids that speak English and do all the shopping and cleaning for them, a social circle already in place for them. A couple others complain about their hangovers. A Marine walks by with a Brazilian girlie cartoon emblazoned on his t-shirt.

It is a co-ed league that requires a minimum of two females be on the field at all times. My team interprets that as a maximum of two females and leaves the rest on the bench for most of the game, even though there are men on the team who have played the entire game. Now there is no doubt in my mind that this team is here to win, not to have fun and make friends.

208

I have not played softball in a long time, and can scarcely get the eye-hand coordination going at all. My muscles feel too weak to flex, despite my strict attention to water, bananas, and oranges. The dry season is shriveling me into dust like the parched countryside, and I can barely move. When I have to run, it is like those nightmares where you are screaming at your legs to move, but they will barely move at all. My only on-base is a fluke swinging bunt. I make no put-outs. Either I am aging faster than I suspected, or I need to start taking more drastic rehydration therapies. At least my shoulder has finally gotten better, after a month of physical therapy.

I depart the softball field and head off to begin my quest for window screens, figuring if I start now, I probably have a couple months in which to look for them before the returning heat requires them. I stop first at the office to telephone my friend: she had a girl, delivered in the car before they made it to the hospital. They are doing well, and I smile.

When I get home, I can no longer deny that the ants have, indeed, sent a large contingent of scouts through the back of the kitchen wall and into the bathroom. I kill them sporadically, halfheartedly. I do not want them to overrun my bathroom, but I do not, by any means, want to scare them back into the kitchen, either. I have already found ants in my water jug and pot of black-eyed peas, and my daily nightmares about ants crawling all over my bed are escalating in horrific detail and frequency.

It is no use. They are as equally desperate as I. Our instincts for survival are evenly matched, and I will have to call upon my superior destructive abilities. I tried to warn them this was an inhospitable place, I tried to keep them out peacefully, but I am giving in to my kill-or-be-killed instincts: I am going to annihilate them. Yes, I have got the name of an ant poison, and as soon as I find it in the stores, I **will** drop the bomb and nuke them all. Maybe I will end up with ovarian cancer ten years from now, but for now, I am favoring my mental health over my physical safety.

Before I fall asleep, my thoughts return to my loser of a car. The steering has gotten very lurching again, and I am appalled at the thought that my expensive alignment job has already gone bad. I guess I will take it back to the mechanic. It suddenly occurs to me that the tires might just be low on air; I get up and write on my calendar "put air in tires".

I spend Sunday cleaning, reading a book, and writing letters. I had thought about going to the park, but decided I was too tired, and would dehydrate too fast in the quasi-desert conditions. In the evening, I dress to go to church: for the first time in the four months I have been in Brazil, I have the missal, the time, the desire, the energy, and the list of churches and mass schedules necessary to go, and I am very, very happy about it.

When I get downstairs, the *porteiro* tells me I have a flat tire. No, no, no, no, no, no, no, no.... My luck is never going to change here. Never. Never ever. I, who have never had a flat tire in my entire life, have four nails embedded in my left rear tire. I will sink and drown here: I cannot bail out the waters of Brazil as fast as they seep into my fragile little boat.

When I get home, I stare out my windows, across the seared field that was burned down to black by a careless cigarette last weekend, and gaze now in only mild amazement at the pier currently on fire across the lake. Can it **get** any drier? I thought these people were **accustomed** to the dry season: why are things burning down all around me? Why are things right **next** to the lake burning down?! Can my apartment building burn down, too?! It is a beautiful and mesmerizing sight, this dock blazing away, pointed like a fiery finger over the serene night waters. I will never feel safe here.

Chapter 36

It takes me several days of searching, but I finally locate the ant poison recommended by a coworker. Out of all proportion to the vast improvement to my life it could achieve, it scarcely costs fifty cents. I buy four. I cannot help wondering, however, if the ants are not, in fact, in retreat already. They are still sending large scouting parties into the bathroom, but the rank and file have not followed suit. I have killed no more than a dozen in the kitchen in, perhaps, a week.

I am faced with a Trumanesque decision: should I drop the bomb anyway, just to be "sure"? Just to show them I **do** have the power of mass destruction, have crossed the moral threshold of outrage and hatred and am now ready to kill off any and all enemies? I leave the poison in the bag for now. I will not deliver a first strike.

I turn my attention to the other bug issue looming: when winter is over, I am going to have to leave the windows open at night, and I will be eaten alive by the lakeside mosquitoes. After several days of hunting, I find somebody who constructs this rare and precious commodity--the window screen--and he comes by to measure my windows and design the screens. I nearly have a heart attack at the price quoted: $200! Now I know just what a rare commodity this item really is here. I only hesitate for a couple minutes: I know the mosquitoes love my skin. If I cannot open my windows at night, I will be miserable. I tell him to do it, and wonder idly if the landlady will pick up the tab. Two-hundred dollars for screens, fifty cents to annihilate ants: I will never succeed in planning a budget here.

***

Work is a turbulence of turnover: people are coming and going at a suddenly alarming rate, and I struggle to read the writing on the wall. Something seems to be changing here, but I cannot put my finger on it. I leave a lengthy memo for my boss to broach the subject of my future projects, and I can scarcely imagine what his response will be. My perceptions and goals for my time here may be far afield of the new wind blowing, whose direction I still have not ascertained.

On Friday night, the receptionist inquires about my praised masseuse, and so I take her there, my one little haven of comfort in cold Brasília. We take turns in the "oven" and on the massage table, initially gabbing incessantly about the chaos at the office, and then slowly subsiding into placidity as the heat and fingers force the tension out of our aching bodies.

We walk home to my apartment on air, and I make her my version of an American dinner: grilled cheese and tomatoes, black-eyed peas, and fried okra. She is pleasantly surprised by the okra, and I am thrilled that I have finally had a guest in my home...three (?!) months after I got my apartment. We end up talking about music, and I play some tapes for her, then play some songs on the keyboard. Do I have a friend? I can scarcely believe it. We are baring our souls to each other. A few months ago, we could scarcely communicate at all! The first time I met her, it took me two minutes just to tell her my name.

***

I plan a fun weekend. I start with softball, proceed to the newly discovered Dunkin' Donuts, then shop for electrical parts in the revelry district. Then I take my new roller skates to the city park.

My childish enthusiasm is sapped within minutes: the bicycle paths are not smooth enough for my wheels, and I have to strain with all my might to skate the path. Ten feet later, my calves are already aching, and I am broken-hearted again. I get off the path and stomp through the grass until I reach the artificial lake. It has

212

rentable paddle boats and no water fowl. I clunk off again, skating a little on the occasional sidewalk, walking a little, on and on, searching desperately for a better surface to skate, until I collapse on an uncomfortable lounge chair at the lakeside bar and grill. The live band is not bad. I order some booze in my rage, but have to go home less than an hour later as my stomach is engulfed in flames.

I nap, then head out to see a rockumentary on one of my favorite bands being shown in my very own neighborhood--what luck! I decide to put cologne on for the occasion. Who knows? It is Saturday night. I arrive to find the theater completely closed, with no explanation posted anywhere. Some other would-be patrons are staring forlornly through the windows at the inexplicable darkness within. I am destined not to have fun in this town, no matter how hard I try, ever.

I retreat to my apartment. Cleaning, writing letters, cooking, reading: this is my mundane life, and I am flippant to expect more. Yes, a good day is a day on which I can count the ants on only one hand, and I shall no longer hope for more pleasure than that.

On Sunday, I head off to mass. No flat tire, no dead battery, no exploding timing belt, no nothing: I am going! I step into the church just as the priest is proceeding up the aisle to the altar. He is flanked by altar **girls**! The entrance hymn is truly divine, and I take my seat, enthralled by the evocative music. What sweet voices! What instrumentation! What a soothing melody! The altar is stunning--a triumph of modern holy art. I glance around at the unusual carved stations of the cross. This is a very inspiring church.

I turn my attention to my written crutches as the priest begins to say the mass. I keep getting lost, but I manage to read along with a few things, and join in a few of the community prayers. I realize I do not have the right music handout, and I will not repeat that mistake again: I am dying to sing along with this youthful choir of angels. They serenely strum guitars and blow into wind instruments, and the congregation sings its heart out. Occasionally, they spontaneously clap along! Yes, this group is good. They even have birds accompanying them.

213

When it comes time for the handshake of peace, the children of the congregation bolt from the pews and run full-speed-ahead, up the altar, to line up for their turn to greet the priest and all the people helping him celebrate the mass. They then race back to their parents, as happy as kids coming off of Santa's lap. Who taught these kids to be so loving? It could not possibly be the people who have nearly run me over every time I ventured my car out onto the streets of Brasília, the city of motor murder. I look around at the people, trying to guess who they are, what they are. If I keep going to church, will I feel their Christian kinship?

The mass ends, and I try fruitlessly to pray. I am tired of praying for the same safe things--the paltry things my faith is strong enough to believe possible. When I was younger, I did believe faith could move mountains, did I not? Somewhere along the way, I got it all wrong. I read every single word in the Bible, but I failed to read between the lines. I walk out of the sanctuary, scan the bulletin board announcements for social clues, then head back to my car, alone. I hate going to church alone.

***

The week is a blur of cramps and fatigue--some hormonal, some seasonal. It is so dry now that my stomach is pained by the quantities of water I am downing. On Saturday, I finally get around to buying new car speakers--which I have been putting off for months, alarmed at how much money I was sinking into my cursed car. The mechanic admires my car--it **looks** so good, yes, it fools everybody-- then promptly points out to me another problem: some mysterious hose has ripped open. I proceed to softball, then to the library to try to find some books in English.

By the time I get home, I am convinced my car is scraping speed bumps. I bend over to scrutinize the underbelly of the beast: am I imagining it, or is my whole exhaust system...sagging? Alright, now there is no doubt in my mind: somebody was murdered in this car, and continues to haunt it, enraged, breaking different parts of it every week, maybe every day! This car has had more problems in four months than my previous car had in seven years. The only thing

214

stopping me from trading it in is my fear that I could, in fact, end up with a car even worse. That is how my luck runs in Brazil.

My office friend, my only friend, picks me up Saturday night to go out to dinner and a movie. We see "The Flintstones". She knows the Flintstones, to my surprise. Surreal. When I get home, I discover that the ants tunneling in my kitchen/bathroom wall have found the bag of cough drops on my medicine shelf. Damn, those bastards are good! The plastic bag and twist tie were not enough deterrent. I mop them up and trash the bootie, but cannot fall asleep until 4:00 a.m. I keep feeling as if ants are inside my pajamas, and I keep feeling that I am lonely and old.

Sunday, I decide not to touch my car again until I can get it to a mechanic on Monday, so I set to work scrubbing out my long-neglected shower stall, then finish hanging some final touches of decoration that have been sitting on my bookshelf--a clock, a Peruvian hand-painted mirror I recently bought at a boring international festival, some final pictures, and my brand new giant dolphin poster.

I decide my apartment cannot look finished with the phone still sitting in its box, so I take it out of the box and hook it up to the dead phone jack just for aesthetic effect. Nostalgia leads me to pick up the receiver...and it has a dial tone! I am shocked! I attempt a phone call to the office--the only Brasília phone number I know by heart--and it rings! Am I hallucinating? My boss picks up the phone--egads! I am stunned--too stunned to think to hang up, too stunned to know what to say to him, too stunned to do more than fumble an incoherent explanation of how I came to be telephoning him at the office on a Sunday...and that I really could not possibly come up to do any work there...uhh...because of my car problems. Stunned.

Have I had a phone line for months without even knowing it?! Where is the phone company sending the bills? No, this must be a recent hook-up, an accidental hook-up. Who owns this line? What will happen if I just go ahead and telephone Washington or Illinois or North Carolina...? No, I am too honest. I call the landlady instead to

215

ask her about it, but she is not home.

This is the final supreme irony, the icing on the absurd cake which has been moving to Brasília: I do not know my own phone number. I do not know anything in this town.

***

On Monday, I go mechanic-shopping again. I discover that, yes, my entire exhaust system is sinking because one of the brackets holding it up has broken off. It is a quick and easy repair job, but my malaise over this car worsens. I proceed to spend two hours walking in and out of auto parts stores and telephoning Chevy dealerships to no avail: the damned ripped hose the stereo mechanic pointed out earlier does not have any counterpart in Brasília, and I still have not even learned what its function in my car is, or if I am in danger driving without it intact.

The 1.5 million people around me are just an illusion: I am in a one-horse town in the middle of nowhere. I burst into tears, sobbing into my own arms like a child. I cannot take care of myself in this town: I cannot, I cannot, I cannot.

On Tuesday, the landlady finally calls me back. She is mystified, having thought the previous owner had transferred the phone line. She will contact him and get back to me.

My boss leaves me an illogical memorandum about my future work projects, and it really pisses me off. He is obviously too busy to give me the attention I need, and I leave him a brief note asking for some clarifications. He finally calls me to his office late in the afternoon and insists that he cannot get more specific if I do not explain to him what I believe I can do at the Institute. I look at him in stunned amazement, having given him a three-page detailed statement to that effect ten days ago. When I point this out, he insists it was not specific at all, and he still does not understand what I am offering to do for the Institute. I ask him if he read it **carefully**. He insists he did. Bullshit!

I seethe inside. My existence here, my function, my role: it is all just an afterthought to him! He cannot be bothered with me! He is too busy now that the beloved President has resigned his position at the Institute and let my evil boss take over the glorified helm. He goes on to to complain about my "generalist" background, and how it is difficult for him to ascertain what unique contributions I can make. My face glazes over as his words sink like little daggers into my heart. Did he not read my curriculum vitae? Did he not read and praise my writing samples while he was courting me? Did he not understand the whole purpose of the donor agency's program, and why the University sent me here? What the hell did he expect from me?

I tell him stonily that I will prepare another memo, as the visitor from the World Bank pokes his head in to inquire if, in fact, my boss is coming to "the meeting". I storm out of the Institute in a rage. Angry--oh, my God, am I angry! That little bastard! That little shit! He brought me to this hellish existence and **then** has the gall to tell me, four months later, that he is not sure what I am capable of! **That damned bastard!** My anger is raging, scarcely under control.

I drive home shakily. He just wanted a freebie. He just wanted the University to pay someone to do pissy little translations and statistical gruntwork for him for two years. He does not give a **shit** about what I am **supposed** to be contributing. He does not give a **shit** about what this program was funded for. **He** sure in hell will never let me get involved in **his** dealings with the World Bank, as the former President did. He is not interested in my opinions about anything--nor my training, nor my background, nor my expertise, nor my interests.

I storm around my apartment, fighting back the tears since I do not want to be crying when the handyman arrives with my custom-built window screens. Custom-built window screens! God, I am pissing away all my money just to **survive** here! What the hell am I **doing** here? When am I going to start to **live** again? They have robbed my money, my Spanish, my peace of mind: God, what will I have left, what will I have to show for this?

The ants have discovered my toothpaste. This is the final straw. I will **not** tolerate invasions of my dental corner! I pull out the poison: I will kill them all! I read the instructions, and am almost too terrified to open the packet after reading the horrific warnings on it. I open it gingerly and sprinkle it carefully: it looks like harmless black dirt. Eat, you bastards. Eat, drink, and be dead.

The ants are attacking my food cabinet again, and I cannot find their entry point. I recheck all my foodstuff packing and decide to empty a brand new package of cornmeal out of its paper bag and into a plastic storage container, so that it gives off less aroma. As I empty it out, I recoil in horror: it is full of live, black bugs! A brand new bag! I dump it into the garbage and quickly remove the crawling trash from my apartment. God.

The handyman comes at long last with my beautiful, wooden-framed window screens. It takes him an hour to shave them down to an exact fit that I can slide in and out. They have arrived in the nick of time, with winter making a sudden departure last week, and heat quickly returning to Brasília. The fresh night air feels wonderful-- wonderful! Yes, I can get wonderful things in Brasília...if I pay through the nose for them.

He leaves, and I am alone in my misery again. I eye the phone. Oh...it would be **so** easy to dial a stateside number...hear a friendly voice...cry out for love and sympathy. I cannot do it! Not until I know who the owner of the phone line is. I clean up the wood shavings, close my blinds, and straighten up. My apartment is now, unequivocally, officially, furnished. What else can I lack?

I jot notes to myself about how I should write a new memo to my boss tomorrow. Maybe I am overreacting. After all, he **is** insanely busy, and I am not the only person or matter at the Institute suffering from extreme neglect. I think wistfully about the ex-President. He understood what I had to offer, and appreciated it. I should not have to write memos justifying my existence! I am not a fraud. I am not a useless object!

But I am. I can scarcely recognize myself in the mirror anymore. When did I get so old and ugly and useless? Nobody wants me...for anything. Every day I get more and more depressed. I am losing my mind: perhaps I have already lost it? Just last night I bolted out of my bed, 100% convinced that a rat was running through my sheets. I spent five minutes poking my covers with an umbrella before realizing it must have been a nightmare. And every night I am scratching away, convinced of the ants in my pajamas--despite repeated undressings and examinations revealing nothing.

Then there was the nightmare I had of Stephanie getting murdered--and how I thought, in my dream, that, not only do I hardly ever get to talk to her, I will now **never** again get to talk to her, and how, in my dream, I tried to let this understanding sink in, but I just could not grasp it, because, well, she hardly exists for me as it is. Hardly anyone exists for me now. I am alone.

Chapter 37

Just when I am sure there is no hope left, inspiration springs forth like a suddenly gushing geyser from the most unexpected of sources: Northern Ireland. The Irish Republican Army has declared a cease-fire, after twenty-five years of desperate guerrilla warfare that failed to accomplish their goals. It took them twenty-five years to realize that slaughtering innocent and/or guilty Britons was not a smart tactic. Now will Britain take the high road and do the right thing? Is peace possible?

The landlady stops by the office to collect my rent, and I wonder if I will survive my one-year lease, or if the University will relocate me someplace that can make better use of this program. The landlady tells me that she spoke to the previous owner, and he said my current phone line is not his phone line. My phone line has appeared by magic, it would seem.

After using an acquaintance's caller ID program to ascertain my phone number, I talk to three different people at the local phone company who all insist that this phone number is **not** located at my address. I decide to devote **one** more day to trying to straighten this out legitimately: then I am going to go on a telephone call binge this weekend!

I succeed in getting my phone line...disconnected. They refuse to put me in contact with the owner of the line, despite my attempt to reason with them: surely the owner wants to sell the line if she is not using it? Obviously it is not being missed! No dice--they will not reveal that information. I pick up the receiver to silence. I will have to battle through the jungle of confused classifieds, where the new currency has driven the price of telephone lines into a hundred standard deviations from the mean. I will never run out of complications at which I can throw my money here.

***

The ants have now retreated from my bathroom, disheartened by the relocation of toothpaste and cough drops to the refrigerator. In the meantime, I have discovered that a chilled toothbrush is a pleasant experience on a warm day. The ants occasionally send additional forays of scouts into the kitchen, and I continue to mop them up and seal off their attack tunnels. Maybe I can live with it--killing ten a day, twenty on a bad day.

Yet, they scare me still, the way they resolutely march straight past my generous heaps of poison powder. Are they, in fact, more cunning than I? That was supposed to be my last resort--this horrific utilization of death dust. Even my cellophane tape has netted some direct homicides--I can see the ants who have gotten stuck on the sticky side of it--but this ghastly black substance with all the warnings on the label has killed nothing and no one.

I have lost my own life. It is buried in a thousand concerns with which I do not wish to be concerned. When it surfaces occasionally, I see it for what it is--a useless lonely nothingness--and quickly bury it again under books and music and dusting and mopping. My boss has finally picked a new project for me, and it is 100% less interesting than what I had hoped to be doing at the Institute. I have sacrificed my Spanish to Portuguese, my money to corrupt economics, my health to the tropics, my time to quicksand, and my sanity to dissolution--all for nought?

At night I pray the same prayer I have prayed, word-for-word, every night for what seems decades, ever since I ran out of original things to say to God, ever since I decided God was not interested in unique prayers, ever since I got fed up with that admonition that God answers all prayers--"yes", "no", or "later". I, for one, think God should be able to handle more than just a multiple-choice quiz. God should answer some tough essay questions. I have posed so many....

221

I pray the "Our Father" because it is good and I like it, but it leaves out things that I want to say to God, like "comfort us". Comfort me. God has written essays and essays, but they were written such a long time ago, and it is so hard to understand what they must mean now. Every day that goes by in which I pray the same thing, I feel as if another brick has been mortared into the wall rising between me and God. God does not want to talk to me, does not want to respond to my prayers, not even with a polite but clear "no". Just another slather of cement followed by the clunk of another hard brick. Why should I go to sleep, for tomorrow will just be the same, and I will end tomorrow by saying the same unanswered prayer I have said just now.

***

I find a friend--an American--for one day. She is sweet and smart and adventurous. Now she is in New York because her father is dying there. I do not know if she will return. It was a platonic one-night stand. I met her at the laundromat.

The Brazilians continue to elude my friendship. They are like the landscape itself--beautiful, lush, warm at first sight; jagged, unreceptive, ambivalent upon closer inspection. Under the green Amazonian canopies lurk the snakes and spiders and jaguars; within the wide flowing rivers lurk the piranhas and anacondas and crocodiles. I am taught to believe the system is all in balance, and every seeming monstrosity has a purpose, yet I cannot add it up. The Brazilians seem like the scribes and the Pharisees--capable of loving their own flesh and blood and nobody else. Has this deceptive land shaped them in its own image?

They must be in balance--it is I who am out of place. Like so many ignorant travelers before me, I fear I will be devoured in Brazil; like so many earlier explorers of Brazil's magic and romance, I and my ineptitude and starry eyes will be pummeled. I have made the ants so desperate that they now seem to be living off the toothpaste I have gargled and regurgitated onto my bathroom sink; I see them swarming desperately over the toothpaste-speckled ceramic every day, and I still feel defeated.

I break down and hit the music stores. My office phone bill for two calls to the States was $150, and, after more car repairs, I have realized I will not have enough money this month to buy a phone line. The stars are now in music store constellation: work sucks, my life sucks, and self-pity is maxing out.

I enter the danger zone, knowing I am capable of dropping a fast hundred here. I am saved by the fact that the first two stores do not have any of the artists I want, and the third store has much cheaper prices. I cannot find everything I want, but depart with a reasonable purchase of four cassettes.

I head home and ponder which to listen to first, then carefully peel off the cellophane wrapper. I am immediately pissed off at the miniscule lettering of the lyrics and the locket-sized photos of the musicians--the music business's punishment for the poor and the nomadic who do not own compact disc players. I recline in my recliner and hold the lyrics one inch from my eyeballs as the tape starts. Trepidation, always--will it be magic and transport me faraway, or will I curse the cash I laid down for it? Have they written the songs in their sleep? Are they, in fact, **songs**, or simply musical belches they needed to expel before they could communicate the good stuff?

It is an uneven lot. Just when I am sure so-and-so is asleep and these folks have run out of things to say, the isolated gems of pure inspiration emerge. Yes, the stars were in song constellation when they made **that** one...and **this** one. There are songs that matter and songs that do not, songs that pull you out of whatever you are doing and catapult you into their emotional universe, and songs that can play without your even remembering what they were two minutes after they are gone. And then there are the ones you hate, but those are just on the radio, because I never err that badly at a record store.

I do not feel better after the four cassettes have played. There were some good songs, and even some great songs, but there was not enough magic. I need that artist that none of the stores had...and maybe that other one, too. I need more. I rearrange my tape case to accommodate the new arrivals in alphabetical order: they have earned their places, but they will not become my new favorites. I am running out of little affordable indulgences to buy in Brazil: I am now wracked with visions of lavish oceanside vacations. I stare at my silent telephone and think about warm sunshine on my head, and the beautiful, wide-open sea caressing my body, and my spirit soaring....

Chapter 38

The weeks creep by--barren, infertile--and my ovaries have finally taken the clue and shut down operations, too. At long last I get another paycheck, and so I finally shell out the thousand bucks for my very own phone line. I fax the number stateside, and wait for installation. A few days later, Stephanie calls, giddy. She is practically hollering into the phone. She pumps me for news, but I pump back, repeatedly.

"What's wrong?" It did not take her long to figure out I did not want to talk about myself.

I tell her some of the frustrations I am having, trying not to be overly whiny. She gives me some encouragement, then calls Michael to the phone. I start all over again, trying even harder to explain without explaining.

"Are you enjoying **anything**?" I ponder this silently. "Something good will eventually come out of this," he continues.

"I think I can sing better now," I finally offer.

"What?!"

"I think I can sing now," I repeat, mentally lashing myself for bringing up such a ridiculously sentimental and idiotic subject. Why did I say that? He is my ex-boyfriend now; only current boyfriends put up with sentimental nonsense like that.

"What are you talking about?!"

"I think I can sing now! I never go flat anymore, I never hit the notes wrong anymore." He knows I was always obsessed with my

225

singing defects: why can't he understand the momentousness of this?

"You could always sing: you just **thought** you couldn't."

"No, I always went flat--"

"You only went flat when you were nervous. I heard you sing perfectly loads of times when you did not realize I was listening." The words slowly sink in.... I have lost my fear to sing out because there is nobody listening.... I can fill up my lungs and belt it out, or croon it sweetly, fearless and alone. "You there?" His sweet voice brings the tears to my eyes.

"Yeah--tell me what's up with you."

He has not found a "real" job. Peter got him hired as a part-time messenger for the law firm, though. I try to visualize him weaving a mountain bike in and out of Connecticut Avenue traffic.

"Do you know your way around D.C. now?"

"Mostly--it's kind of fun, now that the weather has cooled off." I try to

visualize him striding sweatily into chrome and glass offices to deliver contracts, briefs, and depositions to overeducated, underpaid, bored young receptionists who admire his soldier muscles and flirt with his vaguely exotic smiling face, hoping he will have to come back again real soon.

"Are you still job-hunting?"

"Sort of--I'm also doing volunteer work for Amnesty International." I try to visualize him stuffing the envelopes of the mass mailings. "They're trying to figure out if I can do more public stuff without getting in trouble with my parole officer. I'm not supposed to do anything on conscientious objectors, but I might be able to talk about other stuff, like human rights violations I saw in Panama." Now **this** I can visualize, and am glad. "Hang in there," he concludes. "I'm sure the University will sort it out, and when you're happier at work, everything else will start falling into place."

"That's what you think?"

"C'mon! You can't give up: that won't accomplish anything. Live each day as if it might be your last!" Where the hell did **that** come from?! Does he have any idea how scary those words are to me? He puts Stephanie back on the phone.

"Steph, does Michael have enough money?"

"Sure! Don't worry!"

"You never did start taking rent from him, did you?!"

"We're like family now! It doesn't matter."

"Steph, I'll send you money as soon as I have some saved up again."

"Forget it! C'mon, we're fine."

"But your paying roommate moved out!"

"I can pay the rent myself!"

"What does Peter think?"

"What do you mean?"

"His girlfriend has a male roommate who doesn't pay rent: don't you think that bothers him?!"

"He trusts me!"

"I didn't mean that! I meant, maybe he thinks you're being too nice--"

"You want me to throw him out?!"

"**No**!! I want you to admit you're worried about the money: I want to help, but I just can't this month."

"Look, stop worrying about it! Peter really likes Michael. In fact, we're thinking of getting a house where we can all live together."

"The **three** of you?!"

"Not like **that**! Geez, I'm beginning to think you're getting some weird ideas about us!" She laughs.

"I just can't believe Peter would go for that: maybe he'd like to get married and be like normal newlyweds."

"Oh, puhlease! Just because he's a lawyer doesn't mean he can't do something different. Anyway, he really **likes** Michael. It was Peter's idea to get a house together. Anyway, I'm not ready to get married.... I think I need to figure out some things first." She is falling in love with Michael--I mentally kick myself as soon as the thought pops into my head. No--YES! No--YES! She is lying. No, she does not even realize it herself.

"What do you want to figure out?"

"I don't know," she replies. "What I'm doing with my life. Maybe I should be doing something more important with my time--like you and Michael."

"ME!? Are you crazy?! I'm not accomplishing anything!"

"Yes, you are!"

"What?"

"You're standing up for something...and so is Michael. What did I ever stand up for?"

"Me!"

"That's not what I'm talking about!"

"Well, it's a damned good accomplishment, Stephanie!" She is silent. "Maybe we should hang up: we've been on the phone a long time, Steph."

"I don't stand up for you just because you're my sister, you know: it's not some horrible sacrifice! I believe in you, you know!"

I start crying again and say goodbye as quickly as I can. She believes in me? In what exactly about me? My dreams? My dreams whose emptiness cannot be hidden forever?

***

Brazil's elections come and go, and the boy next door has won--the boy next door to our office. A couple weeks later they start dismantling the campaign headquarters that sat a scant stone's throw from our own building. They tear down the larger-than-life placards trumpeting "EDUCATION", "HEALTH", "EMPLOYMENT",

228

"PROGRESS". I hope they store them somewhere and do not dump them with the city trash. A sociology professor who spent three years in political exile during the military dictatorship, he would surely be considered too liberal to win in the U.S.: here, he is suspected of abandoning his leftist roots. How could anyone forget being forced into exile for three years?

***

Another paycheck comes, and I have been here six months. I ask for a couple days of vacation, and my boss tells me that, in Brazil, one must wait an entire year before taking any vacation time--he does not want others to think I am getting special privileges. I stare at him in disbelief. Special privileges? **SPECIAL PRIVILEGES**?! And what exactly do those include? Moving to a strange city in a strange land without understanding the language or the transportation system or the banking system or the shopping system or the health care system? Pissing all my money away because nobody tells me what I need to know not to? Not having any friends? Not having any family? Not having any lovelife? Being the only researcher on the entire staff who never, ever, ever, ever, gets to go anywhere for meetings or fieldwork? Being the only researcher on the entire staff who has never been outside of the Federal District itself?! Being the only person in the world pretending to study Brazil's demographic and environmental situation without setting foot in any one of its most populated cities, not to mention the Amazon region? God forbid I should take a **couple** days of vacation time off--my God! They might mutiny in jealousy of my merry life!

I hate his guts. It is the final straw, and I now, unequivocally, hate his guts. Hypocrite! The other researchers have exciting projects, field visits, international conferences, and he wants me to sit twelve months **straight** in this damned office like a piece of furniture. He magnanimously offers to **let** me work on a holiday in order to take some other day off to create a three-day weekend. Oh, thank you, great Poobah! Shall I kiss your ass for that favor?! Fine, I will come in on some holiday and sleep all day through my boring work to earn the chance to recharge my batteries, God forbid.

No ocean for now. Not for a three-day weekend. Not unless some airline is giving away tickets. I do a little research on nearby resorts and decide on a lake some five hours to the south. The bus schedule is bad, and I cannot really do it unless I take off a Friday **and** a Monday. Fine: I will work the next **two** holidays. What difference does it make: nobody ever invites me to any holiday festivities. I must have been too much of a wet blanket at that first World Cup party--when I was exhausted and menstrual and unexcited by soccer--to warrant more invites after that.

The eve finally arrives, and I pack slowly, reminiscing about other trips I have taken in the past. Hours go by, and I still have not finished packing. I am nearly hysterical. What if I forget something? I cannot forget something: this is the Third World, and you had better take it with you. I need so much more than I used to need to pack--products for my lousy hair, my lousy skin, my lousy allergies, my lousy stomach.... What if it rains and gets cold? What if my shoes get drenched? I need extra everything...and a book...and my portable radio...and extra batteries...it will never end. I will never get to sleep, and I have to get up at six a.m. to catch the bus. Finally, it is done. I could be kidnapped and live quite a long time on this suitcase, maybe even a couple months. I go to bed scared: I am going on vacation alone.

Chapter 39

I try to sleep on the bus, but cannot. I could not stomach eating anything so early in the morning, and, with little food to slow it down, the meager ounces of water I allowed myself before departure have hurtled rapidly to my bladder. I warily head to the back of the bus and am shocked to discover that the water closet is immaculate, sterilized stainless steel, cleaner than my own bathroom, stocked with the works: it even has a self-flusher! Astonishing.

I still cannot sleep, and so I gaze out at the Serengeti Plain passing by my window. So far from the Amazon...so far from the ocean.... This is the landscape that makes it so easy to believe that South America **did** split off from the African continent eons ago. Farther from the city, I will surely start seeing zebras and giraffes. As I get farther from metropolitan Brasília, what I see are lots of cows: live cows, skeletal cows...**dead cows**! It is not Kenya after all, but Ethiopia. The return of the rains has been deathly delayed this year, and it is a wasteland.

I switch buses in a tiny town and, after a two-hour delay, hit the road again on a nightmarish urban bus full of commuters and rural shoppers heading...home? We pass over ten-thousand speed bumps, to which the driver grants scarcely a pause on the gas pedal, and I bounce all the way to my destination. I am the last one left on the bus, and the driver points to a dirt road and tells me where to go.

"Is it far?"

231

He assures me it is not, but then asks how much I will pay him to drive me to the door. I start walking.

My suitcase wheels accomplish little on the dirt road, and, with increasing frequency, I must pick up the suitcase for short stretches. It is not unbearably heavy, but...God! Where is this place? I walk on and on, and suddenly realize anybody could rob, rape, and murder me on this God-forsaken road. The sun is beating down mercilessly and I am soon crying my eyes out from despair and dehydration and exhaustion. I can see the lake, but I see no signs of human life.

I finally reach a sign for the resort, but it is over a barbed wire fenced-off entrance, and its arrow points back from whence I came! Now I am crying full-blast: I do not think I can make it back **up** that hill, and what if that sign is wrong? I see movement in a building on the next lot, and walk downhill a little further. Construction workers! One comes over and verifies that the entrance has been moved.

"I can't walk any further!" I wail. He pulls apart their own fence wires, takes my suitcase, and then helps me through, pointing out how to cross their property to get to the resort. I thank him profusely. Now I have to carry the suitcase over a rocky, grassy field.

I collapse in the shade of the first building I get to. After a few minutes, a man pokes his head around the corner inquiringly. I ask him where the entrance is, and he points. I walk on until the owner himself--as he declares himself to be--stops me in my tracks. I lash out at him, demanding to know why I was told the bus passes close to his hotel. Instead of explaining or apologizing, he lashes back at me! He "**never**" told anybody the bus passed near here!

"Well, **somebody** answered the phone here, and **somebody** told me it was easy to get to on the bus, and **somebody** made reservations for me, and **somebody** knew I was coming all the way from Brasília...!" I am still crying hysterically, and he ushers me to a shaded veranda. I look out on the wild and beautiful lake and realize I am not at a resort. I am at a patchwork of tiny cottages next to a lake, but this is no resort. I cannot stop crying.

232

I tell the owner how I arranged the whole trip through a travel agent: a nice Brazilian young man made the phone calls for me, asked the questions, made the hotel reservations, got the bus schedule. No, **this** was not **my** mistake! This was **not** stupidity; this was **not** poor Portuguese comprehension! Not **this** time!

The owner finally figures out which of his underlings made the reservation, but neither he nor she apologizes for claiming it was on the busline. Then he explains that it is just a simple bed and breakfast inn for people who drive into town with their own boats! I look at the beautiful lake in exhausted horror: if I want to eat, boat, jet ski, do **anything**, I am at their mercy, stranded, too far to walk to anyplace else in town. Totally at their mercy. These rude, lying people's mercy. They have no other guests. It could be the Bates Motel, for all I know. I cannot stay here--not as the lone guest of a manager who will not even apologize to an hysterically sobbing foreigner. Right or wrong, he should at least pretend he feels some sympathy, even if he does not.

He telephones another lake hotel to see if they have a vacancy, assuring me they are better equipped with a swimming pool and so on. He gets the information: it is over a hundred bucks a night, more than twice his price. I wonder if he is making this up, trying to scare me into staying. A hundred bucks a night?! How could **any** hotel in this rural area cost that much?! A four-star hotel out **here**?! I ask him to leave me alone to think it over.

I just want to cry, and I have to shake myself mentally to stop. Think! Decide! Act! Nobody else is going to figure this out for you! The lake is beautiful...but I do not want to spend days here like a prisoner, wondering if or when they will bring me purified drinking water or food, let alone arrange any way for me to get some recreation here. They do not even have a swimmable shoreline.

He comes back and offers to arrange a ride for me back to the bus station, and I accept, forcing myself to act profusely grateful. Two friendly young men in a rickety pickup truck take me to the bus station, and I wait for the next bus back to that little town from whence I recently came. The bus is nicer this time, but mysteriously

233

fills up with only the opposite sex. I am the one and only female passenger in the midst of three dozen males between the ages of eighteen and thirty. I struggle to force the fear of gang rape out of my mind. It sometimes happens. It could happen to me.

I arrive safe and exhausted. I check the schedule for a bus to the only other resort I have heard of that is within a couple hours' drive: only one bus, 7:00 a.m.! Part of me is tempted to return to Brasília instead, but I force myself to fight for my vacation. After some questions and phone calls, I am whisked by taxi to a small hotel to spend the night.

It is like a little heaven, this hotel. For twenty-seven dollars a night, I am tempted to enjoy the lovely room, friendly staff, good food, and cute swimming pool for the remainder of my vacation. Instead, I ask them to give me a wake-up call at 5:30 a.m. I got up at 6:00 a.m. today and did not check into a hotel until 6:30 p.m. No, this is no way to start a vacation. My arms are already sunburned, but only from bus windows.

Am I crazy to ask for a wake-up call? I could just stay here, cry for several hours, sleep until noon tomorrow, read my book and take little walks and swims to pass the time. I take an allergy pill which I do not need now that I am getting shots, but it will help me fall asleep. I dream I am a teenage cowgirl in love with a teenage cowboy. It is a wonderful dream, full of horses, though it actually has no cows--dead or otherwise.

The phone rings to wake me up, and I gather my things together and force my queasy stomach to take in lots of starch and very little liquid. I arrive at the station and learn to my horror that the ride will take three hours! When I learn this bus has no water closet, I down some diarrhea medicine and make one last pit stop.

The road proves to be merciless: not only is it impossible to sleep, but the constant bone-jarring bumps and holes quickly reduce my bladder to a state of hysteria. What little quantity of liquid is there bounces up and down so fiercely that my bladder walls scream for tactile relief. I put on my headphones for distraction, wondering if the driver would stop for me to pee, wondering if there is enough

234

shrubbery to find privacy along the side of the road. All the fields are fenced off: it looks like wilderness, but somebody seems to own it all, including the occasionally inviting tree behind which I would gladly pay money to urinate away my few drops of tidal wave action.

After 105 minutes, we stop at the bus station of a small town, and half the females on the bus bolt for the restroom. So! Brazilian bladders are **not** necessarily stronger than mine!

We continue on and at last reach the tourist haven. I hop a cab to the hotel recommended by my trusty (hah!) travel agent back when we were discussing this option, and, at last, enter a world built for rest and relaxation. This is the city of hot springs, where every pool is one giant bathful of hot water. I change immediately into my bathing suit and head out.

Aaaaaaahhhhhhhhhh! Sylvia Plath Heaven. I sink in. Hot water. Amazing. I have not been totally immersed in hot water since I left the U.S. I have spent over twenty-four hours just to get to a big hot bathtub. I head over to the waterfall and put my bus-contorted spine under the mother of all shower massages. The water pounds me with so much force that I casually speculate as to whether it could break my neck. Well, if that is my biggest fear here, I am in good shape now. I turn slowly, directing my shoulders, my shoulder blades, the hollow of my back, and my neck, to the cascade, then backfloat slowly away. I cannot stay in long: the weather is too hot. I will return.

I swim, I wander out of the hotel, I window-shop, I eat, I read, I nap, I swim, and so it goes. Little thoughts and anxieties keep grabbing hold of me, but I forget everything when I enter the hot waters again. I am hot and nothing else.

At night I try to take a cold shower, but they do not have cold water. I soap off and shampoo out all the day's sweat and chlorine, rub cream all over my body, then stretch out on the white linen feeling as clean as it is humanly possible to feel. I try to visualize myself tramping through swampy Amazônia and bathing the mud off in the river, and cannot. Yet I cannot visualize myself sitting at my desk for the next eighteen months, either. I cannot see the future.

I try to tell myself that the ants on the bathroom sink here just make me feel more at home, but I have never felt more homeless. I think about the last letter I got from my Chapel Hill roommate saying she had sold the townhouse and moved to Atlanta. I cannot go back, I wanted to go forward, but now I just want somebody else to figure it out for me. No men chase me around, no teachers tell me what to study, nobody tells me...shows me.... Is my life over already? The ascending part? The learning part? The growing part? The adventurous part? Am I as old and ugly and useless as I feel?

On Sunday afternoon, I overcome my reluctance to cavort with the adolescents and actually try out the water slide. I hurtle down on my back, terrified I will slide sideways over the edge and plummet twenty feet to the concrete. I finally see the water coming and sink in like a torpedo. I emerge slowly, wiping the chlorinated water from my eyes. Did I hear somebody call my name? I look around at the water slide spectators.... Fernando?! I cannot believe it. He puts out his hand to help me out.

"I cannot believe it! I was hoping I would run into you again! I wanted to call you, but I lost your business card."

I hurl telepathic javelins at him: CROCK OF SHIT! CROCK OF SHIT!

He visibly winces. "Well, actually my girlfriend threw it away. She did not believe you were just the sister of an old friend! She had once asked me if I had ever been in love, really in love, and I told her just once, in America. So she was sure it was you."

"You need to work on building trust in your relationships, Fernando."

"Well, I only knew her for a month! I broke up with her when I realized she had stolen the business card and thrown it away." I look at him doubtfully. "No, really!"

"I really don't care."

"Please! I really want to talk to you. Are you going back to Brasília on the 2:00 bus?"

"Not until tomorrow."

"What hotel room are you in?" I give him the number. "If I come by after lunch, you can give me another card, OK?" I frown. "Please? I am serious: I will call you this week."

"Fine. Tchau." I walk away. I glance back in time to see a bikini-clad beauty being helped out of the water slide pool by Fernando. After he finishes kissing her, I can see her face--not very different than the last girlfriend's.

I would normally be in my room after lunch anyway, so I am there, but I am surprised when Fernando actually shows up. I silently hand him the card.

"You think I'm a shitty liar, don't you?"

"I just wish you did not pretend you wanted to call me," I reply. "I am tired of encountering that particular personality flaw here."

"Ah...you are suffering from one of the many misperceptions Americans have of Brazilians. Let me explain--"

"You'll miss your bus. Believe me, there is too much to explain."

"OK, I will surprise you and call you: you'll see!"

"Tchau."

"Tchau!"

I close the door and return to my novel and cease to think about him. In the night, my reproductive system reasserts its cycle with a vengeance, and I cannot swim on my last day. I moan and groan from the cramps. I have relaxed **just** enough for my uterus to think me criminally guilty of non-conception, and remember it has not punished me for the crime in many months. I leave for Brasília, tired and writhing in agony. The bus has no water closet: I am doomed. On the way back, I feel a virus start scratching apart my throat.

237

Chapter 40

When I get home, I check the kitchen to see if the ants have taken over in my absence. There is nobody there. It must be too dry for them, since I have not been here to spill water for them. My cold grows rapidly, and I am too exhausted to unpack all week. I drag myself around the office, the laundromat, the water filter repair shop (again!), the produce market, the drug store; I am a cursed outcast among human beings, and no one will take care of me and my leprosy.

Too tired to fight back, I am helplessly distressed when I notice spiders spinning webs in all the corners of my apartment: apparently **they** noticed my four-day absence...and made good use of it. Sudden bursts of torrential rain awaken large quantities of Brasilia's larvae, and bizarre insects appear in mass. I see them swarming over the floors and ceilings of the neighborhood shops, and on the ground around our condo, and I am thankful for my expensive window screens.

On Friday, my supervisor at the University finally telephones me--two months after I first started complaining to him about my work. He says he spoke to my boss a week ago, and was told my future here is now planned out pretty well. **Huh**?? What has that lying piece of shit been telling him?! Lying or demented.... Lying or...well, either my boss is crazy or I am crazy, because my future here is stupid and boring, not "planned out pretty well". I am burning with rage and fever and despair. He continues speaking to me, from his northern university office, over the gazillion miles of telephone line. He offers me verbal sympathy but no advice beyond "try to make the best of it". Too little, too late--like the rains. The cows are already dead.

***

I sink into an abyss of fever and phlegm, headaches and bellyaches, pains in my ass and pains in my ear. I feebly try to nurse myself back to health to no avail. I stay home and watch afternoon movies and try to avoid the news broadcasts. I alternate between sleeping endlessly or being completely unable to sleep. I am cold, then hot, then cold, then hot.

I swat at the mosquitoes multiplying in my apartment-- hanging like vampires on the ceiling. What the hell is wrong with my screens?! I shall seek out the vampires by daylight and drive stakes through their hearts. How can there be so many Daddy-Long-Legs in this apartment? Has a nest of spider eggs hatched? I have killed one in **every** corner, and **still** there are more. Bastards! My Greenpeace guide says to let spiders be because they kill other insects, but they are not killing any ants or mosquitoes!! Now I see something marching over the windowsill--termites? Shall my apartment be eaten out from under me now?

By night I sleep erratically--five hours one night, ten another. In between, I stare at the familiar red digits of the clock radio, the red digits that have borne silent witness to my illnesses and insomnias in a score of cities for years and years on end. I know those red digits, for they have been my constant nighttime companion--shining forth mockingly or kindly in a host of different darknesses.

By day, I lie down over and over again. My head cannot maintain elevation for more than a few minutes at a time. I run out of food and order Chinese vegetables and rice delivered, which I force-feed to myself in bits and drabs as best I can for what seems a week. Glimpses of news on TV--something is happening out there. A total eclipse of the sun. I think I already missed it. Martial law in Rio de Janeiro--the army is invading the *favelas* to root out the scourge of drug traffickers in the slums. Yes, we all know that the slums will be pleasant middle class neighborhoods if those irritating drug dealers would just leave them alone.

239

I take a taxi to the stupidest doctor in town. It does not occur to him to examine my ear until I specifically ask him to do so; no, indeed, he thought getting my height and weight measured would tell a lot about this feverish infection. Oh, yes--the ear **is** inflamed! Surprise. I take the antibiotic prescription and flee before more desperate mothers can assail me for further financial contributions to pay for the medical care of still more ailing children being carried around the clinic corridors like begging bowls. My head is ready to explode.

The taxi driver takes the stupidest way home and we get caught in the rush-hour traffic. I lie down in the back seat like a pregnant woman, except that the contractions are threatening to hurl something out of my cranium rather than out of my pelvis. Some enormous virus has taken over my entire brain and will outgrow my skull any minute and explode to freedom.

Home, I pop the pill and sink into my recliner and tilt back. Clankety-clank. I look down at the floor: an enormous nail has fallen out of the chair, and my recliner is slowly falling forward. I have apparently exceeded the recommended dosage of reclinings. I close my eyes and try to count how many times I telephoned the office receptionist, how many times I heard the cheerful voice saying "if you need anything, just call!", how many times I felt worse after hearing that, how many times I felt that they would not even have noticed if I had replied to "how are you?" with "my arm was bitten off by a Rottweiler yesterday."

They are content in their world: they never asked me to come, no, not them. The man that beckoned me down here has already dumped me, and signaled my worthlessness to everybody else. I have been gone from the office for an entire week, and the absence matters less to them than a breakdown of the photocopier, a lapse in telephone service, a poorly brewed pot of coffee.

I no longer have any career illusions: it is a job to which I will return for the paycheck and nothing else...if I ever get better. After I have recomposed myself, I strain to push over the recliner and reattach the loosened hinge. When I have righted the chair once again, I collapse into it in a state of dizziness, and hate my own bitterness more than I hate anything else.

***

Another Monday morning--this one begins at 2:30 when I awake hacking up my guts. Two hours later, I fall asleep again and have a nightmare about my supervisor at the University. I drag myself out the door at noon after force-feeding myself bran flakes and Tylenol. Nauseous to be sure, but only diarrhea today. I can go to work with diarrhea. No fever, no headache--yes, I will go to the office, at least to get my mail.

I walk outside to find a collapsing tire and drive wobbly to the nearest gas station, where a new inner tube is put into it. Even Brazilian rubber is conspiring against me, despite my having devoted some of the prime of my life to the study of its struggling tappers.

I stagger into work. I do not care what nice things anybody says **now**: nobody visited me in a whole week, nobody sent a card, nobody called. To hell with them. Within five minutes, my unsteady muscles have dropped and broken a full glass of water right into the fax machine--my contribution for the day.

My mail is cheery: in between the written and computer correspondence, I have heard from two long-lost friends. Somebody out there likes me. I read the news reports over the computer line: the world has not collapsed in my absence, but the NRA, death penalty, and that Congressional Liar/Constitutional Spitter are all poised to sweep the U.S. elections and turn the country into some sort of military dictatorship. I learn from the ten-pound candy box and brand new cordless phone on the receptionist's desk that my boss actually went **and** returned from the U.S. during my sick leave. If it really becomes a dictatorship, I am sure they will not let him back in.

I leave at 4:30, on the verge of fainting. I carry home the two message slips representing phone calls from Fernando: I will have to regain my senses before I know what to do about those.

241

The week drags on painfully but surely. A half-dozen U.S. soldiers have died from drinking from a mysteriously fouled water container. Another soldier had a heart attack when he, curious, just took a **whiff** of the fumes emanating from the clothes of one of the corpses. The chemical analyses reveal nothing. Panicked by my lack of recuperation, I go see my allergist--a doctor I **do** trust. He gives me some prescriptions and advises me not to swim in hot springs without waterproof ear plugs. I believe; I only wish somebody had told me sooner.

On Friday, I call Fernando, hoping he is not there–and he is not there, on a business trip! Successful telephone tag. I rest all weekend and now I know I will recover.

***

I scan the online news on Monday and read about a maniac machine-gunning the walls of the White House. I am still wondering whether he is a card-carrying member of the National Rifle Association when my connection is inadvertently hung up by the receptionist, who transfers to me a call from Fernando. "Why haven't you called me back?! I left three messages! I sincerely want to talk to you!"

"I was at home...sick."

"I'm sorry! They didn't tell me you were sick. You should have called me!"

"Uh-huh."

"Are you better?"

"More or less." I may get my body back, but I do think I have lost my mind. Wait, I will soon be turning thirty and losing my body, too.

"Do you want to have lunch?"

Not really. "OK."

"Do you like barbecue?"

"I'm trying to be a vegetarian."

242

"In Brazil?! Ha, ha! Hmmmm.... Well, how about...hmmm...pizza?"

"Sure." I'll eat it, but please stop calling it pizza. There is no real pizza here.

A couple hours later, I am standing in the lobby of one of Brasília's thousand pseudo-pizzarias, wondering if I will really get pizza this time. I should have gone for the barbecue: this different drummer thing is really not working for me. I am yawning when he walks in. He still has his sunglasses on, but I recognize the smile--the smile that slew my sister. He takes off his glasses, kisses me on both cheeks, and begins prattling at me in Portuguese.

An hour later, I am depitting the olives in my last slice when he finally mentions Stephanie. We have talked about the weather, soccer, food, and the elections in Brazil and the U.S.--not my job, not his job, not Stephanie.

"I really loved her, you know." He squirts more mayonnaise and mustard on his pizza. "I did," he adds. I say nothing. "It just all seemed different when I came back here." We munch in silence for a few minutes. "Brazil is like French wine: if you're raised on it from youth, you can handle it and love it, but if you try it out later, it either makes you sick or blissfully and overwhelmingly alcoholic." I stare at him, dumbfounded. "Brazil is like a speeding train: if you succeed in hopping it, it's the ride of a lifetime; if you don't, you get run over."

I find myself nodding. Wait, is he talking about me or about Stephanie? I start to ask, but he continues.

"Stephanie wouldn't have gotten run over: she would have hopped it. At least, that's what I thought. I've seen Americans come here and turn more Brazilian than me, and swear they would never live in the U.S. again." Yeah, I know the type.... "I didn't want her to get like that." I drink some mineral water. "I didn't want her to change so much. I was afraid she wouldn't have wanted to marry me anymore." I put down my fork and knife. "Well, that's what I thought...but maybe I...well.... All of the sudden I was back here, and it all seemed so different. I mean, I didn't realize that **where** you fall

243

in love makes such a difference. I thought it was **when** you fall in love.... I didn't believe we could stay in love **here**."

I can contain myself no longer. "You cheated on her, didn't you?"

He fidgets for awhile. "Yeah...I...I had forgotten...well, I mean, I hadn't been around Brazilian women in so long. It all happened so fast...but I guess I had already decided not to marry her."

"So, did you fall in love **here**, then?"

He looks up, surprised. "Not really. I'm too busy." Now I look at him, surprised. "I'm traveling a lot. There are fewer political prisoners now, but there are so many other things: the street kids, the Indians, forced sterilization of the poor." He notices my shock. "Oh, I'm not a computer programmer anymore--well, I sort of am: I do some database statistics for the National Human Rights Committee. But mostly I do a lot of traveling, lobbying, reports." Oh, God, why does he have to be doing that?! How can I hate him **now**?! "Anyway, what do you do? You sort of told me, but not really."

I tell him about my job...sort of, but not really. I am sick of thinking about it, and it shows.

"You don't seem happy with it?" I grimace. He reaches out and clasps my hand. "You're not happy here at all, are you?" Electric shocks run all the way to my ears, and I tremble. Someone has touched me. "You see, you're the opposite of Stephanie: I can tell. You don't know how to get used to Brazilians. You've been shell-shocked."

The tears spring up, and I look down. He is silent for awhile, stroking my hand. I think about my American bosses, the Brazil-alcoholic expatriate down here and the silent watcher up in that cold, northern university: it is not Brazil's fault. But Brazil will not comfort me: she did not beckon me here, and will have nothing to do with me.

"You need to meet more people," he finally offers. "I'm having a barbecue on New Year's Eve: why don't you come? Oh, I'll make sure there are some beans and rice for you, OK?" I have stopped giving a damn about the rainforest-eating cows: I will go anywhere somebody will hold my hand. New Year? I will take a new **anything**.

Chapter 41

The trauma I have dreaded for ten years strikes: I turn thirty. My boss does not show up for work: now **that** is a nice present. The accountant stops by my desk to comment on how horrible it must be to celebrate a birthday all by yourself, far from home. *Gee, thanks for pointing that out.* I get kisses from several of the staff, but no invites for lunch, so I dine alone like an eccentric old spinster in a French restaurant. Chain-smoking businessmen and socialites eye me curiously. It is somewhat delicious, but does not hit the spot.

In the afternoon, I am told that I will have to move my desk once again, this time for a reshuffling of computers and consolidation of office space. The Institute is shrinking, and I am one of the furnishings that will be shoved into a corner. I seethe over the number of large private offices vacant almost every day, their occupants traveling and busy, while I come in here, day in and day out, spreading my files on the floor around my desk. I refuse the lousy corner offered to me and demand the better corner of the suite--the one that is quieter, more remote, near the window. I am an absurd mouse fighting for bigger crumbs.

I have never made such an assertive demand at the Institute before, and this at-first paltry demand for a "quieter" corner continues to hang in the air around me like smoke from a firearm I discharged. I feel uncomfortable in the smoke, even though they acquiesce to my choosing which corner I want to be cornered into. Are they angry? They **do** see that I should have a quieter corner than a part-time computer station, right?

246

I stage a private rebellion as well: I will not work on this depressing family planning project on my birthday. I am thirty, and my ovaries are dying a slow and painful death, and I really do not want to read one more article about teenage pregnancy and excessive tubal ligations. I have already become nostalgic for the tropical timber survey that was boring me only a couple months before. After this many articles on forced sterilization, the topic of charcoal is suddenly looking appealing.

I receive some stateside calls as cheerily as possible, sick of long-distance friendships. I have dinner with a friendly nuclear American family I have been gradually befriending, but feel an outsider in their Norman Rockwell scene. I hold their toddler on my lap during the birthday song, and can only think that I should be out trying to get my own baby before it is too late.

When I get home, Stephanie calls. I am concentrating so hard on not crying that I can hardly follow the conversation. Quietly, she turns over the phone to Michael. "Hey, it could be worse, you grump! At least you got a cake, right?"

I know he turned thirty in prison, and feel guilty about my silly complaints. "Yeah, I got a cake." Except that then I had to change the stinky diaper of the toddler who took a dump while sitting on my lap during the birthday song, which would have been a glorious act of loving care had she been my own, but it killed me to think that someday that little girl will have no memory of me, as so many other children who have come and gone from my lap, but not my womb. I try to rally. "It was a very nice little party." I just would rather have been in a singles bar, living my true desperation, rather than being a parasite on someone else's domesticity.

He changes the subject. "I'm working full-time now at Peter's law firm. Mostly I'm still couriering, but sometimes I help the paralegals look things up. One of the lawyers used to work for the Bureau of Indian Affairs, and he gives me stuff to read on my lunch hour."

"Why doesn't he work there anymore?"

247

"Well, it was mostly red tape, too political, underfunded, underpaid. He wanted to get enough money to buy a house. Y'know, Peter and Steph have decided on a house in Tacoma Park. Peter's been doing pro-bono work for a Hmong refugee family, and if they move in there, the kids can go to a good school."

"What?!"

"Oh....Stephanie's giving me a look. I guess we weren't supposed to tell you yet...."

"Yet?!"

"So...I've been doing some more volunteer work at Amnesty, but it's not so great. Their donations are really falling off: they think the donors are sending all the money to the rainforest now."

I do not want to talk about the rainforest. "Stephanie, Peter, and a Hmong family?!"

"Well...Stephanie can tell you about it. Bye! Happy Birthday!"

She gets back on the phone. "It's not a big family--just a mother and two kids--and they're going to pay a little rent. And Michael's going to help out, too."

"You, Peter, Michael, and three Hmong?"

"It's a four-bedroom house!"

Oh, that explains it. "Are you nuts?! What if she can't find a job? What if the kids get sick? What if--"

"You used to work with refugees! How can you be so heartless?!"

"I'm not being heartless: I'm being realistic! You can't just put them under your roof like stray cats!"

"We're not idiots!"

"I know--I'm sorry, I'm just worried that...well, a four-bedroom house! That's gonna cost a fortune in that county!"

"We can swing it."

248

"You're really going to buy a house without getting married? Are both your names going to be on the mortgage papers?"

"Yeah.... I think we'll get married eventually...in a couple of years." We both fall silent. For the first time in my life, I wonder if I really know my sister. And Michael! What is keeping him going? What is keeping him there? Her?

At midnight, I lie in bed trying to remember all the birthdays of my life. I surprise myself by remembering all the way back to my seventeenth--yes, they have been somewhat memorable, usually for the wrong reasons: the year of the gargantuan practical joke, the year Benny passed out on my couch, the year Derf stole my Christmas music, the year of the musician, the year of that horrible fight. I watch the red digits roll over to 12:03 a.m., my birth moment--8:03 p.m. in Illinois. I wonder if my mom remembers the hour, the minute. Probably not--I am the one constantly reminded every time a new employer, a new country wants to see my birth certificate...as if anybody else would choose to masquerade in my moronic life.

***

Rumors are afloat that the office will close between Christmas and New Year's, and I scramble elatedly and belatedly to reserve a flight to Chicago. My hopes are dashed as quickly as they are raised: 25,000 Brazilians are heading to the U.S. for the holidays, and everything is booked. I am stunned. I continue checking more and more agencies, to no avail: it would be horrifically expensive, if not altogether impossible.

I dejectedly turn my attention to sending my Christmas cards. Should I dare another Brazilian vacation alone? The thought frightens me: with my luck, it would either end in robbery, malaria, or rape. The travel agents tell me all the in-season beaches are already booked up: only the hot, rainy ones are available. Why must everybody in this country go on vacation at exactly the same time?! Only hot, rainy beaches...pneumonia, cholera, heat stroke--something would get me.

249

The postal service goes on strike–I cannot believe it. Not **now**! I will still be getting birthday cards in January, Christmas cards in February. I cannot bear it! What do they want? More money? There are 1,000 people in this country controlling 95% of the wealth, and 250 million others fighting over the remaining 5%.

The weeks drag by. We wait and wait for the official announcement that never comes: the office, as it turns out, will **not** be closing for the week in between Christmas and New Year's.

***

Christmas: another invasion of my American friends' nuclear family. I have never before missed a Christmas in Illinois. I float through the day surreally: the Christmas tree and cookie cutters are mocked by the mangoes and oranges falling off the backyard trees onto the summer grass. The one and **only** holiday song they do not cease to play on the radio is "White Christmas", as if affirming the absurdity of a tropical Christmas. It is make-believe. Jesus might not have been born on a wintry day in Illinois, but His birth here seems even less likely. But these people are becoming good friends, as close as a nuclear family can get to an aspiring spinster, I guess.

I do not go to church, exhausted from a long string of Sundays spent hurtling out of one church after another, trying to flee the omnipresent sermons glorifying marriage and children. Over and over again have I sought spiritual inspiration, only to find one pastor after another reinforcing my own worthlessness with vaunted sermonizing praise of motherhood. Is this my fault? Does this prove God does not love me? I cannot face the Holy Family anymore, not even on Christmas. The Brazilian priests have convinced me that God frowns upon single people.

I return home and await my family's phone call. *No, I have not gotten the packages, I explain. The strike has ended, but too late.* Stephanie gets on only briefly, since there are so many other relatives there, and asks what I will be doing for New Year's Eve. I tell her about the party, without actually telling her that it is Fernando's party. She is going to meet Peter's folks over New Year's, and I am selfishly glad to hear that Michael has gone alone to see his folks in

250

North Carolina.

Jesus, Jesus, Jesus, Jesus. I keep reminding myself. Is He the Lamb or the Shepherd? How can He be both? It used to make so much sense, but it keeps getting more confusing. Happy Birthday, Jesus.

***

Back to work. I am nearly alone: most of the people are taking vacation leave. The office is like a tomb. My Christmas packages have arrived: I am elated! My favorite toothpaste, my favorite peanut butter, that hard-to-find cassette, Sunday comics--I am astonished at how delightful these little things are.

Outside at lunchtime, I give a dollar to a tiny beggar boy--the first completely naked beggar I have seen in Brasília. On his way back from the store, he happily waves his bag of potato chips at me, and I bolt after him, horrified.

"Why did you buy this? This is garbage! You need to buy bread, vegetables, rice, beans!" He runs off, crying. "Where are your parents?" He screams at me to leave him alone, but I chase after him, not sure if I should be ashamed of myself for terrorizing this child or resolute in confronting his parents. He winds his way past the stores and across a vacant lot. At the far end of the field, I see the tent he calls home. How long has he lived here? Are these people among the transients who have come to Brasília to beg during the time of holiday good cheer only, or are they permanently ensconced in these tents?

The child is wailing hysterically, and I wonder if my complaining will result in a beating: is that what he really fears? I eye the growing number of homeless bystanders gathering near as the mother approaches me: they could easily encircle me, rob me.... I hold the bag of junk food up to her. "Look, I gave him a dollar, and he bought **this**: it has no vitamins, no nutritional value." She shrugs and smiles. "The children will get sick eating this crap! They need fruits and vegetables. Do you know how much bread you can buy for a dollar?" I stretch out my arms to illustrate. Why am I doing this?

251

Do I really think this destitute woman does not know how much a dollar can buy?

"The kids don't eat bread," she explains, smiling again. Is she being insolent, or is she smiling from nervousness?

"You need to tell them what to buy!"

"Well, they get money: everyday he goes and buys that."

I argue with her for five minutes, and finally leave, still not sure if I should have done it at all. Potato chips! And at the jacked-up price of the convenience store! He could have bought bread for his entire family. He could have bought underpants. Maybe I should walk around Brasília with a basket of underpants and bread, and stop giving out dollars.

I cannot stand it anymore, and do not rest until I track down a city orphanage where I might do some volunteer work. God knows my projects at the Institute will never be of any use to anybody out here on the streets. When I meet with the director, she summarily dismisses me: "We are not accepting volunteers until February," she declares, frowning at me as if I should have **known** that, "but you can make a donation." I am stunned at her rudeness and ask if I can at least look around before I make a donation. She frowns but calls over a teenage resident to show me around.

It is decent--better than the orphanage I saw in Mexico--but I am reluctant. You cannot tell how they are treated by the number of library books or dining room tables. Is there abuse? Neglect? Upon questioning, the receptionist tells me they get plenty of donations at this time of year, and so I leave, undecided. I am tired of throwing dollar bills around: I want to get involved in something.

My job was supposed to involve me in something meaningful--something about "population and the environment", I believe--though the mandate of my program was obviously of interest to my boss only until he actually succeeded in getting me sent down here to perform free labor for him. Grunt labor. Math problems and book reports. I was doing more interesting research in my first year of graduate school...long ago. I cannot see the point in

252

any of this. No, I need to get involved in something that has a clear goal...a good goal.

Chapter 42

I cannot sleep at night, and have used a seasonal bout of hay fever as my excuse to return to the little red pills that stop up my nose and lull me to sleep. What if nothing happens at this party? What if the New Year really has nothing new? If there is nothing new, I am already dead, right? Has my life stopped? The paychecks are still coming, though: I earn, therefore I am.

***

For the first time in a long, long time, I pull out the old makeup bag. New Year's Eve: serious stuff. Cover up everything that looks bad or old; brighten up everything else. I frown at the mirror: I am undoubtedly the palest, whitest creature in Brazil. I slide on my party dress, pull out my most danceable shoes, and squirt goo into my hair until it has a respectable shape. I almost forget the perfume--crucial, crucial. I frontload some antacid, then drive off to the party across the lake.

It is an enchanting night--warm, not rainy. It reminds me of spring evenings in Charlottesville...a decade ago. It only took me two minutes then to do my makeup and hair. I always had an hour or two to spare, and would dance around the room to the radio, warming up my legs and my hopes. Then, I would sail out into the beckoning starlit night, caressed by the gentle, clean breeze of the Appalachian foothills. Now, I look suspiciously at the sky, wondering if a frigid downpour will spoil the party, wondering if I have stretched out my old leg muscles enough to dance a few songs without cramping up, yawning because it is already so close to my bedtime.

I have resolutely avoided thinking about Fernando, but the hour is upon me, now. I am not going for **him**--I am going to meet **other** people! I pull up to the curb, rechecking my directions in surprise: he lives in this **huge** house? I ring the bell, wondering if a butler will appear. A woman appears, and I ask if this is Fernando's house. She giggles, "Yes! Well, it's mine, actually! I'm Verônica." I introduce myself and go in. This is the third woman I have seen with him, and he is already **living** with her!? "Fernando is out by the grill." She takes my case of proffered beverages and points me toward the backyard.

I know nobody here, and make a beeline for the grill. Fernando is all smiles, kissing me on both cheeks without putting down his enormous knife and fork. "I'm so glad you came!" Small talk--slurred small talk--he is already blitzed! Maybe he should not be playing with fire. "You almost look like Stephanie in the moonlight!" I do not look like Stephanie in any light. "I love that dress!" I look around: all the other women look better...much better. All the other...? I suddenly realize there are over a dozen women swarming all over the small handful of men present. Shit! What is he saying now? "A soybean hot dog! Just for you! I found it at an import store!" I watch him triumphantly toss the dog on the grill. He winks.

Verônica returns to the party with a couple of bottles of wine, and I am quickly downing a chablis. I will **not** get sick, I will **not** get sick, I **will** get drunk, I **will** get drunk. The party drags on: I am slowly meeting everybody, and I hate myself for wanting to hurl the women aside and seize the men for myself. How drunk are they? I used to avoid drunken men: now they are my only chance. No...they are not drunk enough...no chance. I make a stab at conversation with one of the men. "What do you do?"

"I just show off!" he shouts, then he laughs uproariously at himself. Then again...maybe they are *too* drunk....

At midnight, the champagne corks pop in synch with the faraway firecrackers. I am bored out of my mind. Everybody starts to dance, and I let myself go. We are a flock of women dancing around the Christmas tree, with a handful of men looking on, amused at the spontaneous pagan fertility ritual. Fernando is one of the few men working the female crowd. Verônica seems amused that he is taking turns dancing with every female guest. I head to the bathroom before he can reach me. I look in the mirror: Happy New Year.

I open the door to leave, and he is there. He pushes me back in, shuts the door, turns out the light, and is all over me in two seconds flat. Boozy, fraternity-style kisses, sophomoric squeezes. I feel...so...good. Mmmmmmmmmmmmm. A loud knock on the door, and I bolt backwards. "Use the upstairs bathroom!" he hollers. He is groping for me again, but I slither around him. I try to think of something to say, but I am not even sure why I am leaving, so I just slip out silently and head back to the party. I will wait until 12:30, then leave.

Ten minutes later, Verônica asks me if I have seen Fernando. "No," I answer truthfully: it was dark in there. She goes off to look for him. What is he still doing in there: waiting for some other female to show up? They come back two minutes later, and I decide I cannot stand one more minute and prepare to leave. I halfheartedly hand out business cards, knowing that none of these women will ever call me, and only made my acquaintance while the outnumbered men were unavailable for conversation. Fernando is all party smiles as I bid farewell. My God! He does not even remember--already! He is blitzed out of his mind!

I drive home, right hand on the steering wheel, left hand wiping the tears out of my eyes. Why, why, why, why do I keep waiting for something better? I will never have anything better, anyone better. I feel as if somebody has just dropped 365 telephone books on my head.

I lie in my bed, my throat dried out from allergies. I instinctively suppress my coughing because it is so late at night. I almost laugh at myself--actually thinking a mere cough would be enough to catch my neighbors' attention, to catch anybody's attention. I can cough quite loudly here.

I wake up by myself for the thirtieth New Year in a row.

Definitely not my holiday. I think Halloween is my strong suit. Will Carnival be like Halloween? I fear Carnival is probably more about dressing down than about dressing up. I shudder at the thought of parading around in a sequined g-string and boa feathers. What am I doing in this country? What am I doing here? I am just doing time. I try to think of something good to think about so that I do not have to think about how I cannot think of any good reason to get out of bed. There is nothing good to think about. There is no reason to get out of bed. I finally get out of bed hours later, when my parched throat cannot wait one more minute for water.

I think about Brasília--scarcely older than me, a baby among cities. But its space-age-ness did not fool the Brazilians: they came with mule-drawn carts and built their shantytowns anyway, just as traditionally poor as any of the slum dwellers in the Latin American cities that are hundreds of years older than Brasília. I do not know why I am thinking about slums today. I turn on the television to see if there is anything new in the world, if there is anything for me to think about.

The New Year's Day news is all about the inauguration of the new President of Brazil--who will either prove to be the same as all the rest, or a too-good-to-be-true philosophizing sociologist progressive enough to revolutionize Brazilian society. I root for him, and wonder if he is really a savior, and if so, how he can find enough honest and loyal disciples to spread the good news.

The newscast moves to Princess Helena, who has opened an AIDS hospice in Rio de Janeiro. At her side stands her new Brazilian beau--an executive from the Globo television network--and her two sons. "I want to devote my time now to something important," she states in the television interview. The camera follows them into the hospice, where we see the first sixteen AIDS patients who have been admitted. She embraces all sixteen of them and engages in simple bits of Portuguese conversation while her beau beams in the background. The camera follows her to her office, and the interview continues.

257

"It has been five months since you received political asylum in Brazil: how do you feel now?"

"She smiles glowingly, "Marvelous!"

"Maravilhosa!" echoes the interpreter. They turn to her eldest son, "How do you feel?"

"Óptimo!" he shouts, not needing the interpreter. He will never be king.

"Do you miss your dad?"

He frowns, "Sometimes." Helena is frowning, too. "But this is better."

"He doesn't want to be king, anyway," pipes in his younger brother. He wants to be a fireman or a soccer player!"

The news story moves to a statement from Buckingham Palace. "The situation is completely unacceptable, illegal, and against all international norms of protocol. We will not desist in our efforts to have the princess and princes extradited." The story then shows a photo of the recently divorced mistress of her philandering husband, the prince that Helena might never be able to divorce without royal consent.

The interviewer asks Helena one more question: "Any regrets?"

She embraces her children tightly and smiles, " **NO!**"

The news cuts to other New Year's Day stories, the old stuff-- drug raids, car accidents, flooding, soccer. I am about to turn it off when they splash photographs across the screen, claiming they are snapshots of Nick Constantine's new ranch in the Amazon. It is variously rumored to be near the Ecuadorean border, near the Peruvian border, near the Venezuelan border. His spokesman in London offers no comment, other than that Constantine is on an extended vacation while his lawyers are preparing his appeal against Swiny, and that the photos are a hoax.

They move onto the international news--ethnic cleansing, currency fluctuations, evidence of global warming--and I shut it off. I turn on the radio while I clean my apartment. This is what **really** distinguishes us from animals: we are not in harmony with dirt. "What's Going On?" blares the radio. I mop and scrub and lie down on my bed, back aching. I rub my tired eyes and watch the kaleidoscope under my eyelids. Dust, earth--I am allergic to the Earth itself. I blink and stare at the wall and remember in grade school when I learned about molecules and then always thought I could see the molecules of the wall, even though the teacher told us molecules were too small to see. I always suspected she was wrong, as I scanned my bedroom walls and saw millions of pinpoints of light. I do not see them now.

My eyes alight on my dolphin photograph from Mexico. It looks different now: Alejandro, Antónío, and I are all still smiling, but the dolphins look as if they are in agony, perched absurdly on the pool deck, out of the water. Why on Earth did I make them pose with me like that? How could I be that cruel? I get up to take down the picture, but I cannot bring myself to do so. I loved them so much. I hope they are alright. I hope they are happy.

I lie down again and close my eyes, and I suddenly remember the wonderful dream I had about Michael last night. He was so beautiful--smiling, laughing. We were on a huge swing that hung from a giant magnolia tree. We kept swinging higher and higher. Soon we could see the Bell Tower, then the Planetarium, then we were arcing high above the entire campus. The UNC students trundled around like ants beneath us. I clung tightly to him, terrified of falling off.

I push and push myself to remember how the dream ended, but I cannot remember. It was so beautiful, so breathtaking. I open my eyes again. How do blind people dream? Do they have beautiful dreams of sounds and scents and touches? They do not know what they are missing, I guess.

The telephone rings, and I jump up with a start. I look at the clock--3:00 p.m. I was lying in bed redreaming a dream that happened half a day ago, already hoping for another good dream tonight. My days are just countdowns from one little red pill to another. I pick up the phone: it is Fernando.

"You left so early last night!"

"I was tired. I hardly ever go out: I'm not used to being up late."

"Did you have a good time?"

"Oh, it was great--a fantastic party! Thanks again--it was really great!" He obviously does not remember the party.

"Verônica thinks you didn't have a good time."

"Well, you know, sometimes when you don't really know anybody at a party...."

"Verônica really chewed me out for not inviting more men. She hates starting the New Year without a boyfriend."

"Aren't you...and her...?"

"Oh, no! We're just friends. She let me move in when I was having some problems...money problems. Anyway, she thought you were really enjoying watching the samba last night and told me to call you to tell you her sister is a dance teacher and you should take some samba lessons!"

"Well...." My mind is moving too slowly to process this. Verônica is not his girlfriend, Verônica is just a friend, but I do not care anyway because he is a drunken lecher, but he is Stephanie's ex-boyfriend anyway which is worse, but she has my ex-boyfriend, no, she does not really have my ex-boyfriend....

"Interested?"

"Yeah!" In the dance lessons. I take down the telephone number.

"I need to go: I'm leaving tomorrow for a long trip through some indigenous reserves. I'll call you when I get back. Have you ever been to Carnival?"

"No...."

260

"Oooohhhh--you're going to love it! Get some samba lessons: you're going to love it! I'll call you in February."

I hang up the phone, and lie back down on the bed. Did he just invite me to Carnival? I close my eyes and puzzle over this. Geez! Carnival must be two months away, at least! Useless. Two months! I open my eyes to look at the clock--3:10 p.m. I close my eyes again.

Chapter 43

Two days later, I find myself on a patio learning the Portuguese words for heels/toes/hips/step/kick/slide. This woman is a fantastic dancer, and it is sheer torture to see our contrasting images in the wall-to-wall mirror. A small, fluffy white dog keeps invading the dance floor, and Fabiola keeps shooing him off. Another is chained in the yard. Another is locked in the dog house. I see the maid out of the corner of my eye, and there is another dog scampering at her heels, too. I want a dog. "*Já!*" She again stamps her foot impatiently at the white fluff, and he moseys off.

I try not to think about my disappointment that the men in the class are decades and decades older than me. How on Earth could a Brazilian get to be that old without yet knowing how to samba, anyway? During a rest break, I hear the divorce story of one of them--married before I was potty-trained. When the teacher reconvenes the class, she pairs me with him, and I am scared to make any eye contact with him at all. He comments that the song is a good song to dance with a girlfriend. "All slow songs are," I reply, flatly. Drunken men in bathrooms and desperate elderly divorcees on the rebound: this will really be the year of romance for me. How did I get over the hill before noticing I was on top of it? Did something I cannot remember catapult me over it?

I arrive home tired, but glad: it felt really good to dance. And it felt **really** good to have somebody telling me what to do. This foot, that foot, 1-2-3, 1-2-3, stick your hip out further....Ninety minutes, twice a week, somebody else will tell me what to do, and I will not need to think for myself. Thank you.

The phone is ringing as I walk in--Stephanie. "**We closed!**"

"What?"

"We bought the most **beautiful** house! You're going to love it!" I sit down. "It has so many azalea bushes! I can't wait to see it this spring! It's going to be so pretty!"

I try to think of something to say. "You really did it...wow...I can't believe it...congratulations."

"Gee, thanks for sounding so happy for us!"

"I'm sorry! I just...I just can't believe you did it. It must be so expensive! And...what if...what if...."

"We're not going to break up, OK? We're just not ready to get married yet. And Peter would **never**, **ever** break a commitment to me, not on this mortgage, not on anything."

"But...you're depending on other people to help pay the mortgage, too."

"It's not too bad. Peter's parents loaned us some money, and we came up with a pretty big down payment."

"But you need to pay **them** back, too!"

"Yeah, but not every month--that can slide for awhile. Anyway, Michael's working steady now, and Lizzie just started a job--"

"Lizzie?"

"Lizzie! I told you about her. Oh, that's not her real name, but we can't pronounce her Hmong name. You're gonna love her kids: they're just adorable!"

Stephanie, Peter, Michael, Lizzie, and two Hmong refugee children. "Can I talk to Michael?"

"Actually, he's not here. He's speaking at some Amnesty conference in Philadelphia; I think it's on prison reform and some other stuff. But you got his Christmas letter, right?"

"No, everything is coming late: the postal service was on strike for a third of December."

"Oh. Well, he had a good Christmas in the mountains, and spent New Year's in Chapel Hill." I am relieved.

"I should let you get off the phone: you really need to watch your budget now."

"Stop worrying!"

Stop worrying?! I spent ten minutes today watching two skinny little boys empty out half of a garbage dumpster onto their horse-drawn cart, then drive home with the prized finds. Are there really people in this world who do not worry about money? "OK! Congratulations on the house!"

The next day, I finish the first draft of my family planning paper, and print it off for my boss. Thirty-seven pages of concise analysis: sex education, teenage pregnancy, pre-natal care, post-natal care, sterilization, on and on. Oh, please, please, please, please just OK this paper; I cannot bear the thought of having to read about other people's reproductive lives anymore. Give me a new project-- **please**. Poverty and environmental destruction would be nice-- something I am **good** at.... Not ovaries; no, not ovaries.

I plunk the tome into his box, and head dejectedly back to my desk. He will not like it. It has Catholic undertones and romantic idealism peeping through the clinical and sociological "reproductive health" jargon. What will he say? Oh, well--it will take him at least six weeks to say it. From this day forward, I will cease to study uterine issues. This is even a bigger relief than the day I got to put aside my exciting study of Brazilian charcoal.

I log into the computer network and scan the online news reports. I blink twice at the headline: GUNMAN GOES ON RAMPAGE IN CHAPEL HILL. I call up the story, my fingers trembling. Henderson Street, 2:00 p.m. (two in the afternoon!?), man just walking down the street shooting and shooting and shooting, two people dead, victims identified as--I freeze. I am scared to advance my gaze further. I have the names of two faraway dead people on my computer screen, but they are not just glowing letters. They are in Chapel Hill. They could be anybody I know in Chapel Hill...anybody at all...in Chapel Hill. Anybody.

I force myself to keep reading.... Big sigh: I do not know them. Immediate pang of guilt for rejoicing in their unknown names. I close my eyes. No, I cannot picture it. Blood does not get shed on the streets of Chapel Hill, in the middle of the afternoon, around the corner from the post office. No. It is just a story on my computer screen. If it were real, it would be somebody I know. I read some more: a Gulf War veteran subdued the lunatic. I close my eyes again. For the first time ever, I am glad that Michael is not living in Chapel Hill.

I open my eyes. No, he is working in D.C., the crime capital of America. But...he is moving to a nice house in the suburbs. But...but...but what? Why can I never picture him safe, happy? Things are going great for him! Great! He deserves it.

I mechanically finish scanning the news reports--Mexican currency crash, Japanese earthquake, Italian political scandal, Peru and Ecuador at war over contested border territories--oh, just give that stretch of rainforest back to the Indians, for God's sake! I log off, wondering what on Earth I will be doing here for the next--I check the calendar--fifteen months. Fifteen more months! I have only been here **nine** months? An eternity has passed: the calendar must be wrong!! Nine months: I could have had a Brazilian baby of my own by now. But I am empty-wombed. Instead I have a 37-page report on everybody else's reproductive status in this country.

I look out the window. The incessant rain has suddenly created a tidal wave rushing down our street--a flood of muddy water shooting through hubcaps and over sidewalks. The rusty tide rises and rises. The bankers next door come hurtling out of their building, pants rolled up above their bare feet, arms loaded down with boxes of...what? Money?! No, that is all electronic, or in a vault, right? They are not carrying **my** money around in those boxes, are they?

265

The water continues to rise. Surely it will tip over that motorcycle! The hot dog vendor flees the hot dog stand, and I breathlessly anticipate its imminent collapse. There is no more traffic moving now--only a horse and cart. I almost laugh at the genius of it: high-spoked wheels, powered by an animal unafraid of a couple feet of muddy water. The horse pulls the cart safely down the street, while all the automobiles sit it out. I hear someone in the hallway say there is a leak in the Institute's library.

The water starts to subside: the hot dog stand is safe, the motorcycle is still upright, the hubcaps are drying off, and the sidewalks belch water into the gutters. The murky waters will run to the lake now, then slowly through the dam, then out of Brasília, then across Brazil's countryside, then all the way to the sea.

Part III

The Long Arm of the Law

Chapter 44

The University calls after Martin Luther King Day. My supervisor's voice is strangely solicitous: "How ya doin'?" They have not answered half of the faxes or electronic mail I have sent them complaining about my professional functions at the Institute. They have shown even less concern about my health and financial problems. However, now they want to know "how" I am "doin'". "It seem like things aren't working out there," he continues. **Oh, my God**! My heart stops beating: I am going to get fired. No, he is saying something else. I will be transferred somewhere–oh, God, here it comes, Timbuktu, and I will have to learn a brand new language and a brand new everything all over again--"Chapel Hill".

The words are registering, but I do not understand. A professor at UNC wants me to work for him again? I can do the second year of the program **there**? I will be **at** UNC, but doing an Institute project on a Brazilian subject, while still formally employed by the other University? Huh? Still funded by the Washington donor agency? Still employed?

My head is reeling. How is this possible? Chapel Hill? **Chapel Hill**?! He is silent, waiting for a response, but I am too shocked to answer, and tell him I have to think about it. He is surprised: he thought I loved Chapel Hill, and loved working for that professor years before. Yes...but this...this is too weird.

I spend days trying to picture this transition, and, with difficulty, gradually start picturing it. Chapel Hill. I would arrive in April or May, during the enchanting loveliness of a North Carolina spring. I still have a few friends there. I remember it all like the back of my hand. I want to smell the honeysuckle. Michael could come down for a long weekend....

What is this? This is insane! How can I do a good project for the Institute a million miles away if they cannot even find a good one for me while I am right under their nose? My hard-fought and won Portuguese will erode quickly. I will not be able to travel around Brazil. I will not get to know Brazilian professionals in my field. I will not be able to learn anything else about Brazil. The second year would have been the good one, I **know** it! By then, I would have had my apartment and car and banking and Portuguese and everything else under control. By then I would have known my way around, rebuilt my savings, learned the samba, made some friends. All the fun would have been in the second year! I **know** it! How can they take me away now, **after** I have worked and struggled so hard!

What would I **really** be doing for the Institute, anyway? Digging up good stuff at the UNC library and faxing it back to them? Exploiting UNC computer programmers to crank out more and better and still more statistics for the Institute? Does my old professor really want to do this, or is he just trying to throw out a safety net for me? Wait.... Is this a safety net for me...or for somebody else?

I finally sit down to talk to my boss, and he immediately launches into his ideas for what I can do for the Institute while at UNC. "**Whoa!**" I interrupt him, stunned. Why is he already talking about UNC as if it is a done deal? **Is** this a done deal? Was I the **last** person consulted on this idea? Is he **that** eager to have me working for him...across the sea? I do not like this murkiness at all. No. I want to understand this. I look steadily at him, and say in a level and polite voice, "If you want me to leave Brasília, you need to say so, and you need to tell me why."

He sits back in his chair, frozen. Maybe he **has** become more Brazilian than the Brazilians. Maybe he is no longer accustomed to gringo frankness. But I am tired of guessing and trying to figure out what is going on here. Just tell me. I stare at him, silently, awaiting his response, getting angrier with every passing moment, wondering why it is taking him so long to formulate a reply. What does he think, anyway?! That he can just fling me around like a paper clip?! I want to scream, "I am a human being! I have put more blood, sweat and tears into this than you will **ever** imagine, and I at least deserve an explanation!" I scream inside, only.

"I didn't want to get into that," he finally offers.

"**I** wanna get into it!" I am surprised at my quick and sharp response. Slow down, girl.

He squirms a little, composing his thoughts. "Well, you haven't seemed happy here...." I feel my eyes blazing. This man-- **this man**!--has never spent **one** minute of his time even **inquiring** about my happiness, let alone lifting a finger to do something about it! And does he want to pretend all my unhappiness has arisen **outside** of his little fiefdom?! Well, buster, you had some stiff competition, but the Institute is definitely on the misery medal podium, too!

We are really going at it, now. I demand to know why I was not allowed to work on one single project listed in the Institute's original proposal to the University and to the donor agency.

"What project list?"

I storm back to my desk to pluck from the bulletin board the ten-page fax that I had read with such delight a lifetime ago in Mexico, and stomp back into his office, practically flinging it into his face. "All **these**!"

He starts looking at the list...and slowly starts commenting on each project. "Well, this one ended before you got here, this one we never got funding for, this one was just...."

I listen to ten excuses, then stop him. "You got me sent here with **that** list of projects. The donor agency liked it, the program administrator at the University liked it, and I liked it. I have never gotten a project **remotely** similar or even slightly connected to **anything** on that list! **What** were you **really** planning for me to do here?"

He waffles, "Well, ummm, I guess the immediate things we were thinking of were mapping and demographics." I knew it. I figured that out a long time ago but struggled not to believe it could be true. They never wanted me to be a researcher--only a mindless number-cruncher. He goes on the offensive again: "Whenever you did a task, you did it in a sort of perfunctory way, sort of...rude. Part of it is cultural...like...it was very rude of you to refuse to eat those chicken hearts at my girlfriend's barbecue...."

Rude? **RUDE?** Now I totally lose control. "Chicken hearts? You have the nerve to bring up a stupid thing like that?! At a **party**!? **Chicken hearts**!? You treat me like shit, and then wonder why I am not Little Miss Sunshine around here? How do you think I felt compiling tedious demographic statistics for two months, and then seeing them sit in a cardboard box on my floor for seven months because nobody is interested in them?"

"Well, that project scope changed: we originally thought the contractor would require those statistics, but then they didn't. If it was bothering you, why didn't you ask about that?"

"**I DID!**

"When?"

"In three different memos, which you never answered!"

He frowns. "Yes, sometimes memos get misplaced." *I bet the God-damned World Bank memos never get misplaced!* He goes on the offensive again. "People don't like the fact that you come late and leave early all the time."

"**I am bored out of my mind**! I do **not** have enough work to do here! And I have to spend eighty hours a week **outside** of the office just fixing up my goddamn apartment, my cursed car, going to the doctor all the time....What do you think? I was leaving early or coming in late because I was out partying every night?!" I burst into tears. "I'm exhausted out of my mind, just trying to figure out how to **survive** here!" If he were really concerned about my happiness, he would now say something, hold my hand. That's it. I lost it. I became a woman. No, a little girl. I have become a little girl sobbing, and he has won.

272

He is silent for several minutes. "Well, I need to go to a meeting at the Ministry. Think about everything, and we will talk later."

I walk back to my desk, shell-shocked. He hates my guts. He hates my guts because I would not eat the chicken guts lovingly cooked by his girlfriend. He did not give me enough work to do, but expected me to spend eight hours a day pretending to work. He told me not to feel pressure!! What happened to **that**?! Even playing with every program on my computer, and reading newspapers, journals, and books from the Institute library, could not fill up the hours that have ticked slowly away in the last nine months. I could dump my box of auto mechanic receipts and household repair receipts and medical and physical therapy bills into his lap to account for a zillion of those hours "coming in late and leaving early." Yeah, goof-off city.

But what does it matter? He has confessed. He wanted me to crank out statistics for him, nothing more, nothing less. He never cared about the donor's program objectives. He never cared about anything I could bring to the Institute. He never wanted to look at Brazil from a new research perspective. He never cared if I learned anything important about Brazil while I was here. I will go to Chapel Hill: I may have to crank out statistics there, but at least I will be working for a professor who took pride and joy in teaching me and developing my skills. Is **he** still the same?

A co-worker stops by my desk. "We need to rearrange the suite to make space for library books, and we need to know if you are leaving or not." **HA**! And he thinks **me** the **rude** one around here? Cultural differences?! How the hell did **this** guy know I was supposed to be leaving, anyway?!

"I don't know," I say flatly, "but you can move me somewhere else if you need to." Out the window, if that helps! Please, let me oblige! Heaven forbid I should stand in the way of some library shelves!

***

273

A young man shows up at my dance class this week--cute, charming. By the end of the class, I am biting my lip not to cry. I have pissed away another year of my life. I have only just begun to samba, and now I shall be leaving. Stop caring, stop trying to make friends, stop trying to meet guys, stop buying groceries and soap. Start selling things, start writing letters, start undoing all the things that it took you so long to get done.

I pop in my new cassette on the way home--the best Christmas present I had gotten, which I have been playing every day in my apartment, all week long. "Were you lying all the time? Was it just a game to you? And I'm mi-hissing you. You know I'm such a fool for you--" Kkkkkhhhhhhh. It is stuck! I try fast forward and eject, but it will not come out! By the time I get home, half the tape has spilled out of the tape deck, onto the floor of the car. I cry for my mutilated tape--the cassette I could not find anywhere in Brasília. Gone so soon.

Chapter 45

"Chapel Hill?" I hear Michael's voice in the background, eavesdropping on Stephanie as she listens to me try to explain what is going on.

"This is totally amazing!" She stumbles for something to say. "It's so...so...."

"Weird?"

"Weird!"

Michael gets on and congratulates me. "You really deserve this! Another year in Chapel Hill! We'll all come visit you!" **We**? Does he think I can afford a place big enough to host a family of six? "Wow! I'm so happy for you!" I am not happy; I am uneasy.

***

Day after day passes by without further communication from either my Institute boss or my supervisor at the University, and I begin to approach a state of panic. I just want to lie in bed all the time...all the time. I imagine their secret telephone conversations. "She made a horrible face when my girlfriend offered her the chicken hearts! I have never seen such a shocking display of cultural insensitivity!" "I see what you mean. It would be hard to justify firing her for that, though: let me try to come up with something sneakier, something that will confuse her."

February arrives and Fernando returns, and, much to my surprise, telephones. "Do you have plans for Carnival yet?" Yeah, hundreds of invitations. "We're all going to Olinda--can you come?"

275

Yes--**yes**! A four-day national holiday! I can finally get out of town...see the ocean! "Four days? You have to spend at least a week!"

"I can't get vacation time until April: I can only go for the four days."

"I don't think you'll be able to book a flight if you aim for those exact four days. It's too late: too many people want those Friday night and Tuesday night flights." My heart sinks. "You'll have to do it stand-by." Stand-by? No, no, no. This is not the time to risk my boss's wrath by returning to work a day--or two, or three--late. "Is your boss that uptight? Geez, it's Carnival!" He has not given me a single thing to work on in the past three weeks, and has not commented on my family planning masterpiece. Oh, God, I want to go to Olinda, but I must sit here, reading more books, playing with my computer, acting busy. "That is really too bad. Look, when you get vacation time, do you want to visit some Indian reserves in the Amazon?"

"Yes, absolutely!" I say it without thinking. What am I saying? I am never going to see anything else in this country. Please, just invite me to another party, anything, just **something, now**; I am so tired of waiting and waiting and waiting. "Great! I gotta go: I'm way behind at the office. I'll call you next week."

***

On Monday I get a phone call from the U.S. embassy: the new Overseas Development director wants to meet me, since the funding of my program is loosely connected to his own program in Brazil. Why now? These people have not called me since my courtesy visit to the embassy nine months ago. A couple days later, I head through the Marine gauntlet again, and enter the embassy for the meeting.

I carefully answer questions about my work, the objectives of the program, and what the University hoped to accomplish in sending me to the Institute. After the formal meeting with the director, I have a more informal meeting with some of the other Overseas Development staff, and am quickly surprised by a pointed question: "I get the feeling things aren't going well there; how are things going?"

I freeze. Good God! What do I say now? Does it matter? Does she have influence with the donor agency in Washington? She has not shown interest in me in half a year: why now? **WHY NOW**?! When in doubt, honesty is the best policy, right?

"Actually, things aren't going very well." I sidestep the core of the problem, and discuss the peripherals instead. "The Institute has lots of financial problems right now: they even have to close the library because they can no longer afford the rent for that much office space."

"The library! Oh, my God! Things must be **really** bad there." She obviously knows how much pride my boss takes in the library. My departure will not cause a ripple, but the books--the books!

"He has too many other things to worry about. I just cannot be a priority for him right now."

"Well, I'm not really surprised," she responds. *Huh?* "I was always worried about your placement there: I was afraid they were too unorganized to make good use of this program. I was also afraid they would not have money to send you out in the field: have they?"

"No." She frowns and shakes her head. A thought is slowly creeping into my mind: is she sympathetic...to **me**? What the heck: "The University has decided to pull me out." Her eyes open wide. "They are planning to send me back to the University of North Carolina to work with a professor I had previously worked for there. We would still do some sort of research on Brazil, connected to the Institute."

She asks for more details, and continues to shake her head. "I don't think you should have to leave Brazil before having a good overseas experience! There is plenty of work you could do right here in the embassy--project management, reports....The Amazon program just got a budget increase, and we have plenty to do here. Or we could place you in a different NGO in Brazil."

277

She calls in another co-worker to discuss the Amazon program in more detail. I am too dumbfounded to do more than smile and nod. I recross my legs in a more professional manner, suddenly feeling as if I am in the midst of a job interview. Hope slowly rises inside me as I contemplate the prospect of working in this exciting program, doing the things I always thought I could do, meeting Amazonian specialists from all over Brazil, visiting the Amazon!

"She should go to the program's second annual meeting in Belém next month."

"She should! I bet we can pay for that." Pay for me to go to a conference in the Amazon? Pay for me to meet Amazonian specialists in the flesh, instead of just on the printed page? I am delirious with anticipation. The wheel of fortune is spinning so fast I nearly have an epileptic seizure trying to watch the bouncing ball.

We are walking out, much to my surprise, since I did not believe my legs would actually move. I have to say something--say something! Does she understand how bewildered I am? "I think this is an awkward situation. I'm going to be frank with you: I don't think I have the political savvy to handle this."

"I'll handle everything! I'll call your supervisor at the University, and the donor agency. I'm sure we can resolve everything in a couple weeks." **A couple weeks**?! My eyes almost pop out of my head. "I think it would be great to have you working here."

I float on air, out the embassy gates. The embassy! The last place I expected to find salvation! The embassy contingent on the softball team sure thought me a useless and talentless acquaintance, but the Overseas Development staff **wants** me!

I get in the car, too agitated to start the engine. I want to lean back and close my eyes and try to understand what is happening to my life. If I stay in the car, will the Marine guards get suspicious of me? I start the motor and drive slowly back to the Institute. Do **not** get your hopes up, do **not** get your hopes up, it could not **possibly** be as good as it sounds. I will be disillusioned. It will not happen, anyway! If it is good, it will not happen. If it is bad, it will.

I am losing control of my feelings. The hopes are demanding to rise: I can feel them heaving and pushing to escape up through my throat. Yes! I want this! Could it be? Could I really end up in a job managing Amazonian projects, writing reports on something that really matters to me, something I am really prepared and suited to do? Working with NGOs who are out there--extractive reserves, indigenous territories, economic alternatives for traditional forest peoples, hope for the Amazon! All my studies--finally put to use! All my job experience--finally utilized to the maximum! And the chance to get outside of a library, outside of my nine square feet of cubicle space and actually meet the people I always wanted to meet, to work with, to learn from? Could everything finally fall into place? Has learning Portuguese--learning Brazil--had a purpose after all?

I park the car and walk slowly into the office. I am wearing my best dress--my interview dress, now my embassy dress. I feel desired, for the first time in a long time. People are complimenting my dress, and I feel obligated to explain that I had dressed up for the embassy. God forbid they should go complain to the boss that I disappeared from the office for two hours, and am inexplicably elegant.

But the boss already knows I was at the embassy: the receptionist already told him, I learn from one of my co-workers, who compliments my dress, then tells me that the boss wants to know why I was at the embassy. I tell my co-worker that the new director of Overseas Development wanted to meet me.

"It had nothing to do with your current situation?"

I cringe at the words "current situation" and assure him it did not, even as I wonder why my boss sent him to ask these questions.

"You should have a conversation with him: he may interpret it badly if he thinks you decided on your own to go to the embassy."

WAIT A MINUTE! **HE** IS **WORRIED**?! He must think I went there to complain about the Institute! He knows the embassy has some influence with that donor agency! He is scared! **Scared**! It is

279

NOT my fault, and he **knows** it...and he **knows** he cannot finesse his way out of this now! My University supervisor is too far away to understand what is really going on, but the Overseas Development staff are right here in Brasília, and he is as surprised as I was that they are suddenly interested in how my placement is working out!

"If he wants to talk to me, he can talk to me." My confidence is soaring! "He ended our last meeting and never rescheduled another one," I conclude. Ha! My boss is scared! He does not want the U.S. embassy thinking ill of him or his precious Institute! He is desperate to know what I said there!

My co-worker is not satisfied. "If he gets a telephone call from the embassy, he is going to be really angry." That reins me in. My God! Would he have the **right** to be angry? My confidence starts slipping, and I feel confused again. What did I do wrong? Nothing! Why should I have to tell him about the meeting? She specifically told me to sit tight and let **her** "handle" it. Oh, God, I really do **not** have the savvy to handle this. Should I trust her? Is she on my side? Does she know what might happen? Who is really on my side? Whose side should I be on: the donor agency, the University administrators, the Institute, the embassy? Who has the biggest claim on me? How is it that I have felt so alone and abandoned all this time, and now they are rearing up to fight over me?!

No! Nobody is going to fight over me. Nobody ever fights over me. I will get fired, end of problem. I will end up a pawn on the wrong side--the weak side--then get fired for choosing the wrong ally. Then I will end up on my own, abandoned.

I thank my co-worker for his advice, and he finally leaves me in peace. No, I will not willingly talk to anybody of my own volition. I am mentally paralyzed. I have absolutely no idea what to do, and now the choice is therefore clear--do nothing. The gods are discussing my future, and I will await the oracle.

Chapter 46

I lose my appetite and sleep less and less as each day goes by. Minutes drag into hours only after long and tortuous processes. I have no work to do. I try to read, but fall off into daydreams constantly, "awaken", check my watch again, then try to refind the paragraph I was just reading. Silence, silence, silence, and more silence.

I pack up my things and move to a new office space to make room for the library shelves being stripped from the forfeited library space. I end up, to my great surprise, not tossed out the window but placed in a much better office space. My new officemate is one of my favorite co-workers: how did they know that? I painstakingly rehang my maps and posters and calendar for the fourth time, even though I know they may all come down within a month. I might as well hang them up, since I am spending hours and hours a day just staring at the walls, anyway.

The library is getting scattered all around us, with bookshelves being inserted in every spare space available. Not all the books will make the cut, though: some will have to be given away, or stacked in employees' home closets and garages. I feel guilty wasting a valuable chunk of floorspace, because I know now that the books are worth far more to the Institute than I am. The books have taught me more than the Institute has, too--more of what I expected to learn, anyway.

I pick up my travel book--the only book I can concentrate on. If I go to Chapel Hill, I may get to take a vacation before I leave. If I end up working at the embassy...well, I will see these places later, I guess. In any case, if I am going to that conference in Belém, I must get a yellow fever shot for that region, and so I decide to head off to the Ministry of Health to get it. I leave work a couple hours early, with no shame, casually telling the receptionist that I am heading to the Ministry of Health. Maybe she will assume that, at long last, I, too, have important business with a "Ministry". Or maybe I will return tomorrow to find my boss has designated another employee to grill me about the purpose of this expedition, too. The shot hurts like hell, within minutes, and I can barely hold my arm up to drive my car home.

***

Every weekend, now, I give into despair. I return to bed every two hours, incapable of any activity. I want to lie very still and not have to think about anything or decide anything. After all, it never matters what I decide: I never get what I want, and when I do, it turns out I was wrong to want it. I just want to close my eyes all the time. I want somebody to kiss me and tell me I am alive, even though I am just lying here doing nothing. I cry every day--scared, scared of everything.

***

The oracle is proclaimed at last, and it is the University that delivers it. I am to give two weeks' notice to the Institute. I may or may not end up in Chapel Hill. I may or may not end up working at the embassy. I may possibly end up in another country, on another assignment. I will, without doubt, no longer be working with the Institute. I will leave Brazil and go to the great northern University until they decide where to place me for the second year of the program.

The phone is silent as the program administrator waits for my response. "I do not understand," I say weakly, scarcely breathing, feeling faint. I tried to take notes with my pen, but dropped it feebly, minutes ago. "If working at the embassy here is still a possibility, why can't I wait in Brasília until it's decided?"

282

"Program requirements: if you leave the Institute, you have to repatriate." He delivers the word "repatriate" like the punch line of some legalistic sermon. Requirements? I am on the verge of passing out, but my barely functioning brain still has enough blood to know that there would be no diplomatic incident if I sat around my apartment for a few weeks while this was sorted out...or traveled around Brazil until they decided.... Repatriate? Requirements? From the donor agency? What the hell difference does it make?! This is not an exchange of prisoners under the Geneva Convention!

"Leave my apartment, sell my car and telephone exchange and everything, close my Brazilian bank account, **move**--even though I might end up **back** here?!"

"We don't really have a choice." Who the hell is sticking a gun to your head? What are you--mental morons? You let some stupid by-law dictate insanity? I cannot believe that! They must have some leeway.... He must be lying.... The embassy must not be a possibility after all.... Why won't he just say that?

"Are you telling me that the embassy is an **un**likely possibility?"

"They have to submit a proposal to the program; it needs to go through the regular channels--the board, the donor agency, etc." He pronounces "regular" again, as if the donor agency would dismantle the entire program if we do one single, solitary thing not authorized in the manual. I grasp for straws, desperate to derail this nightmare before it picks up steam.

"Couldn't I take a one-month unpaid leave of absence while we are waiting?" Oh, God, I want so badly to work at the embassy. I don't want to be sent to Timbuktu. I don't want to sit in a hotel in the cold north, surrounded by boxes and boxes and boxes of my life, waiting for some clue as to where and when I can unpack again.

"No, but you can take your vacation."

I do not know how the conversation ends, but it ends. I close the office door and lie down on the carpet, thankful my officemate is not around. Am I fired? Is the Institute fired? Are we both fired?

283

The tears are choking me, but my breathing is too shallow and sporadic to draw them to the surface. I gasp for air and swallow them back down over and over again.

The driver's seat must be occupied by the donor agency--the link I know the least, the most obscure piece of the puzzle. It is a new program, and the University is scared to bend the donor's rules. What will happen when I get there? An inquisition to see if I deserve a second year, to determine where the fault **really** lies? **Move** to the University!? Relocate--**repatriate!**--to the University!? For what, two days perhaps? Or another plane ticket to Brasília, and another nightmarish round of buying all this crap again?

No, they would not **dare** do that: it is completely insane! They are not planning on my working in the embassy. Nobody would be **that** unwilling to bend the rules enough for me to stay around a couple weeks while the embassy faxes up a quick proposal. Maybe my supervisor up there does not have the **power** to refuse the proffered proposal, but has secretly rejected it in advance. Maybe, maybe....

My thought process gets nowhere, and my anxiety rises. I get up off the floor to write the resignation letter: he specifically asked me to submit it immediately. He said my Institute boss was expecting it. So...they **have** been having secret telephone conversations about my fate. To them I am a parcel delivery to be shipped back to the manufacturer for warranty-covered repairs. To them I am not a person with bruised flesh and spilled blood and broken heart: I am just a resumé that will be transferred from one filing cabinet to a different filing cabinet. Tonight they can each go home and make love to their women and gaze lovingly at framed photos of their children and have no boxes to pack.

My head is spinning. Who is really under the gun here? They have decided I cannot do further Institute work, not even in Chapel Hill. Does that mean the Institute has been kicked out of the program, or did the Institute want out of the program themselves? **They** are out of the program. **I** am **not** out of the program. **I** am **not** fired. Why do I feel I am being punished without being pronounced guilty? Or is it just that the jury is still deliberating on my own case?

Oh, let me go to the embassy! They **want** me there! **They want me!** Don't make me have to start job-hunting all over again! I can't bear it! I can't! I can't!

I call the embassy, trying to sound casual. "Well, I was wondering about this conference in Belém--"

"Well, that's not really a possibility now, due to your situation." *There's that word again! What "situation"?! I do not have leprosy! Please, explain my situation! I can go to Belém, I can go! I got the yellow fever shot! I've got the time! I can go to Belém!* "I've been on the phone every day to the States trying to convince them to let you work here. We are submitting a proposal but, to tell you the truth, they are very resistant to the idea. But we're trying."

They who? The University? The donor agency? **Who is resistant!?** My brain is too feeble to comprehend this. "Thanks--I really appreciate it." I fumble out some other niceties, then say goodbye. The donor agency did not set up this program for the purpose of staffing embassies, I know, but they also did not set up this program for the purpose of turning my life into a nightmare. Come on! Look at the alternative! Bend your damned rules! I can do good work at the embassy: I know I can! I know I can! Give me a chance!

The shock wears off and I finally burst into tears. She said they have been on the phone **every** day to the States, trying to convince them to let me work at the embassy! They want me, they need me, they love me! On the phone **every** day! They are fighting for **me**! Fighting to give me a chance to do some tiny little thing for Brazil--**in** Brazil--before I get "repatriated"! They are fighting to enlist me to help in their Amazon program, and, God, I will never have a chance like that again. Please, please, please, please, please. I do not want to see it only as a tourist, take some photos, and go home! Home? No, go to University purgatory. I have no home. God only knows what my future holds now. No, I do not even believe that. I think even God has lost interest in my--"life" is too rosy a word--in my existence.

285

Chapter 47

I stumble through my existence. I have no right to hope for anything. I have no freedom to plan anything--except the grand moving sale. I do not know where to begin. I find myself diving back into my bed over and over and over again. I am "consulting my pillow", as the Brazilians say. A year from now, will I remember how to say "consulting my pillow" in Portuguese? After five-hundred consultations, I still get no diagnosis, no prognosis, no prescription.

The news that I am leaving the Institute spreads like wildfire, and various people comment upon it to me. A couple of them say that they are happy **for** me, but the rest.... I am not sure what they really feel and cannot discern it by what they say. And many, many others have been quitting the Institute, not just me....

One woman tells me she knows somebody looking for a furnished apartment. Within a couple days, he steps across my threshold and declares love at first sight--with the apartment. Yes, that is how I felt when I saw it...empty as it was. I saw its potential. He is in love with the results: men do not fall in love with potential. What took me five months to put together, he will get as soon as the apartment owner agrees to transfer the lease. He looks over my furnishings carefully, agrees to buy the majority of my stuff, and makes me an offer I cannot refuse. When I finish out my last two weeks at the office, I will put up the rest for sale.

***

My last day of work arrives without fanfare, and I lug to the car my books, papers, maps, posters, and computer. I have not used

286

my books since the assignment I did many moons ago for the former President of the Institute. I never needed my books for anything I did for the new one, my boss. My papers are a pathetic assortment of unfinished, ill-conceived projects, mixed in with the remnants of my days doing real research in Charlottesville and Chapel Hill, and points in between.

My maps and posters were the most used items I had in the office: my eyes were constantly on them, thinking of other places I would have preferred to be, other things I would have preferred to do. The computer is an expensive telephone now: I will keep using it to link up with the University in the next few weeks...to link up with whomever I can.

I have already sent letters to everyone, telling them to send future correspondence to me in care of the University. Journals, banks, insurance companies, friends.... The entire exercise will have to be redone again, probably within a couple weeks of arriving in the States, maybe even twice more before I am really resettled somewhere. I tell myself I must do this so that the Institute will not be financially burdened with forwarding my mail, but the truth is I cannot bear for my personal letters to be delayed one day more than necessary. They are my sustenance. And maybe a pile of personal letters stacking up at the University will prove my humanity to the program administrator.

I am entering a letter warp: people might be writing to me at the University address long before I actually get up there. If I am stuck here for weeks and weeks, unable to sell my car or my things, they will not know. The people who care about me will not know-- these scattered remnants of past friendships, past homes, past lives. I wish they could always be with me. I wish more of them had the money to telephone me here. I do not want to be here if nobody knows I am. That is too alone, even for me.

Stephanie calls in the evening. "Was this really your last day of work?"

"You got my letter already?!" I am stunned and amazed.

"No--one of your old roommates got an email from you and called to ask what the latest was. Why didn't you call me?!"

"I wrote you a letter."

Why didn't you call me!!!? She is practically shouting. "For God's sake, I told you to call collect any time!"

"I just...." Oh, God, why is she so dense?! Do I have to spell it out?

"Come on! Talk to me!"

"I explained it all in the letter."

"I don't want to wait for the Goddamn letter!!!" I am stunned. She is furious, really furious.

I tell her everything that is going on, and not going on, and how I really do not know what is going to happen.

"Why didn't you call me?" Her voice is softer now, calmer.

Because you are living with the man I love, because I don't know why that makes me feel the way it makes me feel but I get depressed every time I talk to you, because sometimes I think I will never get out of this country alive and well. I have to say something. "Well, for one thing, there's nothing you can do, and for another, I still have lots of time left here. Getting out of the apartment, selling my car--this is all going to be slow. I figured you'd call me after you got the letter. There was no rush."

She is quiet for a moment. "Did you already plan your vacation?"

"Sort of. I have six cities in mind. The University owes me vacation money, so I think I can do it if I stay in cheap hotels." And what does it matter if I spend every penny from my moving sale traveling around Brazil? I have no other plans, no future purchases, in mind.

"We want to come with you." My mouth opens, but no words come out. I want to say "**WHAT**??!!", but nothing comes out. She is quiet for awhile, but then continues. "Actually, we have been talking

288

about this for awhile--doing a trip to Brazil, I mean. We thought we'd have more time to plan for it, but we'll just have to do it now." **Have** to do it? **WE?** "Is one of your cities in the Amazon? Michael really wants to see the Amazon. And he **really** wants to meet some Indians there."

"You and Michael have been planning a trip to Brazil?" My intermittent nausea rises up. No, this is not the vacation I want.

"And **Peter**!" My stomach subsides. "Well, I hope this cheers you up!" Her, Peter, Michael, and me--on vacation. No, this does **not** cheer me up.

"Steph, you must be joking! This will cost you a fortune! You just bought a house--remember?!"

"Don't worry about the money! We have that all taken care of!" What the hell is she talking about? A four-bedroom house in that county–they'll be paying off that mortgage forever! "When do you think you'll be ready for the vacation? We need to ask for time off at work." Oh, my God, she's serious!

"I don't know. Everything moves so slowly here."

"Well, let me know as soon as you can--call collect! And what cities did you pick? I'll tell Peter and Michael about them when they get home."

I tell her my tentative plans, and we finally get off the phone. I lie down and try to think of one thing in my life that still makes sense, but fail.

Chapter 48

The owner of the apartment gives me the runaround about getting out of the lease, the University gives me the runaround about paying my way out of the lease, and my apartment suitor gives me the runaround about making a deal with me to take over the lease. Days stretch confoundedly into weeks as I play telephone tag with everyone, ship some stuff to the States, give some other stuff away, sell odds and ends, and schedule a massage for every single night of the week in which I am not at dance class. I am dancing up a storm now--pagode, bolero, foxtrot, cha-cha-cha, salsa, meringue, forró, and half a dozen varieties of samba--but Fernando has invited me to no more parties.

I try not to think about my future, but strange imaginings vent themselves night after night in my dreams. I dream my best friend in Chicago has a miscarriage, and am wildly relieved the next day to reach her on the phone and hear she has delivered a healthy baby boy. I dream that the entire World Bank staff has been relocated to Cuahtemoc, Mexico, and awaken the next morning thinking what a financial boom that would be for the Bank now that the Mexican peso has crashed. I dream that one of those stars from some new vampire movie I do not want to see asks me out on a date, and takes me to a bar mitzvah where pancakes and maple syrup are being served, and I am stunned to learn that bar mitzvahs have a food in common with Fridays in Lent, and I ask my date if he himself has had a bar mitzvah, and he laughs out loud, declaring that he does not even know which side of his family is Jewish; I start to ask him how he could not know a thing like that, but he just laughs again and pours more maple syrup on. I awaken the next morning completely bewildered, but cannot forget the mischievous smile on his face when he asked me out, nor my uncharacteristically relaxed, carefree, instinctively automatic reply, "OK", and how happy I felt when we were smiling at each other, and I knew he was definitely not a vampire, and I knew he would be nice to me.

Fernando calls weeks after Carnival and tells me what a wonderful time they had and how much he wishes I could have gone. He asks how I spent Carnival, but I have already forgotten.

"Probably watching TV," I reply. I vaguely remember seeing some parades on the tube, but they were not nearly as entertaining as the new soap opera I am totally engrossed in or one of the rare American imports I can catch dubbed into Portuguese. I watch TV religiously now, justifying it because it is contributing to my geometrically increasing Portuguese vocabulary, even though it skews my vocabulary towards that of heroic Brazilian underdogs in Minas Gerais and heroic FBI agents in Washington, D.C. I can understand just about anything on TV now, though I would be hard-pressed to explain how learning to say "throw down your weapons and come out of there with your hands up"--whether it is being said to fugitive *garimpeiros* or furtive supernatural lunatics--will prove particularly useful to me.

He hears something in my voice, and asks what is wrong. Yes, what **is** wrong with somebody who spends Carnival home alone, watching TV? That was not the plan. I have hardly talked to him--**really** talked to him--ever. He did not know that for a few weeks of my life, I thought I was returning to Chapel Hill. He does not know that for a few weeks of my life, I thought I was staying here after all, to work in the U.S. Embassy's Overseas Development division. He does not know that for a few weeks after that, I thought I was fired until the University said it would send me the airline pass for my vacation in Brazil. He still knows nothing about me.

"I'm just sort of tense. My life is really confusing right now. The University decided to pull me out of this placement, but has not yet decided where to send me. After I sell everything, I get a long vacation, then I head north to find out what is happening."

He is silent for a moment. "You mean, you're leaving Brazil?"

"Yeah."

He is silent again, for a long time. "I feel so bad. I've been so busy....I never showed you the things I wanted to show you, I never--"

"It's OK. It wasn't your obligation."

"Yeah, but you're Stephanie's sister, you're here all alone, I wanted to help you out more--I **should** have helped you out more."

"You have much bigger things to worry about! You have an important job."

"Sometimes....Sometimes I'm not so sure about that....Look, what about this vacation? I can show you a beautiful place in Amazônia, take you to an Indian reserve: I mean, I will be working, but I think you will really enjoy it. You have to see the Amazon before you leave!"

"Yeah...." My mind is racing. No! Yes! No! Yes.... He can introduce Michael to Indians-- **really** introduce Michael to Indians. He knows Indians. But Stephanie! She will not be able to handle this! What am I thinking? There is no way he will do it if he finds out Stephanie is coming--Stephanie and her quasi-fiancé.

He interrupts my thoughts. "You know, I have been really busy, but I could have called you more, I could have taken you to some parties. The truth is, I just can't stop thinking about Stephanie when I'm with you. I have never been really religious, but I started thinking you were sent here by God to remind me what a huge mistake I made breaking up with Stephanie." He is quiet for a moment. *Is that why I'm here? Did I have to use up a whole year of my life just for this, God?* "Well, I know it's too late. Anyway, she deserves better than me....Sometimes I thought, if I helped you enjoy your time here, she would appreciate it, and maybe somehow forgive me." *Forgive him?* "It scared me to be with you, though, I mean, it made me think of her and it hurt....Has she...has she forgiven me?"

"Actually, I haven't told her I met you here."

292

He mumbles an understanding affirmative, but I know he is misreading my motive for not telling her. "Well, none of this matters now. I can't believe you're already leaving! But I suppose you are glad?"

"I don't know. I still don't know what my next job will be. Anything could happen."

"You'll get something good! I know you will!" Sure you do. "So...how about the Amazon? I think I can really make an interesting trip for you: I have been visiting the *Waiãpis* a lot, and they are really fascinating. They are struggling right now with gold prospectors invading their lands. We are trying to get the situation resolved peacefully. It is a beautiful area: there are a million things to see there. Do you want to go?"

"I would, but--"

"No `buts'! There won't be any problems! I know how to do this right: you'll have clean water, protection from malaria and dengue, safe food, no tarantulas, no piranha, nothing to worry about!"

"Yeah, right!"

"Well, almost nothing to worry about! But, really--"

"Fernando, the thing is...Stephanie wants to go to the Amazon with me." Silence. "She has a wonderful boyfriend--it's not like you would have to feel guilty for leaving her--but, well, I think neither of you would enjoy seeing each other again." Not to mention that Peter would probably drop dead if he saw this gorgeous guy and had even one iota of a suspicion that Stephanie might still have any feelings for him...or vice versa...or both....

"Well...it's OK with me. If it's OK with her, it's OK with me. I never showed her Brazil, either: I owe her that."

"I don't think she'll enjoy thinking of you `owing' her a tour of the Amazon."

"I **want** to do it! I want to give her something wonderful, something adventurous, something dreamy....Is **he** coming?"

"Yes."

"Perfect." *Perfect?!* "I will make this an unforgettably romantic vacation for them. That will be my penance. And that will be my proof to her that I never wanted to make her unhappy." I say nothing, trying to understand this. My vacation-- **my vacation**--but Stephanie will be the one with three adoring guys, and I will have nobody. I instantly pray to God to forgive me for that selfish, evil, and unjust thought...but I am still pissed.

"Well, I'll ask her what she thinks."

"What's **his** name?"

"Peter."

"You think he's the jealous type?" Jealous?! He didn't even complain when Michael was living rent-free with Stephanie! But...as she hinted...Michael was an ex-convict half-breed.... Of course, Fernando could be an ex-convict, and he is certainly sprinkled with Brazil's racial spices...but he is Stephanie's ex, not my ex.... Maybe Peter **will** be jealous? "I take that as a yes?"

"Oh, ummmm, I don't know, Fernando. They're pretty serious, I think. They bought a house together." Low whistle. "Maybe he doesn't worry about other guys anymore, but I don't know him. I know that he knows Stephanie was engaged to you, and that it was not her idea to break it off."

"Well...look, if you think it will help, I can give her a call."

"No!" Geez, it's **my** vacation! "I will talk to her...I mean, first I have to tell her that I met you here."

"Oh, right."

We finally get off the phone, and I consult my pillow again. Good thing I am selling this pillow: it has never given me any answers. I roll over to stare at the wall whose posters have already been removed. I cannot bear the bleak whiteness of the wall and roll onto my back to stare at the ceiling. The ceiling light quickly blinds me, and I shut my eyelids. I need to call Stephanie. I need to call Stephanie. I cannot move. I cannot move. I cannot move one muscle.

The light is burning through my eyelids. The phone rings.

I bolt off the bed. It is my apartment suitor. He is cheating behind my back--I know it--looking at other apartments, other people's goods, stringing me along, keeping me on the back burner. It has been three weeks since he first said he wanted to take over the lease and buy all my stuff.... He now announces he will not take over my lease but **is** willing to buy my stuff. Fine, I reply, **if** I can get out of my lease. He does not understand.

"Look, if I sell all my stuff to you, I can't keep living here! I'm not going to pay for a hotel at the same time that I am still paying for this apartment! Stop pressuring me!!"

"OK! I didn't mean to pressure you....I'll put my proposal in the mail."

I hang up, alarmed at myself. How could I lose my temper with **him**? I need his money: if he falls through, it could take weeks to sell all this crap. I need to call the landlady again.... No, I need to call Stephanie and get it over with. I will just lie down and close my eyes for a little while longer.

Chapter 49

I dig out my telephone book to look up her new number in the Maryland suburbs. Not that I actually remember her old number in D.C. I cannot remember anybody's phone numbers now: Mexican and Brazilian long-distance rates took care of that. I look at the clock: yes, she should be home from work by now. I call collect, and the Hmong woman answers and slowly deciphers from the operator "Brazil".

"Yes! Yes! OK! Jussaminnit." I hear some hollering, kids' voices, a TV, then somebody picking up a different extension, then the first extension being hung up.

"I don't know anybody in Brazil--not anybody that ever **calls**!"

"Hi, Michael!" I am already smiling. "I've written you a zillion letters: doesn't that count!?"

"Of course it doesn't count! You write three letters for every one of mine: it just makes me feel guilty!"

"I have more time on my hands: I have nothing but envy of people too busy to write letters!"

"It's not like I'm busy having a **good** time!" He has already lost some of his drawl, but his voice is inexplicably softer than it was before, sharper but quieter at the same time. "I've been doing more and more stuff for Amnesty International: things are really heating up!" I cannot believe his enthusiasm: he sounds ten years younger than we are. "And I'm still working full-time, and we had a lot to do with the move--but that's all boring, you don't need to hear about

296

that." Don't you know I could spend an entire day just listening to you read from an auto manual? "When do we go on vacation??!!"

"Michael, you **know** I'd love nothing more than for you guys to all come down here, but I just don't understand how you can afford it."

"Don't worry about that: we're rolling in the dough!"

"I'm serious!"

"So am I! Look, we have the money, so don't worry about it! Now, when do we go? I can't wait to see you!" Me? **ME?** I thought he wanted to see Indians. **ME?!**

"It's still touch and go. I am fighting with this family to get out of the lease. I almost had this guy lined up to take over the lease, but that fell through, so I need to wait for the family to decide about letting me out of the lease."

"Just leave! What the hell: you think they're gonna send bill collectors to the States?!"

"Believe me, I would, except for the fact that my boss is co-signor on the lease."

"Ho-HO!"

"I just don't want to stick him with **that** as my parting gift."

"Sounds like he deserves it!"

"Don't tempt me! I just can't do it. He's probably already written horrible reports about me. I don't need to piss him off anymore."

"You're the one who should be pissed off!"

"I **am**! But getting him more pissed off is not going to make things any better for me....So...I need to talk them out of the lease. Then, if that ever happens, I still need to sell my telephone exchange, and then after I sell that, I'll sell my car. It could still be a few weeks."

"Well, move like ya got a purpose, girl!" I start laughing, remembering the way he used to tease me with that macho army crap on those rare occasions when I actually let him talk me into

297

hiking in the mountains. He felt bad, later, when he learned about my knee operations. He kissed and apologized to each scar individually. He could not believe I had not told him.... I was so afraid of him thinking me a wimp.

"I'm moving as fast as I can! Everything is slow here: I don't know how to explain it to you."

"Well, I hope things pick up soon! I sure don't want this damned yellow fever vaccination to wear off: it hurt like hell!" I laugh. "We've been reading about these places you picked, and we're totally psyched! Do you think we'll really meet Indians in Rio Branco? I mean, not just sail by 'em in a canoe?"

"Well, actually I am leaning towards Macapá now."

"Ma-kuh-what?"

"Macapá--it's in Amapá."

"A-muh-what?"

"It's at the other end, the northern border. I know somebody who has been working up there: actually, he's been doing human rights campaign work for the Indians."

"Oh, my God! You're kidding?!"

"No. He can introduce us to some Indians in the reserves, but the situation is sort of complicated. Actually, I need to talk to Stephanie about it: she will probably not want to go there."

"Is there violence?"

"Well, that would make **me** not want to go! Stephanie will have a different reason."

"Typhoid? Cholera?"

"No...ummm...is she there?"

"Nope."

An evil thought pops into my head: make Michael tell her. I seize it before my conscience can talk me out of it. "Michael, do you remember hearing about Stephanie's old boyfriend from Brazil?"

"Fernando? Yeah."

"Well, it's him: he's the guy."

"The guy-what?"

"The guy who can show us around Amapá."

Silence. "You know Fernando?"

"Yeah."

More silence. "Why didn't you ever tell Stephanie you knew Fernando?" His voice is more than accusatory.

I am not totally sure myself. "Well, I hardly know him at all, actually." True enough. "I have only seen him a few times." True enough. I pause. "Mostly, I just didn't see any point in telling her: she would have wanted to know a million details about his life, it would have just upset her."

"Are you dating this guy?"

"No! Of course not!"

"C'mon! What are you holding back?!"

My heart is pounding. "I just feel sort of...guilty. I mean, nothing happened, but...I just...sort of liked him, and I felt guilty about that....I don't even really like him....It's just that....I haven't met any guys here, I mean, none that were available and interesting and....It was nice to get some attention."

"How much attention?"

"Michael! Geez!"

"Look, you can't just fool around 'cause you're lonely! Shit! Do you know how many cases of AIDS Brazil has?"

"AIDS!? All he did was kiss me! And, yes, I know **exactly** how many cases of AIDS Brazil has. Didn't I tell you about that long family planning project--"

"So you **were** dating him!"

"**No!** It was New Year's Eve: he was bombed out of his mind. He probably thought I was Stephanie. He didn't even remember it

299

afterwards." He is silent. "He's not interested in me at all. In fact, I'm not sure he's really over Stephanie." He is still silent. "He knows about Peter, though, and he still wants to take us to Amapá. I think he's being sincere: I think he wants to do a good deed for her, you know?"

"How do you know he doesn't want to do a good deed for **you**? Maybe he **does** remember New Year's Eve! Maybe he **didn't** have you confused with Stephanie! Hell, you don't look like her at all!"

My God! Is he jealous?! I thought he was angry on **her** behalf! "He met me five months ago! Don't you think I would have gotten more than a New Year's Eve drunken kiss by now?!"

"I don't know! Maybe you're sending him mixed signals! You sound kinda mixed up about him."

"Mixed up?! Look, he's a cute guy that was nice to me when I hardly had any friends: that's all. I would have felt the same about any other guy in those circumstances."

"No, you wouldn't have: you would have grabbed any other guy that nice. You held back because of Stephanie."

"No, I didn't! I held back because...because...there was nothing there! There never was! God, don't you know how hard it is for me to find a guy?!" Oh, shit, why did I say that.

"I'm sorry....I'm sorry....I was just...so surprised by all that. I'm sorry."

"It's OK."

"Oh, God....Things...things have gotten so crazy for everybody....I know you're worried about your career and money and where you're gonna end up and everything, but I'm glad you're coming back....I mean, that job was just all wrong for you...and you'll find something better....And you'll find a good guy, too: you will, believe me, you will." I cannot think of anything to say, nothing that would not be interrupted by my bursting into tears halfway through it. "Look, I'll talk to Stephanie. Actually, it would probably be good for her to see Fernando once more, close that door once and for all. Pete's the guy for her." Pete's the guy for her?! Is Michael really saying that?! "I'll just tell her you never told her about meeting him because you didn't want her to start thinking about him again."

"And he's had two or three girlfriends just since I met him! Tell her **that**: I mean, tell her that if you think it will help."

"OK. Wow...this is going to be an interesting vacation." Tell me about it.

"She's never going to agree to this, Michael."

"Yes she will."

"And Peter?"

"He doesn't give a shit about her old boyfriends. He just looks forward in his life." Wow. "We'll call you back soon, OK?"

"OK."

"I'm sorry I got kind of--"

"It's OK! It's OK. It was really nice to talk to you, Michael."

"Look, I mean, if you did like some guy, you wouldn't be afraid to tell me, would you?"

"You never tell me when **you** like anybody."

"I would if I did."

"Would you?"

"Yeah!"

"There's such a shortage of good guys in D.C.: women must be hounding you!"

"No...it's not like that." He is so quiet I can barely hear him. "We'll have plenty of time to talk when I get there-- **really** talk. I've wanted to talk to you about so many things, for so long. God, I've missed you." I shove my right fist into my mouth to muffle my cry.

"I've missed you, too," I mumble.

He is quiet for a moment. "We'll talk soon."

301

I lie down and roll over to stare at the blank wall through the blur of tears. I am crying my eyes out for somebody who now has a phone number I do not even know. Why do I feel as if he is the only man who I have ever understood, and never understood? Why do I feel that he is the only one who has ever understood me, but has never understood me? Maybe he does understand me...well enough to know he does not want me. When will I get over him?

Chapter 50

Things slowly come together. After I leave increasingly frantic messages on their answering machine, the family finally agrees to let me out of the lease. I call back my apartment suitor, and, a few days later, he arrives at my condominium with a moving truck and a fat check. With the help of a cheap and extraordinarily talented maid, I cart the remainder of my belongings off to the vacated apartment of a vacationing co-worker, and do a thorough cleaning job in my own apartment. I leave behind one painting, two buckets, two kitchen towels, one sponge mop, several cleaning supplies, the one window screen I did not manage to sell, and immaculately gleaming floors. I am sad when I shut the door. I will miss the dark wood floor. I will miss the view of the lake.

Moved, I quickly announce for sale my telephone exchange and car. After a few unsuccessful days, I realize the prices in the newspaper are mere fantasies, and start dropping my prices until I finally sell the telephone exchange and Chevy at the end of the week. I wonder if I should feel guilty as the man drives off with my cursed car, but maybe it **is** all fixed up now...and he will know better than I how to keep it that way.

By the weekend, I am ready to make airline reservations and call Takoma Park. Stephanie accepts the collect call. "So, what's the deal?"

"I'll be ready to go next week."

"Next week?!"

303

"Yeah--well, I really didn't know until now that all my assets would be liquidated." She laughs. "I had a shitload of assets here! Things here are expensive, I'm telling you!"

"I know! I just thought it was funny, hearing you talking about `liquidating assets'!" She does not sound upset with me in the slightest. Surely he told her about Fernando by now?

"So, what do you think, Steph: when can you go?"

"Pretty soon! Our bosses knew it would probably be next week, or the week after."

"Great! Ummm, Steph, did you talk to Michael?"

"Yesssssss....So...you ran into Fernando five months ago and never told me?"

"Well, I guess I just didn't see much point in telling you: it would only have upset you....Wouldn't it have?"

"Not as much as wondering why you never told me."

I am silent, trying to remember my rehearsed explanation: I should have written it down. "He was really nice to me, and I didn't want to tell you that, especially after I forced him to explain breaking off your engagement."

"He explained it to **you**?" I offer a quiet affirmative. "Gee, how nice! He never explained it to **me**!"

"Well, I don't think he really could have put his finger on it when it happened. I think he must have needed to reflect on it awhile to understand why he did it." I try to repeat the things he said, how being in love in Brazil was different than being in love in the U.S., how Brasília would not have matched Stephanie's expectations of Brazil, and, finally, how he could not resist Brazilian women after not seeing them for so long.

"Uh-huh." She sounds nonchalant. "Did he put the moves on you?"

Shit! Why did she ask that? "Only once, when he was really drunk on New Year's Eve: and he even said I looked like you, and he

304

didn't remember it afterwards."

"You were afraid to tell me **that**?!"

No, I was afraid to tell you how much I **enjoyed** kissing him.... "I just didn't see the point."

"OK, we'll talk about this when we get there." Great, this is going to be such a fun vacation. "I'll go to Ah-muh-pah: the damn bastard owes me this!"

"Steph! C'mon! Don't agree to this just to torture him! What about Peter?"

"I'm not going to torture anybody. And Peter's cool about it. The important thing is that Fernando can introduce Michael to some Indians." Yes, you have made it abundantly clear to me that **that** is the important thing in **my** vacation. "Let's work out the details."

"I was thinking of going to the Northeast and South first, so do you guys want to meet up with me in Amapá later...?"

***

That night, I go to a birthday party for the daughter of a friend of a friend. It is a lovely party, in the lovely garden of a lovely house, full of lovely people. I am not supposed to be getting emotionally involved in Brazil anymore, so I try to avoid meeting anybody. I just came to help with childcare, really. I walk clunkily around in old shoes that I will throw out before I pack for the trip. Despite my best efforts not to be, I am introduced to many new people, though they ultimately fail to get to know me because I have no answer to any of their questions. "Where do you live?" "What do you do?" "Where are you from?" I don't know. I don't know. I don't know.

On Monday, I am ready to pick up my tickets and buy travelers' checks. The bank tells me they can only sell back half the number of dollars I have previously exchanged in Brazil. The shocking news explodes simultaneously in my brain and in the pit of my stomach, and I burst into wild, hysterical tears. **Oh, my God!** I may have to leave money **behind**??!!! I scramble around to three different tellers in two different departments trying to sort it all out. They are all so calm: they could care less! Damn them all!!! I will sell my *reais* illegally if I have to! I scramble to add up my money exchange receipts. How many dollars have I sold here? How many *reais* do I have to sell back?

The panic subsides as I realize that I have enough dollar exchange receipts to prove my worthiness to buy back several thousand American dollars. My liquid assets. They tell me which bank branch to go to, and they tell me to bring my Brazilian currency in cash! I withdraw thousands of dollars worth of *reais*--leaving a few hundreds' worth for my vacation--and hop straight into a cab, terrified we will have a car accident and all my money will burst into flames. We make it, and I move my wobbly legs back to the correct money exchange department, clutching my fanny pack snugly against my womb. A half an hour later, I leave the bank with U.S. travelers' checks and their serial numbers scattered strategically around my body and bags. I am mobile now. I am liquidated.

I return to the travel agent, but the tickets are still not ready, and he sends me to another office instead, but at long last I can return to the apartment to pack. I am going on vacation.

I stop by the office in the morning to send a fax to the University with the details of my itinerary, and discover they have already sent a fax to me about my itinerary for my visit up north. I read it with trepidation: Spanish Inquisition at 11:00 a.m., torture chamber at 1:00 p.m., guillotine at 3:00 p.m.? No...no...it does not say anything about what will happen after I get there: only that they have made reservations for me to stay three nights. **Three??!!** What does **that** mean? Will they take three whole days to fire me? Do they have another assignment for me and need only three days to orient me? If they have an assignment, why don't they tell me **now**?! NO! NO! No, they must be planning to fire me! Why do they need three days to fire me?! I take a cab to the airport and begin my vacation full of dread.

Chapter 51

Four hours later, I touch down in the colonial Northeast, the part of Brazil first settled by the Portuguese. I am looking for the "hundreds of kilometers of glorious beaches" and the "most African culture outside of Africa". The gang will not join up with me for awhile, and I will have to enjoy the first legs of my journey all alone. It is pouring rain as the cab driver takes me to my carefully chosen, moderately priced hotel, near a "swimmable" beach.

I unpack and wait for sun...and wait...and wait. Finally, it momentarily lets up, and I race down to the beach as the sun begins to set in the west. I have not set foot in the Atlantic Ocean since...I do not even remember...years. I step in gingerly...but this is not a Carolina shoreline after a hard rain in the fall: **this** is **bathwater**!

I dive fully in as the warm ecstasy encompasses my body and the fantastic waves lift me up over and over again. I am lost--finally outside of my head. I think of absolutely nothing other than the imprecise calculations needed to ride each wave to its maximum pleasure. I love the water, and am starting to believe in God again.

I reluctantly get out as darkness falls, and head back to the hotel, exhausted and hungry. I fall asleep in that ethereal state of believing my body is still being rocked by the waves. I fall asleep peacefully and quickly, and wake up for the first time in a million years **eager** to get out of bed. I open the curtain to look out on my "glorious beach": my heart sinks at the sight of pouring rain. I will **not** waste my vacation! I make arrangements for a city tour; surely I will have a sunny day tomorrow.

It is a dreary city--gray and wet. We are herded onto and off of the bus over and over again, dutifully photographing blurry images of the special places we are shown: a fort built by the Portuguese to guard against Dutch invaders, colonial-style government buildings, renovated docks and lighthouses. We stop at a crafts store full of mysterious Indian artwork manufactured in other states where Indians still reside. The Afro-Brazilian art is far more authentic-looking. I buy some African musical instruments after seeing them impressively demonstrated. I buy some tiny paintings, too, then get back on the bus.

They cart us off to the ecological park. Three-quarters of the crowd refuse to get off the bus because of the rain. I tramp off to photograph the mangrove swamps. The glistening green lushness almost makes me cry after a year in the high, dry plateau of the Federal District.

The air conditioning on the bus comes even closer to making me cry. Those of us wet from the ecological park plead for the AC to be shut off, but the majority who stayed on the bus and are drier demand that it stay on. I am chilled to the bone by the time I retreat to my hotel. I spend the evening reading up on the variety of beaches I can explore: white dunes, pebble beaches, black "radioactive" (?!) sands. What shall it be?

I awake to pouring rain. God! My throat hurts, and my ears are smarting. Just a cold? Or worse? Should I have worn ear plugs at my "clean, swimmable" beach? I envision microbes and parasites burrowing down my ear canal, down my esophagus, down into....

I will not even bother finding a doctor. I go straight to the pharmacy--bundled up in slicker and rubber boots--to buy antibiotic eardrops. I will **not** be sick on my vacation! I head back to the hotel and book another excursion--this time to a more historical town a little further away. I board the bus in the rain, and disembark two hours later in a town square surrounded by the impressive governor's mansion, an historic museum, and two colonial cathedrals. Wow! I suddenly feel I am in Latin America--the one I thought I knew so well, before I came to Brasília.

I click and click, knowing the photos will be lousy but wanting to capture it anyway. So beautiful. Click. We are being led up and down quaint old residential districts now. Click, click. The Portuguese built these houses long ago--back when it was politically correct to steal South America from the Amerindians and Africans from Africa. Slave labor wrought beautiful things on blood-stained land. Click. I pause to watch an African-Brazilian dance being performed. Click. A hat is passed, and I toss in a dollar.

We are ushered quietly into the world's most gold-laden cathedral. No clicks allowed. Gold-painted walls, gold-coated candle holders, gold-covered pillars, gold-overlaid statues, gold-adorned altar. I would not click it if I could: I am appalled. I look around in amazement, trying to figure out what a solid gold cherubim and emerald-eyed seraphim have to do with the Good News. What did the slave laborers of this cathedral think of this tribute to the white man's God? Did they know how many Africans were enslaved in the gold mines to make this possible? I remember the cathedral in Cuahtemoc, whose bishop stripped the gold off the walls to sell it for the poor. This place is long overdue.

I get back on the bus, gloomy. It is still raining, and my ears feel worse. I tilt my head to the left, squirt in my ear drops, wait ten minutes, tilt to the right, and squirt again. The tour guide smiles at me. I guess I look pretty ridiculous. One by one, everyone is dropped off at their hotels until only I am left. The guide sits next to me. "How are your ears?"

"I have an infection."

He shakes his head sympathetically. "You know, I can take you to see a *Candomblé* ceremony tonight, if you like?" I look at him dubiously. I do not want to spend gobs of money to see the tourist version of an African religious ceremony. "It's **very** interesting." He does not give up easily. "I'm Marcos Antônio," he says, smilingly. "What's your name?"

Wait a minute here.... A suspicion is creeping into my mind.... Maybe it's not **money** he's after.... He starts telling me about *Candomblé*. He is part African...and part Indian...and part

309

Portuguese...and actually very interesting-- **whoa!** His hand is on my knee, and waves of heat flood my body. God, he **is** cute. I want this. I want it bad. No...no, I don't. This is crazy! I won't even be in this town after tomorrow. I am leaving Brazil at the end of the month. He slides his hand up my thigh as I stare into his warm brown eyes. He could be a lunatic. He could be planning to drug me and steal all my stuff. He slides his hand up further. We are nearly at my hotel now.

I have said nothing beyond my name. Marcos Antônio continues speaking. I understand all the Portuguese words, not that I need to. "I live really close to your hotel. I could come back and pick you up--take you somewhere."

"OK." I get out, wondering if the bus driver had figured out what was going on. Maybe he knows. Maybe the tour guide always picks up one of the gringas. It is not raining at this end of town. I go to my room to get ready and figure out what I am going to do. A date! It's a miracle! I should not be doing this. This is not really a date. I would just be using him. But **he** wanted the date so badly. Should I change my clothes? No--he must have liked what I had on already. I put on some perfume and brush my hair and change to dry shoes. Should I let him take me "somewhere"? The desk calls to tell me I have a visitor. I go downstairs, determined to be disciplined.

He smiles at me and starts telling me about the places he is planning to take me...in his van!

"Ummm, I would rather just walk down to the beach."

"The beach?"

"Yeah." He is crestfallen, but acquiesces. When I see the perfect spot, I spread out my towel. Yes...there is privacy here, but it is still close enough to the street that I could let go some blood-curdling screams if he turns into a violent rapist, robber, murderer.... He is looking around dejectedly.

"Maybe we could find a place with more privacy?"

"No, this is fine." I do not want to get **more** private than this. He looks at me, puzzled. I think he is hurt. How can I explain to him my fears? I cannot. I smile at him and put my arms around him. He smiles and moves closer Mmmmmm.... I had forgotten how luscious this can be. Mmmmmmmm.... Wow.... This guy knows what he is doing. It feels so good to be in his arms.... Mmmmmmmmm.... "**NO!**"

He is puzzled again. I have stopped him from undressing me any further.

"We're not going to do **that**." Yes, I am going to be selfish. I pull him tight against me and get what I want and it feels marvelous. When it is over, I hold on longer because I know he has not gotten what he wants and will have a much more difficult time getting it than I did. His kisses grow monotonous, the sweetness evaporates, and suddenly it just takes like **spit**, and soon I want him to stop kissing me, and by the time he does, I am nearly nauseous.

I tell him I am cold and put my shirt back on, and he walks me back to the hotel, pleading for a second date. I feel evil when I say no, but the truth is I do not even like him anymore--or something about this--even if I were not leaving town soon. I emphasize to him that I am leaving town and leaving Brazil and that he just has to face the facts. I muster a very tender goodbye kiss, and go upstairs to my room to brush my teeth for five minutes. I do not remember ever getting kisses that tasted so much like spit before! What is wrong with me? I go to bed feeling a freak.

Morning dawns brightly, and I book a quick morning boat ride before my afternoon flight. The sky is an extraordinary-- virtually impossible--shade of blue. Is this the same sky that has ruined two dozen photographs? The boat whisks us up and down the--and I can affirm this now--"glorious" coastline. Mmmmmm. I wish Marcos Antônio had his hand on my thigh right now. No, that is a lie. I wish Michael had his arm around me. Spit?! **Michael** never tasted like spit! It is suddenly beautiful here, but I have to leave.

Nine hours later I touch down in the deep southern hemisphere--in a very cold rain. **Really** cold. It must be only fifty degrees here! In my hotel room they turn on the heater for me--the first heater I have seen in Brazil. My ear infection has worsened, and I gloomily shoot more ear drops before unpacking. I open my suitcase and discover shrimp juice from some traveler's food crate has leaked into my suitcase and everything stinks of prawns. I squirt jasmine cologne over all my clothes and go to sleep, too exhausted and penny-pinching to think about whether I should pay the hotel launderers to wash every item of clothing in the suitcase. I sleep through the night and half the next day before mustering the courage to face rainy Curitiba. It is the dry season here, and I am really, really pissed at the rain. I head out to see the "ecological capital" of Brazil.

I am impressed: parks, plazas, pedestrian malls, aesthetic street vendor booths, street musicians, European and colonial architecture blended into modernity, high rises scarcely noticeable, more parks, more and more parks. I am clicking up a storm. I want to live here. I want to work here. Look at these great bookstores, artists on the street, musicians on the corners, flowers, trees, buses instead of cars: why, it **is** an urban planner's paradise! I should march right into the mayor's office and ask for a job....

I snap back to reality: I **have** a job, ha, ha. Anyway, what would they hire me for? They have obviously got the planning of this place under control: I could only screw it up, now. What do I have to offer such a perfect place? Click, click. No, it is too good to be ruined by me. It would probably rain every day, if **I** lived here.

I wander around for a few more rainy days, trying to stop loving this city and trying to get psyched up for meeting the gang in Rio. Well, at least we do not have to deal with Fernando until Macapá. At last the day arrives and I fly to Rio de Janeiro to rendezvous with Stephanie, Peter, and Michael in the airport. I keep thinking I need to plan what I will say to them: why am I so afraid of our spontaneous reunion? Peter will be suspicious, Stephanie will be peculiar, Michael will be unfathomable. I give up and go back to my earphones. The plane touches down in pouring rain. It is not supposed to be raining here at this time of year.

312

Chapter 52

I go to the restroom to freshen up. I sniff for prawns and administer some more jasmine. I should have splurged and spent the two-hundred dollars it would have cost to launder all my clothes at the hotel, instead of just laundering the ones that got the direct hit of shrimp cocktail. I should have thrown them all out and sold the suitcase and bought a lightweight duffel bag and the "couple changes of clothes" travel experts always talk about, except that I could never figure out how to do that when you are going to go from ninety degrees down to fifty and back up to ninety, from rain to sun and back to rain, when you do not want to waste precious vacation time doing handwash in the sink every night or waste precious money paying hotel launderers over and over and over again.

I go to the commode and squeal in horror as my bracelet drops off my wrist and into the toilet--not the Senegalese bracelet Michael gave me! I gingerly pull it out and race to the sink to wash it off. Can bracelets harbor cholera? I soap and rinse and resoap and rerinse, and by now the cleaning lady is eyeing me with curiosity. I tell her what happened and ask her if I can use her bathroom disinfectant to clean it. I scrub and rinse and rescrub and rerinse, and I can tell she is inwardly laughing at me. She can probably smell the shrimp, too. I want to smell like jasmine and wear the bracelet for Michael to see.

I head out to discover where their arrival gate will be. Their flight is not listed on the monitors. Oh, God! What happened to them? Don't panic, we have a back-up plan, we know what hotel we are going to stay at.... I finally find an airline employee who can look

313

up their flight on the computer system.... It will be four hours late. Shit! No, this is good, late is good, crashed is bad.

I could buy a magazine or a newspaper...or work on some crossword puzzles...or open up my suitcase in a smoking lounge to disguise the lingering prawn scent...or read my book...or spend four hours psychoanalyzing myself and preventing an emotional earthquake when I see Michael. Well, my psychoanalysis usually only works in unrehearsed spurts of inspiration: I had better not push it. I buy an American newspaper and try to catch up on my once and future world.

I finish it with plenty of time to spare--which I know for certain since their flight out of Miami has now shown up on the monitors--and start perusing postcards of Rio de Janeiro. My...God.... They are not kidding about this place. Wow. This is soooooooooo beautiful. I look out the window at the rain--please, please, please.... I look at more postcards. The architecture is not very impressive: it is the nature. They call this the "Marvelous City", but they never should have built a city here. It is an extraordinary place.

I buy a snack because my head is light, but my stomach is not in it. I am nervous. Stupidly nervous. You are never going to get back together with Michael. He is "just a friend" now. God, it will be so good to get a hug from him. It will be good to get a hug from Stephanie, too. I hope I become friends with Peter. Brother-in-law: boy, does that sound stodgy.

I work on crossword puzzles to occupy my mind until my hand cramps up and the hour is upon me. I sit expectantly at the customs gate, my heart pounding. Whom should I hug first? I guess I had better hug Stephanie first. Well, I guess I should hug whomever is closest, first. Why must I rehearse this in my mind?! This should be easy. They have all come to see me. They will all be happy to see me.

I return to the bathroom every ten minutes that pass without the plane's touchdown being announced on the monitor. It is later than the monitor predicted. I look out at the rain, trying to hold the panic down in my guts. Finally, on my fourth return trip from the

314

bathroom, the monitor says the plane has landed. Now I must wait for them to get through immigration and customs. Ten minutes later I decide I need another trip to the bathroom, but swear this is the **last** one. Fifteen minutes after that, I go again. I return to the throng of people waiting at the customs gate, dig out my hand lotion to soothe my raw, over-washed hands, and suddenly remember to put Michael's bracelet back on: it has been in my fanny pack since I first returned to the commode. Now I am ready.

I stare and stare and stare and stare and finally see them emerging. They are looking around for me, but I do not feel like flailing my arms like the people around me. I get a good look at Stephanie first, and she looks the same, except her haircut is a little different. Peter looks the same.... No, his haircut is a little different. I cannot see Michael's face. God! I start laughing because his hair is so long that it is covering his face. I always hated his short army haircut. He is not pushing it out of his eyes because both his hands are occupied with baggage. I start repositioning myself, weaving my way through the crowd. They are looking around for me, but cannot see me because I am coming to them from the side. "Stephanie!"

"Hey!" She abandons her luggage and throws her arms around me, squeezing me tightly, chattering in my ear. "God, it's so good to see you! You should have gone to the hotel to wait: I can't believe you sat in the airport all this time!"

"It was only a couple hours."

She pulls back and takes my face in her hands to give me a good look. She smoothes back my hair and smiles radiantly. "Wow!"

"OK, Steph!" Michael wants her to stop hugging me. He wants to hug me. She steps aside, and I gaze into Michael's face. His black hair is tucked behind his ears now, and I can see his beautiful brown eyes. He is smiling his biggest dimpled smile at me, but...but...he looks pale...or tired...or--"God, I've missed you." He crumples me in his arms before I finish gazing at his face. He does not chatter, and I do not chatter. He just holds me for a long, long, long time. He rubs his hands up and down my back, then strokes my hair, then kisses my head, then, after an eternity, pulls back to cradle

315

my head in his hands and gaze at me. "You look great!"

I want to say the same, but...he looks...different. He seems smaller, thinner, tired.... Prison must have taken a much, much worse toll on him than I had ever expected. But he has been out for a long time now! And I thought he was so happy and busy! God, Washington is killing him! Why won't he go back to North Carolina!? I put my hands around his face, unembarrassed because he is doing the same to me. "I'm so happy to see you, Michael!"

He finally pulls away, and Peter gives me a hug, too. We head out to the taxi stand, and I answer questions about my recent trips, and they tell me about their flight. We have difficulty locating a taxi big enough for four people with luggage but finally head out into the night. It is rainy and foggy, but we gaze out the windows as best we can at the manmade environment--lights, cars, roads, buildings. We turn a bend and spot the famous statue of Jesus, gigantically placed high above Rio de Janeiro, arms outstretched to all who come to Him. We can barely see His face through the mist.

As we start snaking our way through the human zoo of Copacabana, Peter asks me if I am sure I have picked a hotel in a "good neighborhood". I do not have the heart to tell him how much it would cost us to stay in a "good neighborhood" in this city, nor that Fernando is the one who has given me all my hotel recommendations, and they have been pretty good. "You have to be ready for pickpocketing in Rio all the time, but the hotel itself should be perfectly safe." I see him squeeze Stephanie's hand, obviously determined to defend her from any danger. Michael is seated in the front seat.

We arrive, and I check everybody in, though they are all obviously enjoying playing around with their Portuguese phrase books. By prearranged plan, Stephanie and I head to one room, and Peter and Michael take another, down the hall. Stephanie turns to Peter and Michael before we split into two parties. "You guys wanna go out for a drink or something?"

"Yeah!" says Michael.

316

"Come get us when you're ready," says Peter.

Stephanie closes our door, and we move furnishings around until our luggage is happily settled. She cracks her back, then stretches her legs and arms. "I am sooooooo sick of flying!!!!" I bet she does not realize that the flight from Rio de Janeiro to Macapá will be some eight hours. I feel hungry and tired. I feel loopy, as if I will soon be getting a corsage and heading out on a double-date to the prom. She flops down on the bed, and I flop down beside her. "Sooooooo?"

"So, what?"

"How does it feel to see Michael?"

"Why are you asking that?"

"Because I want to know if it hurts or if you're happy."

"Does it hurt **him** or make **him** happy?"

"I asked you first!"

"Whose side are you on?!"

"Everybody's!"

"It hurts **and** it makes me happy. Is that a big surprise?"

"No....It hurts him and makes him happy, too. Is that such a big surprise?"

"No, I guess....I still can't believe he doesn't have a new girlfriend already."

"Well...there's a reason for that...." What? He's in love with **you**? I cuss myself out the moment the thought pops into my head. "He's been going through a lot of changes...in prison...and since then....But he'll talk to you more about it later."

"Steph, just tell me, please....I mean, you obviously know him better than I do now--"

"No, I don't! I just happened to be around during a really rough year of his life."

"He **is** over me, though, isn't he? I mean, **totally** over me?"

317

She shakes her head. "God, you don't even know how much he loves you, do you?" My heart quivers. "He'll never get over you."

I sit in silence for a minute, but she does not continue. "Steph...do you think we have a chance...to get back together?"

"Oh, sweetie!" She pulls my head to her chest and hugs me like a baby. "I know you don't really mean that. You're just feeling that way because you haven't found somebody else yet, but you will."

"But you just said--"

"You didn't understand what I said. You guys have a really special love, but...God....It wasn't strong enough, hon...and it's too late now. I thought you already knew that. I didn't mean to say something to...confuse you....Y'know, I'm so jealous of you and Michael in so many ways....I think you had this raw closeness that...women and men hardly ever have. I mean, Peter really, really loves me, but...I never felt like...God...like it **hurts** how close I am to him...like....I don't know what I'm trying to say." She is quiet for awhile, stroking my hair. "It was like you too got so close so fast, before you were prepared for it. Like, you and I are really close, but we had a lifetime to get there. You two...you just sort of ran into a head-on collision, you know?"

"So why can't we slow down now and--"

"No, no, no, no. It's too late. He still considers you his best friend, you know, so...just...hang onto that. He's been out of his mind waiting for this trip. I know he wants to talk to you about a lot of stuff that he has trouble talking to me and Peter about." She is silent for awhile more. "Let me braid your hair, OK?"

I sit up obediently, and she starts gathering wisps together. "It's gotten thicker!"

"I know. I don't know why. Maybe because I eat fresh food all the time now. I don't know."

"I thought it would be really, really blond now."

"I haven't actually been out in the sun much."

She is quiet for awhile, weaving an intricate pattern that will be spoiled by shampoo within a few hours. I feel my neck muscles relaxing as all the hairs on my head get moved around in turn. "You have to think about what love really means now." What? "Love is patient, love is kind, love is...." She recites the whole Biblical passage to me, much to my amazement. "I know you **feel** love for him, but you have to **give** love: and that's a lot harder. Believe me, I know. Here, hold this." She puts the ends of my hair in my hand and heads to her little suitcase to dig out a band to tie it up with. She quickly returns, ties off my hair, but continues to hold it in her hand. "He really needs you right now." My heart crashes 10,000 feet. "He doesn't need you to fall in love with him again. He needs you to be his best friend....You have no idea how much he suffered in prison....He still hasn't gotten over it yet...."

I turn around to look at her. She has tears in her eyes. "He always acted like it was no big deal--"

"I know." She shakes her head. "He didn't want to burden you with anything while you were in Mexico and when you were here. You were going through so much shit of your own." She looks down for awhile, then looks back up at me. "You have to be strong for him--**really** strong! Don't even **think** about falling in love with him again! Just **love** him...unconditionally...like a....Just...." She cannot complete the sentence and looks down again for awhile, then finally looks at me once more. "C'mon! We're going to have lots and lots of fun! This is going to be an extraordinary trip! And maybe none of us will ever return to Brazil again, but we're here now!" She puts her hands on my upper arms. "You **will** have fun!" she says, mocking my father's stern warnings when we departed on childhood vacations. "It'll be OK," she says, softer. "He loves you more than you think he does....But he needs your friendship now, more than ever, and nothing more complicated...and difficult. Just talk to him, OK?"

"OK." I am totally bewildered and not even sure what I have agreed upon.

"C'mon--let's get going. What are you going to wear?" We rummage around for something fun to wear out in our first evening in the Marvelous City, and Stephanie is quickly wrinkling her nose towards my suitcase. "Do you smell...shrimp...or something?"

I tell her the tale of the prawn marinade, and we are soon giggling hysterically about it. She lends me a blouse, and I lend her a jasmine-scented Brazilian skirt, just for the hell of it, and we sail out the door to pick up our dates. No: she has a date, and I have a "best friend". I am not sure why she is jealous of that.

Chapter 53

We go to the fellas' room and compare notes on our multiple guidebooks, debating whether to go for live music, or good dancing, or some quiet piano bar, or.... After awhile, I put my book down and start staring at Michael. He has a black bandana tied around his head now, holding his hair in place. His hair is even blacker than the bandana. His face is definitely paler, though. I guess he probably has not gotten much sun during the D.C. winter, but...I thought his skin was naturally darker than this. He has definitely gotten thinner. I guess he really did spend a lot of time in prison just reading, burnt out on years of pumping iron in the army. No, it is more than that: he looks as if he has been ill or something. But still so beautiful. The quasi-Indian cheekbones, the quasi-African nose, the quasi-Scottish dimpled smile, the deep eyes and long dark eyelashes. He puts down his book and smiles back at me. We sit quietly, looking at each other, waiting for Peter and Stephanie to decide where we should go.

Stephanie looks up, "How about--?"

"OK," Michael and I say, simultaneously. Stephanie laughs, and we head out.

We end up at a really good nightclub, order some drinks and food, and chat about travel stuff. I tell them about the Northeast and Easter in Curitiba, and then we start planning how we want to spend our days in Rio de Janeiro.

"I thought it was not supposed to be raining here," Peter says.

"It's global warming," I reply, assuming the implicit question was directed at me.

He looks at me, furrowing his eyebrows. "You really think so?"

"The dry seasons and rainy seasons have been totally screwed up all over Brazil the past year. It's probably the end of the world."

Stephanie shakes her head at me, laughing. "Thanks for your expert opinion, Dr. Doom!"

"Could **be**," Michael pipes in.

"Well, let's enjoy it while it lasts," says Peter, hoisting his glass up and saluting us.

They start playing some American rock and roll music, and we get up to dance. Michael and I fall into our easy pattern, though we are both less frenetic about it then we would have been...three years ago? No, four.... The music switches back to Brazilian. Stephanie and Peter return to the table, but I impede Michael's escape.

He moans. "C'mon! You know I don't know this stuff!"

"Just fake it!"

"I can't even understand this rhythm!"

"No foreigners do: just fake it!"

"Just because **you've** been studying Brazilian dancing is no reason to make a fool out of **me**!"

"Shut up and dance!"

We move somewhat awkwardly, but have a good time. He even twirls me around a few times. We get a round of applause at the table when we return.

We chatter away for a couple more hours, then head back to the hotel. It is really late, but the rain clouds have broken up a bit, so we decide to take a walk down to the beach. Stephanie breaks off alone with me.

"Everything OK?"

"Yeah. You and Peter having a good time?"

"Great! We'll probably head back to the hotel, give you two a chance to talk."

We join up for awhile. Peter and Michael are trying to recognize city landmarks through the mist. After a little while, Peter and Stephanie go.

"You wanna sit down?"

"OK," I reply. He used to be the one who never got tired. "Do you have a cold or something?"

"Something."

"Well, what is it? Do you need to see a doctor?"

"I got some medicine: don't worry about it." He lies down on his stomach and props his head up in his hands to gaze at the Atlantic. We can see a sliver of moon above the ocean. "This isn't how I pictured it...from your letters, I mean."

"I didn't live here!"

"Yeah, but it's hard to imagine how one country can have so many different places." Sometimes I forget how much of his life he spent in North Carolina alone. I curl up on the wet sand, perpendicular to him, and rest my head on the small of his back.

"What does the law firm think of your hair?"

"Well, usually Stephanie puts it in one of them there French-braid swirly things you got going, and they like it pretty good." We both convulse with laughter. My head bounces gently above his vibrating rib cage. "Oh, I just tie it in a ponytail. I think I'm fulfilling some equal opportunity quota for them--maybe a couple quotas."

"C'mon! Stephanie says Peter raves about how hard you work there!"

"I work pretty hard, but I only do eight hours. Lawyers do like twelve hours of work a day."

"Well, when they raise your salary to eighty K, you can start working twelve hours a day, too."

"Puhhh. It's a lot more than eighty K. But I like my evenings. It's so wonderful to get to the end of the day and think, `Wow, I can go anywhere I want...do anything I want.' God, I love that feeling. One week, I went to a different Smithsonian museum every night. God, there's so much to learn. There's so much to do."

I want to ask him if he is thinking about going back to school, but I know it would be virtually impossible: he has probably disqualified himself from any kind of financial aid that might have been available. The only reason he is affording Washington is obviously because Peter is one of those lawyers working the twelve-hour days; I wonder how much money he has spent on Michael...and Stephanie.

"It's weird to think you might be sent somewhere else," he continues. "You've been gone so long already."

"I just don't know what else to do. I feel like I have to do whatever the University tells me to do, or they'll never give me a good recommendation and I'll never be able to get another job again."

He rolls over and puts his left hand under the back of his head, and he wraps his right hand around the hand with which I am drawing circles in the sand. My head is now resting on his stomach, and I stop drawing circles in the sand. He looks at me, then gazes up at the sky. "Maybe...God wants you to do something else."

"Like what?"

He is quiet for a moment. "I'm not sure. He must be trying to get you ready for something."

"Well, it's not working. I've never felt less ready in my entire life."

"Neither did I, but...."

"But what?" I lift my eyes to look at him, but he is still looking up.

"As soon as you have one thing figured out, then something else comes along, y'know? I don't think God **wants** us to figure it all.

324

I think God wants us to keep learning new stuff all the time."

"Why do we have to suffer to learn?"

He shakes his head. "I'm not sure. Sometimes I think it's the only way God found to get people to really pay attention to each other."

"It just makes me curl up inside myself."

"For awhile....Then you come out again, different....And you recognize...I mean...you see how a lot of other people are curled up inside themselves, too."

I am quiet for awhile. I am sick of abstract thought. "So what did you learn in prison?"

He lets go of my wrist and starts stroking my hair with his right hand. "I didn't think I learned anything while I was in there, but now...I don't know....It seems like I did....It's hard to explain...." My body shudders from his gentle touch in my hair, and the feeling of cool, wet sand under me. "I'm really tired; let's go back to the hotel."

We get up and swat at the wet sand clinging to us, then head back. He holds my hand as we walk back silently. At my door, he kisses me on the forehead. "I'm really glad to see you!"

"Me, too."

"Goodnight."

"Goodnight."

I walk in slowly, figuring Peter might be in the room, but Stephanie is already in bed. She clicks off the TV. "Did you guys have a good talk?"

"Sort of."

She smiles wanly, "Well, it's been a long time, I guess." She notices the wet sand clinging to me and furrows her brow at me. "Did you fall down?"

"We were lying on the beach, talking. I'm gonna take a shower."

"OK, sweetie."

I stand in the endless supply of hotel hot water for a very, very long time. When I come out, Stephanie is already asleep. I crawl into my bed and stare at the ceiling. I can hear the rain beginning again.

Chapter 54

It rains the next day. We diligently truck around the whole city, determined to see everything, as best we can--cathedrals, government buildings, parks, beaches. We spend a soggy couple of hours in the botanical gardens, then head to the racetrack for the Thursday night races. Michael has never been to a racetrack, and this one is supposed to be one of the most beautiful parks in the world. Despite what our guidebook says, the park is not open. We beg the guards to let us at least look at it, and they finally consent, but warn us it is illegal to take photos.

We walk through the jockey club and gaze out on the track. Stephanie and I went to Arlington Park a few times when we were young, until I started having doubts about how much horses actually like to race. The memory of it still stirs me, though--the beauty and the glory of horses pounding their way around the track. They do not even know why they are running. They simply run: scared into a false panic, they flee in raw terror. The jockeys cling to them, united not in love but in adrenaline. Sometimes betting a couple dollars unites you, too, to their adrenaline rush. If only you could ride a horse that loved you, that really wanted to take it with you.

The clouds break up a bit, and we see the crescent moon has risen near the escarpment of Christ the Redeemer. The sky hovers between blue and black, with just enough light for us to see the water in the background to one side and the mountains in the background on the other side. The moon shines down on the empty race track. "No pictures!" One of the guards has followed us in, and repeats the stern warning. The scene is breathtakingly beautiful, and he knows it. I ask him if we can see some horses, but he says none are boarded there--they only come on race days--so we leave.

We take a taxi to the guidebooks' highest-rated vegetarian restaurant, but it has apparently closed down, so we wander around the Ipanema neighborhood until it starts raining hard again, then scramble to find an inexpensive restaurant in the midst of high-rent Ipanema. We finally settle on a Chinese/Japanese restaurant.

Peter turns to me. "What should we do tomorrow if it rains again?"

I do not know why he is asking me. I have never been to this city before, either, and they have read more in the guidebooks than I have. "Well, I guess we should hold off on Pão de Azucar and Corcovado until it clears up."

Michael suggests we take the ferry out to Paquetá tomorrow, and we head home for the night, damp and exhausted.

The next day it rains some more. We catch a cross-town bus to the ferry landing, then start riding to Paquetá. It is an enormous harbor, with many little islands. Paquetá is a half-hour ride. We can see the beauty of Rio intermittently as the sun peeps in and out. When we arrive at Paquetá, we hire a horse-drawn cart to give us a tour of the carless island.

Most of the trees are enormous, and most of the houses are tiny. The guide points out all the curiosities of the island--the bird cemetery, the beach cave with the legend, the quaint little pastel-painted cottage that some old soap opera was filmed at--but he seems oblivious to the extraordinary natural beauty around him. The lushness overwhelms me--the island sounds and smells and colors. So much greenery...but so many flowers too...and precious little cottages painted in yellows and pinks and blues. Enormous trees stretching out wider than the houses behind them, draped in creeping vines and drooping lianas. And every turn of the road brings another beach and another view of the ocean.

"God, what a paradise," says Peter, after we complete our circuit of the island.

328

"Doesn't it remind you of Mackinac Island?" Stephanie asks me.

"Yeah, but this...this is...incredible."

We order some lunch at a seaside restaurant--all the restaurants are seaside restaurants--and gaze silently around us at the picturesque downtown with its little shops and tiny cathedral, listening to the gentle clipclop of horses pulling carts past us.

Michael turns to me. "Did you notice that house for sale?"

"Yeah!"

He just smiles at me.

"What?!"

"God, that would be fantastic," adds Stephanie.

"What, are you guys crazy? I can't buy that house!!"

"You could get a house loan," says Peter, with a serious look on his face.

I look around. They are all looking at me, seriously! "I can't buy that house!!"

"Why not? You're in love with this island! You're head over heels in love with this island," says Michael.

"What would I do here?"

"Maybe they need a planner," says Peter.

"It's already a paradise!"

"Well, it'll take more than luck to keep it that way," says Michael.

"You guys!"

Our food comes, and they drop the subject. It's just silly.... Just because it looks like a paradise doesn't mean it is. And I don't want to find out the hard way. Better to remember just this one perfect trip to paradise.

We take the ferry back and try for Pão de Azucar since the clouds are partially broken up. By the time we get there, it is raining again, but we wait for the cablecar anyway.

"Do you think it's safe in the rain?" Peter asks, turning towards me. Why is he asking me? How do I know?

"C'mon, Pete! It's now or never!" Michael answers for me.

Our turn arrives, and we enter the cable car. Peter grabs a rail with one hand and wraps his other arm around Stephanie. Michael wraps both arms around me, and lets me grip the rail for both of us. He whispers in my ear, "Are you scared?"

"Hell, yeah!"

"**Really** scared?"

"Average scared." Average for Brazil. Always scared in Brazil.

We sway in the wind but glide past the first jutting rock. We can see some of the harbor through the fog, and then we suddenly see Pão de Azucar looming in the mist.

"It doesn't look like a sugar loaf," says Peter.

"I don't think they named it for a sugar loaf," says Stephanie. "Didn't the book say that was just a phonetic version of an Indian name?"

"I think so," says Michael.

When we get up to it, it is too covered in fog to see anything at all. We are supposed to have a panoramic view of the coastline up and down Rio de Janeiro, but we see nothing but the big gray cloud enveloping us. It is cool and damp, and we gladly take the first cablecar back down.

"We'll just have to buy the postcards," says Michael.

The rain is picking up, so we head to a shopping mall for dinner and browsing. Peter buys Stephanie a ruby necklace, Stephanie buys Peter a colorful t-shirt, and Michael buys a book about the founding of Rio de Janeiro, written in English. He is already reading about the Indians the Portuguese discovered there

330

by the time we walk out of the bookstore. "Did you know...?"

The next morning, it is still raining, but it is our last day, so we take a bus to the Tijuca National Forest, and start the slow train ride up the mountain of Corcovado. All around is dense green jungle, with rain pouring down.

"God, it's like we're in the rainforest!" exclaims Peter.

"We **are** in a rainforest, right?" says Stephanie.

"Yeah, it's called Atlantic rainforest. It's more endangered than the Amazon, actually. There aren't many patches of it left."

We see occasional bright specks of flowers, but mostly just wet, dark green trees. At long last we get to the end of the tracks, and start climbing the numerous flights of steps that lead to the base of *Cristo Redentor*--Christ the Redeemer. It is exhausting, and many of the elderly tourists have to keep pausing to regain their breath before proceeding up the stairs. We climb slowly but steadily. It is only misting now, so we do not need to raise our umbrellas, but we feel wet through and through.

When we get to Christ, we can see his body, but not his face, which is lost in a cloud. We walk out to the scenic overviews and read the placards and diagrams to learn about the panoramic view we cannot see whatsoever in the gray wall of fog.

"We could've seen all the way to Petropolis?!" exclaims Peter.

"I'd settle for just seeing the bay or the ocean," replies Stephanie.

"We'll just have to buy postcards," says Michael.

We walk back down and peruse dozens of postcards while waiting for the train to depart. Peter emits whistle after whistle as he and Stephanie exchange favorite finds with each other. Michael hands me a card with an aerial view of *Cristo Redentor* looking out over *Pão de Azucar*, the bay, the ocean, the escarpment, and the city of Rio de Janeiro. A rainbow reaches from the Heavens across the Carolina blue sky and down to what must be Copacabana beach. "I think the pink part is landing on our hotel," he says to me, a twinkle in his eye. I smile back, and take the card up to the cash register. God, it would have been beautiful.

We take the train back down, then a bus back to the hotel to collect our bags, then a taxi to the airport. The clouds are scattering as we approach the airport, and we crane our necks to look back at the suddenly sunny city. What a gorgeous place. The Marvelous City. My heart aches as I think about how different my life might have been had I been sent to **this** city for a year, instead of the high, dry plateau and space colony of Brasília. But maybe it would have just been worse. I have never seen a place more beautiful.

Chapter 55

Our flight out of Rio is late, so we pick up an American newspaper. They cannot believe how much I enjoy the comic strips. We people-watch for awhile, and they practice some Portuguese phrases, letting me correct their pronunciation. I have warned them that far fewer people will speak English in Amazônia, and they all have phrase books zippered into their fanny packs with their passports and tickets.

The flight goes on and on and on, and they finally realize just how enormous Brazil is. Michael sits next to me in my row for awhile, then Stephanie asks to trade with him so she can talk to me for awhile. Then Michael comes back; he is very sleepy and desperately trying to be polite and not take a nap, but I finally tell him to take one. He offers me a new tape to listen to on my headphones.

"Who the heck are Hootie and the Blowfish?"

"You haven't heard them yet?"

"No," I reply.

He smiles an enormous grin. "You're gonna looooooove this. This guy's voice....God! He has such a beautiful voice. And the lyrics are so...real. And they're from South Carolina, so that's close to cool."

I pop it in as Michael closes his eyes and drifts off. The voice pulls me in immediately--a rich honeyed voice from the depths. It is real. The pain is real. The sadness is real. The guitars have a clean and simple approach but build up a surprising wall of warmth and friendliness and sentimentality. The voice. "I'm gonna love you...the best that...the best that I ca-han." God, are there still men out there who think love is something worth making an effort for? He really sounds as if he means it. He is not bragging about being the only guy who can make her happy, or belittling her by saying nobody else will ever love her. He is just saying he wants to try.

"...I could not believe...she was the same girl...I fell in love with long ago." Now he has tried and failed. No, she has failed. He can do nothing but let her cry and sing for her now. Totally honest. Totally empty and hurting. It is the most astonishing album I have heard in a very, very, very long time.

I play it through twice, watching Michael sleep, wanting to understand why two people who feel so many of the same things cannot stay together. I put it away, pop my ears, and reach for the ear drops. I am on my second ear's application when Michael awakens.

"What's wrong with your ears?"

"Don't worry about it." I smile sarcastically and fondly at him, still annoyed he will not tell me about his own illness. It is one of those invisible break-up rules, I guess: *just-friends* do not converse about their illnesses. He rubs his eyes. "You had a **really** long nap. How ya feelin'?"

He looks at his watch. "Wow." He pops his ears. "Are we descending?"

"Yep. How ya feelin'?"

"Groggy." He stretches his back and his legs. "Do you still have some water left?" I hand him my bottle, and he pours some into his mouth. "You want the rest?" I decline, and he pours it all into his mouth. "How'd ya like Hootie?" I just shake my head in amazement, and he smiles at me. "I thought you would!" He puts the bottle away. "How long do you have to sit like that?"

"'Til the drops soak into my ear and won't drip out."

He takes my tilted head from my own shoulder and pulls it over to his, then fingers my tilted left ear. "Does it hurt a lot?"

"No, it's almost better."

334

My sister comes over to our row. "There's no way we're gonna make the connecting flight."

"Don't worry about it, Steph. It'll probably be heading out late."

"What if it's on time?"

"Maybe there's another flight," says Michael.

"Just don't worry about it until we get there, OK?" Today has enough of its own troubles.

We touch down in Belém in pouring rain. It is the rainiest city in Brazil--one of the rainiest in the world--and airline employees are waiting at the bottom of the steps to hand us courtesy umbrellas as we slosh our way into the airport. We have missed our connection to Macapá. The next one is at midnight.

"I don't wanna arrive in this God-forsaken town after midnight," wails Peter.

"I'm sure it's not **that** bad!" says Michael.

We do not have a hotel reservation there because the cheaper hotels in Macapá did not make them, and we did not want to stay at the spanking new multiple-star jobber. "I don't want to arrive that late, either. Why don't I ask them if we can fly out on tomorrow evening's flight, instead?"

"But we don't have a hotel reservation **here**, either," says Stephanie.

"It's a big city: I'm sure we'll find something. I'm sure it'll be easier here at 9:00 p.m. then there after midnight."

"Yeah, and if not, we'll just have to find a stable," says Michael.

Stephanie and I start laughing, but Peter doesn't get it. "`Belém' means `Bethlehem', she explains. I explain to the airline staff that we do not want to arrive in Macapá in the middle of the night, and they agree to change all our tickets over to the next evening. We hop a taxi and ask him to recommend a good three-star hotel.

335

It looks all right, so we check in and consult our guidebooks for how to make the best of our one day in Belém. Most of the tourist spots seem to be pretty close together, so we write out a fairly simple itinerary in the hotel dining room. I notice that Peter and Stephanie have gotten progressively less picky about the "weird" Brazilian food, making an adjustment that took me weeks in just a couple days, and they have all fallen in love with my beloved cashew juice. Michael would always eat anything, as many people from very poor families do. Soon we are all in bed, exhausted and damp again.

The day dawns with only minor cloudiness, and we head out into Belém optimistically. This is the city for which I got my yellow fever shot, improbable as it would be to get yellow fever right in the city itself. I wonder, now, if the odds are more favorable for me to contract yellow fever or to meet--by some outlandish coincidence-- one of the Amazonian specialists I might have met had I been allowed to attend the conference here. I always dreamed someday I would get paid to attend important conferences on subjects that interested me. We enter the gate to the city's tiny jungle preserve, which houses a lush reminder of how the area of Belém looked before it was built up in the ashes of the trees. We enter as tourists.

We take dozens of photographs, enthralled by the massive formations of fern, bamboo, liana, and wood. We see a few rainforest critters scurrying around in the undergrowth but do not manage to photograph any of them. We are enchanted by the little castles of stone built by sentimental Europeans, the walls now covered in vines and blending into the scene with a surprising loveliness. We enter the museum and learn more about the state of Pará--about its Indians, flora, fauna, and minerals.

When we come out, the sky has burst open in a torrential downpour, and we gaze out at the little fraction of rainforest. From where we stand, we can see nothing but dark greenness drenched in water, and it is both easy to picture and impossible to imagine living out in the rainforest. I am sure I would have cut down the jungle, too.

When it slows to a gentle rain, we head over to the harbor for lunch amidst the hustle and bustle of actual people doing actual port things. Michael wants to head into the market to see what there is to buy, but I am too claustrophobic to go, so Stephanie sits at the café with me while we watch the guys weed their way into the throng.

"Is Peter having a good time?"

"Oh, yeah, he just doesn't like rain."

"Yeah. If we could only get **one** sunny day! It doesn't even seem like a vacation: it's like some difficult field trip."

"Do you remember when we went to the Field Museum?"

"Yeah, that was the best," I reply.

"Nah! The Museum of Science and Industry is the best!"

"Geek!"

She laughs. "You loved pressing the buttons just as much as everybody else!"

"Yeah, I like pressing the buttons. I just don't like spending the hours necessary to program the damn buttons."

"Try **days**."

"Really?"

"Well, maybe not then, but they put some pretty complex displays into museums nowadays. This museum made me think of the Field Museum, y'know? God...those dramatic renditions of cavemen and everything."

I sip the last of my mango juice. "I wish you guys had been able to read some of the stuff I've been reading at the Institute on Amazonian Indians. Their culture and beliefs are a world apart from American Indians...in a lot of ways...I think....I mean, some stuff you read really romanticizes them, but their lives are so difficult out there....They've really had to adopt some pretty harsh practices to survive."

"Like what?"

"Like killing children if their mother dies." Her eyes open wide. "Their belief is that a child should not grow up without a mother, but it is not too hard to figure out that this is just a justification to kill the kid so that nobody else has the additional burden of gathering food for the orphan."

"Do you think that's wrong? If the tribe didn't have enough adults to gather food for orphans?"

"I don't know....It makes you think more about other things, y'know? Like why men would use shotguns to hunt down the fathers of their teenage daughters' babies. Like maybe they didn't really care about the disgrace of the girl or her family: maybe her dad just couldn't afford to feed one more mouth."

"Or these people who have abortions because their baby has spina bifida or something, saying, well, they'll never have any **quality** of life. Not many of them have the guts to say they don't want to take care of an invalid for the rest of their lives."

"I don't know. It's so horrible to think that somebody else might have to die so that you can live." We fall silent for a little bit. "Steph, do you ever wonder why we hardly ever heard anything about our ancestors' coming to America?" She nods. "I know there's that one story about one of them running from the mafia or something, but there must have been a lot more stories than that. People desperate to find land or a job or something. Maybe some of them had even done desperate things. Maybe we wouldn't even be alive if they hadn't done something desperate...selfish...cruel--"

"God, I hate thinking about stuff like that," Stephanie says, shuddering.

"So do I," I say, staring out at the market, where I can still just make out Peter's Baltimore Orioles baseball cap. I have suddenly remembered that European ferry that capsized in the North Sea and how the only survivors seemed to be young men, and how obvious it was that the women and children and elderly must have been shoved aside in the race for the lifeboats...or maybe they just fell to the side without even being shoved. I almost mention it to Stephanie, and then decide not to. "I think about that stuff all the time here," I finally say.

338

"Why?"

"Don't you feel it?"

"What?"

"Like death is all around you in this country?"

"**No!** The people are so a-**live**! So vibrant!"

"I know. It's as if they're living each day like it could be their last."

"You're just depressed: it's not that bad."

"I'm not saying it's bad. I feel like....I don't know. Maybe they're more tuned into what life is all about because they have to struggle so hard to hold onto it."

"Yeah...."

"I mean, there was this one woman at work who, whenever I said `see you tomorrow', would say `God willing', and she had this look on her face like she really thought God might strike her or me down that very night. It's like, they're always waiting for it to happen--not waiting for it to happen, but just sort of realizing that it might happen."

"Is that how you feel?"

I look at my sister, feeling it would be ridiculously melodramatic to tell her I think I am dying. After all, I might just be crazy, instead. Or maybe I am not dying but my life is over anyway. Is that possible? A begging child interrupts our thoughts. Stephanie reaches for her money, but I hold her back with my left hand while using my right hand to offer the remains of the bread basket to the child, who takes it promptly and heads off. I change the subject to Fernando, the subject she has avoided for a long time.

She hesitates a moment. "I talked to Michael about this a lot, you know?" *Michael? Oh, God.....* "I think he's right. This will be good for us. We can sort of finish wrapping it up now that the hard part is behind us. Michael said you guys had a long time to ease out of it...just become friends...and it was too abrupt for me. It was like

339

he died, y'know? Because I loved him, and then he was gone. I had to grieve by myself, instead of sharing the grief with him, like you and Michael did." ***Did? Is that** what we did? What are we doing now?* "I love Peter a thousand times more than I ever loved Fernando, but even if I didn't have Peter, I think I could do this now, y'know? Say goodbye to him in a nice way. I don't regret our relationship. Maybe he regrets what happened, but my feelings can't go back now. I just wish you had told me you met him here: you shouldn't have been afraid to tell me that."

She looks at me quizzically, but I do not know what to say. I am still not ready to tell her how desperately lonely I felt that I actually let him kiss me in a bathroom. I would like to save that confession until she is married with two kids, I think. "I just didn't see any point in telling you. I'm sorry. I didn't mean to upset you."

"It's OK."

By the time we see the guys coming back, we are just staring quietly at the ships in the bay. I think about how my first language was English, and then I metaphorically crossed the English channel to learn French, then headed down the Iberian peninsula to learn Spanish, then Portuguese, finally sailing off to the New World to arrive in wild Brazil. How did it feel to be a European sailor then? Scary? Was it just a job--a lousy job? Were they terrified of the naked Indians living in the wild dark jungle? Did they **have** to kill them, the way I **have** to kill the cockroaches and ants that terrify me? Did they really not know they were human? Did they love to come back out of the jungle to this Europeanish city? Did they gaze at the ocean and cry for Portugal? Or did they take Indian wives so fast that their loneliness was assuaged?

Michael and Peter hold up their newly prized possessions: exotic fruits, jewelry, shirts, and hammocks.

"We're not gonna need hammocks," Stephanie tells them.

"We will when we get back!" Peter exclaims enthusiastically. "We've got the perfect trees in the backyard for these!" Stephanie gives him a kiss, and we hail a taxi for the historic district, to finish up the day taking photos of old colonial government buildings and the graceful whitewashed cathedral--exterior only, since it is locked up. We then head back to the airport in a drizzle, grab some dinner, then fly off to Macapá.

Chapter 56

We land in Macapá in dry weather, and rejoice. We head out to the taxi stand and ask for the hotel Fernando had recommended. It does not look too good, but we figure maybe that is about the best we can get in the sticks.

"Oh, God, it's one of those electric showers that can electrocute you!" Stephanie looks at me, terror-stricken.

"Don't worry," I tell her, even though they still make me nervous.

"Don't worry?! **Look** at it! If it falls down, I'm fried!"

"Just wear rubber flip-flops in there."

"You think flip-flops could kill the current in **that**?"

"Probably." Please don't tear apart one of the few remaining comforting illusions I have here.

"I don't think so! The current must be at least--"

"Look, if you're really terrified of it, just don't turn it on: shower in cold water. That never killed anybody."

"I was hoping to avoid that as long as possible!"

"So am I! That's why I'm going to shower in flip-flops and hope for the best!"

The bellhop knocks on the door again to bring in some more towels and a lightbulb for the nightstand lamp. When he turns on the light, we see a giant cockroach scurry across the bed. I scream at ten decibels, and Stephanie screams at about one-hundred. The bellhop swishes the covers around until it lands on the floor, then steps on it.

"I can't stay here," Stephanie says.

I look at her, hesitantly. If it were not so late at night, I would be inclined to agree with her. After all, roaches in your bathroom is to be expected, but **in** your **bed**?! That is a real nightmare. What if there are food crumbs all over the mattress? What if....? "Well, maybe we can find a better place, but maybe not: it's kinda late."

"Oh, **please**! I don't care if we have to spend a hundred a night. I know, I know, I know: I am going to have to deal with this soon, but I just want to ease into it a little more gradually! Let me start with the cold showers, OK? Then I can work my way up to roaches in my bed!"

"Sorry? No like?" The bellhop apparently understands a little English. I tell him that we would not mind roaches in the bathroom, but are quite disturbed at seeing one on the bed. "Little more money, better room up stair." He nods his head, smiling with encouragement.

"Could we look at it?" It turns out to be a bigger and cleaner room, and after a thorough inspection of the bedding, we decide to take it. While he is bringing our luggage up, we check on the guys to see if their room is OK.

"No problemo," says Peter.

"Are ya sure?" asks Stephanie. "The rooms upstairs are much better."

"I wanna start getting accustomed to roughing it!"

Michael laughs good-naturedly at him. Michael is the king of roughing it. We split up for the night, too exhausted to investigate Macapá's nightlife, which we expect nothing from, anyway.

The next day dawns gloriously hot and sunny. A quick call to Fernando's contact in town reveals he has not shown up yet, so we map out our day. First stop--before it gets any hotter--the equator! A jolly taxi driver takes us on the twenty-minute trip out of town to see

343

the memorial marking the hemispheric equator. We climb the stairs
to the roof of the gigantic memorial--apparently built large enough to
accommodate a whole charter flight's worth of Japanese tourists, or
maybe entire soccer teams--and puzzle over the marker.

"This side must be north," says Peter.

"I don't think so," says Stephanie.

I ask the taxi driver to tell me, but am confused by his
response until I realize we all had perpendicular switched with
horizontal in the marker.

"Huh?" says Michael.

"North is on **this** side."

"Oooooooooh!" We make various straddling poses--click, click,
click.

"This is the most touristy thing I have **ever** done," announces
Stephanie.

"I think it's great," says Michael.

"What's that stadium?" asks Peter, pointing to a structure a
stone's throw from the parking lot.

The taxi driver explains it is also built to straddle the
equator: the center line of the field is on the equator. "Oooooooooh!"
Click, click, click. He takes us to see "the beach" on the way back--a
popular stretch of shoreline near the mouth of the Amazonas River.
There are plenty of young people swimming in the muddy-looking
water and hanging out on "the beach", jamming to boom boxes. The
jeans and bikinis at first seem oddly out of place here, yet, well, this
is Brazil now.

"How can they swim out so far?" asks Michael. "Isn't the river
moving fast here?"

It's so wide, too, I think...so dark. The taxi driver explains
that it is very shallow in this spot, which is why people come here to
swim. We can barely see across the water to the other shoreline--one
of the dozens of islands that split the Amazonas river into a half-

344

dozen fingers before it empties out into the Atlantic Ocean.

"Aren't they scared of piranhas and stuff?" asks Peter.

I translate the question to the taxi driver, who tells us that those kind of things usually live in the interior tributaries, not out here, where the river has grown wide and is heading for the sea.

We head back to town to look around at the handful of historical buildings, which were really put up for no other reason than to guard this hinterland of Brazil against an invasion from French Guyana. Brazil had no further interest in the state of Amapá until a large vein of bauxite was discovered a couple decades ago. Now the bauxite is gone, and they are talking about turning the bauxite boom town into an ecotourism center; Amapá is one part of Amazônia that still has a lot of unspoiled nature.

Now we are boiling hot and taxi back to the hotel to eat lunch and take a siesta. We call for Fernando again, but he still has not gotten into town, so we decide to check out Curiaú--the village founded by runaway slaves.

After forty-five minutes of driving out of town in the opposite direction from the equator--the last half hour on what felt like one gigantic pothole--we arrive at what is clearly not a tourist spot. The occasional people out and about eye our car with not entirely inviting visages. I ask the taxi driver to get out and ask them if they mind tourists looking around. He comes back and says it is OK, so we park the car and start walking around.

Michael's face shows he is totally enthralled by it, and I am, too. Apparently the Portuguese really did not know where the slaves had run off to, or just did not want to bother hauling them back to Macapá, and so the runaways simply set up an African village as best they could, and as best they could remember, without interference from anybody. It is very scenic, nestled into the curve of one of the Amazonas River's latecoming tributaries. It is absolutely beautiful, and I ask the taxi driver to request permission to take photographs. He goes off to talk to some villagers again, and then comes back to tell us it is OK.

345

We walk past a collection of simple wooden buildings to a sort of farmyard--an expanse of grass and weeds with cows and chickens feeding side by side. We walk out to the water. Some of it is shallow enough to reveal some sort of water lily, but much of it is deep, and we quickly spot some children taking turns jumping merrily off a bridge to swim away the hot afternoon. We walk out on the bridge, and the kids take turns doing daredevil dives to win our admiration and our snapshots. From the bridge, we can look back at the little village of simple houses surrounded by a random assortment of jungle/coastal transitional trees, very green grass, well-fed animals, and peaceful looking people.

I turn to Michael. "How many runaway slaves do you think had it **this** good?"

"How many **Portuguese** do you think had it **this** good?! Fish, horses, chickens, fresh water to drink, alluvial soil to farm, hard to get to by land, unlikely to find by water. They were **really, really** lucky to find this place."

"Don't you think they would get malaria here?" asks Peter.

"I don't know," I reply. "Mosquitoes don't carry malaria **everywhere**. And they're not **that** far from the ocean breezes. Anyway, Africans would be more immune to malaria, wouldn't they?"

"Yeah, I think so," says Michael. "But I think they would not have been immune to some of the other stuff: like, isn't dengue just in the Americas?" We all shake our heads, not sure. "I don't think they would have had it any worse here than in Macapá: and here they would have had more food to help them stay healthy."

On the drive out, we can see Portuguese names written on the storefronts and the school building. The taxi driver tells us that they are trying to get the government to build them a health clinic and a better school. It has been a long time since their secret African village was discovered by the Brazilians...and absorbed, sort of, into society.

As we bump and grind along the dirt road, Stephanie and I exchange pained sympathy glances: we both want to pee. I pull off

346

my hat to let the perspiration in my hair evaporate, and Michael exclaims about my sunburn. "Didn't you put sunscreen on?!"

"I thought the hat would be enough," I reply.

"We're at the equator!" He holds my loosely woven straw hat up against the window for emphasis. "Look how much sun can get through this!"

"But this is not even as hot as North Carolina!"

"It doesn't matter: we're **at** the equator! The sun is **closer** to us!"

"It **doesn't** feel hotter than D.C. in the summer, either," says Stephanie, who has taken off her hat. Peter carefully examines her face; he looks like a doctor. I take out some lotion and share it with Stephanie.

"You don't feel as uncomfortable because it's not as humid," says Michael. "But you **have** to be careful with the sun!"

At long last we get back to the hotel and bolt for our room. Stephanie lets me pee first, honoring a long-standing acknowledgment of my inferior bladder. When I come out, Michael and Peter knock on the door to tell us that Fernando has left a message at the desk for us to call him at his colleague's house tonight. I telephone while Stephanie is still in the bathroom, but there is no answer.

Stephanie comes out, and we slather on gobs of the good facial moisturizer, then loll around, downing bottles of mineral water out of the *frigobar*.

"I guess we should wait and have dinner with him, huh?" asks Peter.

"I don't wanna wait very long," replies Stephanie, sitting down in Peter's lap now that she has stopped sweating.

"Let's wait awhile: I think Michael's asleep," I say. They turn to look at him, sprawled out on the bed beside me.

Stephanie looks at Peter. "Let's go down and order some juice or something."

They leave me alone with him, and I lie down beside him, gazing at his face. He is sound asleep. I get out my ear drops to put in the final dosage. I do the right ear first, and tilt my head to let it drip in for awhile. I watch his chest go up and down. He had torn off his shirt when he entered the room, and I look admiringly at his hairless chest. It used to be more muscular, though. He really must have totally stopped pumping iron when he got out of the army. I stuff a wad of cotton into my right ear, then lean it on his chest while I put drops in the left ear. I should have put the ears on alternating dosage schedules from the start: why has this obvious thought only popped into my head now? A few minutes later, I feel his left arm sliding around me and look up to see if I have awakened him, but he is doing it in his sleep. I rest my head again and go to sleep.

I awaken to the rumble of Michael's stomach growling. I lift my head up groggily, and he apologizes.

"That's OK." I rub my eyes. "Let's go find Steph and Peter and have some dinner."

Instead he pulls me close to him again. "It felt nice to wake up with you in my arms." I do not protest. "I had this dream about Rio. You had bought that little house on Paquetá, and I had bought a little house up on Corcovado. I visited you, and it was so beautiful, and then you visited me, and it was so beautiful." He is quiet for awhile. "I'll always love you, y'know."

"Me too."

"But...." *But what?* "We weren't meant to stay together....You know that, don't you?" I cannot answer. "Someday you'll fall in love again, and everything'll be OK." He is quiet a little while longer, but I still cannot answer. "Your friendship means more to me than you'll ever know." I lift my head to look at him. "You need somebody who has all the answers....And so did I." I pull away from him and sit up on the bed.

"I don't believe anybody has all the answers," I say.

348

"You hope for a lot of things you don't believe can happen, and believe in a lot of things you don't hope for." I just stare at him, trying to understand what he is saying. "You really want somebody who can take away what you don't want to believe and make happen what you do want."

"But I'm not that idealistic anymore!"

"No, I'm not saying that. You were **never** idealistic. You always hoped for the best and expected the worst: that's not idealism."

"I **try** to be optimistic!"

"I know! You try a lot of things that go against your nature."

"What nature? I don't even know what I believe in anymore."

"You believe that someday some guy's gonna show you what to believe in. Sometimes you think it will be somebody like me, sometimes you think it will be somebody like God, but that's what you believe in."

"You think I'm crazy?"

"No!" He takes my hand. "I just wish I had figured that out a long time ago, before I tried to be the one to show you what to believe in when I hadn't figured it out yet."

"You have it figured out now?"

He laughs and squeezes my hand. "I think I do...but I can't explain it. I think everybody has to figure it out for themselves...because it's different for everybody."

"So who helped you figure it out--a girl or God?"

He laughs again. "Both, and a whole lotta other people and places and things."

"Why won't you tell me about this girl?"

"I just did."

Me? "But I'm not the love of your life."

"Whatever that means....You loved me more than anybody else ever did. You expected more from me, that's for sure. I wish I could have been the love of your life." I open my mouth to speak, but he does not let me. "Don't say I am, because I'm not. Somebody else is going to come along someday, somebody whose love gives you only joy, somebody whom you'll know was put on this Earth to love you and bring you good things and raise kids with you. Then you'll know. 'Cause best friends don't share a lifetime of joy: they share a lifetime of pain, and love each other in a different realm."

My mind is reeling, trying to grasp this, when Stephanie comes in to tell us that they have just reached Fernando on the phone and he is on his way over to pick us up for dinner. Michael goes to the guys' room to find a clean shirt, and Stephanie and I change clothes, too. I hope he brings some cute friends, I find myself thinking. I immediately get angry with myself--not because of Michael, but because I should be thinking about how Stephanie feels right now. Yet, she does not look ruffled in the least. I am the ruffled one. I am the one who has been bewildered for three decades. I am the one who always wants to cry.

Chapter 57

Ten minutes later, we are fanning ourselves in the downstairs lobby, waiting for Fernando to show up, slathered with Avon Skin-So-Soft to repel the evening mosquitoes. We have purchased stronger stuff for the interior, but this is good enough for the coast...and it smells so sweet. I am not hungry, but feel weak, and hope my potassium pill kicks in soon. I suddenly see Stephanie turn her face towards the door, and look to see that Fernando is walking tentatively towards us.

"Hello, hello!" He smiles broadly, glancing around at everyone, obviously nervous.

Stephanie has not gotten up, so I get up first. "Thanks for recommending this hotel--and the others! They've worked out really well!"

"I'm glad you liked them! Everything OK?"

"Yeah, everything's great. Let me introduce you." Michael has now gotten up, so I introduce him first, and they shake hands. I am thankful to see that Stephanie has now gotten up, and the glazed expression is fading from her face.

"Hi, Fernando. How are you?" She sounds as if she is talking to any former co-worker.

"Fine, fine. How are you doing?"

"Fine, fine. This is Peter." They shake hands, more limply than the other introductory handshake we just went through.

"Well," Fernando toys with his straw hat. "I know a nice little restaurant that looks out on the bay. The food is not very exciting, but it's clean and has a nice view."

"Sounds perfect," says Michael. "Is it close enough to walk, or do we need a cab?"

"We can walk...sure." Fernando seems perfectly content to accept Michael's acquiescence on behalf of the entire group, and we all head out into the night.

"How do you like Brazil?" It is strange to listen to Fernando speak in English. He always spoke in Portuguese to me, after that first meeting. His English is still quite good.

Michael replies for the group, again. "It's great! It rained the whole time in Rio--"

"*Puxa vida!*" Fernando interjects.

"--but it was great. Beautiful place."

"Best in the world," responds Fernando.

"Have you been all over the world?" asks Peter, sarcastically.

"No, but I have seen pictures from many, many places...and I have never met anybody who disagreed after seeing Rio." Peter looks unconvinced. "I am sure you would agree if you saw it on a sunny day."

"I agree," says Michael. "It's astonishing! Rainforest-covered mountains sloping right down to the ocean! The curve of the shoreline between the ocean and the bay! Everywhere you stand there, you see water and trees and mountains behind you! They couldn't **build** enough city to obliterate it."

"No, but the poor people will continue to build their *favelas* further and further up the sides of the hills unless something is done for them. Maybe they will even start building shacks out on crappy piers and create *favelas* in the bay, too, like in Salvador."

"Do you really think it could get that bad?" Stephanie has finally entered into conversation with Fernando.

352

"Maybe. Maybe Michael is right, and they can never obliterate the beauty."

"It's more important for the poor people to survive," responds Michael.

"Yes, it is," replies Fernando. "Look at this town," he continues. "Do you see beggars here?" We shake our heads. "There **will** be. They have already made it another `free-trade' zone, and the rich businessmen have already started crawling all over it with their precious little tax breaks to in-**vest**, and the poor will follow them, begging to wash their cars and clean their toilets and shine their shoes. Nobody will ever teach them how to get better jobs."

"What about the ecotourism plans?" I ask.

"*Ecoturismo*?!" He rolls his eyes and gesticulates with his hands. "They will screw it up, be-**lieve** me. It might be good for a little awhile, but then it will be screwed up."

"What makes you so sure of that? It's a fast-growing industry," says Peter.

"Oh, they will screw it up. They will do it so that a few rich people and a few government officials own and control everything. They will not give the Indians one penny of compensation to thank them for keeping Amapá so wild and beautiful and unspoiled. They will have strict laws against hunting the wild animals--like the jaguar--and they themselves will be secretly buying the skins and selling them for lots and lots of money in the black market. And as soon as the tourists start coming, lots and lots of poor people will come, too, to set up little vending carts to sell food and drinks and souvenirs, and they will build *favelas* all over the place, and they will all get malaria and parasites because they will not know how to avoid it, and then they will be living in such lousy conditions that they will get cholera and spread it to the tourists, and then it will all fall apart."

He turns around triumphantly to see if we are all impressed with his sweeping, acidic assessment of the situation, but we are all speechless. I fear he is right, though I desperately want the ecotourism project to succeed.

"Well, this is the restaurant," he announces, pointing into a simple place with a simple sign announcing `Comida Caseira'. "Crazy place: owner is a German from South of Brazil, cooks are all Negros from the Northeast. They get along OK--lots of fish on the menu, some good pastries, too." He looks at me. "Beans and rice, too...salad." We go in, and he asks for a window table. We are duly impressed with the view of the mouth of the Amazonas.

"Wow, it's beautiful," says Stephanie.

They pull a couple tables together. I sit on one side with Stephanie and Peter, and Michael sits with Fernando across from us.

The waitress hands us menus and asks us what we want to drink. Fernando suggests we try some of the exotic fruit juices available fresh here, so we let him order them. Then he gives us pointers on which fish are really caught fresh near here, and which are shipped in from far away. "And don't order the beef--too tough here." After we get our drinks, and order our dinners, Fernando distributes the juices according to who wants tart and who wants sweet, then congratulates us on how quickly we got equatorial sunburns.

"Y'know, we **went** to this equator thing, but how do we **really** know it was the equator?" says Stephanie. "Maybe some of those corrupt rich guys just built it there because it wasn't too far from town for the tourists to get to."

"No, no, the government built that, and it's in the right place: believe me, **hundreds** of civil servants probably got a full year's salary locating and building **that**!"

"The Army Corps of Engineers could've done it in a month," says Peter.

"Ah, yes, those are the people who go around damming up rivers so that Dan Quayle can have an easier canoe ride, right?" Everybody laughs but Peter. I wish he would not get so wound up about Fernando.

"I love it here," volunteers Michael. "The city is so small and quiet, just so simple, y'know? And Curiaú was like a dream!"

"Curiaú! Very nice, huh? You are part African, right?" I wince and look at Michael to see if he is irritated that I had told Fernando that, but he just nods. "You don't really look it, but most of us don't, either. We have this Portuguese blood which is probably half Moorish anyway." He sips some of his *maracujá*. "You **do** look part Indian, though."

"Mostly Indian," Michael answers.

"And you wanna meet some Amazonian Indians, huh?" He nods. "Well, I know a lot of them, but...well, I hope you are not too disappointed."

"Oh, no!"

"Well, sometimes Americans are disappointed if they see an Indian with a radio or something. They feel like they've been cheated."

"That's ridiculous," says Michael.

"Yeah, well, they're almost all out of isolation now. Settlers and miners and hunters have gradually fanned out all over the place. Most of the Indians know now that if they defend their territories with bows and arrows, planes search out their villages and bomb them. So now they try to learn to trust people like me to fight for them."

"What do you do?" asks Stephanie.

"I try to get to know them, find a good interpreter I can trust, which is really hard since a lot of interpreters are wicked thieves. I try to find out how many people they have, where they hunt, where they grow their food, how much land they really need to survive, then I go back to Brasília, and we try to lobby *o Congreso* to de--what is the word for drawing the new lines on the map?"

"Demarcate," I reply.

"Yes, demarcate the lands for the various tribes. But then the ranchers and the other people complain, and so we have to

355

compromise and change the lines, and then I go back and talk to the Indians again and say, `From now on, you cannot go past this river or this hill or whatever', and they get angry, and I have to convince them that it's not my fault or they'll stop trusting me--"

"Have you ever been attacked?" asks Michael.

"Couple times, but interpreters protected me, splained that I was **weak** man with **little** power with whites, and that killing me would only make things worse--give excuse for bombing or something." His English gets worse when he is emotionally charged, I see.

"God," says Stephanie.

"Other Indians, they know whites longer time, it is different. Then I have to tell them to avoid miners or *seringueros*--"

"Rubber tappers," I explain to the others.

"Yes, rubber tappers--and not share food and not let their daughters go with those men because they can end up with, you know, these diseases, and they don't have any now. And I keep track of when people attack them, and try to figure out whose fault it was, and get the police to arrest people who invade their lands and stuff."

The food arrives, and we dig in. It tastes better than Fernando led us to believe.

"So," says Michael, "who can we meet? Some of the Indians that know whites better? Will that be easier?"

"Actually, I want to take you to meet the *Waiãpis*, because not enough of the Westerners know about them. They are in a very remote place, but now many men have gone there because gold was discovered in their hills. And these miners use very old ways, and spill mercury in the water, and it flows down and accumulates and makes the fish and everybody sick. The Indians attacked them a little while ago, but the men had lots of guns and fought back. It was horrible. The new government was getting inaugurated at about this time, so they could not respond very quickly. They have sent some army people in to separate the Indians from the miners while they

356

negotiate re--what is that word?"

"Redemarcating," I respond.

"Yes, redemarcating--while they negotiate redemarcating the Indian reserve not to include the gold hills."

"That's not fair!" exclaims Stephanie.

"Well, they do not need the gold: it will only encourage them to buy stupid things they don't need like cars and clothes. They need to be left in peace."

"How come you get to decide whether they get cars and TVs?" asks Michael.

"You think that is good for them?" asks Fernando, incredulously.

"I don't know. It seems **they** should get to decide what's good for them."

"Well, yes, in theory, but it's not like that, you know. If some tribe gets a lot of money for selling mahogany or diamonds or something, it is the chiefs who get all the money, you know? And the chiefs go to Belém or Manaus or someplace, then come back with these cars and TV and satellite dish and fancy clothes and beds and stuff, and they don't bring back things that can be shared with everybody, and then there is a lot of jealousy and fighting. It is horrible. I have seen some of these villages after there has been a rebellion and cars and TVs were smashed and chief and wife and kids killed and stuff. Horrible. I don't know Michael. Seems better just re...redemarcate."

"But what if somebody talked to all the people, found out if it might be good to get them farm tools or books or medicine or something useful, for all the people?"

"Well, they are very good farmers, and don't need white medicine if they don't get white disease, and don't have a written language--"

"But there must be something good that can help them!"

357

"I don't think they need our help: I think they just need their land protected," replies Fernando.

"But what about the rest of the Brazilians?" I ask. "I mean, these gold miners are poor, desperate people, aren't they?"

"Yes, they are. That is why I want to see it re-redemarcated."

"But what if somebody else finds something else useful in other Indian lands? Even if the cattle ranchers have lost their subsidies, there are always going to be desperate Brazilians struggling to find some land to farm, or timber or minerals to sell, and now the roads are all there to get in, and they're going to keep exploring Indian lands."

"I know." He resumes eating.

"Why doesn't the government see that they need agrarian land reform, and irrigation projects for the Northeast, and job training in the cities--"

"Because it is simpler to tell the poor to stop having babies! What a lie--the biggest lie! When there were only five-hundred Portuguese in this country, four-hundred fifty of them were poor sailors and servants. When there were five-thousand Brazilians, four-thousand five-hundred of them were poor sailors and servants. When there were five-hundred thousand Brazilians, four-hundred fifty thousand of them were servants and slaves and cheap farmhands. And now they throw condoms around and tell us we are too poor because we have babies! The rich landowners kept bringing in more and more and more slaves and poor people to have lots of cheap labor, and now they tell us to stop having babies! The government likes to say the simple things, and not do the difficult things, so the rich people who own everything won't complain to the army and start another military dictatorship."

"But Brazil can't continue like this indefinitely!"

"I know," he says, returning to his food. He has no answer. Nobody has an answer.

358

"You had said that you wanted more Westerners to see the *Waiãpis*: why's that?" asks Michael.

"Well, I think it would be good for foreigners to write letters to the government to ask them to move more quickly to redemarcate and pull the army out of there. Things are happening, Indians who go on long hunting expeditions are disappearing without a trace, even if they go nowhere near the gold miners, and they are getting angry, and think they are getting tricked into being slaughtered."

"What do you mean, disappearing?"

"They go on these trips to the far edges of the reserve, to hunt meat or fish, and then they never come back. They are not even close to the gold miners, and so they are angry, because they think the white army is encircling the reserve and killing whatever Indians go off in small groups."

"Do you think it's true?" asks Stephanie.

"I don't know," Fernando shakes his head. "Before, maybe, under the military dictatorship...but with this President, I cannot believe it. He seems a pretty good guy. Maybe the army is just doing things, you know? Without the President knowing. Or maybe settlers are exploring other hills, hoping to find other hills of gold. I think the *Waiãpis* will go to war soon if things do not change. They need to send their young men out to hunt, and then if they die, they will have no young warriors, but if they don't go hunt, they will run out of food in the rainy season."

"Will it be safe for us?" asks Peter.

"Sure, we will not be in the remote area: we will only be in the main villages. And we are whites. Now, would you like to fly there, or would you like to take a trip up by boat?"

"Boat!" says Michael.

"Before you answer, I am talking about a very long boat trip, starting all the way back near the ocean."

"Boat!" says Michael.

"The only reason I am suggesting this is that I know one of these guys trying to put together some ecotourism, and he wants to try out this trip where tourists could see some different things, so if we try it out with him, he can point out a lot of the animals and stuff that I don't know."

"Let's do it!" says Michael.

"How long a trip up the Amazon is it?" Peter asks.

"No, not the Amazon River," says Fernando. "We can't get there from here. We would have to take a boat **up** three giant waterfalls! We either fly all the way to the *Waiãpis*, or we sail up from the Araguari River--only little waterfalls."

"Whaddaya mean little waterfalls?!" exclaims Peter.

"Well, more like, uh, rapids--but we can get up them in a powerboat. They are not giant waterfalls like on the Jarí out of the Amazonas River. We can get up the Araguari to the *Waiãpis* in about three days."

"Boat!" says Michael.

Stephanie and I are consulting the map. "Isn't the mouth of the Araguari where that loud water thing is?" I ask.

"Yes, that is why he thinks the ecotourists will like to start there. Very unusual place. Here, where we are, the Amazonas gets really, really wide before reaching the Atlantic, but, even though the Araguari is only a small river, it gets so narrow right before it reaches the Atlantic that it comes out really hard and fast, and it crashes out in this place where the tide is very strong coming back, and it is like they crash against each other. The river is trying to get into the ocean, and the ocean is slamming back at the river, and the water sprays way up in the air, and it's really loud and totally amazing!"

"How do we boat **that**?" says Peter.

"No, we don't boat **that**. We would fly over to Ilha Juruá and then rent a helicopter to fly over the, uh, tidal slamming place--I don't know how to translate that word--to São Miguel to rent a boat."

Peter is now looking at the map. "That would be totally out of our way! It makes no sense!"

"Brazil was totally out of our way, too, Pete!"

"Well, what is the point of starting from way over there? How many miles of the same river do we need to see?"

"C'mon!" Michael says earnestly. "This guy can point out animals and trees and fish to us!"

"Well," I say, "I would love to see that--what's it called, *porarroca*?--" Fernando corrects my pronunciation. "...I mean, it might be worth it just to see that."

"So you vote for that?" asks Stephanie.

Well, then again, I will probably faint from fright just being in a helicopter. "Well, I don't really care: you guys can decide. But, Michael, if we take the boat, it's much less time with the Indians."

"I know--but if they need to be left in peace, maybe we should only visit them a couple days, anyway. And I'm tired of seeing all these movies of the Amazon where they just fly over it all and it's just one big green thing: I want to crawl my way in and **see** it!"

Stephanie looks at Peter. "Well?"

"What do you want to do?"

"I don't mind doing the long way on the boat, and I think I'd like to see that thing with the water," she replies, "but not if it really bothers you."

He frowns. "Well, I guess it's OK if he thinks he can find a **safe** helicopter. I really don't wanna be flying over some gigantic tidal wave in a flying tin can."

"So, you are all agreed on that?" Fernando asks. We nod. God, I never would have agreed to this for anybody but Michael. I will have to overdose on motion sickness pills and anti-diarrheals. "Wow! I was afraid you wouldn't agree! And he'll be so excited to have some test tourists! He won't go all the way up the river, but he'll go about halfway, then wait for us to come back and pick him up in

361

Ferreira Gomes. He wants to see if that's a good place for a jungle excursion. Wow! This is going to be fun!"

We depart the restaurant and head to a cantina down the street, at Fernando's suggestion. He orders up a pitcher of beer and tells us little tidbits about Macapá, whose population has tripled since it became a free-trade zone. "We can leave tomorrow, if you guys want."

"Don't we need to buy some stuff for the boat?" I ask.

"No, these boat owners have everything they need to take people up the river, and I've got the tents and stuff for the villages."

"Fernando, we're **gringos**!" whines Stephanie. This is the first time I have seen her smile at him.

"Don't worry, my dear!" Oh, God, Peter winced at 'dear'. "They have all the mosquito nets, medicines, water, boombox, insect repellant: believe me, they have to take politicians around who are probably much **less** accustomed to roughing it than you are! People who have never even cleaned their own toilets!"

"Well, I don't **mind** cleaning a toilet!" I say. "I really like having them, actually!"

Fernando laughs and asks me if I want to dance.

"Which one is this?"

"I thought you learned all the dances!?"

"Well, I did, but I can never recognize which one to do to which music." He laughs and rolls his eyes. "It's so obvious!"

"No, it's not!"

"C'mon, it's forró."

"Oh, God, this one always cramps up my legs."

We dance for awhile, then he says they have switched to pagode, so we switch to that. I cannot help laughing and enjoying myself; he is a much better partner than the fellow beginners I danced with in the class.

362

"Fernando!" Somebody is hailing him, and it turns out to be his ecotourism buddy, so we go over to greet him, then bring him back to the table to complete the introductions.

"This is Adão."

He shakes hands all around. "Little English...very bad!"

"His English is getting better all the time! He'll have tourists eating out of his hands in a few years," says Fernando.

We sit down, and Fernando tells him we have agreed to give his budding ecotourism enterprise a shot. He is delighted, and hoists his glass for a toast. "To ecotourism, salvior of Brazil!"

"Savior!" laughs Fernando, correcting him.

"Savior of Brazil!"

We all hoist our glasses, then go home to get a good night's sleep.

Chapter 58

The next morning we are sitting in the lobby again, this time with our luggage strewn around us, waiting for Fernando to pick us up. Stephanie had gone straight to sleep last night after assuring me that seeing Fernando was "fine" and "no big deal", while I had tossed and turned for hours, trying to understand what Michael had said. Maybe there is no point in trying to understand it. He was trying to tell me in the nicest way possible to find another guy. But why did he come here? If he loves me so much, why can't it happen for us?

Peter has also apparently not slept too well, obviously frazzled by gorgeous and charming Fernando, despite the fact that Stephanie has been constantly holding his hand and reassuring him verbally. Peter heads to the bathroom again.

Stephanie shakes her head at me. "He doesn't like taking much medicine."

I have purposefully dehydrated myself, and stoked myself on potassium pills, anti-diarrheals, and motion sickness pills. I have never been afraid to take medicine. I want my body limp and entirely immobilized throughout this entire thing. "He won't even take one anti-diarrheal?"

"He says if you obliterate the symptoms, it's harder to diagnose the illness."

"But he might just be tired or nervous."

She shakes her head again. "I don't know. I think he's more scared of the helicopter than he wants to admit."

I think he was up all night brooding about Fernando, personally, but I do not say that. I glance at Michael who is totally relaxed, browsing through his book on Indians of Amazônia. Peter emerges looking wan, and I offer him some anti-diarrheals; he hesitates for a moment, then takes one, thanking me. Thank God! If he had gotten sick up in the air, I would have gotten sick just seeing him getting sick. Stephanie never gets sick on anything. Michael never got motion sickness, either, though he still looks a little under the weather.

Fernando comes in the door and lets out a long whistle at our pile of luggage. "Oh, my God! You have so many bags!" We say nothing, knowing we are guilty as charged. "Do you really need all that stuff?

"Well," I respond, "some of my stuff was warmer clothing for Curitiba--"

"OK, let's get rid of that."

"I don't wanna **dump** it!"

"No, no--when we go pick up my friend, we can leave extra bags at his place. Whatever you can dump off, dump off there, then consolidate the bags, OK?"

We take a taxi to Adão's house and dutifully sift through our luggage, setting aside dressier clothes, warmer clothes, makeup, jewelry, and books, until we are all down to one bag and one backpack each.

"OK, that's **much** better! Now we don't have to rent an extra plane just for the luggage!"

"Are you sure it's safe to leave our stuff here?" asks Peter.

"I would leave my own mother here!" declares Fernando.

Adão comes in from tidying up his kitchen, sees that we are ready, and heads outside to flag a couple taxis. Soon we are at the Macapá airport, and Fernando and Adão are negotiating with various pilots to see who will fly us to Ilha Juruá. I stare at Adão, trying to fall for him, but he does nothing for me. Not my type. Not that "my type" has ever really done me any good. I have no idea how to find what I seek, the elusive cure for my emotional cancer, the mysterious ingredient which could be lying dormant in any uncatalogued specimen of the male species anywhere in this world. Why is Michael so sure somebody exists out there for me? Some illnesses have no cure.

"OK, ladies and gentlemen, step this way!" Fernando starts ushering us towards the hired plane, and I nearly faint when I see how small it is. The pilot greets us cheerily and loads our luggage into the hold. I ask when we will take off and mentally locate the bathroom so that I can take a last-minute pee.

Forty-five minutes later, we are all aboard the plane. Peter seems satisfied with the look of the equipment inside the plane, and his facial color returns to normal. Michael is sitting next to me and squeezing my hand tightly. "It's gonna be great! I've flown in planes like these--really smooth!"

I close my eyes during take-off, not opening them until the plane is finished banking. Fernando and Adão are already pointing out things below us. "There is the original fort, before they built a better one and moved the town. See, there is Curiaú over to the left: you see how isolated it is and how hard it would have been for the Portuguese to find the runaways? See all those islands on the right? That is the Amazonas River. See how it gets all split up before arriving at the ocean?"

Before I know it, we are descending on Ilha Juruá, and I close my eyes again. "Now, you have to admit, that was smooth, wasn't it?" Michael is very encouraging, and I squeeze his hand in gratitude. "I'm really proud of you." You wouldn't be if you knew how doped up I was to get through this. We bounce our way to a jerky stop, and are soon huddled around our luggage in another airport, waiting for Adão to find his helicopter pilot friend. It can hardly be called an airport: it looks to be about two runways, a grassy field, and a small building. We can see water all around us.

"This island is so small!" exclaims Stephanie.

"It's even smaller than Paquetá," I say.

"And Paquetá didn't have an airport!" says Peter.

"Well," says Michael, "this hardly qualifies as an airport. You can see over there the deep-water port they have. They must only use this airport for shuttle flights here and there, for people in too big of a hurry to sail all the way into Macapá or wherever they're going."

Adão returns to tell us his buddy is not around, and we are going to have to wait awhile. He tells us to take a taxi into town and relax at a seaside restaurant called ` Cantina do Mar', and says he will telephone us there when the helicopter is ready.

"What about our stuff?" asks Peter.

"Leave here--no problem."

I look at Fernando for confirmation that this is a good idea, but he is already picking up bags and following Adão to wherever it is Adão is planning to sit with the bags and wait for the helicopter pilot to show up. I shrug my shoulders and follow him. I was already prepared to die in Michael's arms in a fiery crash: what do I care about my bags now?

We taxi to "town" and order drinks at a little café looking out on the enormous Atlantic Ocean. After a few minutes, we realize we can hear the faint humming of the waters colliding to the west of us, but we cannot see it from here. I sip conservatively from my tiny bottle of mineral water, trying to keep my bladder empty for the helicopter ride, even though I am dying of thirst. Nobody seems to have anything to say, so we just stare out at the waves. We can see some ships in the distance, ships coming from both up and down the coast of Brazil.

After an hour and a half, we get a telephone call from Adão and grumble when Fernando tells us the pilot has shown up but needs to make a run somewhere else first. We should plan on coming back to the airport in three hours. There does not seem to be anything to do on this island, so we order some lunch, and I finally order a large bottle of water. After we eat, Fernando asks if anybody

367

wants to take a walk, but we are hot and decline. He puts his hat on and heads off. We are silent for a couple minutes, then Peter pulls some cards out of his backpack. "Anybody want to play some euchre?"

He is barely finished dealing when the waiter comes out to tell us gambling is not allowed there, but I assure him that we are not playing for money, and he finally leaves, mollified. We switch seats around so that Peter and Stephanie can sit across from each other and be partners, and watching Peter and Stephanie make eye signals to each other nearly makes me burst out laughing several times. Michael knows I always bid conservatively, and I gave up trying to read his body language a long time ago.

After an hour, we are a little behind. Stephanie turns up a heart for trump, and I despair because all I have is the queen. I pass, and Peter passes, then Michael tells her to pick it up--and that he is going to "go it alone". I fold my hand and hope he really has enough hearts to do it. He wins trick after trick until he is down to one card. The suspense is killing me, even though we are not playing for money. He lays down an ace of clubs, and they cannot trump it. A little while later, we have won the whole game.

Fernando returns to show us some seashells he has collected.

"You aren't going to pack **those** are you?" I tease him. "Extra weight!"

He laughs. "No, I thought we could use them to tip the waiter!"

"Let's play poker for sugar packets," says Stephanie.

After an hour, Peter looks at his watch and tells us it is time to head back to the airport. When we find Adão, he says the pilot has just landed and is refueling and adding oil. "Who wants to go first?" Of course--I should have realized we could not all fit in one trip.

"How many can go at a time?" asks Peter.

"Depends on luggage--but my friend says two trips. Either three people each time with luggage split, or two and four, with extra

368

luggage with the two people."

"Does the pilot speak any English?" I ask.

"Uh, not really," replies Adão.

Fernando says, "Well, I can go alone with Adão and the luggage, and you can all stay together: her Portuguese is better than Adão's English, anyway."

Peter looks **really** perturbed now. "Peter," I say to him quietly, "if Adão were gonna steal our luggage, he would have done it by **now**!"

"OK, OK."

"Do you want us to go first?" asks Fernando. "That way, if there is any problem, we can come back and you don't have to go." We all nod OK, realizing that our discomfort at being left alone in the airport is not as great as our discomfort would be at braving the helicopter ride first. They quickly load the luggage in and get ready to go. I really want to hug Fernando goodbye in case they crash and die, but I do not want to irritate anybody with my melodramatic feelings, so I quietly retreat to the edge of the airstrip with the others to watch the chopper lift up.

"Looks pretty smooth!" says Michael. "Smoother than some army rides I've had!" I look at him dubiously, and he laughs. "I'm serious!" I pop some more motion sickness pills so that they will be at peak efficiency on our own trip, and sit down on some type of crate to await completion of the forty-minute round trip, checking my watch to note when I should visit the bathroom at optimal pre-departure time.

Peter and Stephanie decide to walk around the airport and stretch their legs a bit, but Michael stays with me. "I know you're nervous, and it's not about the luggage." I do not say anything because I know that he knows about all my fears. "I'm really proud of you for being willing to try this."

"It can't be more dangerous than driving in the streets of Brasília."

369

"Yeah, but it's different when you're the pilot than when somebody else is."

"I would be so disappointed in myself if I didn't try this," I say.

"I know," he replies. "I wouldn't have lobbied for it if I didn't think it would be worth it." He takes a swig of orange juice. "I think it's gonna be unbelievable."

"Can I lean on your shoulder?"

"Why are you asking that?"

"`Cause I want to," I say, feeling stupid.

"You don't have to ask!"

"But you...."

"You don't have to ask, OK?" He pulls my head to his shoulder. "I know what I said hurt you, but not saying it would have hurt you more." Not as much as it is going to hurt when you fall in love with somebody else.

We sit quietly until Peter and Stephanie come back, then Stephanie and I go to the restroom. "Is Peter OK?"

"Yeah, he just doesn't like Fernando much, which is no big surprise since he had already thought of the guy as the jerk who dumped me after we were engaged. I'm trying to tell him that hating Fernando is unproductive: Peter's loving me is what I need. I think he'll come around."

"He's not worried about you starting to like Fernando again--"

"**No!** Well, maybe he's worried about Fernando making moves on me or something, like if he's drunk, but he knows I'm not interested. Fernando's not interested, anyway; I don't know why Peter can't see that."

"He doesn't have 20-20 vision at the moment!"

"Yeah."

We get back from the restroom with perfect timing, our helicopter having just landed. The pilot tells me the trip was really smooth and, in some sort of Portuguese expression I do not know, appears to tell me the equivalent of "they got quite a rush". I translate the good news, and we pile in as soon as the pilot is finished drinking some mineral water. We are lifting up before I have even finished saying my prayers. I close my eyes and do not open them until Michael pleads with me to do so.

"Look, we're coming up on it already!" I look out and see where the ocean seems to be frothing up.

"There's the river!" shouts Stephanie, and suddenly we can see it. The Araguari seems to be flowing straight into a white wall. Water must be flying hundreds of feet into the air! The thunderous roar now overpowers the helicopter racket, and we have to cover our ears against the din. We are quickly right above it, looking straight down into a mammoth spray of water where the tides are slamming into the draining river. Just as I think I am about to die of fright, we are past it.

We look backwards to see it from the river's vantage point. It is flowing into an enormous tidal wave! We are speechless, craning our necks to gaze at it as long as possible. Gradually, the roar and sight recede, and we sit back in our seats, too overwhelmed to look down on the peaceful river winding its way to its yet unknown violent introduction to the Atlantic.

"I knew I should have brought the camcorder!" Peter exclaims at last.

"You're never gonna forget this!" Michael says. "Who needs a video?! God!"

I desperately want to see it again, even though I know he is right: I will never forget it. Then I am comforted realizing we will probably see it again on our way back. I look at Michael, wishing I could kiss him on the lips. He smiles at me and squeezes my hand for the hundredth time, trying to keep my circulation encouraged during the helicopter ride. I squeeze back and look out the window.

371

Our beeline for São Miguel has placed us over land, but the river's curve will soon be under us again. There are few human settlements of any kind to be seen, and no boats at all because none can enter the Araguari from the ocean. A few minutes later we are above land again, and we can see the small port town of São Miguel, where dozens of river boats are docked in another curve of the river. Stephanie suddenly starts laughing. "Look! Fernando is waving his arms at us!" I take a quick peek at him, then close my eyes for the landing.

"Stay relaxed," Michael whispers in my ear. "Sink into your seat cushions. We're almost there, get ready, it's gonna be...now." **Wham!** We are on the ground. I open my eyes. "I'm so proud of you!"

We pile out, and Stephanie hugs the surprised pilot in her exuberance. "Fernando, it was fan-**TAS**-tic!" She is exploding with excitement. Even Peter cannot help but tell Fernando and Adão that it was utterly astonishing.

"You liked, too?" asks the erstwhile ecotourism guide to me and Michael.

"*Maravilha*!" I shout.

"Whatever she said!" Michael exclaims. "**Un**-believable! I have **never** seen anything like that!"

"So," continues Adão, "American tourists, they like, and come?"

"Hell, yeah!" shouts Peter. "Sign **me** up as an investor!" Fernando laughs.

Stephanie shakes her head at Peter. "You see, Fernando is **right**! Whatever works well, the rich businessmen will come in and take over! They'll come in and build deluxe helicopters that seat ten or twelve people and knock pilots like this right out of business!"

"Or they'll build a ski-lift right over the whole thing!" says Michael, and we all laugh at that, except the pilot, whose laughter is delayed as Fernando struggles to translate the comment into

Portuguese.

Adão takes off to look for his favorite riverboat captain, knowing if he delays any longer, we will probably have to wait until tomorrow. Fernando tells us to sit down and fetches us some bottles of pop. We look around at the hodgepodge town in whose center we have apparently landed. There is no airport: the helicopter just landed in a big field not too far from the docks. Fernando seems to be buying the drinks from a little vendor cart near the boats. I am glad my bladder is empty and everything else is plugged up.

The helicopter pilot returns shortly after Fernando does, and gets ready to depart for Ilha Juruá again, having ascertained that nobody else is interested in a helicopter ride this afternoon. With the shade of the helicopter departing, we get up and head over to the trees shading our luggage, earlier deposited by Fernando and Adão. I am so glad he talked us into ditching half of our stuff; I am already dreading carrying it down to the boat.

A small child in rags comes out of nowhere to ask if we want to buy some "souvenirs". He holds up some old coins of an earlier permutation of Brazilian hyper-inflated currency, now worth nothing. We each buy one coin for a dollar a piece, and he races off to share his good fortune with...somebody. Michael lays his head on my lap and promptly falls asleep. Stephanie lays her head in Peter's lap, and we all sit quietly, finishing our drinks, until Adão returns to tell us his favorite riverboat captain is available and we can leave tonight. He is going to go into town to buy some more food, but we can take our luggage down because his son is waiting for us on the boat.

Twenty minutes and twelve sore arms later, we are lugging our bags onto a decent-sized powerboat, and Adão is introducing us to an eight-year old boy named Betinho. Betinho knows no English, apparently, and Fernando and I interpret what he says to the others. We ask where to put our luggage, and the boy brings us down to the hold. He explains that there is not enough room for everybody to sleep below deck, but they have plenty of hammocks and mosquito nets to sleep above deck. The guys quickly insist that Stephanie and I take the only "guestroom", and we store most of the luggage there as well.

Then the boy points out to us the "water closet", which is actually a storage closet that also has some toilet paper and a bucket to dump in. Fernando explains that during the day, people usually dump straight over the side, and the bucket is really more for times when privacy is too difficult to come by, or nights when the rain is so hard that everybody is huddled in the hold, and so forth.

"They won't be **upset** if we use the bucket, will they?" I ask.

"No, no!" replies Fernando.

"No running water?" asks Stephanie.

"We are on top of **miles** and **miles** of running water, my dear!" says Fernando.

"Very funny."

"Don't worry: he will bring back plenty of bottled water to drink, and we will bathe in the river everyday, and you will love it!" Thank God my ovaries have gone on strike in the presence of Michael. I wonder if Stephanie will have to deal with **that**?

Betinho then points out the "kitchen" and food storage. He says we can eat whatever we want, whenever we want, but we will get charged for everything eaten. As we climb back up on deck, Fernando assures us that boat captains always buy tons of food for gringo passengers, and not to worry about that. "And it's cheap out here--what he will buy, I mean. You will not be getting any fancy stuff, but he will not charge much for the rice and beans and canned stuff he'll have. And we can catch fish every day."

Adão has already returned with some supplies and begins rearranging things on deck, hanging hammocks and readying mosquito nets for the approach of dusk. Betinho has remained below deck to rearrange cabinets to make room for the supplies of food his father will bring back to feed us until we reach Ferreira Gomes. I sit down on the side and look out at the Araguari River, wishing I did not like to frequent indoor plumbing several times a day. I never did go camping with Michael because of that, but here I am now.

Peter is trying to talk to Adão about attracting ecotourists. "Y'know, **some** people would totally go for this, because they're used to camping and everything, but if you want to get the tourists with lots of money, you need to get really **nice** boats, really clean, with a flush toilet and lots of beds." Adão just nods politely. I know there is no way for somebody like him to get a bank loan in Brazil. He probably cannot understand what Peter is saying, anyway.

Stephanie hands me some Skin-So-Soft and I slather it on, maybe for the last night. Tomorrow night we will be further inland and be more afraid of the interior mosquitoes, and will probably switch to the toxic stuff. I wipe some oil on Michael's limbs for him, then on his neck. "This is soooooo fantastic, isn't it?" he says. "I know you hate camping, but, I **really** think it'll be worth it."

"I know it will," I say, and I do.

Soon the captain returns with a vendor and his entire rolling bicycle-powered vendor cart, and the guys unload the groceries. In the process, we are introduced to the captain, Manoel, who wastes no time in pulling the anchor and taking off. As soon as Betinho has finished storing the tie ropes, he and Adão go downstairs to prepare dinner. They emerge with a small propane grill and a box full of food and plates and silverware, and we all join in helping to prepare a meal. They grill some fresh fish, and heat up some beans and plantains, and pass around fresh bread to eat. By the time Betinho pulls out the imported chocolate chip cookies to our immense delight, the sun is already setting--almost straight in front of us. We take some photos of the sun sinking into a mesmerizing orange splash on the river.

Adão points out some waterfowl along the shore, eating for the last time today before they go to sleep. He points out the nighthawks already starting to circle. "There will be much more to see in the daylight, when we get further in."

When darkness falls, Adão takes over the skipper's wheel and lets the captain and his son go to sleep in the back, explaining to us

375

that they will be up at the crack of dawn to eat breakfast and get the boat started again.

"You aren't going to drive all night?" asks Stephanie.

"No, only a couple more hours, until I get sleepy," he says.

"Then you'll drop anchor?" asks Peter.

"No, then I will stop motor and just let it float by self."

Fernando bursts out laughing, and we realize Adão is joking. We sit around chatting for a couple more hours, then decide to try to go to sleep, advised by our ecotourism guide that there is a lot to see in an Amazonian dawn.

Chapter 59

Stephanie and I gradually awaken to the sound of squawking...something or other. At least, I assume that is what has awoken us. Maybe it was the restarting of the engine, because we are definitely motoring our way upriver again. We throw our cotton dresses back on and bring our baby wipes for our trip to the "water closet". Neither of us believes that the six guys on board want to close their eyes every time one of us were to make a river dump up on deck.

"Should we take the bucket up to dump it overboard, or do you think Betinho will do it?" asks Stephanie.

"I guess we should do it."

We carry it up the ladder carefully, and Betinho rushes out of nowhere to grab it from our hands. "*Não, senhoraś! Não é preciso!*" We hand it over sheepishly, and I see Michael chuckling at us while he eats a banana. Peter gives Stephanie a big kiss and hug and asks how her night was.

"Fine! How was yours?" she whispers.

"Fine!"

"C'mon!" shouts Fernando. "You are missing the show!" He and Adão are sharing the binoculars back and forth as Adão points out some animals in the trees, mostly birds.

"You slept **very** late," he scolds us. "Already missed many morning things!" I look at my watch--6:00 a.m.! This is like a personal best for me! No alarm clock, even!

377

"Why didn't you wake us?" wails Stephanie to Peter.

Michael and Peter both laugh. "You are both **way** too grumpy in the morning!" says Michael.

"Don't worry," says Adão. "In a few hours, we will stop for lunch in one of the...uh...." He stops to consult with Fernando for the word.

"Like a feeder stream?" Fernando says tentatively.

"You mean a stream that flows into the river?" I ask.

"Yes!"

"Yeah, that's a feeder stream."

"Feeder stream," repeats Adão. "We stop for lunch in feeder stream--see lots of things."

"What did we miss?" I ask Michael, as I settle in for some breakfast.

"Huge flocks of birds, and some monkeys, and some flying fish, and some turtles, and a giant water snake--"

"Gross!" shouts Stephanie.

Michael continues listing some other wildlife we missed, even as Adão is pointing out other passing scenes to us, identifying different types of trees and monkeys and birds. He points out occasional hills in the background and the waterfalls cascading down them. Occasionally we can see smoke in the distance, where settlers must be burning or cooking something; we are too deep in the rainy season for them to be clearing land. We are all clicking our cameras like mad, eating breakfast simultaneously.

The wildlife breakfast crowds thin out as we finish up our own breakfasts, and we set aside our cameras and sit back to relax a bit. Betinho puts on the radio to one of the satellite stations that play American-style rock and roll, and we listen drowsily to an old U2 song, haunting and mesmerizing: "Walk on by, walk on through, walk 'til you run, and don't look back, for here, I am...." We are starting to get clammy and hot. Seemingly in answer to the

378

unspoken question, Fernando tells us we can swim before lunch.

"Does Betinho go to school?" Stephanie asks Fernando.

"I doubt it."

"Is his father teaching him how to read?"

"I don't think Manoel **knows** how to read."

"Is his mother dead?"

"Probably. Never heard of a Brazilian woman abandoning her baby unless she was crazy or had no money. And if he had left her, he wouldn't have taken Betinho."

We fall silent, watching this small boy take the admiral's wheel so that his father can...clean his **guns**?

"Why is he cleaning his guns?" I ask.

"If you shoot a dirty gun, it blows up in your face," replies Fernando.

"I **know** that! What is he planning to shoot?"

"Well, he just needs to be ready, in case."

"In case of **what**?" asks Peter.

"Well, the captains are always like that: it is how they are, you know? They still act like jaguars and Indians are going to jump out of the jungle and attack them, even though the jaguars and Indians have almost been hunted to extinction already." He looks around at us, trying to gauge our level of credulity. "I am sure he will not shoot anything at all--maybe a monkey to eat."

"A monkey!" exclaims Stephanie.

"Yeah, they taste pretty good."

"But they're so cute!"

"Not as cute as lambs and veal!"

"OK, let's not argue about that," says Michael.

Adão finally puts down his binoculars to eat some breakfast, satisfied that the peak wildlife morning performances are over.

"Everybody happy? Very beautiful?" We all nod, drowsy in the sticky heat, even though we are all sitting in the shade of the boat's overhanging roof. We watch the trees glide by us silently for a long time, sipping water and juice. We seem to be on a tiny thread of water in between two endless walls of green. Stephanie and Peter and Michael have all picked up their Brazil guidebooks to read what they can about this region. I know very little will be in their guidebooks about it. I walk to the back of the boat. I feel like crying, but I am not sure why. I stare at the water and the humming trees.

A few minutes later, Fernando comes up behind me. "Are you ill?" he asks, in Portuguese.

"I'm OK," I reassure him.

"You and Michael--it makes you very sad?"

"Yeah, but...I need to learn to deal with it."

"Seeing you with him...makes me understand maybe why you were so unhappy in Brazil." I look at him, expectantly. He leans on the rail. "He is...like an open book. He is like the warm blanket you wrap around yourself. Now you are in a place where people are all closed books, very hard to open. And the blankets must be unfolded first. And foreigners do not know how, and nobody tells them. The lucky ones figure it out. The lucky ones find a way to get inside a clan--for we are a clannish culture--and then they are all right."

"You think Stephanie would have figured it out: isn't that what you said?"

"Yeah, I think she would have. She figured **me** out, better than she thinks." He is quiet for a few moments, scratching some mosquito bites. "You got to know Michael, then you loved him. In Brazil, you have to love the people first, then they let you get to know them. If you are not born into a clan, you have to love your way into it. You never found a clan."

"Or I didn't have enough love to get inside it?"

"You wanted to understand first, then love."

"Why doesn't anybody explain anything?"

380

"Because if you are not already in their clan, they see no reason to help you. It is not malice: it is simply how we are. How the Portuguese or something or somebody has made us."

"Did Stephanie love you before she got to know you?"

"Yes, absolutely. But I could not bring her into my clan."

"Why not?"

"Because I am a different person in Brazil than I was in the U.S."

Aren't we all, I think.

We hear some screeches from the front of the boat and race up to see what it is. Betinho is at the admiral's wheel shouting, "*Botos! Botos!*", Manoel has his rifle raised, Stephanie is struggling to stop him from shooting, and Michael and Peter are trying to pull Stephanie away from the gun.

"Please, OK!" shouts Adão to Stephanie. "He will only shoot defense boat!"

"They're just dolphins!" wails Stephanie.

"*Boto vermelho!*" shouts Manoel, trying to push her aside.

"Stephanie!" Fernando's shriek makes her wince. "Calm down! He won't shoot them unless they try to capsize the boat!"

"That's crazy!" she shouts.

"I **know**! So don't **worry**! He won't shoot them! He's just scared! There are horrible myths about those dolphins attacking boats, knocking them over."

"How could dolphins knock over this boat?!"

"They **can't**! He's just being cautious, OK?"

She finally calms down, and Peter pulls her away from Manoel, who still has his gun aimed at the river dolphins bow-riding in front of us. I listen to Adão talking calmly to Manoel, explaining to him that, even if the myths were true, those myths are about dolphins capsizing little fishing boats and canoes, not enormous

381

motorboats. Manoel does not lower his arm or his gaze.

We stare at the two pinkish/grayish dolphins in amazement. They are much uglier than the bottlenoses we are accustomed to, with grotesquely enormous sonar melons in their foreheads. They are now flanking the wake of the boat, swimming very fast, occasionally leaping clear out of the water just for the hell of it. When they jump, we can see strange bristles on their snouts. They abruptly peel off, and we turn to watch them swim off into a small feeder stream. Manoel lowers his gun and wipes his sweaty brow with his shirt sleeve. He quietly uncocks the gun, puts it back in its place, and takes the steering wheel from Betinho, who silently resumes his chore of resewing some torn nets and hammocks.

We all sit down, and I ask Adão to tell us why Manoel is so afraid of the dolphins.

"You splain, Fernando."

"Well, this kind of dolphin-- *boto vermelho*--or, uh, red dolphin, is a very strange dolphin, and there are many myths about him. They are sort of, uhh, naughty? Playful? People say they knock over fishing boats all the time. It is probably just to play, but people sometimes think they're evil."

"Evil?!" exclaims Michael.

"Well, you know, people are scared of things they don't understand, you know? They see these fish come up, and breathe air, and so they think they are like people, and have a secret city under the water--"

"No way!" exclaims Stephanie.

"Yeah, and they think the *boto* can turn into a handsome white man and seduce girls at parties."

"What?!" says Peter.

"Yeah, they say that. Like, when a fisherman is gone for a few months, and comes back, and his wife is two months pregnant, she says it was the *boto*, and the *boto* took her to his underwater city, and usually she describes a place that looks like Rio de Janeiro or

382

something, which she probably saw on TV, and everybody believes it." We all laugh at that. "No, I think they **really** believe it."

"Well, it's better than stoning the woman to death," says Michael.

"Sometimes they want to kill the *boto*, but they are afraid to do it. Some people think the *boto* has many supernatural powers and controls all the rivers in the forest." We just shake our heads in amazement. "It is very confusing, because sometimes they talk about the *boto mesmo*, which is like the simple dolphin, but then they talk about the *boto encantado*, which is like the naughty supernatural one. I think they are afraid that killing the *boto mesmo* is very bad luck, but sometimes you **have** to kill a *boto encantado* in self-defense. And then you keep one of his eyes for good luck, or sell it for lots of money, as a, uhh, talisman. But sometimes you have to ask the *boto encantado's* permission to hunt or fish, and be nice to him."

"That doesn't make any sense!" exclaims Peter.

"Yes, it is very confusing. I think different people believe different things, you know? Everybody has different stories, and they try to put them together to make sense out of it. Some anthropologists think dark-skinned poor people equate the dolphin with rich white people who have an easy life. Sometimes they feel like they are competing with the dolphins for the fish and everything."

"Tell them about the *tucuxi*," says Adão.

"Ah, yes, there is a second kind of river dolphin called *boto tucuxi*, which are more like, uhh, harbor porpoises--small and dark and bluish/grayish. These ones nobody is afraid of. There are no bad myths about them: maybe because the other ones are so ugly and strange!" He laughs. "But these littler ones, they are less curious and mischievous, and they do not come near people's boats much. Some people say the *tucuxi* are very good, and will even save drowning people and carry them to shore, or carry dead people back to the shore or the boat. They swim in big groups, you see? They act more like friendly fish, not like the *boto vermelho*, which always

383

seems to be sneaking around one or two at a time."

"And *tucuxi* no take the fisherman fish," adds Adão.

"Yes, see, this is the thing," says Fernando. "When the rainy season comes, the rivers all rise up and flood all over the place, and the fish can scatter all over the place, and it is very hard for the fishermen to find them. These *boto vermelho* are big but very flexible, and they will swim into the flooded places and wiggle around the trees and take fish everywhere, but the *tucuxi* stay in the deep part of the river, they are less aggressive, and so the fishermen do not get angry at the *tucuxi*. You see?"

We all nod slowly.

"What do **you** think, Adão?" I ask.

He shrugs his shoulders. "I see some *boto vermelhos* jump around and look very crazy. I am not surprised people think they are with crazy spirit. I see *boto tucuxi* push dead fisherman to shore."

"Really?!" we all ask.

"Yes, like, did not want poor man to get eat by *piranhas* or something."

"You saw **that**?!" asks Fernando. Adão nods earnestly. "*Mesmo*?" He nods again.

We sit in silence for a long time, watching the forest go by, occasionally discussing things we are reading in various guidebooks, until Adão signals Manoel to pull the boat into a feeder stream for lunch. I wait impatiently for the all-clear signal to jump in the water.

Chapter 60

Manoel and Adão consult and point in various directions until they nod in agreement on where to moor the boat. As soon as the anchor is dropped, Michael pulls off his shirt to jump in the water.

"Wait!" I grab him. "There could be barracudas or crocodiles!"

"I don't think so," says Adão.

"How do you know?!"

"I just don't think so. We'll check, though."

Betinho brings a piece of raw fish and a hunk of raw chicken up from the kitchen and throws them into the water, then agitates the water with a pole to attract attention. After a minute he stops moving the pole and we watch the stream carefully. It is not very clear, but we can make out the shapes of some fish swimming around. Nothing comes near the bloody bait.

Adão uses binoculars to scan the flood fingers of the stream to see if there are crocodiles hidden in the trees. "*Peixe-boi*," he announces, cheerfully.

"What?!" exclaim Stephanie and Peter simultaneously.

"No *jacarés*, uhh, alligators. OK!"

"What about the 'peshee' thing?" Peter asks.

"No problem," he shakes his head.

"It's a mammal," says Fernando. "You have them in Florida, too: I can't remember the name."

"Manatees?" I ask.

"Yeah!" says Adão. "Manatees! Cute!"

With that, Michael jumps in the water. I pull the binoculars from the hands of Adão and look out at the manatees. I do not know much about manatees, but they do not seem to be stirring. I can barely see their eyes. Splash--I turn around to see that Fernando and Adão have already jumped in. I look back at the manatees, and they are swimming away now.

"Let me see," says Stephanie, but they are already gone. Stephanie and I go downstairs to put on our swimsuits. "Do you think I can use my shampoo here? It's organic: I bought it at the rainforest store in the mall!"

I look over the list of ingredients. "I guess!"

When we come up, Peter has jumped into the water, too. Manoel and Betinho finish setting up some fishing poles and whatever other chores they were doing, kick off their flip flops, and jump in the stream, too.

"Is it cold?" I ask.

"Yeah, can't you see that mountain glacier it's coming from?" replies Michael, laughing at me. I take Stephanie's shampoo bottle and throw it at his head, but he puts up his hand to catch it. "You must be joking!"

"It's organic rainforest shampoo!" shouts Stephanie, and jumps in.

I take one more peek with the binoculars, then jump in after her. Ahhhhhh! Sooooo warm! Manoel is flipping Betinho up into the air. Fernando and Adão are swimming along the shoreline, apparently talking about plants and birds near the water. Stephanie retrieves her shampoo bottle from Michael, suds up her hair, then passes it around to all the gringos. Soon Betinho has swum over to us to beg for shampoo, too, so Stephanie squirts some in his hair and

386

lathers it up, and he giggles in wild amusement. Is this really his first shampoo? She offers some to Manoel, but he declines, even though he is obviously quite amused by Betinho's bubble-capped appearance.

We all duck under the water to rinse, then swim off lazily in different directions, except for Peter and Stephanie, who swim off together to kiss somewhere discreet. I float on my back and see the sky in between the trees arching over the stream. It is a thin sliver of blue sky, with a couple puffy white clouds. The rainy season must be nearing an early close: we have not gotten any rain in Amapá at all, even though we should have. I swim for a long time until I am hungry, then return to the boat, where Manoel and Betinho have already started cooking up some lunch with the fish they pulled from their hooks.

The smell of warm food brings everybody else back to the boat, and while we eat, Adão points out some wildlife on the shorelines. Our swimming scared off quite a few critters, apparently, but they have returned now--turtles, crabs, frogs, and various types of waterfowl. He points up in the trees to identify some monkeys and parrots and macaws.

"*Tucano!*" shouts Betinho triumphantly, obviously proud that he has spotted the toucan before Adão did.

"You see," says Adão, "my idea is take tourists like this, and then see water stuff along river, and then I pick out good place inland to take them around in canoe and walk so that they see monkeys and maybe some other things-- *tamandú*, uh,--"

"Anteater," offers Fernando.

"Yes, anteaters, uhh, deer, and little things, not rats, but like rats, umm, tapirs, maybe jaguar, and lots of insects and flowers. Need to learn more English so I can splain, don't touch frog, poison!"

"The frogs are poisonous!?" exclaims Stephanie.

"Some of them," he replies.

387

"People have to go **deep** into the woods to see some of these animals," adds Fernando. "People have to rough it and they have to take risks and they have to listen to the guides. The problem, I think, is that, to make money, the guides want to take a big group, you know? But then they have to watch all these people at once, and sometimes people don't listen, and they walk off by themselves because they don't see any jaguar, but they don't know that there could be a big snake hidden right in the tree next to them, you know?"

Not **my** idea of a vacation, I think. But I **am** enjoying **this**, I guess. It is really special. Not fun, not lie-on-the-beach relaxing, but really special. And I hate to admit it, even to myself, but it is hard to be very scared of the jungle when I am surrounded by so many men. I have this crazy idea that men would instinctively defend the women from anything. It is no longer true in modern, urbanized society, but in the jungle, surely they would....

The guys curl up on their hammocks, and Stephanie and I retreat below deck for a siesta. We wake up when the engine revs up again, visit the water closet, then join the guys on deck. They are drinking pop and kicking a miniature soccer ball around the deck with Betinho.

"Fernando," says Stephanie, sitting down with a bottle of Guaraná in her hand, "how did these dolphins get here?"

"Into Amazônia?" She nods. "Well, the Indians have a very strange myth about it, but I do not know if I can tell it right. Something about a great rainy season when it rained and rained and did not stop raining for a single day for ten moons, until the Sulayapo could find no land left anywhere. They were clinging to the tops of trees, starving to death, when their leader had a vision of where they could find dry land. He told them to follow him, but they would have to swim very far. Some of the people refused to go, but most of them went and swam all day and all night until they found the dry top of a very high hill. They ate many fruits from the trees and lived on the top of the hill for one moon.

388

"Then the rain stopped, but they had to live up there for another moon until the waters started receding. Gradually, the waters went down, and they were able to return to their original home. They expected to find skeletons, assuming that their kinfolk would have died and been devoured by animals when the waters went down. Instead, they discovered the kinfolk that had not gone with them calling to them from the river. The big pink ones with the funny heads were the stubborn adults who did not go, and the little blue ones were the children who had had no choice but to stay with their parents. They called and called to the other Sulayapo to join them in the water, where they would never have to run away from the floods again, but the Sulayapo were afraid and did not want to live in the water.

"From that day on, the pink dolphins would always make trouble for the Sulayapo, capsizing their canoes, and trying to get them to join them in the water. The Sulayapo were a little afraid of them and a little sorry for them and sometimes angry at them. The little blue ones got tired of their parents', uhh, antics, and went off on their own, because they were just children, and had already stopped missing the other Sulayapo. They were happy to play by themselves, except that if they ever saw a Sulayapo in trouble, they would always help it, because they knew the Sulayapo were their ancestors."

"That's totally amazing!" I say. "That has so many similarities to what the Brazilians say about the blue ones being better behaved and everything."

"Well," Fernando says, "I think many of the Indian tribes have similar myths about the dolphins, and so settlers probably heard them all over Amazônia, when they moved here."

"The Cherokee have a myth like that, too," says Michael. "At least, I think they do. I don't remember it so well. They didn't let us study those myths in school, and so we would only hear them occasionally during holiday celebrations. The adults always seemed sort of embarrassed to tell them in front of us, because they knew that in school we were all being told that the Cherokee myths were pretend. But I remember a story like that, about a great flood....I

389

think it was to explain why turkeys don't fly." He furrows his brow. "No, maybe it was to explain why frogs sing when it rains....No....Shoot! I can't remember! But I know I've heard a story like that!"

"But it is still just myth," says Adão. "People always make up stories to splain things they not understand. Now we have science, and we understand nature better."

"So how does nature explain the Amazonian dolphins, then?" asks Peter.

Adão struggles with his English to tell us the story that I had once heard my Institute boss mention, about how the flow of the Amazon river system had shifted from westward towards the Pacific, to eastward towards the Atlantic, but it still confuses me. Ancient geology, shifting plates, the emergence of the Andes mountains...it makes me dizzy trying to understand it all.

"So the dolphins were **suddenly** trapped inside the continent?" asks Peter, incredulously.

"Well, maybe," replies Adão, speaking slowly to remember the words in English, "but some people think they had choice, that they could have escaped back out to Pacific when the Andes were only beginning to rise, but they liked the fish inside land and stayed. Maybe they just kept swimming, ummm--" he consults with Fernando for the correct word, then continues, "--downstream because it was easier than swimming, umm, upstream, and they liked the fish they found, and then later they could not find their way back to Pacific Ocean because Andes got too tall."

We sit and ponder that in silence for awhile. I try to picture the Andes shooting up into the air, right under the unsuspecting dolphins who had swum a little bit into the river to hunt fish, and all that water that had been flowing to the Pacific suddenly flowing downhill--down the new hills--to the Atlantic. I did not understand it when I first heard it, and I am still not sure I understand it now.

"I don't know," says Stephanie. "I think the Indian myth makes more sense than that stuff about the Andes!"

390

Adão shakes his head. "I will find book to show you. My English is bad."

"No, your English is very good," I assure him, "but we have no training in geology!"

"Which story do **you** believe, Fernando" Stephanie asks.

"I don't really care," he laughs. "I like all the stories."

"Sometimes I wonder about these geologists and archaeologists and all these experts telling us they know what happened five-thousand years ago, or five-million years ago," I say. "I think they do a lot more guessing than they admit."

"Oh, I'm **sure** they do!" says Peter. "We read some of the archaeology books about Mexico while you were over there, and every other sentence began with `it is assumed' or `it is believed that'. I mean, what about those ruins at Campeche? They have changed their minds about those plenty of times, already, haven't they? Did you read what the <u>Smithsonian</u> wrote about it last year?"

As I enter into a discussion about Mexican archaeology with Peter and Michael, I notice that Stephanie has quietly followed Fernando to the back of the boat, to the "men's room". Did he ask her to follow him, or was it her idea? They have not been alone yet, the entire trip. About ten minutes go by without Peter's noticing their absence, and then Adão shouts to us that he has spotted some alligators in a feeder stream.

Manoel turns off the motor, and we stop to watch the alligators snapping at some birds on the edge of the river bank. The birds are running frantically, trying to build up steam for take-off, but about a half-dozen of them are caught; dozens of luckier ones escape into the air to search for a different stream without alligators. By the time the show is over, Stephanie and Fernando have blended back into the group.

The guys launch into a macho discussion of hunter and prey, and it is very easy for me to take Stephanie aside and ask her what happened.

391

"Nothing," she says. "I just wanted to talk to him alone for a few minutes, thank him for arranging such a special trip for us and everything."

"Are you OK?"

"Yeah! I'm totally over him, and I wanted to tell him that, too, so he would feel more comfortable around me...and Peter. Maybe if he feels more comfortable, Peter will feel more comfortable. Peter says they're getting along OK, but I don't know. Fernando definitely does not think they are getting along OK."

"Well, they're getting along pretty well, considering," I say.

"Yeah, considering....But, I wanted a chance to talk to Fernando alone. It was nice. We said some things we should have said a long, long time ago. I mean, part of it was my fault, too. Not the break-up, but I never wrote him **after** the break-up, and I should have. I should have told him how I felt, and given him a chance to explain things. I didn't want him to **have** a chance to explain things. If I had given him a chance, I think I would have gotten over him a lot faster."

"Yeah, but it sounds as if he didn't really have it all figured out right away."

"Yeah," she says, "but even knowing **that** would have helped me. I would have thought of him as confused, whatever...not just malicious or something, which he wasn't"

"You really feel OK about all this now, huh?"

"Yeah."

Peter departs the hunter/prey conversation and comes over to Stephanie, and I unobtrusively leave them alone, wondering how fast she would have gotten over Fernando without a Peter to come along and pick up the pieces. Michael resumes kicking the miniature soccer ball around with Betinho, and all I can think is what a great father he would be, and how the first time I ever saw a wild dolphin was with Michael, on the Carolina coast, and how I had screamed, thinking a shark was approaching the beach, and how Michael had

392

laughed, and pointed out to me how many fins there were, and how they were bobbing in and out of the water, which meant they were dolphins, and how enchanting it had all been.

It had wrenched my gut somehow, that sudden exhilaration of going from thinking a shark was after me to realizing I was surrounded by friendly dolphins. Two kinds of fin...a thin line of emotion. Seeing the dolphins pluck António from the depths of that Mexican pool had wrenched my gut again. Now I know it was not the same thing at all. António could do that trick over and over again. It was good that I had left Cuahtemoc while I still could feel some of that magic feeling, before totally losing it, as I would have, eventually, when I realized that doing the trick over and over again would not guarantee getting the gut rush over and over again. I can still remember it with the rush, and I always will.

Chapter 61

We spend the rest of the afternoon answering Adão's questions about what American tourists would prefer on an inland trip. Lots of wildlife? Rapid travel, or slow travel, with scientific descriptions of the most interesting flowers and animals? Would they like lots of handouts with this information, or just hear some little speeches about it? Should they have a professional video cameraman recording the whole thing, to sell copies of to the tourists, so that they can relax and enjoy it without worrying about their own camcorders? How much money would people be willing to spend?

On and on. I let Peter and Stephanie answer most of the questions. I have no idea what the average American tourist would want, except that I suspect the average American tourist probably is not going to come here, anyway. And God only knows what these adventure-type tourists want. They sound suicidal, the things they like to do. They would probably want to wrestle the alligators and take on the pythons.

Or maybe this will become one big Everglades National Park, with all the malaria mosquitoes bombed out of existence, and comfortable hydroplanes zooming everybody from four-star hotels out to see waterfowl, and back again to their four-star hotels. Everybody likes four-star hotels...even me.

But, God, this is beautiful, I think, even more so as we start to see faint forms of human settlement appearing oddly out of place as we approach Ferreira Gomes. I will miss Adão; I wish he could make the whole trip with us, but I know he needs to do some research for his ecotourism business plans. I wish I had the guts to try something like that.

Ten minutes later, we are docked in Ferreira Gomes. We put the strong insect repellant, long pants, and long sleeves on, and prepare to enter the dusk of this sleepy port town. We will have dinner in town while Adão helps Manoel buy enough groceries for the next leg of the journey, and makes some arrangements for his stay in this town. Fernando has volunteered to guard the boat, letting us take Betinho "out to dinner". Betinho has donned a New York Yankees t-shirt, apparently his best shirt.

Adão points to us his culinary recommendation, "Restaurante Joaquina", before turning the corner to get to the grocery store. The restaurant is heating up fast, now that they have closed the doors and shutters against the twilight mosquito onslaught. We sit in puddles of perspiration, and would not enjoy the meal at all were it not for Betinho's obvious ecstasy at being lavished with such an unexpected kindness from the gringos. He really is adorable...and boy, does he know he is getting a free meal! He eats and eats and eats as if there is no tomorrow.

We walk around town for a little while, but feel uncomfortable the way people are staring at us. They are not malicious stares, but...do they know an ecology entrepreneur is scouting their sleepy little town out for imagined hordes of tourists? Would they like that? We buy some candy bars and old Brazilian magazines at the drugstore to try to win some smiles. The biggest smile is from Betinho, who has received a gift of a new t-shirt from Peter--a t-shirt celebrating Brazil's World Cup victory the year before. Betinho puts it on immediately and prances around, suddenly king for a day.

We return to the boat, bearing carry-out and candy bars for a grateful Fernando. We play soccer on deck a little until Adão and Manoel return with the groceries and fresh mineral water bottles. Adão tells us he will spend the night in town with a friend, but will come by at dawn to bid us farewell. I hear Manoel make a quiet comment in Portuguese to Fernando about Adão's "friend", and they both chuckle.

We sit around talking a little bit longer, then go to sleep, hot and exhausted. The next morning, Adão comes by at dawn as promised, and spreads goodbye hugs and kisses around to everyone. "Remember, if Indian trip no good, come back early, go on jungle tour with Adão!" Manoel starts up the motor, and we begin our second day on the Araguari River.

It seems much duller without Adão to point out every little thing. We try scanning the shorelines with our binoculars, but we are not as adept at seeing the camouflaged animals. A couple hours out of Ferreira Gomes, we start ascending some rapids, which suddenly rock the boat fiercely. We all drop to the deck except for the captain, who appears unfazed; evidently he has taken his boat up this river many times. The river calms down for another half-hour, then froths up again as we do another ascent.

"OK!" Betinho calls to us. "OK!"

"There won't be any more rapids for awhile," says Fernando.

We lounge around lazily on hammocks until it is time to dock for our noontime swim and lunch. Then we sleep for awhile. When Manoel starts the boat again, we stay in our hammocks. With every bend of the river, the water seems narrower, and the trees arching above our faces seem ever so slightly closer and closer to fusing together. We all feel it--the hot jungle closing in on us as we get closer and closer to the river's narrow source, the temperature going up a degree for every foot of river's width we lose. Or am I imagining it?

We lounge on the hammocks for the rest of the afternoon--only getting out of them to look at a manatee that Betinho has pointed out to us. Near dusk, we put on mosquito repellant and longer clothing again. As dusk approaches, we reach the town of Pedra Branca, which is even smaller than Ferreira Gomes was. It has a rough sailor-like look about it, and the gringos are happy to stay on board the boat as Fernando accompanies Manoel to buy our final groceries for the long haul.

396

We sip our last bottles of pop, knowing we will not be taking anything that bulky and heavy for the rest of the trip. No more jugs of mineral water. No more bananas or bread. No more meats or vegetables. From now on, we have to use all the storage space for a cautious three ("just in case", Fernando had said) weeks' worth of dried rice, beans, and milk, in addition to the ladies' request for more toilet paper, and the extra cans of gasoline Manoel will need to get back. Some of the storage space is already taken up with gifts for the tribe (more radio batteries and vitamin pills and a few baubles for the chief) and a special bag of goodies for the Brazilian anthropology student living with the *Waiãpis* who will be interpreting for us.

Every day we will boil water for at least ten minutes before we drink it, or use iodine drops if our matches get wet for some reason. We will only eat fish and meat we can hunt, and turtle eggs and crabs we can dig up, and only eat fruits and vegetables we can find. This will be easier for us once we are with the Indians, Fernando says.

We lie in our hammocks, gazing out at the darkening town.

"I hope they get back soon," says Stephanie. "This town gives me the creeps."

"Why?" asks Peter.

"I don't know."

"I think it's because it looks so small, and the jungle looks so enormous and dark behind it," says Michael.

"And we're so deep now," I say, even while realizing how absurd the statement is, because I know from the map that we have penetrated a mere corner of the Amazon basin. "It's so much jungle. It just goes on and on and on."

"I'm not surprised they wanna burn it down: it looks really scary at night," says Stephanie.

"That's not why they're burning it down," I say.

"I know--slash and burn agriculture, cattle ranches. But it gives me the creeps at night."

397

"It should," says Michael. "You don't know how to survive in it at night." At night? That's generous: I don't think I could survive in it by day. "It doesn't scare the Indians. A big city would scare the Indians."

I crawl into Michael's hammock, not caring if it is inappropriate, to gaze at the moon coming up. He puts his arm around me and whispers, "Do you think the river trip was a mistake?" I shake my head. "Do you think they regret it?" I turn to look at Stephanie and Peter, stretched out together in a hammock, with Betinho sitting on their lap showing them the many tricks he can do with a bit of string. I shake my head. "I can't believe how much he plays with them, and they can't even speak a word of Portuguese to him! I expected him to be playing with **you** all the time."

"Maybe he thinks they're normal for not speaking Portuguese. Maybe he thinks I'm weird because I try to speak his language and it just comes out goofy." Or maybe he senses instinctively that they are the ones with the light hearts.

"It doesn't come out goofy! Fernando says your Portuguese is fantastic: he can't believe how fast you've become fluent."

"He's exaggerating."

"I don't think so."

"You were right about the plane trip: that would have been wrong. We would not have felt it the same way."

"It's so beautiful and sad." Yes, I think, and we have not even seen the Indians yet.

Fernando and Manoel arrive at last and stow the provisions. They have bought a fresh food feast for our last night of fancy eating--chicken, ham, sausages, lettuce, cucumber, tomatoes, onions, green peppers, watermelon, bananas, fresh-baked bread, fresh milk and cheese, and some sort of pastry made of *açai*. We eat slowly, relishing the variety of things we will not see for awhile.

"Some of the men said they could not believe we were going into *Waiãpi* territory," Fernando remarks, casually. "They are really angry at whites right now." He looks up from his watermelon to gauge our reaction. "I wasn't telling that to scare you! I was just saying it to prove my point--that the *Waiãpis* are near the breaking point, and the redemarcation must be completed soon, and enforced."

"Are you **sure** there is nothing to be scared of?" asks Peter.

"Absolutely! This is not like old times when Indians shoot every white person they see! They **know** me! And Luis is there with them, and they know he is a good white person."

I am not worried about the Indians, but about reckless prospectors, which is silly, because they would have no reason to attack a bunch of white people on a large boat. And it would be stupid for them to...even though we only have one gun...as far as I know. God! I hate guns. I should not even be thinking about the gun. Our real danger is boa constrictors and the like.

Fernando chats a little more about the town, what kind of people live there--failed farmers, former ranch hands, tired prospectors who have given up on looking for gold and diamonds and settled into an easier life of trading skins or white men goods, poor young girls from the countryside turning tricks for sailors and occasional soldiers because so few men around here want the financial liability of marrying and raising children. Maybe that is why the people of Ferreira Gomes had looked so proprietary about their town--afraid it would go downhill if too many outsiders came into it too fast, and end up like Pedra Branca.

We clean up the greasy mess and retire for the night. "Are you scared of meeting the Indians?" Stephanie asks me, after we have turned out our lantern and gone to bed.

"No. I think I'm more scared of snakes and stuff. Are you scared?"

"A little, but it's an OK kind of scared, I think. Like before the first time you jump off a diving board, or something. You're scared, but you know you wanna do it. I can't believe we'll be there tomorrow night. I mean, I can because we've been on the boat so long, but it's still hard to believe."

"Goodnight, Steph."

"Goodnight."

I lie in bed for a long time, listening to the hum of mosquitoes and other things outside, wondering what it would be like to awaken in the morning to find all the guys have been stabbed to death in their hammocks. God, I'm a gruesome person. I make my way cautiously to the water closet, hoping insanely not to see a cockroach, but there are about twenty in there, scurrying about. I shudder and try to pee, but it is difficult to relax enough to do it. I wish I did not have to squat down so close to the cockroaches to pee. I wish I could stand straight like a man and just shoot urine down on them.

At long last the urine comes, and I rush back to my bed, amazed that my desire to get rid of half a cup of urine overwhelmed my distaste for cockroaches. I think about Michael and how badly he had wanted to meet Indians. He has greeted every other aspect of this trip with endless joy and good humor, but he will probably get very serious there. I listen to Stephanie's breathing and think about how I always had to hear her sleep-breathing before I could go to sleep myself. My little sister. When did she grow up? She is so far ahead of me. I am still a child.

***

I awaken to the sound of Stephanie screaming at the top of her lungs, "**snake, snake, snake!**" She lunges through our doorway, her underpants at her ankles, and slams the door. I throw my arms around her to comfort her, trying not to scream myself. "It was **huge**!" She is slipping through my arms to climb up on top of the bed. I climb up and put my arms around her, wondering if the snake can slide under our door, wondering if someone on deck heard her screaming.

We soon hear many feet racing down into the hold, and a cacophony of English and Portuguese exclamations and swear words, then a gun shot makes us both let out a blood-curdling scream and jump so high we bang our heads on the ceiling and fall down on the bed. The door comes flying open, and Peter races into the room.

"It's OK! He got him!"

Stephanie jumps into Peter's arms, and I walk out of the room in a daze, into the arms of Fernando.

"OK, got the snake, don't worry." He gives me a big hug. I hear Manoel speaking in Portuguese to his son, telling him the snake is not poisonous to touch: he can feel it if he wants. I pull away from Fernando to look at the snake and see Michael looking at me, a smoking rifle in his hands. He looks down at the snake, and I look down at it, and recoil in horror at its enormity.

"*Anaconda*," Manoel says, poking it with his knife. It must be half a foot in diameter; it is at least ten feet long. I start shaking, and Fernando puts his arms around me again. "*Puxa vida!*" Manoel is apparently inspecting the storage and kitchen areas now, assessing how much food the snake ate last night while we were sleeping.

We hear the bedroom door creak, and I let go of Fernando to see if Stephanie is OK now. They come out together, with Peter's arm around her. Her chest is heaving. "I can't believe Michael killed it with only one shot," she says, her eyes glazed over. "It's so big."

"That makes it easier," replies Michael, quietly, before uncocking the rifle and putting it down.

"It probably wouldn't have bitten you," says Fernando. "It was eating all night and was probably full. They usually sleep during the day."

"Well, it wasn't asleep when I went to the water closet!"

Peter scoops her up in his arms and carries her across the snake, and up and out of the hold. Manoel gestures to Fernando to help him carry the snake out, too, all the while muttering about how much food the snake ate, amazed that it would eat dried rice and beans. It must have still smelled the grease from the meat we ate last night, Fernando replies: there must have been grease on the floor and the counters. Betinho picks up the gun to carry it up to the deck, and I walk over to hug Michael.

"You saved our lives," I say, burying my face in his chest.

"Don't be silly: nobody's life was in danger."

"I can't believe you grabbed the gun and ran down here before Manoel did."

"She was screaming in English: he didn't know what she was saying."

"Well, I can't believe he didn't come, just hearing her screaming!"

"He **did** come! We **all** came! I was just the one closest to the gun, that's all."

"How could you get it in one shot?"

"It wasn't even moving; it was half-asleep, digesting." As far as I know, it has been at least four years since he fired a gun. It is a horrible type of comfort to think how easily it was for him to remember how to cock it and fire it in a matter of seconds...and not miss.

"Why don't you go up on deck until this is cleaned up?"

"I want to use the water closet." I look at him, forlornly, and suddenly start to laugh, and he starts to laugh, too.

"I'll scout it out for you," he offers. He walks around the water closet and comes back out again. "Not even a cockroach! Hell, the snake probably ate 'em all in the night." He gives me a kiss on the forehead. "I'll see you on deck, OK?"

I do my business, then join them on deck, where they are all apparently drinking rum and orange juice. I decline, knowing it would make me vomit.

"We need to go buy some more supplies," says Fernando. "Betinho is going to clean up the mess while we're gone."

402

"We'll all help clean it up," says Peter.

"The good news," says Fernando, "is that we'll get lots of money for this snake in town: it will pay for all the supplies."

"Who would want to buy that disgusting thing?" asks Stephanie.

"Lots of people," responds Fernando. "There's a lot of good meat on it, good skin for selling to traders, eyes for a talisman--"

Stephanie and I groan.

"OK! You asked! *Vamos lá, Manoel*." They wrap the snake around both their necks, and march off to town to barter if for more supplies. What if they do not have more supplies for us to buy? It is not that big of a town.

We follow Betinho down the stairs and help him collect the torn bags of food and mop up the snake guts and spilled food. He does not seem fazed at all. I notice, though, that he changed out of his brand new t-shirt before starting the clean-up operation.

A little while later, the provisions are restored, and Manoel motors us out of Pedra Branca, much to everybody's relief. We munch on fresh bread and fried eggs and bananas, and try to relax.

"By the way," says Fernando, reaching into his pocket. "Who lost a watch?" We all check our wrists, then Fernando tosses Peter his Casio. "Nice, waterproof watch, huh? The snake did not even mangle it at all. Good thing the guy who bought it skinned it right away and found it, huh?"

Peter looks incredulously at the watch. I am glad I have already finished eating.

Chapter 62

The rest of the morning passes uneventfully, aside from the fact that the river is getting narrower and narrower, and the heat more and more sweltering. Our lunchtime swim and siesta stretch to three hours before Manoel can cajole himself back to the skipper's wheel, and then only because Fernando scolds him that we will not reach the Indian village before dark if we do not get going soon.

A couple hours later, we ascend through another rapids--a long, gradual stretch of whitewater. When it is over, Fernando declares that it is the last, and that we only have a couple more hours to go. Peter suggests some more euchre, and so we team up again. I think we are all getting nervous. Occasionally Betinho and Fernando point out animals and birds in the trees, or flying fish, but we are just ready for the trip to be over.

At the approach of dusk, we slather on our insect repellant, get dressed, and eat a simple dinner while Manoel navigates the last leg of the journey under the careful directions of Fernando. We leave the main part of the Araguari now, and head up a labyrinth of feeder streams. We have gradually risen to a higher altitude, and the heat has let up a wee bit. The orange ball of the sun is hovering directly in front of us, threatening to sink, when Fernando announces we have arrived. We look around; we have arrived at a swamp.

"OK, help me blow up the raft," he says, and Peter and Manoel take turns with an old bicycle pump to blow up the rubber raft. "I will take the gifts for the chief and make sure everything is OK, then come back with them in some canoes to bring the rest of you there."

"How long will that take?" asks Stephanie.

"I don't know--maybe half-hour to get there, twenty minutes to talk, half-hour to come back."

"If you don't come back in an hour," says Manoel in Portuguese, "I will take them out, and we will go call the police."

"Wait at least three hours, please," says Fernando to him.

When he has a chance, he whispers to me, "there is no reason to be scared. I do not want to argue with Manoel about that, but if I am delayed, it is only because I do not want to be rude to the chief. He may want to give me a little feast or something, and it would be rude to say `Wait! I have friends in my boat!' I am not sure that they would understand this, but if I am late, tell them, OK?"

"OK," I say.

He paddles off in the rubber raft, and we all watch him silently, listening to the drone of night insects beginning, and nightbirds, and monkeys calling goodnight to each other. Thank God it is not raining--not even cloudy. When he is out of sight, we go down to the hold to pack up our things, being extra cautious to put our valuables in water-tight plastic containers.

When we come back up, Manoel and Betinho are sitting side by side, fishing poles extended over boat's rail. "What do you think you'll catch here?" I ask.

"I don't know," Manoel says. "Never came here before."

"How do you think Manoel will find us to pick us up again?" asks Peter.

I just shake my head, completely baffled. "Well, I guess if Fernando could memorize this spot, Manoel will memorize it, too. Manoel must be much more of a sailor than Fernando is."

"If he leaves in the morning, it will be easier for him to memorize," says Michael, who has a military training in reconnaissance and survival skills. I know we have flares and radio equipment and all sorts of things, but the gravity of our situation is finally dawning on me: without a boat or a plane, we are in the middle of nowhere.

About thirty minutes later, Manoel hauls some sort of catfish-looking creature out of the stream, and guides Betinho through the cleaning and gutting process. About thirty minutes after that, Manoel lifts his rifle and cocks it. I do not know if he is gunning for dolphins or Indians.

"Hey! We're back!" calls Fernando cheerily, and Manoel lowers his gun, and I resume breathing. In the gathering darkness, we can barely see the canoes or the dark-skinned Indians, but Fernando's yellow raft reflects the light of the rising moon. We stare in silence as two canoes pull up, flanking Fernando's yellow raft. "Hey!" he calls again, pulling up close. "This is Luis," he says, pointing to the Brazilian in his own raft.

"*Oi!*" Luis calls to us. We wave to him.

"He doesn't speak much English," adds Fernando.

Luis points to the four Indians in two canoes, giving the name of each, and, when called, they hold up their hands to greet us, and we hold up our hands in turn, as Fernando points to each of us and calls out our names. They are very skinny and do not seem to be wearing anything at all. They have strange hair cuts.

We load most of our bags onto the yellow raft, wedging the rest with ourselves into the two canoes. The *Waiãpis* smile at us as Michael and I enter the canoe on the left. I feel civilization slipping away from me as my foot pulls away from the motorboat. Betinho and Manoel had kissed everybody goodbye, but Betinho gives Stephanie a big hug, and it makes me want to cry, even though I can hear Fernando and Manoel confirming that we will all rendezvous here a week from tomorrow afternoon.

Luis and Fernando are chattering away in Portuguese, but too quietly for me to understand what they are saying. Maybe I will fall for Luis: he looks kind of cute, though it is too dark to be sure. Michael puts his arms around me as we are paddled away, and I lean back against his chest, wondering what he will kill snakes with now that Manoel and his rifle are gone, wondering if we will be put in the same tent, wondering why I suddenly feel so peaceful.

***

A half-hour later, we are helped onto a shoreline, and the canoe and raft are dragged up to rest beside other canoes. There are a dozen Indians waiting there, and now I can see in the moonlight that they are all men, and all have the same bowl-cut hairstyle, and all wear nothing but belts around their waists. We all hold up our hands in greeting, and the *Waiãpis* pick up our luggage to carry to the village, despite our protests that we can carry them ourselves.

"They would be insulted if you did not let them carry the bags," says Fernando, so we march behind them. After a couple bends in the path, we see the clearing where their village is, and smoke rising. After another bend in the path, we can see the thatched huts encircling the smoke. Soon we are inside the circle of homes, getting stared at by the whole village.

Luis, with Fernando's reminders, points to each of us in turn, calling out our names, and we dutifully hold up our hands in greeting. An older Indian approaches us, and Fernando explains that this is the chief, and we go through a long and formal introduction to him--long because it has to be doubly translated, back and forth, in and out of English to Portuguese, Portuguese to *Waiãpi*, then back again. I know Fernando's translations are quite good, but I have no way of gauging Luis's *Waiãpi*. I hate not knowing what people are really saying.

After the introduction, the chief turns to the people to address them, and Luis simultaneously tells Fernando, who tells us, that the chief is telling them to retire to their hearths and not bother the visitors, because there is going to be a council meeting with them tonight, then they need to set up their white men's tents and sleep. The Indians dutifully disperse, except for a half-dozen men who precede us as we are ushered into the chief's home. A few women are in there, setting out food and drinks in coconut shells, but they leave after exchanging a few words with the chief. We all sit down and accept the chief's offer of food and drink. I am not hungry at all, and can only pretend to nibble at the strange mixture of food. I know

407

some of it is manioc flour, but it must be mixed with fish, and I hate fish; I sip my tangy juice instead.

After a few minutes, and a signal from the chief, Luis begins summing up what has happened since Fernando's last trip here. He speaks in Portuguese to Fernando, who repeats it to us in English:

"*Waiãpi* are continuing to disappear on hunting expeditions. The people are getting hungry because this is the difficult season to hunt and fish, and the women and children are crying for their missing fathers. The *Waiãpi* do not know what to do. They have been told to stay away from the gold hills and not hunt near the white settlements, and so they have had to go to deeper swamp areas with too much badwater, and if they go more than a day's journey, they must spend the night in badwater places."

I interrupt to ask if he is talking about malaria when he refers to the "badwater".

"Yes." He confers again with Luis. "Yes, malaria and other things. They used to be able to avoid the places with malaria, but now they cannot hunt in some of the good places because of the white settlements. Also, they are now finding the badwater and mosquitoes in places where there used to be good water, and it is getting harder and harder to hunt. They never had malaria here before--they had only seen it when they visited other villages, closer to the white men--but now they have many men sick with malaria, and many who have not come back from hunting."

"Do they think they died of malaria on the hunt?" asks Stephanie.

"No," says Fernando. "You do not die fast from that: if they got it, they would come back to die."

"We have medicine for them, don't we?" asks Peter.

"I have a few things, but I was not expecting this here. And it is hard to cure malaria," Fernando shakes his head. "Especially for them, because they are very thin and, especially during the rainy season, they have some vitamin deficiencies. They are weaker in the rainy season. I have brought some medicines, but I do not know if they will help much. It is much better to take the anti-malarials to start with, but we do not have enough for all these people. Anyway, what they do not understand is why they never find the dead hunters. Before, when *Waiãpi* hunters were killed by white settlers, they would usually be left as a, uh, warning, or their heads would be cut off--"

Stephanie and I gasp.

"--or something like that, to scare the *Waiãpi*, but they find no trace of the hunters anywhere."

"Do they think it's the army?" I ask.

"They don't think so, because they are very good at tracking the army people in the jungle. But they are afraid the army has hired another Indian tribe to attack them."

"Another *Waiãpi* tribe?" asks Michael.

"No, a different tribe. There is no other *Waiãpi* tribe--just different clans of *Waiãpi* living in different villages. They have consulted with all the other villages, and they tell the same stories. They have lost so many hunters, some of the villages are talking about joining together. The ones closest to the gold hills have already moved closer to here, and now there are other ones that are talking of moving. They are very lucky that the rainy season is ending early this year: the waters will recede quicker, and the fishing will get easy faster. The women can fish for themselves."

The Indian chief interrupts and exchanges a few words with Luis, who tells Fernando that the chief is wondering why it is taking so long to finish the story, and why we have not yet gone to see the "sick man".

"OK. There is one hunter who just came back today with bad malaria, high fever. He says they took his companions away--"

"`They' who?" asks Peter.

"Please, let me finish."

"Sorry."

"It's OK. He says they took his companions away. He was lying down and vomiting with fever, and they did not see him, so he came back to the village, but they cannot understand what he is saying because he has so much fever: he is talking about jaguars and snakes and witches and everything, and they don't know what he really saw and what is just the fever talking. The chief thinks maybe if we give him very strong white medicine, his fever will go away, and he can tell us something. I don't know how much it will help, but, I guess we can try."

"Well, of course we should try," says Stephanie. "Why are you hesitating?"

"Because Luis thinks this guy may have seen a boat or a plane or something. If he comes out of his fever and says that very clearly, the *Waiãpis* might assume it is the army and go on the warpath." We sit quietly for a moment, but Fernando cannot wait for us to ponder this. "Look, he is expecting us to bring our medicine to this guy right away, unless you can think of an excuse not to."

"I think we should do it," Michael says quietly.

"Michael," I say, "if they attack the army, we could get bombed!"

"We'll just have to try to talk them out of it."

"How!?" asks Fernando.

"I don't know--maybe by going out to find this boat or plane ourselves." I look at him, incredulously. "I know you've got guns, Fernando: I saw them in your bag." Stephanie gasps.

"I don't wanna get involved in this!" says Peter.

"Well, we are," says Michael. "We can't let them attack the army: it's suicide, for **us**, too. It's probably just sadistic poachers who hate Indians! They can get away with it against bows and arrows, but a couple guns will change their minds!"

I stare at Michael in disbelief. I thought he never wanted to lift a gun again in his whole life. I thought he always wanted to find the peaceful solution.

410

"Michael," says Stephanie softly, "do you really mean what you're saying?"

"I'm just assessing the situation! We're here. If we don't give the guy medicine, they won't trust us anymore, and we can't get out of here for another week. If we give the guy medicine and he talks, and they attack an army base, we could all get bombed in retaliation. I don't see any other way besides giving him the medicine, seeing what he says, returning to where he says he was, and tracking those bastards ourselves." We are quiet for a minute, staring at him. "I'm not planning to shoot anybody, c'mon! I don't think we'll need to. We can probably just shoot their propellers to pieces!"

The chief is gesticulating and obviously complaining to Luis about the delay. "I think Michael's right," says Fernando. "I wish I could tell you how sorry I am about this." I expect Peter to yell at him, but Peter is not even glaring at him. "I did not foresee getting in an awkward situation like this, where they might stop trusting me. They have always trusted me...and Luis."

We look at Luis, and I suddenly realize his credibility with the Indians might be on the line, too. "I think we should do it, too," I say, "but let's only send a couple people into the hut to give him the medicine and listen to what he is saying. I think the rest of us should set up our tent and stay there and discuss how we can talk them out of attacking an army base if he identifies some sort of army vehicle."

"Stephanie?" Michael is looking at her, waiting for her response.

She looks at Peter, who says nothing. "OK, Michael. Why don't you go with Fernando, and the rest of us can wait in the tent--"

"No, I'll go with Michael," I say. "Fernando should stay in the tent with you and Peter--and tell them that you're, I don't know, looking through your medicine box for other things to try on the malaria." I hate to admit it to myself, but, if we are going to split up, I want one of the gunmen present in each group at all times. I am suddenly thinking Fernando might have overestimated how much friendship he has with these Indians. If I were them, I would not be

411

too trusting of anybody right now. "I will go with Michael and Luis and translate to Michael, and Michael might be able to tell if he is describing an army vehicle or not."

Everybody gives a half-hearted nod. Since we have had this entire conversation in English, Fernando turns to Luis to give him instructions in Portuguese: all the Americans will set up their tent and look through their medicine box for the best thing, and will come to the man's tent in a few minutes.

When the message is relayed to the chief, Fernando signals to us to get up, and we walk out to where our gear has been stored. They have already started a fire nearby to smoke away the mosquitoes for us. There are a lot of fires going, I think. They must know that the clean mosquitoes here can bite the sick people and start spreading the malaria around. I am glad we have been dutifully taking our anti-malarial pills, even though I know they are nowhere near one-hundred percent effective.

We quickly set up one of the tents and go inside to open boxes. Fernando hands a pistol with bullets to Michael, who loads it and shoves it down his boot, covering it with his pant leg. Fernando puts the other gun in his own boot and hands me the medicine to bring to the delirious witness.

"This is crazy," says Stephanie, eyes glazed.

"Yes, it is," I say, in a dream of my own.

"I'm sure it's not as bad as it seems," says Peter, suddenly trying to be cheerful.

This time, I give everybody a big hug, then head out with Michael. Luis is waiting outside our tent to escort us to the malaria victim.

412

Chapter 63

Michael cradles the medicine in his left hand, and takes my left hand in his right hand, and we follow Luis. I want to say something to him, but I do not know what to say. I do not need to tell him that I do not want him to use the gun, because he already knows that. I do not need to tell him to be careful. I do not need to tell him how much he means to me. There is nothing for me to say. I just wish he would say something...tell me if he is doing this because he is scared, or because he wants to protect us, or because he thinks it is the right thing to do for the *Waiãpis*. I cannot ask him why he is doing it because there is no time. I have to trust his decision. I could never have decided anything like this as quickly as he did.

We enter the home of the sick witness. The chief is already waiting for us with all of the council members. I am relieved to see they have no weapons, even as I realize what an absurd thought that is: they have no reason to be angry at us. Yet, they have reason to be angry, and they are trying to figure out where to direct the rage.

Luis offers to do the injection, so Michael hands him the objects necessary to prepare the syringe. Luis is talking to the victim and his family in what sounds like a soothing, reassuring voice. They appear nervous but do not protest the injection. The chief gestures for us to join them in sitting in a circle around the prostrate man, who is obviously babbling incoherently. I look at the faces of the family, kneeling by his side. It looks to be a wife and two children, and perhaps a brother and the brother's wife and baby girl. They have paint on their faces, and I quietly ask Luis about it.

"The holy man was here," he says.

I look around the hut to try to focus on anything but their faces. I feel myself a horrible intruder. I see some cooking utensils near a stone hearth. I see a parrot--clipped and tied to a perch-- silently surveying the sickroom scene. I see hunting bows and arrows in one corner. I see hammocks hung from every corner. Perhaps there are other things; I cannot see too well through the haze of smoke. I keep thinking I see tarantulas, but I hope I am imagining them in the smoke.

Why are we sitting here like this? No medicine can cure a fever that fast. I suddenly realize what a headache I have and how much my stomach hurts and that I really need to relieve myself. And my back is aching from sitting Indian-style. Would it be disrespectful to ask to "go to the bathroom"? I whisper to Luis if he thinks I can go, and he tells me it is OK, and calls the sick man's daughter over to take me to the "ladies' room" side of the jungle surrounding the village.

She sticks out her hand for me to hold, and turns her sad paint-covered face to me. I take her hand, stand up, and follow her out to the jungle. I must try to be quick and not let a mosquito bite me while exposed...or anything else, I think, shuddering. She takes me further than I had expected, but at last points out a spot for me. I let go of her hand to pull my pants down, and she stands in the same place, watching me. I cajole and plead with my bashful bladder, and finally it relaxes and opens up, even though she is watching me and I hate that. My intestines rumble and I know there is a mess inside there, but it is plugged up with the immobilizer. I was good and did not plug it up on the boat, but I plugged it up today because I feared it today.

I pull my pants back up, and she takes my hand again and leads me back. I hear a million night voices, and marvel how unafraid she is. I suppose jaguars would not come close to a village with fires burning, but there must be snakes out here...and lots of tarantulas...scorpions.... At last we get back, and I sit down next to Michael. He takes my hand and tells me Luis has gone out to give the injection to some other hunters, at the request of the chief. He will be back soon.

414

It is unbearable sitting in here, and pointless. I wish we could wait somewhere else until the witness is ready to speak. The woman who must be his wife starts chanting something quietly, and the rest of her family joins her, then the chief and the council join in. They all chant it quietly, but it is many voices. It hovers between speaking and singing, and after awhile Michael starts humming the same cadence. I look at him in surprise, but his eyes are closed. I look around to see if anybody has noticed him humming, and many of them have, but they do not show an adverse reaction.

I lower my eyes, trying to think reverential thoughts. I wish I could pray for this man to get better, but I am just not sure about praying anymore. I believe terrible things must happen to everybody sooner or later. I say the "Our Father" over and over in my mind. After what seems a very long time, Luis returns and joins the chanting. After another long time, the chanting stops. I look at Michael. His eyes are still closed, and he is licking his dry lips. He is probably as thirsty as I am.

After a long time, I cannot stand it anymore and squeeze his hand to see if Michael is awake. He looks at me with surprise. "What?" he mouths.

"Are you OK?" I mouth back.

He nods. "Are you?"

I nod back. He squeezes my hand, then closes his eyes again. I guess he is praying. I know sometimes he prays the Christian prayers that he learned in church, and sometimes he prays the Cherokee prayers to the Great Spirit that he learned from his grandmother. He told me that when something needed to be prayed about, and it seemed a thing that his grandmother or another Cherokee might pray to the Great Spirit, he prayed to the Great Spirit, but if he could not imagine that, if the prayer had something to do with college, or his car transmission, or a toxic spill, he would pray to Jesus. He probably thinks I am saying prayers to Jesus and so that is covered and he can just say the prayers to the Great Spirit, so I close my eyes again and say some genuine prayers this time--creative, unique prayers to Jesus, my hero.

415

At long last, there is murmuring from the mat: the sick man is stirring, and he is no longer perspiring. They give him some food and drink, as much as he can take, and his family showers him with kisses. Then he begins to speak pointedly, and everyone falls silent, except Luis, who quietly translates to me what he is saying. I mentally condense the Portuguese into the most precise English I can to pass along the gist of it to Michael without losing the train of Luis's continuing narration.

The beginning part is not very helpful because the man is mumbling a lot, and Luis is not understanding all the words, but when the chief and the council ask more specific questions of the sick man, the story becomes more sharply defined.

"It was sunset," Luis tells me in Portuguese. "They had just finished the day's hunt and did not have much to show for it. They prepared a fire to cook their dinner and smoke away the mosquitoes, although they felt they had chosen a pretty good place uphill from the water. This man could only eat a little, then he had to lie down to vomit, and his companions told him he must have gotten the mosquito sickness, and that the next morning, they would return to the village. Then, this crazy, evil thing came out of nowhere--"

"What?! `Crazy, evil thing'?" I cannot believe he is translating this right.

Luis nods his head fast. "Yes, and these two men popped out of it. One of the men was a white man with ugly hair like dried grass, and the other was a white man that looked more like the white men they have seen near gold hills, or the ones that come to visit--with black hair and dark eyes like the *Waiãpis*. They had on white men's clothes. The dark one spoke to them in *Waiãpi*, but with a funny accent and many wrong words. But they could understand him. He said they looked like fine hunters and could they help these men find a jaguar that was attacking their cattle.

"Well, he thought that was a strange thing to say, because they only had a few animals strung up, and nobody would call them great hunters for that. The two *Waiãpis* talking to the white men said they could not help. Then the white men offered them lots of things--

416

cattle meat and hides and flour and knives and other things, but the *Waiãpis* still said no. Then he heard screaming, and he pulled his head up from where he had been vomiting, and he saw a terrible fight, and he tried to lift himself up to help his brothers, but he was too tired, and the white men hit them on the head with big sticks--he must mean guns--and dragged them into the big evil thing, and flew off like a devil."

Luis pauses to drink something while the wife gives her husband something to drink as well, and I finally catch up in retranslating it to Michael, then take a deep breath.

"How did he describe this 'evil thing'?!" Michael asks me.

"He hasn't yet."

"You need to ask him!"

"I'm sure they will: just wait."

"I'm sorry: he's wasting so much time on these details, it's frustrating me! And the clothes--he needs to describe the clothes."

"I know."

When the man is finished drinking, the chief asks him a question, and Luis resumes translating to me. "I did not see it too well because I was lying down, very sick. It was white or maybe grayish like some rocks. It seemed to come from the water, but it did not look like a boat. It had things that looked a little like wings, but it did not look like the plane that the white men come in sometimes. When it left, he could see smoke coming from it. It left on the water, but it was not in the water. It was like the--uhh, some insect, I don't know the Portuguese word for it--that skims along. It scared him: he thought it was a horrible vision. He had heard of evil creatures that do not swim and do not walk and do not fly but simply, uhh, can get around, like evil wind, and he was terribly afraid."

By the time I finish retranslating it to Michael, the *Waiãpis* are talking furiously amongst themselves. Michael grabs Luis by the arm and turns to me. "Tell him to tell them there's no way that was the army."

417

"How do you know?"

"Just tell him now, so they calm down!" I pass on the message to Luis and he passes it onto them, and all eyes turn to Michael waiting for his explanation. "Tell them it is some type of hydrofoil, it is very expensive, and the Brazilian army does not own any of these."

"What if they own some secretly?" I ask.

"If they had some, they would not be wasting them rounding up stray Indians! They would be using them to infiltrate drug runners and guerrilla camps."

"Well, they don't really have guerrillas to worry about in Brazil," I tell Michael.

"Well, if they could not use them for that or for narcotraffickers, they would not be wasting them on this: they would sell them for big bucks to Colombia or Bolivia! Believe me, these Indians have been nabbed by private citizens--probably to be slaves somewhere. I mean, if it were some malicious army people, they would have just killed them, right?"

"I don't know. I think that about most military maniacs, but they seem to love setting up prisons to torture people."

He shakes his head at me. "Trust me on this! I had to spend a lot of time studying the damn militaries of South America!"

"But you've been out of the army for years-"

"Just tell Luis what I said, please? If I'm wrong--and I know I'm not--it will at least buy us time."

I turn to tell Luis why Michael does not think it is the army, and then turn back to Michael while Luis is retranslating it into *Waiãpi*. "If you really don't think it's the army, should we try to radio the nearest army base for help?"

He shakes his head. "I don't think so. From what we've been told, the *Waiãpis* would not trust any army help, and the army would just assume it was a standard skirmish between Indians and whites."

"Maybe we should go to the federal police?"

"If drugs are involved, they could be connected to it."

Luis has now provoked a loud reaction, and translates some questions back to us. "Why does he think they have been taken as slaves? Nobody ever takes Indians as slaves. If other tribes take *Waiãpis*, they only take girls, and kill men. Who would do that? Where are they? Indians are no good to work on cattle ranches or anything like that."

I translate it back to Michael, confirming that it is an unlikely idea: Africans were brought here in such enormous numbers precisely because the Portuguese completely failed in their attempts to enslave Indians.

"Well, maybe somebody out here is desperate, and there aren't any Africans around here for them to catch!" I look at him and realize he is completely serious. I know he has been reading a lot of Amnesty International material on forced slavery around the world, but as far as I knew, it was not an issue in Amazônia--not for Indians, anyway.

I translate his comment back to Luis, who translates it back to them. Michael does not wait for their reaction. "I think we should go after them--sneak up on the damn bastards--"

"Michael," I interrupt. "Look, I think you should sleep on this before you offer anything like that. Please? Look, I'll tell them **maybe** we can help them find the missing *Waiãpis*, but I won't say anything specific, OK? We need to sleep on this--and let them talk it over and sleep on it, too, OK?"

He squeezes my hand. "OK."

Five minutes later, we are back in the tent, repeating the long evening's events and revelations to Stephanie, Peter, and Fernando. Michael and I each down about a quart of purified water during the process. Then there is a heated discussion about what to do. Michael thinks it would be very easy to catch the unsuspecting white men, who are only picking off surprised Indians.

419

"Yeah, but, after all these disappearances, I can't believe the Indians are letting themselves be such easy targets," says Peter. "They must have been cautious, and they still got nabbed."

"But they didn't have **guns**!" says Michael.

"How are they finding these Indians?" asks Stephanie.

"I'm not sure," says Michael. "Maybe they're using radar on the hydrofoil. They probably find a lot of anteaters and jaguars and monkeys in the process, but, now and then, find a couple *Waiãpis*, too."

"What about the Federal Police?" I ask Fernando. "Do you think it might be a drug thing and they might be too corrupted to ask for help?"

Fernando shakes his head. "I think we do not have enough information to give them: they will just say it is a skirmish with white settlers, they will say the *Waiãpis* are probably wandering out of their reserve because the hunting is difficult in the rainy season....I don't know."

We are silent for awhile, then Michael speaks up. "Look, I'm really tired, and I'm gonna go to sleep. I don't know what you're gonna decide for yourselves, but I think they really need our help. If we can nab this hydrofoil, I can probably pilot it, and I don't think any of the *Waiãpis* can. I'm going to bed." And with that, he walks out to retreat to the other tent that Fernando set up for the guys.

"Fernando, if you tell him to give back your gun, I think he will," I say.

"You are so against this?"

"We don't even know what we're going up against!"

"Yes, but I want to help the *Waiãpis* find out. If a jaguar were paroling outside the village right now, I know they would go out to kill it. I am helpless because I do not know how to hunt a thing like that. Now they are helpless, and I must help them hunt the thing that they do not know, the thing that is threatening them."

420

I do not know how to argue with that. I desperately want there to be some good army, some good policemen we can call, but I am not sure who it would be. Peter kisses Stephanie goodnight, and he and Fernando go to the other tent to sleep. I pull my bedroll close to her, and we hold hands and talk for a long time, but we are tired and cannot think straight and do not know what to do. Finally, we go to sleep.

Chapter 64

We wake up to Peter rushing into our tent. "They're gone!"

We rub our eyes. "What?"

"They're gone! Fernando and Michael left!" We jump up. "They left a note saying they have already left with Luis and--"

Stephanie tears the note from his hand and starts reading it, and I read it over her shoulder.

> Dear All,
>
> Sorry we left without saying goodbye.
> We knew you would be upset and try
> to talk us out of it, but we know this is
> the right thing to do. We have taken
> one of the radio transmitters and will
> stay in contact. Don't worry--we
> won't take any chances, and Luis says
> the two *Waiãpis* going with us are
> really sharp. We'll call you on the
> radio in a couple hours.
>
> Love,
>
> Michael and Fernando

Stephanie crumples into Peter's arms, and I sink back to the bedroll. This is not happening. This is not happening. This is not happening. They are all going to die--disappear forever. This is not happening.

"I'm not leaving Michael in the hands of Fernando!" I hear Peter say. "No way! God knows how worthless he'll be in a pinch! I'm going after them!"

My mind blanks out again until Stephanie starts shaking me. "C'mon! They just left! If we can convince some other *Waiãpis* to take us after them, we can catch up!" I just look at her, dazed. "**Come on!!!!** We gotta get out there and convince somebody to take us after them!" She is barking orders at Peter and forcing me to get dressed, lacing up my boots herself. "It'll be OK: we'll find them!"

I am not sure how it happens, but a little while later, I find myself in a canoe with Peter and Stephanie and two old-looking *Waiãpis*. What has woken me up is Michael's voice crackling on the radio equipment.

"Don't be angry, OK? We woke up early, talked to Luis and the chief, and decided to get going right away.".

"You liar!" shouts Stephanie. "I can't believe you did this!"

"**Please** don't be angry, OK? You're making a big deal out of nothing."

"My sister can't even say a word: do you have any idea how upset she is?!"

"Don't underestimate her: she'll understand."

They close the transmission. I do not think they have told Michael and Fernando we are following them. I stare calmly out at an *anaconda* swimming past us in the water. The sun is rising and getting hotter, and I ask for water, which Peter hands me.

"It's OK," he says. Everybody keeps saying that. God knows how they communicated with these *Waiãpis*, and how they will track a canoe in water.

A few hours later, we catch up to their canoe. Our *Waiãpis* send a signal whistle to their *Waiãpis*, and they stop paddling. Michael, Fernando, and Luis turn around in shock to see us gliding up behind them. Fernando is muttering something, but Michael is just staring at me. I realize there are tears flowing down my cheeks.

A couple minutes later, the canoes are side by side, and Michael has climbed into ours and put his arms around me. "I'm sorry. Don't cry. There's no need to worry about this." I say nothing, just sobbing quietly into his chest, and he starts talking to Stephanie and Peter. "Why don't you guys just go back? Everything's under control." They say nothing, and I can only guess that they are shaking their heads no.

"Come on," I hear Fernando saying. "The *Waiãpis* are here because we told them we have a plan. If we sit here with women crying hysterically, they are not going to have much confidence in our plan!"

"Shut up!" shouts Stephanie.

"I'm sorry!" he says. "Are we going to do this or not?"

"Only if we **all** go," says Peter, firmly.

"C'mon, Peter!" says Michael, but he continues to stroke my hair, and I know he will not make me turn back crying.

A few minutes later, I feel the canoe start moving again. Michael still has his arms around me. I do not know if we are going forward or backward. I am afraid to look into his eyes: I know he is disappointed in me.

"It's OK," he says. "I'm sorry. I didn't think you'd be this worried. I thought Stephanie would be able to calm you down." After a long time, he wipes my wet face with his t-shirt and holds a water bottle to my mouth, as if I am a baby in his arms. I will not leave his arms until I have to.

We finally stop the canoes to eat our hastily packed lunches and stretch our legs, and I have to lift my head from his chest. He cradles my face in his hands. "Are you angry at me?" he asks. I shake my head. "I didn't mean to hurt you."

"I know," I reply. He kisses me on the forehead. "There's really nothing to worry about: it will be sooooooo easy! I know it will be! Trust me!" He leads me out of the canoe, through the swampy shore, to where the others are munching on food and

424

walking around to stretch out their stiff muscles. Stephanie gives Michael a strange look, and gives me a big hug. Now I know I am a baby.

We eat quickly, mostly in silence, and then resume our trip. Michael slides in behind me and lets me rest my back on his chest. He massages my tight neck muscles. He is the one going to battle, and I am the one getting prepared for it. "Michael," I ask, "didn't you want to spend time with the Indians?"

"Yeah."

"It's like, we're not even talking to them, or learning anything...."

"I know...but...it's not our vacation anymore, y'know? This is their life. People are dying. Young men are dying...or disappearing. What am I supposed to try to learn from them now? That village was full of women and children and old people--like a refugee camp. They're desperate. I know I can help them. I have to do it." I pull his arms down around me. "I know how you feel. I'm not planning on shooting anybody." That's what they all say. Yet...when **he** says it, I believe him.

We pitch camp when dusk falls. We have spent all day canoeing through a monotonous network of streams, swamps, and flooded forests. It utterly astonishes me that the Indians can navigate all this like a printed road atlas, completely confident that tomorrow afternoon, we will be in the vicinity of the reported kidnapping. We light a huge fire on high ground and eat some fish that the *Waiãpis* have been spearing along the way. Lunch was sparse, and now I am very hungry, and eat my share of the fish even though I do not like fish. Then I go with Stephanie to stake out a ladies' room because I do not have my little immobilizing pills here. The *Waiãpis* sleep in hammocks strung in the trees, and we sleep in the canoes with mosquito nets over us. I sleep in Michael's arms.

We wake up to drizzle, put on our rain slickers, eat some fruit, and depart. It rains on and off most of the day, but we get too hot in our slickers and take them off. The rain feels good. Mid-afternoon, the *Waiãpis* tell us we are in the vicinity of the trees and hills described by the victim. We look around in bewilderment, having no idea what distinguishes this stretch of swampy forest from any other. We can only guess from the probable number of miles paddled, and direction we have generally headed, that we must be at the far corner of the reserve, near the border of French Guyana.

There should be no white settlers out here. This should not be a narcotrafficking zone either. This **could** be an army zone, however: the Brazilian military has long been obsessed with militarizing the least populated corners of the country. Yet, it does **not** make sense that they would be kidnapping Indians out here-- killing them, perhaps, but not trying to enslave them. The *Waiãpis* help us hide one canoe with our mosquito nets and belongings under a dense grove of trees, and then three of them paddle the other canoe a little ways away. Michael and Luis take turns watching them through the binoculars.

When night falls without anything happening, we light a fire and go to sleep again. The next day, three *Waiãpis* take the canoe for a long meandering "hunting trip", hoping to attract radar attention. It rains really hard in the afternoon, and we have to empty and tip over the canoes, and put our slickers on for a couple of hours. At dusk the "hunters" return to camp again to wait for their kidnapping. I feel I am going out of my mind, but there is nothing to do about it. I am certain we are all going to die here one moment, then certain it is all a dream the next minute, then certain we will be stuck here for weeks with nothing happening.

Then we see it come--a dirty gray phantom gliding out of the sunset drizzle. It seems to float above the swamps, touching neither water nor sky, its motor barely audible above the screeching of forest animals eating their suppers. When it stops moving, I feel somebody grabbing me: it is Michael. "Don't worry, hon. We'll be back in a flash." He kisses me on the lips, and he, Luis and Fernando are gone in the blink of an eye.

Stephanie puts her arms around me, and we watch together. Peter and one of the *Waiãpis* get the other canoe ready as a backup.

426

After a long discussion, everybody had decided they did not want to use poison darts or even sleeping darts to nab the kidnappers because then they would not be able to guide us to their...whatever it was. However, this fourth *Waiãpi* will have them ready, and he and Peter will get within range in case Fernando and Michael have any trouble. I still cannot believe I am watching this unfold. Things like this do not happen to me.

Michael and Fernando and Luis are wading through the swamps, holding their guns above their heads. We are too far away to hear anything, but we can see that two white men have already gotten out of the hydrofoil--or whatever the hell it is--and approached the three *Waiãpis*, who are deliberately standing very close to a stream. We know that Luis will do a certain bird call as the signal to them that Fernando and Michael have the guns in range, and then the three *Waiãpis* will drop into the dark water, and we will all hope to God that the white men do not even try, or fail if they do, to shoot them when Fernando screams at them to drop their guns.

And suddenly it happens. We see the three *Waiãpis* drop into the water, and the white men jerk their guns around in confusion, unable or uncertain about shooting into the dark water or aiming their guns at whomever has just screamed at them from the other direction. Then they shoot, and there are shots fired back, and Stephanie and I take off running for the swamps, walking and swimming and crawling as best we can.

When we are in range to hear voices, we cannot hear what is being said in Portuguese or English because the *Waiãpis* are in a screaming rage. Then we see that the hydrofoil is taking off. Michael and Fernando shoot at it, but it gets away.

"Come on! We've gotta follow it!" Michael yells. He hops into the canoe with Peter and Luis and the fourth *Waiãpi*. "Do you think they can follow gasoline plumes?"

Fernando quickly translates the question and answer between Luis, the *Waiãpis*, and Michael, and their canoe takes off after another Indian jumps into it to help paddle.

427

"Wait!" I scream.

"There's no time!" Michael screams back. "Stay here and we'll radio you."

Fernando grabs my arm. "Come on--we'll follow them in the other canoe." We slither our way through the swamp back to the hidden canoe, quickly arrange ourselves and our gear in it, pull the mosquito nets over us as best we can, and let the other two *Waiãpis* start paddling us away.

An hour later, we catch up to the other canoe, and they report that they are having no problem following the smoke plume in the water: the residue is distinctly purple for some reason. Michael guesses the hydrofoil--or whatever it is--is going twenty times as fast as the canoe, though, so we can only hope it is a short journey.

The clouds let up, and we suddenly have a full moon to light our watery trail. I look around at the well-lit swamps and jungles gliding by, utterly astonished that this is happening. I look at Stephanie, wondering why she has not rationalized a better solution to this, but she is just staring resolutely ahead. I look at Peter, still in the other canoe, wondering why he has not tried to argue us into settling this via the proper legal channels, but he is also just staring resolutely ahead. I look at Fernando, but his face is blank, as well. Perhaps they think it is a dream and are simply waiting to wake up. I cannot see Michael's face because he never looks back. A snake drops from a tree into our boat, but a *Waiãpi* quickly stabs it with a knife and hurls it overboard. The scream inside me does not even emerge. I close my eyes and wait to wake up somewhere else.

Chapter 65

I wake up in a cloud of mosquitoes. They are suddenly droning all over the nets, and the *Waiãpis* are groaning in agony as the mosquitoes bite them all over their unprotected hands and wrists, the only body parts sticking out of the mosquito nets draped over us. Luis tells them to stop paddling for a minute so that they can apply more insect repellent to their hands. I am glad we started giving them anti-malarial pills two days ago, but I am sure we are all going to get it now. I want so desperately to beg them all to turn back, but I hate being such a coward, and cower alone in my fear.

After what seems an eternity, they suddenly stop the canoes: they have spotted smoke. After consultations, we proceed again, slowly. The mosquito hordes have not abated whatsoever, and it is a nightmare trying to see through them. Vampires. I cower down again, and let others do the watching.

The *Waiãpis* begin exclaiming, and then Luis tells us they have spotted what looks like a tiny *Waiãpi* village. I hear Michael and Fernando cocking their pistols as our *Waiãpi* comrades prepare some sleeping and some poison darts, just in case. They pull close enough to send some signal whistles and wait for a reply. Silence. They try again. More silence. They paddle a little closer, then whistle again. This time we hear a whistle back to us; Luis says it is a friendly whistle.

We beach the canoes, and the guys discuss their approach to the mini village--which we can barely make out--encompassing the plumes of smoke which we now see must be coming from several large bonfires. It is decided that two of the *Waiãpis* will approach

429

first, unarmed, and the other *Waiãpis* will follow from a distance with Luis, Fernando, and Michael. They all douse their skin in insect repellent, then crawl out of the mosquito nets. Peter comes over to kiss Stephanie goodbye, and Michael comes over to kiss me goodbye.

"We'll be right back: don't worry!" He brushes aside mosquitoes to kiss me through the netting. He kisses me on the lips and strokes my hair. "I didn't shoot anybody, y'know." He looks into my eyes and smiles. "They got away because I just shot near their feet to scare them, then when they took off, I just tried to shoot something on the hydrofoil to make it inoperable. I think Fernando was aiming for them, but I guess he's a lousy shot!" He smirks. "Or maybe you've had some influence on him, too." He kisses me again, then takes off after the others.

Stephanie puts her arms around me to wait. A few minutes later, Michael emerges from the trees alone. "It's OK! You can all come out!" As we douse our skin with insect repellent, he tells us that the *Waiãpis* here were also kidnapped, but they are not from the same village. They have lots of fires going, and Fernando said it smelled as if DDT had also been sprayed liberally there--the result being no mosquitoes inside the small circle of huts.

Michael holds my hand as we approach. The village looks a lot like the village we had just left, but it is very tiny, and the central plaza is very small indeed. There are a dozen *Waiãpis* standing around talking, with Luis and Fernando listening. I can see into the huts and notice others sitting or lying down in hammocks, and they all seem to be listening, too. Luis is apparently too caught up in the conversation to bother translating for us, but after a few minutes we are gestured into one of the huts, and find ourselves in another tribal council. We sit around in a circle, and it is easy to tell our *Waiãpis* apart from the others because the others are so thin and haggard.

They offer us a beverage which, to our surprise, turns out to be tea, and we drink thirstily, eating the rice and beans they offer us as well. The man who is apparently their chief converses with Luis, who periodically pauses to relay the discussion in Portuguese to Fernando, who then relays it to us in English.

430

"Some of the men have been here only a couple moons--others many, many moons. They cannot get out because there are too many mosquitoes in the swamps. They have never seen mosquito swamps like this. Sometimes men try to escape in the night, but they are found the next day dead, covered in bloody mosquito bites. They cannot escape during the day because the white men circle the area in a helicopter, counting them, and they are too weak and tired to run fast enough and be cunning enough to hide."

Our *Waiãpis* have grown agitated listening to this and begin brandishing their weapons and exclaiming; they are asked to quiet down before the chief continues. Fernando resumes the translation.

"The white men give them medicine sometimes, but they all seem to have the malaria, at least a little bit, and so they are tired all the time. They have to hunt through the jungle for a very rare tree, and pull off the vine that grows only on that tree. They must find ten vines to get a kilogram of rice from the white men, and twenty to get a kilogram of beans, and one-hundred to get any fish or meat. They can eat fruit they find in the jungle, but there is not very much, and it is better to keep hunting for the vines because there is no game here with all the mosquitoes."

"What are these vines?" asks Peter, but Fernando motions to him to wait, then resumes interpreting.

"They do not know how many white men there are. Most of them were kidnapped by the same two men, a few others by a couple different men. They do not seem to have seen more than a half-dozen different white men. They think there are other Indians kept in other places, but they do not know where. They were taken here in blindfolds."

Fernando continues relating other sad details of their existence, and after awhile they get back to discussing the vines.

"They do not know why the white men want the vines. They are inedible and not strong enough to be made into ropes. It is getting harder and harder to find more vines. Sometimes they go

431

back to trees they have been to before, hoping that a new vine has already sprung up where they chopped one down before, but the white men do not give as much food for the baby vines. Once, some of the *Waiãpis* found some good poisons and made some poison darts and tried to kill the helicopter men when they came to trade food for vines, but one of the white men saw them starting to shoot the darts, and he started killing all of them."

Fernando pauses for a moment, straining to hear Luis's translation in the midst of the uproar emerging from the *Waiãpi* visitors.

"I guess the guy had a machine gun. He must have killed ten of them. Then the other guy yelled at him, and they left. The *Waiãpis* buried the dead. Sometimes they talk about other plans, try to think of ways to escape, but they do not know how to get through the mosquito swamps."

At long last the narration seems over. We exchange several questions and answers, but there is really nothing more to say. They think there is some sort of headquarters but they do not know where it is. They point in the direction from which the helicopter generally emerges.

Michael wants to resume following the gasoline trail in the water, and so do our *Waiãpis*, though they are obviously scared. When we explain to these *Waiãpis* that we have nets and insect repellent to go through the swamps, many of them want to come with, but Luis explains to them that we only have two canoes. Nobody says it, but it is also obvious that they are too undernourished and sick to help.

Michael again tries to talk us into waiting behind, or going back, but Peter refuses. I have heard him say several times over the past couple of days that he does not like entrusting Michael to Fernando's partnership. I could understand him being jealous and protective of Stephanie, but his concern for Michael is quite extraordinary. And I know if Peter goes with, Stephanie will insist on going with. I am too dazed to decide anything.

And so we find ourselves bidding farewell to the prisoners, and telling them we will do all we can to free them. We all cry when we leave the mini village. We jog quickly through the waiting mosquito hordes back to the canoes. I go in the lead canoe with Michael, and he silently slides in behind me, pulls the mosquito net down, and puts his arms around me. "Don't worry: it'll be OK." I saw men shooting at him today, and he still thinks it will all be OK.

The *Waiãpis* pick up the petroleum trail again, and we continue winding our way through the streams and swamps of the most God-forsaken corner of Amapá. The mosquitoes buzz incessantly around us, and we quiver under the nets. Michael strokes my dirty hair and kisses my neck. I lean back on him, and he hugs my knees with his knees. I am exhausted, and have no idea what time it is. I close my eyes for a long time, until I hear excited voices in the canoes and know that we are approaching something.

When I open my eyes, I see smoke above the trees. We take some bends in the streams with caution, and then suddenly it comes into view--a ranch on a high plateau. We can see several hydrofoils "docked" to the side, and there is a lot of smoke rising in one of the compounds. The *Waiãpis* maneuver the canoes around, trying to find a more hidden approach, but we do not see any way of entering the compound without crossing a lot of exposed land.

"I think we are going to have to approach from the hydrofoils," says Michael. "I'm sure there's nobody out there: we can pull the canoes over there, and then swim or walk through to the shore, and then crawl up."

I turn to look at him, aghast. "You don't even know how many men are in there! They could be armed to the hilt with machine guns!"

"I don't like the looks of it, Michael," says Peter. "Look, we know the location now: let's leave and radio for help. Surely those half-starved Indians are enough proof for the authorities!"

"I don't know," says Fernando. "There are no chains there, no fences."

"Fernando!" exclaims Stephanie. "How can that not be enough proof?!"

He is silent for a moment. "I don't know how to explain it to you. There are still people in the Amazon who behave like the, uhh, Wild West. Sometimes...I don't know. Sometimes, it is very hard to figure out who are the good guys and who are the crooked sheriffs and sometimes you have to be very careful who you talk to, and sometimes it's better to do it yourself."

"So you want to storm the place with two pistols and a few poison darts?!" I exclaim.

"We never said anything about storming the place!" says Michael. "I just wanna have a look around. Listen, we can stash the canoes and everything in one of the hydrofoils, OK? I can check it for gas and to make sure I can figure out how to drive it; you guys can have it ready to go when I come back. We'll fly outta here like all get out!"

I almost laugh at this sudden eruption of Southern slang, but I am already starting to cry. He really means to do it. We are all silent except for Luis, and I suddenly realize that he and Fernando have already been translating the entire plan to the *Waiãpis*, who are nodding their heads enthusiastically. Stephanie, Peter and I try to talk them all out of it, but everybody else has agreed to the plan, so we pull the canoes slowly around the bend to check out the hydrofoils.

We glide in and out of docking spaces as Michael tries to pick one that is fairly close to the shore, but not immediately in the line of vision from the compound. He finally makes his selection, and he and Fernando start climbing into it, guns cocked while we wait below in the canoes.

They are not beset with mosquitoes, and I realize there do not seem to be mosquitoes in this stream. I can see them clearly in the moonlight, cautiously lifting their heads up and in, and looking around. Then they climb all the way in, and we can faintly hear them moving around. Then Fernando peeps his head out and whispers,

434

"We found a drunk guy in here--a white guy!"

"Oh, my God!" exclaims Stephanie. "We gotta get outta here: somebody'll come looking for him!"

"I don't think so," says Fernando. "I think he lives in this hydrofoil. Come look at this!" And with that he disappears again. Luis waits in the canoes with the *Waiãpis* while we cautiously climb into the hydrofoil. They are all the way in the back, and we walk there slowly. There are things strewn all around--pillows, books, a guitar, rain ponchos, bottles and buckets, boxes, food, jugs, and liquor bottles. Lots of liquor bottles.

Michael seems to be tying somebody up, but the guy is barely awake anyway. Michael finishes putting a gag around the prisoner's mouth, then leans him up against the wall. Now I know I have lost my mind, because the first thing I think is that he looks exactly like Nick Constantine. His hair is long and mangy, and he has a full beard, but I recognize the eyes. He is wearing a filthy t-shirt and khakis and no shoes. He smells awful. He is looking around us now with tremendous curiosity, but he does not look as if he will be able to say anything coherent anytime soon. Then he starts to cry. I kneel down and touch his face.

"Nick?" He looks up at me, and I know it is him. It is either him in reality or it is him in my malarial hallucination, but it is definitely him. I start pulling off his gag, but Michael stops me.

"He might start screaming!"

"It's Nick Constantine, Michael."

"What!?"

"It is: look at him!"

I pull off his gag. "Am I dead?" he whispers to me. I shake my head and wipe the tears from his eyes; then he slumps over. Stephanie drops down to check his pulse, but he has just passed out. I go to untie him, but Michael stops me again.

"Look, drunks can really get out of control: we need to keep him bound and gagged until he sobers up." He puts the gag back on,

435

then lays Constantine out in a more comfortable position. "We'll wait a few more hours to see if he wakes up and can tell us what's going on, but if he doesn't, we'll have to go check it out ourselves. It'll be light in about six hours."

"Let's get some sleep; we can take turns keeping guard," says Fernando.

Stephanie and I go down to sleep in the canoes with the *Waiãpis* so as not to be disturbed by the guys' switching on and off the one-hour watches they have agreed to. They want the *Waiãpis* to sleep the whole time because they are exhausted from paddling for days on end.

When I wake up, it is still dark, but there are voices in the hydrofoil. Stephanie and I climb up. Everybody is awake, including Constantine. He is shaking all over, and they give him sips of liquor under his gag until he calms down. When they are sure that he is not afraid and will not scream, they take off his gag and untie him, and then he begins to speak.

"I tried to leave so many times...but I always got lost. Sometimes I came back. Sometimes I drove until I ran out of gas, and they came and picked me up. I couldn't stand living in there anymore, so now they let me live out here. They're totally mad!" He looks around at us, his bloodshot eyes bulging. "I bought this place because they told me they thought they could find a cure for AIDS out here. They just wanted a stretch of virgin forest that had never been explored before. I didn't know what their plan was." He stops to beg for more liquor.

"What are they doing?" asks Michael.

"They had all these monkeys and rats infected with HIV, and kept trying different chemicals on them--chemicals they would extract from leaves and roots and vines. I gave them a lot of start-up money, and then a couple weeks ago, I decided to come and see how it was going. They're totally mad." He puts down the bottle and stares at his feet.

"What are they doing?" Michael asks again.

436

He bites his lip and starts to cry. "They were surprised by our visit. They shot us down, you see." He pauses. "My pilot's dead. I kept thinking somebody would come looking for him eventually. But you see, I would not let anybody else know where my goddamn ranch was! I just didn't want the press making a big deal out of it. I knew it was such a long shot anyway, but I wanted to give those scientists a chance. They were sort of rogue researchers in England. They had run out of money, but some people thought they were on the right track."

"What are they doing now?" Michael gently prods him again.

"They had all these Indian slaves and...they had killed a lot of Indians. They stuck their...heads on these poles around the compound. I thought I was having a bloody nightmare, but it was real. They're totally mad. I think they were using the Indians like rats in tests before, but that's not what they're doing now. They've discovered some vine that does something to plastic. I don't understand it, but it turns the plastic back into some sort of petroleum. The vine can do it to anything--plastic bottles, toys, bags. I've seen it. It turns into a purple liquid, and then they put it in the gas tank and go. They know there aren't a lot of vines, though, so they're trying to preserve the key ingredients--the genes, I guess--to have some sort of biotechnology. They think they're gonna be bloody rich. Do something with all the mounds of plastic trash in the world. Undersell OPEC and make billions."

He takes another swig of liquor and wipes the tears across his muddy face. I can hear Stephanie crying. I do not hear a word from the *Waiãpis*: Fernando has been quietly translating it into Portuguese for Luis, but apparently Luis has been afraid to pass it onto the *Waiãpis*.

"Maybe they never cared about AIDS....I don't know. Maybe they thought they could get rich off me, but most of my money is in escrow on account of my litigation with Swiny. I think it's more than the money, though. They order these slaves around....God, it's horrible. Some of the Indians just commit suicide. Some of them have malaria--a lot of them. They did something to make the mosquitoes multiply like crazy in the swamps surrounding this stretch of forest to keep people out. They're brilliant."

"How did you learn all this?" asks Michael, untying him.

"I tried to escape in one of these things right away, when I realized they had **not** shot us down by mistake, and saw the...heads on the poles all around. They drugged me for awhile, and I tried to escape again, then they locked me in a room with a lot of liquor. They didn't give me any food for a few days, and I started drinking....I guess I never stopped." He takes another swig. "Then they didn't pay much attention to me anymore. They thought I was drunk. I would hear things that they didn't think I understood."

"Maybe he hallucinated all this," whispers Peter.

"No, I didn't," says Constantine. How could his hearing be that sharp? "There's a high-powered telescope built into that wall over there: just look." We look at the wall in puzzlement, and he staggers over to the console to show us where the telescope is built into the hydrofoil.

Michael looks through it for several moments, then sits down, looking green.

"What?" says Stephanie.

"I could see the...heads," he whispers. We all stare at him, then back at Constantine.

"If you know how to find your way out of here, please, take me with you," Constantine says. He looks around at us all. "Please!"

"C'mon," says Michael, getting to his feet. "Fernando, you and Peter check to make sure everything is OK with the oil and the gas and everything before we start the motor. And tell Luis to tell the *Waiãpis* we're gonna load the canoes and everything onto this, as soon as we clear out some of this crap, and after we're certain we don't need to paddle over to another one to pirate gas. And make sure Luis does **not** tell them about **any** of this until we leave. I'm gonna look at the controls and make sure I can drive it."

438

Stephanie and I start dropping refuse quietly into the water, and it takes a long time to clear out the hydrofoil. It would be much easier to grab a different one--a clean one--but this one is definitely the least visible from the compound. Fernando discovers we have no gas, but that is something they can siphon from another one without climbing up and in, so nobody should see them.

"Come on, come on!" Michael is getting anxious now, probably because it cannot stay dark much longer. The full moon is starting to fade ever so slightly. They pull up the last canoe. "Ask the *Waiãpis* if we just float for awhile, if we will float downstream in the right direction." They say yes, for awhile, so Michael tells us we will just try to float it for awhile, until out of sound range from the ranch, before starting the motor. Peter and Fernando untie the phantom ship, and Michael steers it as we slowly drift away.

Peter comes over and puts his arms around Stephanie, who is seated beside me, holding my hand. Then Constantine comes to sit beside me. Maybe it is because there are so few people here who speak English, maybe it is because I touched his face when he was crying, but it is probably because I am the only other woman here and he wants a bosom to cry into.

I pull him gently to my breast, and we both cry. I cannot imagine how he will survive this...horror...sane. I do not know what sort of policeman you call to the scene of this type of...crime. We float in complete silence. Luis has still not told the *Waiãpis* much. They have a right to know.... They will know soon enough. The *Waiãpis* signal that we cannot continue floating in the same direction, and must start traversing some side swamps, so Michael finally starts the motor as the first faint glimmer of dawn sunlight breaks through the Amazonian mist in front of us.

Chapter 66

When it is light enough to see well, Fernando and Luis start rummaging through the food supplies still on board. Constantine pulls away from my embrace sheepishly and goes to help them clean off utensils and plates, and find a can opener for them. His hands are shaking badly, and Fernando hands him another liquor bottle. I readjust my balance, as Michael drives the hydrofoil as fast as the *Waiãpis* can navigate across the streams and ponds that only exist a few months of the year in Amapá.

Fernando passes out food to the *Waiãpis*, and I share my plate with Michael, spoon-feeding him so that he can keep his eyes and hands in motion. He looks electrified and exhausted, but smiles at me after every mouthful. "It'll be OK," he keeps saying, occasionally taking one hand off the steering wheel to brush my messy hair out of my eyes.

Stephanie begins poking around the consoles, trying to discern some radio equipment, since ours is totally water-logged now. Constantine tells her that it was disabled on his hydrofoil.

"What about the others? Did you ever try to send out radio messages?" Peter asks.

Constantine just stares at him blankly.

Stephanie asks Fernando and Constantine to hunt for screwdrivers, determined to take apart the radio equipment and hook it back up again. I am again amazed at my sister; I have nothing to contribute. Fernando returns with a couple tools, but hesitates to hand them over. "If we send out radio signals, maybe the ranch will pick them up before anybody else does?"

"I'm more worried about them picking us up on radar," she replies, taking the tools from his hands. "We need to have the radio ready to send out a distress signal if their helicopter comes after us."

I drop my plate on the deck. "It's OK," says Michael, but it is not OK. I had completely forgotten they had a helicopter and stare at him in wide-eyed horror. "We can easily outmaneuver a helicopter under this canopy of trees. Their visibility will be lousy, especially if the rain picks ups." Rain? I look out on the water and see that he is right: scattered drops are falling. I look up at the cloudy sky and start to pray, hating myself for wishing we had a machine gun on board...or a rocket launcher. Better to be a victim than a murderer.

"You need to get Luis to try to figure out from the *Waiãpis* exactly where we are--you know, longitude and latitude or something--so that we can radio out our position," Stephanie says to Fernando, who looks back at her dubiously. "Something! I don't know--the name of the river--"

"We're not in a river right now--we're going across flooded swamps," Fernando says.

"Well, you better come up with **some** explanation! Show them the map: show them where the rivers are, and figure out where we are in between them, then!"

Fernando converses for awhile with Luis and the *Waiãpis*, while Stephanie hunts through the exposed circuits trying to figure out where the disconnection is. I look at Constantine, who stares back at me, huddled away from the commotion. He is sitting on the floor, knees pulled up to his chest, arms wrapped tightly around his legs, rocking back and forth. "We are trying to get back to the Mapari river, I think," Fernando calls out.

"Don't tell me what you think! Tell me what you know!" Stephanie yells at him.

He goes over the map again with Luis and the *Waiãpis*, even as they are directing Michael to take a wide turn which has dramatically altered our course. "At this time of year, the sunrise

441

would be...." He gazes around. "We must be northwest of the Mapari river. By canoe they said...." He makes mental calculations in his head. "One-hundred miles northwest of the Mapari?" I look at Stephanie, who takes her gaze from the circuits only long enough to give him a disdainful look. "I'm doing the best I can!"

"I know," Stephanie says, looking at him again, more kindly. "It's just very frustrating."

"They say we have already done a half day's journey by canoe, so we are making good progress. Hey! Did you figure it out?"

Stephanie is closing up the console. "Yep."

"God, you're amazing!" exclaims Peter, giving her a peck on the back of her head.

The *Waiãpis* suddenly point to the sky behind us, uttering loud exclamations. I see the pained reaction of Luis and hear him tell Fernando that the *Waiãpis* have heard a loud noise approaching us.

"What?! What is it?" screams Michael.

"They heard something," I answer feebly, straining my neck to see through the patchy mist and rain clouds. I hear nothing.

Michael looks nervously over his shoulder a few times as the *Waiãpis* continue to point to the sky behind us, then suddenly jerks the hydrofoil to the right to dive under some trees. "Send out the distress call--**now!**" Stephanie turns on the radio, but falls down when Michael abruptly swerves to the left to avoid some fallen tree trunks. As she gets back up, we all spot a glimpse of the helicopter through a break in the mist, and scream. Michael looks over his shoulder and sees it, too, then resumes zigging and zagging the hydrofoil in and out of densely covered swamps.

I feel a tug at my leg, and look down to see that Constantine has crawled across the deck to get to me, and is now hugging my legs in desperation. I stroke his hair and try to say something, but I am choking back my own tears and screams. We hear an explosion of gunfire and turn to see innocent monkey bystanders toppling from their trees.

"Get down!" Michael screams, pushing me down to the deck. "Everybody down!"

I huddle down with Constantine, as Fernando signals to Luis and the *Waiãpis* to take cover. Stephanie crouches below the radio, adjusting knobs and dials, then hands the microphone to Fernando, who starts yelling out a half-crazed, barely intelligible distress call.

"Did you tell them where we are?" pleads Stephanie. Fernando continues yelling into the microphone in a Portuguese so riddled with profanity and terror that I can barely understand it. "Stay **calm**!" she continues to plead with him. "Speak **clearly**!"

"Put Luis on the radio!" yells Michael. "Fernando, get your gun ready. Peter, you wanna drive for awhile?" We all stare at Michael, dumbfounded. "Look, if they get close enough, we might be able to shoot out their windshield--maybe even their propeller or gas tank." Peter gives Stephanie a tight hug and a passionate kiss, then moves forward to the steering wheel. "Just keep zig-zagging it: make it difficult for them," says Michael, handing over the wheel.

He looks down at me as he pulls his gun out of his boot, then squats beside me. "I've gotta try to shoot them down...if they get close." He wipes the tears off my face. "I don't think they can get a good shot at us: it's raining too hard now, and the Apache can't maneuver as fast as we can. But if they manage to get close and have a good look at us...." He does not finish the sentence--just kisses me tenderly on the mouth.

"I love you, Michael."

"I love you, too."

He pulls away and races off to the back of the hydrofoil, pausing only to grab Fernando by the elbow. I watch them position themselves in the back, trying to find a way to shelter themselves while keeping their guns and vision clear. I hear Luis stating our conjectured position calmly and clearly into the radio microphone, even as he looks doubtfully at the crazy zig-zagging we are doing. The hydrofoil takes a sudden lurch as we drop into deeper water.

"Are we getting close to the Mapari?" Stephanie asks. Luis evidently understands the word "Mapari" and shakes his head. He tells me in Portuguese that we are going the wrong way, and must be getting close to the Jari river instead, which I repeat to Stephanie, who consults the map. The *Waiãpis* have made no move to redirect us, evidently understanding that we are just bobbing and weaving now. They have readied their poison darts, though I can tell by the looks on their faces that they doubt it will come down to that.

"Stay near the trees!" Michael yells from the back.

"The water's getting broader!" Peter hollers back to him. "Should I double back?"

"**No**! Whatever we do, we wanna keep moving away from the ranch. The further we get from it, the more they will hesitate to continue. They can't concentrate on following us **and** on keeping track of their own position, and I doubt they want to wander into civilization. If we get far enough, we may even run into some air traffic or something to scare them off. Just hug the side: stay close to the trees!"

"I don't wanna hit 'em!" yells Peter.

"This baby can take some trees, Peter! Stay near the trees!"

The water is broadening all around us now, and we quickly find ourselves in a large stream. Each time Peter thinks he has turned the hydrofoil into a side stream with more trees, we just end up coming out on the large stream again. He dutifully hugs the tree-lined shore, but I can hear him quietly discussing with Stephanie whether they should disobey Michael and double back for denser forest cover. I am too stupid to know what to do and just keep stroking Constantine's hair. I feel as if I am in one of those dreams where I am being chased and try to run, but my legs will not move because they feel like lead, and I finally get exhausted and stop trying and just wait to be caught.

I hear the helicopter swooping in and realize it has broken through the mist on our left and is flying smoothly over the stream, positioning for a clear shot at us. Peter rams the hydrofoil through a narrow gap in the trees and turns back for denser cover, but the Apache is already shooting at us. "Weave it!" I hear Michael screaming, and Peter pulls it left and right like a lunatic, scraping trees constantly. I watch in disbelief as Michael and Fernando take pistol potshots at the helicopter, and a bullet actually cracks the windshield of the Apache. I feel a glimmer of hope erupt in my heart for a brief moment before I see the rear corner of the hydrofoil strafed with bullets and see Michael's outstretched shooting arm turn into an appendage of bleeding, burning flesh.

I jump to my feet screaming his name, but Constantine pulls me back down as bullets start landing all around us. "Let me go!" I scream helplessly. "I want to die with him!"

Peter falls on me, and I hear Stephanie's screams joining my own, and then we are all lurching right and left as the unsteered hydrofoil bounces off several trees before hurtling down some cataracts. The bullets have stopped, and Peter tries to take the steering wheel again, and I hear Stephanie saying that the console is shot to pieces. I pull free of Constantine and jump up to find Michael; I must climb over and around the *Waiãpis* and Luis and the debris that is scattered all over from the hydrofoil's bouncy ride.

Somebody pulls me down again, and this time it is Luis screaming to me in Portuguese, but I am too hysterical to understand him, and he slaps me, and I stare at him in shock as he tells me that the *Waiãpis* think we are coming up to the Waterfall of Despair and should try to bank the hydrofoil, and that I must tell Peter this because Luis cannot speak enough English, and he and the *Waiãpis* start dragging me back to Peter and Stephanie as I scream in crazy Portuguese that I need to get to Michael, but Luis does not care and keeps dragging me. When we reach Stephanie, Luis grabs her leg hard to get her attention, and she looks down at me in amazement as I struggle with the desperate *Waiãpis* all around me. "They say we're coming to a waterfall and...and we should...and we should...ba-ba-bank the boat."

"The motor's not even running!" she screams! "We're just trying to find a way to steer it! Ask them if they can pilot the canoes

445

in this river." I haltingly translate the question to Luis, who blanches upon hearing that we cannot operate the hydrofoil, and then translates to the *Waiãpis*, who also blanche. They talk amongst themselves, then answer him, and he tells me they are not sure, but it would be better to try to paddle to shore in the canoes than go over the waterfall.

I translate the response back to Peter and Stephanie even as Luis and the *Waiãpis* begin preparing the canoes. I get up to search for Michael, horrified that neither he nor Fernando have yet come up front. I didn't want you to die alone, Michael.

I fall to my feet as the hydrofoil starts bouncing and rocking violently and cannot get up again because of the turbulence. I try to crawl, but things are slamming into me, and a canoe nearly broadsides me. The hydrofoil takes another huge lurch, and we all slide forward, and I land in Constantine's arms again as I hear Peter screaming that he can see the waterfall. He drops down beside me, and Stephanie crawls around him to hug him and me both.

"Michael," I whimper.

"He's in God's hands now," Constantine says, "and so are we." I turn to look at him in amazement, but his eyes are closed and his lips are moving in silent prayer. I turn back to look at Stephanie.

"I love you so much, Steph!"

"I love you, too, sweetie!" She hugs me hard, and I feel Peter's arms wrapping around her, and hear him whispering in her ear.

I pray to God for mercy, then feel the hydrofoil leave the water. I look up and see the waterfall we have just sailed over looming behind us, getting taller and taller and more and more ferocious as we continue to drop. Water is spraying all around us, and still we have not hit the bottom. I stare at the waterfall in disbelief as it looms as high as a skyscraper above us. I pray to God to kill us instantly, and then we crash into the water at the bottom. Large boulders rip through the floor, but the current is pushing us too fast for us to sink. "We made it!" I hear Stephanie and Peter exclaiming, then we slam into the side of a rocky cliff and tip over.

446

In a split second I am engulfed in water. I struggle desperately to swim up to the surface, but the current is knocking me so hard that I cannot get enough sense of equilibrium even to know if I am upside down or right side up. My lungs prepare to explode and then I am launched out of the water. I gasp for air and see that I am flying down another waterfall, but it is small. I fill up my lungs for impact, then swim hard to get to the surface. I gasp for air and start swimming for land.

The current has eased up a bit, and I make a difficult diagonal line for the shore, looking frantically around me for signs of life. I see several heads bobbing here and there, and arms flailing away at the Jari river. I swim and swim and swim and finally slam into a fallen tree to grab hold of. I catch my breath and pull myself up. Luis is suddenly by my side, panting heavily, and grabbing my hand to follow him. We race down the shoreline to try to keep up with the people still swimming. Some of the *Waiãpis* are climbing out up ahead of us, and we continue to jog past them as they catch their breath.

We turn a sudden bend, and I scream in delight to see that Stephanie has dragged herself up. I pause at her side, but she pushes me away and points me on. "Make sure everybody gets out," she pants. "I'll catch up in a minute."

Luis and I jog forward, and now the *Waiãpis* who have caught their breath catch up to us and pass us. I scan the Jari for the others and see a few *Waiãpis* climbing out ahead of us, and we keep jogging, and then we see Peter climbing out. He takes a gulp of air, then screams, "Keep going! Fernando is holding onto Michael."

Constantine appears out of nowhere and takes my hand. "Come on!" We keep running, and a couple minutes later Stephanie and Peter have caught up with us.

Then the *Waiãpis* start pointing, and we follow their cue and spot Fernando and Michael in the water. "There! There they are!" screams Stephanie. They are approaching the shore. As Fernando grabs hold of a rock, the current suddenly rips Michael from his grasp.

447

"**Noooooooooo**!" I scream, racing towards the water to jump back in, but Stephanie and Peter hold me back.

"You can't catch him swimming! C'mon!" They pull me away from the water, and we resume jogging along the rocky shoreline, trying to keep an eye on him. The *Waiãpis* ahead of us start exclaiming about something, and when we turn the bend, we see that the Jari has now fanned out much wider...and Michael is sinking into it.

"Oh, my God!" I scream, again racing towards the water, but Stephanie and Peter hold me back, pulling me along in a desperate and exhausted jog along the shoreline. We stumble on as fast as we can, all of us gasping for air, looking forward and backward for a sign of him. Please, God, please, God, please, God....

Then Stephanie pulls me down to the ground, and I collapse into exhausted sobs. Why him? Why not me, God? Why not those monsters back there?! Why?! Why?! Why?! Why?! Why?! Why?! Why?! Why?! Why?!

"**Look!**" somebody screams, and I leap to my feet. The *Waiãpis* and Luis and Constantine are all pointing to some dark movements in the water. "**There!**" I see what seems to be Michael's head bobbing up to the surface, but it drops below the water again. He is not swimming. He is dead. I try to turn away, not wanting to see his dead body, but I am too paralyzed to move.

Suddenly Michael pops up to the surface...and starts floating in our direction.... I feel the horror welling up in me, not wanting to see his corpse wash up ashore, but I cannot take my eyes off him. Then I see the fin...behind him. No! It can't be! He starts to topple back into the water, and then a second fin pops up behind him and he is above the water again, floating straight for us.

"*Tucuxi!*" I hear Fernando exclaiming. "*Tucuxi!*" The good dolphin? **The good dolphin?!**

Then we see several gray faces pop out of the water and start whistling and clicking...and smiling. *Tucuxi!* The river is full of the good dolphins! They are bringing Michael straight to us! Oh, my

448

God! Maybe he's alive! Maybe he's alive!

The pod of dolphins pulls up below us, trying to find some sort of ledge among the rocks where they can deposit Michael. Peter and Stephanie start climbing carefully down the rocks to meet the dolphins, but I cannot wait that long, and decide to jump over the cliff. I hear Stephanie and Constantine screaming my name just as I land in the sea of dolphins. One of the *tucuxi* is under me even before I start swimming, pushing me up to the surface. We break water, and I catch my breath, relieved that the dolphin is pushing me towards Michael. I can see his mutilated arm dragging in the water, but his face is turned away from me, and I cannot tell if he is breathing.

"Michael!" I scream. "**Michael!**" He does not answer, and I try to get off the dolphin to swim over to Michael, but the dolphin just interprets this as an unintentional fall, and lifts me up again. Then I see the dolphins push Michael onto a ledge: their bodies nearly come all the way out of the water as they strain to push him up the slippery rock. He still is not moving, and I know he is dead, but I cannot bear it, and want to rush to him anyway. Finally, my own dolphin gets me to the same ledge, and some other dolphins join in to give me a push up.

I clamber across the wet rock even as I faintly hear Stephanie screaming something about not touching him. I reach his side and turn his head to me, but his eyes are closed. I steel myself to remember what little I know about this, open his mouth, put my mouth on his, and breathe in. "C'mon, Michael," I whisper, as I shakily move my fingers to his neck to check for a pulse. Please, please, please, please--**I feel it!** I press my fingers harder, to be sure. "**Michael!**" I scream.

"Don't touch him!" Stephanie continues to scream at me, and I look up at her and the others descending the rocky cliff, not caring at all what she is saying. "He--"

"He has a pulse!" I pinch his nose and gleefully start breathing more air into his mouth until I am out of breath, then I thump on his chest until I catch my breath, then I start breathing into his mouth again–then somebody is pulling me off him. "No! He's

449

alive! I swear! I'm not crazy! He's alive!" *I felt his pulse, didn't I?*

"Hold her!" Peter screams to somebody, and I find myself being shoved into the arms of Constantine.

I squirm around. "I'm not crazy! He's alive! He needs CPR!" I stare at Peter and Stephanie in amazement, furious that they pulled me off of him.

"He has AIDS," Constantine whispers to me. I turn to look at him, in shock. "They were afraid you'd get messed up with his blood."

I turn back to them. Stephanie is holding a rain slicker tightly around his mutilated arm, Fernando has straddled him and begun chest compressions, and Peter is preparing to give him more mouth-to-mouth resuscitation. I turn to look at Constantine again, but he is looking at Michael now; he has not relaxed his grip on me. I lean back into his chest, and he relaxes his embrace just a little, and rests his head on my head. Sobs overwhelm me as I stare at Michael, trying to understand. They are trying to save his life, but he will die anyway.

Michael's head suddenly jerks up, and he starts spitting water out. "Michael!" I scream, as Peter tenderly holds his head to the side to facilitate Michael's coughing spasms. I squirm to get away from Constantine, but he whispers to me to wait. Michael leans his head back, and I can see him taking deep breaths, his eyes closed. Then he calls my name, and Constantine lets me go.

Peter takes my hand and guides me down beside Michael's face. His eyes are still closed. I look across him to Stephanie, who is smiling and laughing and crying all at the same time. I look back down to him, breathing erratically but deeply, intermittently calling my name.

"Jobie."

"I'm here, Michael." I wrap my hands around his head and kiss his face.

"Jobie."

"I love you, Michael."

"Jobie, Jobie, I love you, too." He weakly opens his eyes and searches until he can focus on me. "Jobie!" He smiles until his dimples show. "Jobie! Thank God you're alive! Thank God." He closes his eyes again, and I nestle my head next to his, wanting to feel his breathing and his pulse next to me, for however long I can. "Jobie, Jobie...."

Chapter 67

When I open my eyes, I see a whitish ceiling above me, paint peeling. I am in a bed with blue curtains drawn to my left and my right and in front of me. I start to remember and try to get out of bed, but I have tubes in both arms, and I am exhausted. "*Oi*," I call out tentatively, hoping I am in a hospital and someone will hear me. "**Oi!**"

The curtain opens and Constantine walks in. "Bloody hell! You've woken up! How are you feeling, love?" He puts a steaming cup of black coffee down on the tiny nightstand, and grasps one of my limp hands. "Everything's fine now, love! We're in hospital in Macapá. Everyone's alright."

"Everyone?"

"Yes! Everyone! Well, you've all got a touch of malaria, but they're very mild cases, thanks to your anti-malarials. Everybody's a bit scratched and bruised, of course, a few sprains and slight fractures and whatnot, but all in all, a pretty healthy lot, considering." He pauses to lift a water bottle to my lips. "How about a few sips for me, dear." He pours a little water into my mouth, and it feels wonderful. He looks bathed and shaved but still very haggard, with dark circles under his eyes. "I'd call the nurse, but they're terribly under-staffed here, it would seem. But I've made the rounds and looked in on everybody. Stephanie's right there, by the way." He pulls back the curtain to my right, and I see Stephanie asleep.

"How long has she been--"

452

"Well, she's woken up on and off a couple times. They say it's to be expected with the ordeal and the malaria and whatnot. You woke up once during the helicopter ride, but you were quite delirious: I suspect you don't recall. The army uniforms scared the dickens out of you."

"Army--"

"Yes, the Brazilian army managed to find us from the radio transmission. It took them awhile, but they did. By that time, everybody was either asleep or delirious or unconscious or somewhere in between...exhausted. Except me. I...uhh...don't have the malaria, you see. I just desperately wanted a drink." I squeeze his hand, and he smiles.

"Did everybody really make it, or are you just saying that?"

"No! Everybody made it, I swear! No thanks to me."

"**What?!**"

"Well, if you had all just left in the canoes, none of that would have happened."

"It's not your fault!"

"Yes, it's all my fault." He says it very matter-of-factly, not a confession to a friend or to God but more like a deposition. "All my fault."

"It wasn't your fault!"

"Shhhh, don't get excited. You need to rest now. Michael's going to need a lot of taking-care-of."

"I wish they had told me."

He shakes his head. "Everybody always waits for the right time to tell it...but there never is a right time."

"I need to see him."

"No, you need to rest."

"He must still be in grave condition: he must have lost so much blood!"

"He's in stable condition. His malaria's the worst case, though."

"Oh, my god! He'll die from it!"

"No, he won't."

"If he's got no immune--"

"The anti-malarials are taking care of it: it's just slower for him because his body can't contribute to the fight at all."

"You're just saying that!"

"No, I'm not." I stare into his eyes, and there is nothing hidden there. It is the truth. There is sadness in his eyes but no lies.

"I still want to see him."

"Later, love. Are you hungry?" I shake my head. "You just need to rest, then."

"How long have I been out?"

"Well, awhile, I suppose." He looks around for a clock, but does not see one. "Seven hours, I think. We were there for quite awhile, debating what to do. We hid ourselves away, in case the helicopter came back, but it didn't. The Indians gathered a few fruits for us to eat, but then everybody sort of fell asleep talking about how we needed to start trekking off for the nearest town, wherever that might be: arguing over what direction to march in just brought the delirium and exhaustion on in everybody, I suppose. Once we realized the helicopter was no longer after us, everyone sort of just relaxed and passed out. I can't tell you how thrilled I was to see the helicopters coming in!" He pauses to give me more water.

"You haven't slept at all?"

"Well, I passed out in the helicopter ride back to Macapá, I guess--woke up later to find somebody had bathed me and shaven me and jabbed me with some needles. I looked around and found all the blokes in the same ward as me. I wandered around until I found a doctor who spoke English, and he told me how everyone was. Chatted a bit with Fernando and Peter: they were awake for awhile,

454

then went back to sleep. Luis woke up too, but he doesn't know much English, so I didn't have much of a chat with him! The Indians had seemed pretty miserable until Luis woke up and told them the doctor said they could go back home in a couple days."

"Did you tell the army everything?"

"Fernando and Luis did, I guess," he says quietly, turning to look at the wall. "I never had a chance to learn much Portuguese. I suspect sooner or later somebody will come to question me about it."

"Have you called anyone?"

"No." He looks back at me and smiles. "I've been busy looking in on all of you, now, haven't I?"

"Will you sing something for me?" I regret saying it as soon as the words leave my mouth, but he smiles.

"What?"

"Anything." He starts singing, and I close my eyes and drift off.

When I open them again, he is gone. I stretch my arm to pull the curtain, but Stephanie's bed is empty. "Stephanie!"

"Jobie!" I whip my head around, realizing I was pulling the curtain on the wrong side. "Hey," she calls from the other bed, pulling the curtain open. She gets up and walks over to me, no tubes in her arms. "Everything's OK, sweetie. Are you hungry?" I shake my head. "Just try to rest, then."

"What about--"

"Everybody's fine. Nick checked in on everybody before he went to bed."

"He went to a hotel?"

"No, he's sleeping in the ward. Go back to sleep: in the morning we can go see Michael."

I close my eyes and dream no dreams.

Chapter 68

The next day, I eat sweet rolls and fruit with Stephanie, and ask her why they did not tell me Michael had AIDS.

"Why don't we talk about this later."

"Later?! **Later?!** How many 'laters' do you think we're gonna get?"

"OK, I'm sorry. There were a lot of reasons."

"When did he get AIDS?" I can already picture the prostitutes in Panama: that would explain everything--

"He got HIV in prison."

"**Prison?!**"

"Yeah....He was...well, you know..." I stare at her, dumbfounded. *Gay? My Michael? No, he must have been raped. Please let it have been rape. Oh, God! I didn't mean that! I'm sorry! I didn't mean that.* "...he was raped." I push away the tray, feeling dizzy and sick. "I knew we should have talked about this later."

"**No!** Tell me now!"

"I'm not going to tell you now--not about that. But that's why he was paroled early. We sued the damn prison for ignoring his requests for a cell transfer and letting him get...abused...and get HIV, and we found out that a couple of the guards in his unit were ex-army, and we proved with telephone records that they had been in frequent communication with his former commander and his military prosecutors, and we were building a hell of a wild lawsuit, and then they all cut a deal for him to get out of prison early."

"Why didn't you tell me this?"

"You had enough shit to deal with in your own life! Michael didn't want to tell you because you had enough problems of your own. And he knew you still loved him too much, and he wanted you to get over him and not worry about him."

"And now he has AIDS?"

She nods. "He just found out a few months ago. That's why he decided to come to Brazil. He got a lot of money in the settlement and....and....Well, he put some of it into the house--like an early wedding gift to us--gave most of it to his family, and, uhh, part of the deal was that the Veterans' Administration would have to adjust his discharge status so that he would be eligible for V.A. hospital care for the rest of his life, so he didn't need to save money for that."

"He gets to go to V.A. hospitals?!"

She nods. "Peter found a really good lawyer on this one, let me tell ya! Anyway, he had put aside some money for you. He wanted to wait and see what happened with you first, you know? See if you ended up staying in Brazil, or if you'd come back to the States, or go to some other country. But he had this money saved up, just in case you needed it. And then...then he thought, well...." She looks down at her tray and plays with her napkin. "He thought," she starts, choking up with tears, "he didn't know how much longer he'd be around to give you the money, even though he wasn't too sick, yet. He wanted to come and take us all on vacation with you so that you'd have some really happy memories from Brazil." She starts wiping her eyes with the napkin, and I pick up mine, too. "He kept saying, `I can buy her a house or something, but it won't make her happy. Let's go visit her there and...figure out what we can give her...so she can forget about the pain. She's had so many broken dreams.'"

The nurse comes in to pick up our trays and is immediately unnerved by the sight of us both crying our eyes out. I try to explain to her, but she rushes off to summon the doctor, who comes in and prescribes sedatives, but by the time another nurse has brought them in, we have stopped crying, and she leaves us alone when we

457

tell her we will go back to sleep.

I lie down and close my eyes, saying nothing to Stephanie, and pretend to sleep so that she will go to sleep. When I know she is asleep, I go to the toilet, wash up, brush my teeth, then wander off to look for Michael. In the corridor I run into Constantine, who tells me the guys are all asleep and that he was just coming to check on us, but I talk him into taking me to see Michael, anyway. We walk past the sleeping *Waiãpis* and the others before reaching Michael, who is at the very back of the room.

He is asleep when I get there. Constantine fetches me a rare visitor's chair, seats me in it, then perches himself on the foot of Michael's bed. We gaze at Michael in silence. He has an oxygen tube in his nose and looks like he has AIDS. Maybe he did before and I was too self-absorbed to see it. I fight back the tears and the self-anger. His left arm has an intravenous tube, and his right arm is in a removable cast. The rest of his body lies skinnily outlined under the sheet, and I realize he must have lost forty pounds since the time I first met him.

"Now I know why you didn't find another girlfriend, Michael," I mumble.

"I wouldn't be so sure about that," Constantine says softly.

I look at him in surprise, having already forgotten he was there. "It's all my fault, you know."

"What?!"

"I was the one that soured him on the military and landed him in jail, and that's where--"

"**Hold on, there!** It's not **your** bloody fault!"

"But it **is**!"

"Look, I've seen a lot of people get AIDS, and the last bloody thing they need is everybody hunting around for the blame. And he sure in hell wouldn't have come to Brazil if he blamed **you**!"

"He **should** blame me."

458

"No he **shouldn't**! Don't start with that rubbish: it's of no use to anybody! He loves you and he needs you **now**...at least to be his friend. Did it ever occur to you that the reason he didn't want to tell you was because he wanted you to remember that you **did** actually break up--wanted you to remember that you are divorced, so to speak, and not widowed? Wanted to make sure you would let go of him and find somebody else?"

"But I can't!" I sob, burying my head in my hands. He gets off the bed and walks over to my chair and starts rubbing my neck and stroking the hair on my head.

"Someday you will, love. Nobody ever believes it when they still love somebody they can't have, but in time, it fades away to a precious, precious sweet part of your heart that no longer makes you sad. And someday you find somebody else, somebody who **can** be a part of your life, somebody who needs you."

"Nobody has **ever** needed me."

"I need you." I turn around in surprise. "I'm sorry! I'm not making a pass or anything! But I **do**: I really do. And from what I know of Michael and your sister, you are definitely a person far more loved and far more needed than you realize."

"They're the only ones."

"Maybe you think they're the only ones because they're the only ones that **you** love. But you've got a bigger heart than that--much more room in it. You just need to open some of the doors."

"No, my life is over."

He hugs me really hard. "You mustn't say that--not now...not now that we've learned so much about it...how precious it is...how precious it is not to be alone...how precious it is to hold somebody and know that they're alive." He holds me for a long time, until my sobs subside, until we hear Michael stirring, then he lets go. "I'll go check on the others now, but I'm coming back in a little while: you really need to go back to bed, love." He kisses me on the top of my head, wipes my face dry with his shirt, and walks through the opening in the curtain.

459

I stroke Michael's hair, waiting for him to wake up, trying to remember everything that Stephanie said to me and everything that Nick said to me. I want to be strong for him. I want to be very, very strong for him. He opens his eyes.

"Jobie," he smiles, weakly trying to squeeze my hand.

"Hi, Michael," I say, and kiss his forehead.

"How ya doin'?"

"I'm fine. How are you feeling?"

"Great," he says hoarsely.

I reach for the water bottle on the nightstand and wet his mouth, gingerly holding his head up so that he can swallow a little bit. "Are you hungry?" He shakes his head. "Do you need pain killers?" He shakes his head again. "I'll take care of you now. You should have told me sooner: I would have quit my stupid job to take care of you."

"I didn't need you to take care of me."

"Do you now?"

He is quiet for awhile, and I look away. "Well...I'm not real keen on the idea of spending the end of my life in a V.A. hospital...." I look at him. "....but I see no reason for you to give up--"

"I don't have anything to give up."

"I don't think that's true, and even if it were, you still have a future." I shake my head. "Look, just give the University a chance, see where they wanna send you: maybe it'll be good!"

"I wanna stay with you," I sob, lowering my head.

"Well, maybe I can go with you..." I lift my head again. "...if they send you somewhere that doesn't have HIV immigration restrictions."

"You've jeopardized your health enough."

"That's a choice I made long ago."

"You let it happen, didn't you? You didn't fight back?"

460

He shakes his head and lowers his gaze. "I didn't wanna spend my whole prison sentence fighting, joining in on all those in-house gangs and rivalries and hatreds, always sleeping with one eye open, wondering if I trusted the wrong person to watch my back. I didn't wanna be at war the whole time! I couldn't take it anymore--fighting and destroying and killing. I thought they'd leave me alone after awhile, but...then I figured out the guards were goading them on....The guards were ex-army...."

"Stephanie told me."

"Yeah...I finally told her what was going on. I knew she had a lawyer boyfriend and asked her to ask him about it...if there was something I could do....So, she told you the rest?" I nod. "She's really the greatest, isn't she? And Peter. I didn't even tell my family until they came to pick me up, but they're OK with it, I guess. My mom cried a lot."

A nurse suddenly appears and starts scolding me, and I have to leave. I return to my own hospital bed, take a drink of water, and pass out.

When I wake up, Fernando is sitting on Stephanie's empty bed, watching me. He tells me that Stephanie is off with Peter, keeping Michael company, that Luis and the _Waiãpis_ have just left for the _Waiãpi_ reservation under the escort of the military police, and that Constantine is in his fifth hour of interrogation. Everybody else has already given a statement--except me.

"Have they raided the ranch?"

"Oh, they did that immediately--when they got the radio transmission. They dispatched helicopters to look for us, and when the hydrofoil crashed, they had a hell of a time tracking us down, but they were easily able to track the helicopter with radar. They warned it to land several times, and didn't shoot on it because it looked to be limping along, anyway."

"You guys actually shot it up?!"

"Well, I guess we shot something! So the helicopter finally landed at the ranch, and the military helicopters landed, and they

461

surrendered immediately. But it's going to take a long time to...clean up this mess. I've called some people in Brasília, and Constantine is waiting on his lawyers to show up...and some British embassy folks, I suppose. And every damn official working in Indian affairs is heading this way, what with the slavery and the murder of Betinho's father--"

"**What?!**"

"Oh, nobody told you that, yet?"

"**No!**"

"Betinho's here, in the men's malaria ward. When they left us, they went off to do some fishing for awhile and accidentally wandered into the *Waiãpi* reserve. Some Indians found them and were furious, because they have been struggling the entire rainy season just to survive. They killed Manoel--"

"**Oh, my God!**"

"Yeah, poor bastard. They killed him and tried to kidnap Betinho, but he got away on the boat, and somehow found his way back to Pedra Branca. He was delirious from fear and exhaustion and a touch of malaria, and somebody brought him here. He was really happy to see us: he was sure the Indians had killed us all, too, and I had a terrible time trying to explain to him why it happened. How do you explain something like that to a little boy?"

"I don't know," I say, crying. "What will happen to him now?"

"Your sister wants to adopt him."

"**What?!**"

"Yeah. She and Peter are talking about getting married right away so that they can adopt him and take him back. Nobody in Brazil adopts kids like that--babies, maybe, but not big kids who have never been to school, don't know anything but fishing. I hope they can do it.

"I want to go talk to Stephanie."

462

"Why don't you eat something first? Wait there." I get up to use the toilet and wash my face and try to leave, but he quickly returns with a tray of food and makes me eat something before I go.

When we get to the men's ward, we find Betinho sitting on the foot of Michael's bed with Stephanie's arms around him; Peter is sitting in the visitor's stool, spoon-feeding Michael. There is nothing left to say now. I know they will get married and adopt him, if they can, and I can tell from Michael's smile at me that he will not shut me out of the rest of his life.

Chapter 69

The next day, some military police officers show up with the belongings we had left at the *Waiãpi* village. Peter and Stephanie kiss their passports, knowing that now they have the IDs necessary to go to city hall to get married. We are all discharged from the hospital, except Michael, who will probably have to remain hospitalized for a couple weeks. Peter has already contacted the U.S. embassy about flying him back to a V.A. hospital in the U.S., and they will probably have that all arranged within a couple days.

Constantine is finished with the first round of interrogations and surprises us all by insisting on checking us into the finest hotel in Macapá; he then hands out wads of money so that we can buy nice clothes and prepare for Peter and Stephanie's wedding. He surprises us again at the courthouse when he shows up with an entourage of flower-bearers, who turn out to be two lawyers and his sister. They set Betinho to work scattering flower petals on the floor, place bouquets all over the courtroom, pin a giant orchid on Peter, and hand Stephanie an enormous bouquet. I serve as maid of honor and Portuguese interpreter, crying softly through the whole ceremony. Stephanie does not cry at all. It is astonishingly beautiful, and I wish Michael could have been there.

Constantine has one more surprise for us: a dinner reception he has had prepared in the rear dining room of the hotel. It is truly an elegant affair, with the well-groomed wait staff out-numbering our small wedding party. We eat and drink and dance and laugh, scarcely believing we are once again partaking of the sweet things in life. The finest toast to the new couple is from Fernando. Stephanie

464

and Peter head off to the honeymoon suite, and I pack off Betinho for my first night of nephew-sitting. We both fall fast asleep in a matter of moments.

***

In the morning, my University supervisor tracks me down at the hotel with a surprise telephone call, extends his condolences on my bout with malaria, gives me the number of a corporate American credit card, and advises me to buy new airline tickets for an immediate return to the U.S. I hang up the phone, stunned. How did he know? I have not even filed with the health insurance company. The Brazilian authorities had asked us not to discuss the ordeal with anybody at all. Peter had not even told the U.S. embassy everything in requesting air evacuation for Michael, but had merely stated that Michael had a severe case of malaria.

Does the embassy actually know more than that? I know the British embassy has been involved in extricating Constantine from criminal indictment, but surely they would not have passed along the information to the U.S. embassy? Or did the U.S. embassy get it straight from the Brazilian military? And, even so, military intelligence officers at the embassy would have nothing to do with the Overseas Development department personnel who know me...would they? Who noticed my involvement in this and contacted the University?

I shudder all over, not feeling at all comforted by the University's mysterious condolences on my malaria, and gaze fondly at Betinho--who has already fallen back to sleep, only momentarily disturbed by the ringing telephone. They have not yet told him they are trying to adopt him, but I suspect he knows it...and wants it. I take a shower, then take the now-awake Betinho to the hotel dining room, where we find Adão eating breakfast with Fernando. He gives us a heartfelt greeting. After chatting for awhile, he takes the restless Betinho out to play in the garden.

"Do you think **he** would adopt Betinho if Steph and Peter are not allowed to?" I ask Fernando.

"Yeah...maybe...but I think it would be better if Stephanie and Peter adopt him."

"Why?"

"I don't think that kid is ever going to want to pilot a boat in Amazônia again...and he doesn't know anything else. I can't imagine what Adão could do for him." I wonder silently if he is thinking about adopting Betinho himself. I tell Fernando about my surprise phone call, and he shakes his head. "Damn bastards."

"Who?"

"I don't know, but I know some damn bastards are involved!"

"Do you think the Brazilian military shares Amazonian intelligence with the U.S. military?"

"A little bit--just enough to be considered partners in the war on communism, I mean, the war on drugs, or whatever they are pretending the war to be right now, whatever the excuse is to have spies all over the jungle, making sure nobody causes any trouble for the big landowners and mine owners and ranchers and politicians."

"So we were causing trouble?"

He laughs. "A little bit!"

"What about the National Indian Foundation? They're not **all** corrupt, are they?"

"Oh, no! It's a real civil war in there. Right now, the good guys are probably spying on the bad guys, trying to figure out if they **knew** what was going on at that ranch, and the bad guys are probably trying to figure out how the hell it happened so quietly that they couldn't even extort any bribes because they didn't even know it was happening. The British embassy is probably dying of embarrassment, and the U.S. military is probably pissing in its pants because its intelligence personnel had no clue. The Amapá state police and Brazilian national police are probably fighting with each other **and** with the military, and not cooperating on the investigation, because nobody wants the blame pinned on them--and nobody is sure yet if there **was** involvement with some corrupt officials. It's a mess."

"But who would have told the University?"

He shakes his head. "I don't know. The military police probably gave all your names to the U.S. intelligence to make sure you weren't drug runners or something, and they figured out you were working in this program that was sort of connected to the embassy."

"Barely!"

"`Barely' is enough! They don't know if they'll be able to keep the media out of it! They sure in hell want to get anybody connected to the embassy 10,000 miles away from the scene of the crime!"

Stephanie and Peter come in for breakfast, and Fernando tells him that Adão is playing in the garden with Betinho.

"Is he thinking about adopting Betinho?" Stephanie asks, fretfully, seemingly jealous.

"No, no--he just came back to Macapá as soon as he heard what happened, wanted to make sure we were OK. Oh, and he brought your extra luggage from his house: it's in his car."

I tell them that the University wants me to leave right away, and they shake their heads in disbelief. "Well," says Peter, "Michael is leaving today, too. He just called from the hospital to say that they've arranged his transport for this afternoon."

So we all go to the airport together. I bid goodbye to Michael with no tears, believing that I **will** see him soon, believing that he will **not** die soon, trusting completely in the U.S. military plane that is waiting to fly him stateside. They carry him up the stairs and into the plane, and he looks as frail as an old man. My plane back to Brasília is next, and I leave Stephanie and Peter in Macapá, trusting in Fernando's able assistance to arrange their application to adopt Betinho. Fernando kisses me profusely and earnestly tells me that he hopes I will come back to Brazil some day. Constantine gives me an enormous hug goodbye, kisses me on both cheeks, and promises to visit me and Michael as soon as his affairs are in order. Then I fly out

467

of Macapá.

***

I touch down in Brasília in a complete daze. It seems like a year since I have been here, yet I know it has only been a few weeks. I take a taxi to my American friends' house and tell them about my malaria but nothing else, wondering to myself why I am honoring the authorities' admonitions not to divulge what happened. I sort through the luggage I had left with them, picking out warmer clothes for my trip up north, and carefully repacking the vacation clothes I have just washed and dried in my friends' utility room. The shrimp smell is finally all obliterated.

The next day, I get my new airline tickets for the U.S., close my Brazilian bank account, and stop at the Institute to say goodbye to my former co-workers. I have a new-found sentimentality for them, and the goodbyes are harder than I had originally expected. I wish my trip through Brazil had come at the beginning, before I tried to "study" Brazil from this crazy vantage point. I might have understood better why they huddle inside their clans. How can you face Brazil without a clan?

Chapter 70

In the evening, I fly out. It is a very, very long flight. We stop in Washington first, and must completely disembark to go through customs, then reboard the plane to fly on to New York. I miss my connection in New York and must take a flight much later. When I finally check into my hotel up north, exactly twenty-four hours have passed since I flew out of Brasília: exactly one day to get from there to here, to get from the rainy autumn down under to the northern spring up here, to get from my past to my future. I go to sleep, having absolutely no idea what to expect tomorrow.

I put on my best clothes and eat breakfast alone in the hotel dining room, staring out the window at the laborious process undertaken by a man in a wheelchair to descend from his wheelchair-equipped van. Buttons and levers and a motorized ramp and a motorized wheelchair. My God. I think I would rather be pampered to death in a home for invalids. That is how I am.

I walk slowly to my morning meeting with my supervisor. Delighted graduates are posing for cap-and-gown photographs all over the wind-blown campus in anticipation of this weekend's commencement ceremony. I see happy faces surrounded by family and friends everywhere I look, cameras clicking away to record this magnificent achievement. There will be no cameras to record what I will be "graduating" to.

I steel my face for cheery nonchalance--aided and abetted by the modern pharmaceuticals that have dutifully locked up my churning insides--and approach the project secretary, bearing gifts of Brazilian coffee and bejeweled stirring spoons for the office. She is delighted, and escorts me to the conference room to await my supervisor, but says nothing about my malaria. Ten nerve-wracking minutes later, he enters the room.

"How are you feeling?"

"OK, thanks. How are you?"

"Fine, fine. You all over the, uhh, malaria now?"

"Yeah."

"Great, great," he says, with no emotion showing in his face. "Well, we, uhh, have made the arrangements, and you're going to Chapel Hill."

"Chapel Hill?" ***What?! I'm not fired?!***

"Yes, to work with the professor whom we discussed earlier. Here's an email message he just sent me about what you'll be doing for him: I haven't even read it yet, actually." He hands me the page. "You'll probably have an end date around October or November."

"That's only six months from now," I reply, puzzled. "I have another year left in my program." If I'm not fired, that is.

"We had to bend the rules as it is: the donor agency never agreed to fund anybody working inside the U.S., so another six months is the most we can get out of them for you. The program was designed for overseas work."

"Why couldn't I work for the embassy in Brazil?"

"Well, uhh, that's not really an option."

"What about other overseas assignments?"

"There really aren't any other options right now. This way you'll be in the U.S. and it will make your job-hunt easier." ***What!?*** "I have to run now, but Mandy will go over all the details with you. Best of luck." He offers his hand, and I dazedly shake it, wondering what the hell has just happened.

Am I fired? No.... Yet...yet...my program has been cut short. When the hell was this decided? Yesterday? Or did they **want** me to spend months thinking I might be fired? Maybe they've been trying

470

to get me fired and failed. What the hell has been going on? **"My"** job hunt? They are supposed to **help** me find a job at the end of my program: that is one of the benefits of the program! I am supposed to become one of the "leaders" of the "next generation" of "professionals working in the field of--"

God! Those bastards! They **wanted** to fire me, but they know they don't have any justification to, so they pulled me out of Brazil on purpose, knowing it would jeopardize my funding! Those bastards! I **could** have had another full year! The embassy **wanted** me to stay in Brazil and work in the Overseas Development department! I could have learned something, done something, advanced somewhere!

I bury my head in my hands. Why did I ever complain about that assignment? When has complaining ever gotten me any redress, ever? They hated my complaining from the start--hated the fact that they had to pass along my progress reports and faxes and email memoranda to the donor agency, hated the fact that I was documenting what a waste of time and money it was for me to be placed at the Institute, hated the fact that I was making waves. I thought the University would be on my side--would want to identify and address problems in my placement. No, they want no problems. They want the donor agency to think they have set up this program without a hitch.

Chapel Hill.... I love Chapel Hill, but...it is like being sent backwards in my life...to work with the same professor again.... How will I explain this on future job interviews? There is no explanation. I cannot hope for a recommendation from these people. I will have to work like hell to produce high-quality research in a scant six months just to have something to show for myself. And the first month will be shot just getting an apartment, furniture, a car....

Chapel Hill.... I love Chapel Hill, and I can take care of Michael there. We can be happy there for a little while. We will not have to think about money or jobs...at least, not for awhile. We can take long walks...if he is not too tired. We can check out new bands...if the bar smoke is not too dangerous for him. We can--

Mandy abruptly walks in and hands me airline tickets to Raleigh/Durham International Airport.

"Ummm, I can probably find friends to stay with, but if not, is there any allowance for hotel for when I first arrive, until I find an apartment?"

"Uhhh, yes, yes."

"How many days allowed?"

"Well, uhh, just stay in a hotel if you have to, and then send us the bill." *What the hell does that mean? Will you pay it or not? Two days? Two weeks? A month? What?* "We made an appointment for you to get a check-up at student health before you fly out." She hands me a couple more papers, and that is that.

I wander off to student health. They hand me a form to fill out. Recent headaches? Loss of appetite? Nervousness? Dizziness? Stomach aches? Yes, yes, yes, yes. The nurse practitioner examining asks me about stress in my life, and I try to tell her how much stress I have...sincerely wondering if I have turned the bend in my life where I am going to have to be put under medication. Instead she consoles me verbally, and vicariously chastises my employer for leaving my job status up in the air for months, and gives me her business card to call her if I need to. I go back to the hotel and start making phone calls to my friends in Chapel Hill to tell them I am coming back.

Chapter 71

It is good to see Chapel Hill, and my old friends...and my old professor. He gives me a big hug, and it soon comes out that he did not know for sure that I was coming until two days ago. He is also surprised to learn that I will only be funded for another six months. We chat at length about Brazil, and he tells me about the research he would like me to help him with on migration and rainforest colonization. He tells me that I do not need to come into the office until I find an apartment and get a car.

It takes me a week to find a car, and another two to find a place to live. After a hundred telephone calls and dozens of visits, I finally find a decent, furnished basement apartment on East Franklin St. The homeowner is a nice old professor who offers rent reduction in exchange for lawn work. Michael will love it. I love it. I gaze in amazement at the rolling hill of a backyard, replete with flower and vegetable gardens, a gazebo, swinging chairs, a couple of hammocks, and my dream magnolia tree. Well, vicariously "my" dream magnolia tree.

I move out of the hotel and into the apartment two years to the day after I first left Chapel Hill for Mexico. Then I return to work...in the same department...at the University of North Carolina. I still have many, many acquaintances there, and it is quite a homecoming, and yet...it is entirely different. I dig happily into my research--poring over books and journal articles on migration and rainforest colonization, comparing dozens and dozens of different socioeconomic and ecological statistics, synthesizing the analyses of a host of different researchers as to why and how people migrate into rainforest regions and what happens to them and what happens to the jungles after they get there. I am finally doing the kind of research I thought this program was all about; how ironic that the donor agency views this as an aberration and an inappropriate use of funding, and will cut me off prematurely.

A couple weekends later, Stephanie, Peter, Betinho, and Michael pull into my driveway. Betinho races to the swinging chair where I am waiting and gives me an enormous hug. "*Tia Jobie! Tia Jobie!*" I get out of my seat and swoop him up, marveling at how quickly kids can bounce back. "*Que saudades!*" He has missed me. They have told me he is learning English quickly, but he is obviously enjoying this opportunity to lapse into Portuguese, and chatters rapidly about all the things he has seen and done in Washington.

Michael approaches me next. His face looks a little less worn, and I can feel a little strength in his arms when he hugs me. "Nice place," he whispers. "Beautiful magnolia tree." We turn to look at the tree--which Stephanie has already pointed out to Betinho, who promptly runs over to marvel at its giant flowers. They are surely the only flowers he has seen in the U.S. large enough to remind him of Amazônia.

After hugs from Stephanie and Peter, we all go inside to have lunch before unloading Michael's things. Afterwards, we lounge around lazily in the backyard, enjoying the warm summer's day. Betinho goes to sleep in one hammock, and Michael lies drowsily in the other.

Stephanie and Peter tell me that Betinho is doing very well. He cried a lot the first couple of days, and didn't want to play with Lizzie's kids, but they advertised in the paper for a Portuguese-speaking babysitter, and found a nice Brazilian teenager to come over. She has made all the difference for Betinho, helping teach him English and little things about America, and helping him not feel that he has totally lost Brazil. They are still hunting for a Portuguese-speaking therapist to help him get over the trauma of seeing his father murdered, and narrowly escaping the kidnapping. They are still not sure what to do about schooling, but they think he is pretty

474

bright and can eventually catch up to other kids his age. He loves kisses and hugs, and trusts his new parents.

I tell them about my job, and they are thrilled to hear that I am really enjoying it. "I still don't understand how they can justify cutting six months out of your contract," says Peter. "If you've fulfilled your end of the contract, and told them you were willing to go on another assignment, and willing to go to another country, I don't see how they can do it. I think you should sue them."

"Peter!" exclaims Stephanie.

"Well, I do!"

"I know," I say, "but right now I can still say I did everything they told me to do. If I have to look for another job in a few months, I don't want to totally piss them off. I mean, I might need them to give me a good reference."

"Well, it sounds as if this professor will give you a good reference."

"Yeah, he will, but he can't comment on my work **in** Brazil."

"I thought you said the former president of the Institute was willing to give you a reference," says Stephanie.

"Yeah, but he was only there the first few months I was working in Brasília, then he left. Things are just really strange, and I don't want to complicate things any further."

"Sometimes a good lawsuit is what you need to clear the air," says Peter.

"Sometimes," I reply. How can I explain to this successful attorney that somewhere between leaving for Mexico two years ago, and coming back from Brazil a couple months ago, that I lost all my professional ambition, that I have grown tired of swimming against the tide my whole life, that I want to spend the rest of my life doing something simple and unchallenging and squarely within the realm of the possible? And how can I explain that I have decided not to begin to think about my next job until after Michael dies?

In the evening, we walk down Franklin Street, stroll around the campus, then give Betinho his first taste of Southern cooking at Dip's Country kitchen. He is delighted to find the familiar okra and corn, and instantly falls in love with blackberry cobbler and fresh cream. On the way back, Michael shakes his head dejectedly when we walk past the place that used to be the Columbia Street Bakery, the place we started dating. He is as disappointed as I was to learn that it is now a "health food" restaurant that serves its food with disposable plastic plates and utensils and cups.

We get up early Sunday morning to take Betinho for a swim in Jordan Lake. He has never seen anything like it--a wide shallow lake, fringed by pine trees. He marvels at the multi-colored sailboats in the distance, and complains when we say it is time to go.

After lunch, they depart for Washington with a promise from us that we will be up to visit soon. Michael returns to the hammock for a nap. I put away some of his things, and tidy up, wondering for the first time what this will really be like. He might not die for a long time. I might fall deeper in love with him, instead of letting go and finding somebody else. I might suffocate him. Is that what happened the first time?

I am browsing through and shelving his books when he comes back in. "You don't have to do that."

"I don't mind. You've been reading a lot."

"Not much else to do in prison. I was sick of pumping iron all day long."

"I was just putting them up in the order they seemed to be in the boxes."

"It's OK: just leave it. It'll give me something to do while you're at work all day."

"You have to work in the backyard, you know--so we can get our rental discount," I reply, smiling at him.

"Oh, right! Do you think they'd let me get a puppy? It'd be a lot more fun working in the yard with a puppy."

"You don't **have** to do yardwork: I was just kidding!"

"No, I want to. It's been so long since I did serious gardening. It'll be good to remember how to plant and weed and harvest. You'd like a puppy, wouldn't you?"

All I can think is that I do not want a dog who will outlive Michael and be a constant reminder of him. "Sure! You know I love dogs."

We spend the rest of the afternoon unpacking his stuff and hanging his posters, then make dinner. He comments on the London postcard stuck to the refrigerator: "Nick?" I nod. It was forwarded by the University with a bunch of other things--months of statements and magazines and letters. "Can I read it?" I nod, and continue chopping my green pepper. "He really likes you!"

"He does not!"

"It's pretty obvious." I have reread that postcard twenty times, and I have no idea where he is getting that from. "He can't wait to visit you."

"He didn't say that! Anyway, he wants to visit **us**--everybody. He just feels obligated to us because he thinks we saved his life."

"He's not making plans to visit the Brazilian military: they rescued us at the end! He just wants to see **you** again!"

"Oh, would you **stop**! We went through a trauma together, and so we feel bonded, that's all."

"You're already in love with his music," he says. *I'm already in love with you, too, but that didn't work out.* "I know he sang you to sleep in the hospital."

"Because I asked him."

"Just give him a chance, OK? Promise me." I look at him, incredulous. "Just give everybody a chance, OK? Don't be afraid to take chances!"

"OK," I say, half understanding what he is saying, half believing I can.

After dinner we turn on the TV news, and there is a report on plans for a large Cherokee-run casino in Tomotla. It will put a lot of Cherokees to work.

"Do your parents live near there?"

"No," Michael replies. "Snowbird is pretty far from there. We should go visit soon, while it's warm. You never wanted to visit when it was cold." He says it without accusation, knowing my terror of winter was genuine, knowing I never wanted to take the time to make the long drive out to the Smoky Mountains of North Carolina when I was in graduate school.

"I'd really like that. How about the Fourth of July?"

He smiles, knowing I hate the patriotic insanity of that day. "OK, let's do it!" We turn off the news and head outside to enjoy the twilight's final birdsongs. "Hey! I think I saw a rabbit under the magnolia tree," says Michael.

We creep quietly under the outstretched branches and peer in. "I don't see anything," I whisper. He covers my mouth with his hand, and pulls me in a little closer, then points. Its whiskers are quivering in fear of us, and at last it risks it all and catapults out. We sit down, leaning our backs against the trunk of the tree, deeply inhaling the extraordinary sweetness of the enormous white blossoms all around us.

"I think you'll really like Snowbird," he says, when darkness starts descending in earnest. "I don't think you would have before, but now I think you will."

"I know I will," I say. No matter how much poverty or misery it has, I am ready for it now. Where I would have seen victims before, I will now see survivors. Where I would have seen unapproachable mountains before, I will now see the source of the fresh water springing forth to renew us all. Where I would have seen alien Indians before, I will now see fellow human beings.

"I hope so," he responds, "because I want you to be there when I die...and I want to die in Snowbird."

478

"I'll be there," I reply.

"I hope so."

"I will."

He is silent for a moment, then turns my face to him. "Afterwards," he says, "you have to go away. I need you now, but I won't need you when I'm dead. You will still be in the land of the living. Don't ever forget that. It's the living who need you, and you need the living. My parents will tell you that you can come back to visit whenever you want, but you can't stay there. You'll have to leave."

"I don't know where to go," I whisper.

"Some people have to wander a long time before they find their place. Don't be afraid of that. Just don't ever stop. Keep going."

I lean into his chest, and he caresses my head. "Why did the dolphins save you if you have to die anyway?"

He is silent for a few moments. "That's not what you're asking, is it? You wanna know why God just didn't let me die quick and easy."

"I don't know."

"I don't know, either. But if God doesn't want to spell it out in neon billboards, I'm sure He has His reasons."

"But He **should**! It's so hard to understand God! How can we ever be sure we are following God?"

"We can't; all we can be sure of is that we're seeking God."

"Why can't we find God immediately?"

"In the space of God's eternity, maybe a lifetime **is** `immediately'."

"Then God doesn't really understand how much we are suffering, if He thinks this is going by quickly for us."

"Or we don't really have faith in how much peace and joy there is to come, and that God knows how to bring us there."

"Where did you get so much faith, Michael?"

"I don't know, Jobie, but it wasn't always there. Just keep your heart open. No matter how much it hurts, always keep your heart open. No matter what else is locked up, always keep your heart open."

The moon rises in the now black sky. In the nests above our heads, the songbirds have ceased singing lullabies to their babies, and all is peaceful in their magnolia home. I listen to Michael's heart beating and thank God for his time on Earth...and mine.

The End

Made in the USA
Monee, IL
16 April 2022

94848764R00272